HELEN

BOOKS BY D. W. BUFFA

The Defense

The Prosecution

The Judgment

The Legacy

Star Witness

Breach of Trust

Trial by Fire

The Grand Master

Evangeline

The Swindlers

The Dark Backward

The Last Man

HELEN

D. W. BUFFA

BLUE ZEPHYR

San Francisco

Published by Blue Zephyr

Helen, originally entitled *Eros*, was first published in Europe under the pen name Jean DuMont.

www.dwbuffa.net

ISBN-13: 978-1495241925

ISBN-10: 1495241920

For Joseph Cropsey
Who Showed Me The Way

HELEN

My first novel, The Defense, was published nearly twenty years ago by Henry Holt in New York. It was not the first novel I had written. Like too many other unpublished authors, I had tried to write stories in a way that publishers might think they could sell. Failure has its lessons. After what seemed an infinite series of rejections, I finally decided to write about something I had been thinking about almost from the first time I stepped into a courtroom, the tension that often exists between what the law requires and what – by any decent standard –justice demands.

There are two trials in The Defense. In the first, the defense lawyer, Joseph Antonelli, uses the law to win an acquittal for someone he knows – who everyone knows – is guilty of a terrible crime. In the second, he breaks the rules, violates the law, to save the judge, Leopold Rifkin, who had presided over the first trial, from being found guilty for a crime he did not commit. Antonelli is the central character in the novel, the gifted lawyer who can do anything with a jury, but Rifkin gives the novel whatever weight it has. A serious scholar on the trial court bench is rare enough, but Rifkin never stops questioning everything he sees and hears. At a gathering of lawyers, he goes so far as to suggest that a lawyer who wants to do the best thing for a guilty client should make sure he gets punished so that he will not continue to do evil. Antonelli loved him.

There were those who noticed that Leopold Rifkin, the character I invented, bore a certain resemblance to Leo Strauss, under whom I had studied at the University of Chicago. This was true, to a point, but only to a point. I had tried to imagine what might have happened, if instead of being born in Germany, Leo Strauss had been born in the United States, and, instead of studying philosophy in German universities, had gone to an American law school and become a judge, a judge who never stopped studying, among other things, the works of Plato and Aristotle.

There were six more 'Antonelli' novels and six other novels as well, all of them either legal or political thrillers. And then, a few years ago, in a conversation with the former head of a German publishing house that had published some of those novels, it was suggested that I consider writing a novel about a Greek philosopher, one of those who taught that the world, and everything in it, could be explained in terms of the smallest quantities, the atoms, of which they were composed. But if I were going to write about Greek philosophy, why someone like Democritus – why not Socrates? Why not try to write the story of what it was like to be there, in that time, at that place, when Socrates was not just a distant memory, a few paragraphs in some dull schoolbook, but alive, and when Athens was not crowded with tourists taking pictures of ancient ruins, but the most powerful city in the world, controlled by the far-seeing genius of Pericles and tempted to destruction by the brilliance of Alcibiades?

There were obvious reasons not to write a novel about Athens from the Age of Pericles to the end, or what was tantamount to the end, of the Peloponnesian war. The history of the war has been written by Thucydides and nearly everything we will ever know about Socrates and the origins of Greek philosophy can be found in the dialogues of Plato and the writings of Xenophon. But there is a curious, not to say strange, absence of connection between the two accounts: there are only a few allusions to the war in what Plato wrote and Thucydides never mentions Socrates. This meant it was possible, and worth whatever effort it might take, to combine both the war and this new thing, this new way of looking at the world, which Socrates had brought into being. The result is Helen, a story about what Socrates was and what Athens became, the peak of ancient history and the peak of ancient, and perhaps not just ancient, thought, both of them together the origin and source of western civilization. Whatever its faults, it has at least the merit of trying what, so far as I am aware, no one has tried before.

This is a novel, a work of fiction, but with the exception of Helen herself all the characters are real. The events, the speeches, the conversations in which Socrates reportedly played a part, all took place, but while the sequence of events is correct, the intervals between them have been compressed to create the necessary elements of a single story. Helen's father, Hiero, was the tyrant of Syracuse, but some years earlier than the narrative suggests. Gorgias, the famous rhetorician, did visit Athens, but in 427 B.C., a few years, instead of a few months, after the death of Pericles. The Sicilian expedition, the turning point in the war, which in the novel takes place a short while later, was launched six or seven years later in 416.

The story is told through the eyes of Helen, a young woman with a passionate desire to learn. The daughter of a tyrant, she escapes to Athens where, because of her great beauty and her astonishing intelligence, she becomes the confidant of Aspasia, first the mistress then the wife of Pericles, and through Aspasia, Alcibiades, with whom she falls in love, and Socrates, who is unlike anyone she has ever known. Helen sees everything that happens, and, such has been her education, grasps the real meaning of what she sees. Everything, or almost everything, Socrates says is taken from either Plato or Xenophon, but Helen hears, and remembers, what from her perspective she thinks important to mention. There are also times what she hears what was said at second remove. In the Symposium, Plato has Alcibiades say what he really thinks about Socrates; in Helen, Alcibiades tells Helen what he has just told Socrates a few hours earlier.

There is a famous British case in which the painter, Whistler, on trial for charging an excessive amount of money for a portrait he had painted, testified that it had taken only two days to do it. The plaintiff's attorney, violating the first rule of cross-examination – never ask a question to which you do not already know the answer – demanded: "Only two days! And you claim your fee was reasonable?" With no doubt a quiet half-smile, Whistler replied, "Two days to paint it, forty years of preparation." Helen took six months to write, and, beginning with the first seminar I attended when Leo Strauss was teaching, nearly half a century of frequently interrupted but never abandoned study of ancient sources. Helen is not a novel for everyone, but it is, I hope, a novel that will lead those who read it to view the ancient authors as proper companions for the present.

This novel is dedicated to Joseph Cropsey who, along with Leo Straus, brought philosophy to life for more than one generation of students. He died two years ago. In one of the last conversations I had with him, just months before his death, he told me something of what he had learned from his study of the Parmenides, that most difficult of Platonic dialogues. He would have liked Helen, not because of anything it says, but because, with the unfailing generosity that marked his life, he would have praised the intention.

– D.W. Buffa

CHAPTER ONE

It had been three years since my father murdered my mother, three years in which I had done nothing that might reveal what I thought and felt; three years the silent observer of a tyrant's domination; three years learning the difference between reality and appearance, the distinction that if I did not want to die my mother's death I had to understand; three years teaching myself the distinction between what Hiero, the ruler of Syracuse, made the world think he was and what my father really was.

The world is full of fools, men who cannot tell the truth because they do not know what it is. That was how my father stayed in power: not because he ruled with ruthless violence, but because he made everyone believe that, more than mortal, he could do things only the gods could do. He made them think that by the murder of my mother he had saved the city from all the evils of a civil war, a conspiracy that would have drowned them all in blood. He made them think that far from casting a shadow over the great things they had achieved, the death of my mother would open a new era in which Syracuse would become the envy of everyone in Sicily and Greece. The tyrant's wife had met her fate, the victim of her own betrayal; the tyrant's daughter, the girl, the woman, whose name alone proved how clearly her father could read the future, would now replace her.

"What else could I have called her?" demanded my father, staring at the great crowd, come just weeks after my mother's death to swear their undying love, their eager willingness to remain the subjects – the slaves if they but had the courage to admit it – of the Tyrant of Syracuse, the greatest man in Sicily and, according to the dreams by which he read the future, someday in all the world.

"What else could I have called her?" His booming, strident laughter echoed through the vast circular chamber and still echoes in my mind; the laughter with which he had watched more than one execution; the laughter, I later learned, with which he had murdered my mother; the laughter with which he now announced that, on this day, my thirteenth birthday, the day I ended my childhood and became a young woman, the name he had given me had now been proven true. "What else could I have called a child that from the moment of her birth I knew would become as beautiful as any woman who had ever lived? Look at her! – A day ago only twelve, and already more beautiful than any woman you'll ever live to see."

Hiero sat on his golden throne, wearing his golden sandals and his gold armor. A shaft of sunlight streamed through the opening in the dome high above, sheathing him in a golden fire. It was, like everything else he did, the studied effect of a great imposture, a working fraud: the rumor, tended with all the care due a fragile contrivance, that unlike other, mortal, men the Tyrant of Syracuse could make himself invisible. I sat on a golden chair just below him, the one my mother had always used, visible to anyone who cared to look.

"And if you hadn't known it, if you had never heard her name – Look at her! – You had to know her name was Helen! – The face that launched a thousand ships and drove men to war!"

And then, while all those fools were looking, all those rich merchants who had grown richer under a tyranny than they had been before; all those tin generals hired to protect the tyrant from the anger and resentment of his own people; all those paid for poets who wrote his praises in ways that would have embarrassed Homer, there was a single, blinding flash and the tyrant disappeared. It was a trick he had learned, a conjurer's device – a handful of combustible material that, thrown on the ground, ignited, harmless but dramatic, a reminder that he could at any moment of his choosing become invisible and pass unseen among them.

I knew what my father was and what he had done, but he had never spoken to me about it and I knew what would happen to me if I asked. And then, finally, just days ago, it all came out, and I knew that everything had changed, that something now would happen, that he would either kill me or make me not want to live. He did not come to make his confession as a way to seek atonement.

Drunk as only he could be, he came into my room, grabbed me by the wrist and pulled me out of bed, dragged me down the marble hall to the room where he had once slept with my mother, the bedroom with the windows that looked out at the wine dark sea, the bedroom with the brass doors engraved with scenes of love, the doors no one had been allowed to enter since the night it happened, that night he filled with murder. He threw me onto the bed where he had brought the final darkness to her eyes, and from the rabid hatred with which he looked at me I thought he was going to take his revenge a second time on what she had done to him.

"Do you know what she did, that whore, your mother?" he cried, his eyes full of fire.

Grabbing the wine jar he had brought with him, he drank until the red wine splashed down across his dark bristled chin. With the back of his arm he wiped it away and with heated, frenzied laughter threw the jar hard against the farther wall. It shattered into pieces and the sound of it, the sound of something broken, hit him like an inspiration, a sudden reminder that the only power worth having was the power to destroy.

"Yes, Euarne, the woman who betrayed me! Named for the goddess 'of the lovely figure and face of perfection' that Hesiod wrote. Better another name had been used from that same author: Echidna, she of the 'fair face and eyes glancing, but the other half a monstrous snake, terrible and enormous and squirming and voracious!' But the name does not matter; what matters is what she did." He stopped suddenly, a puzzled expression on his face. "Or was it the other way round?"

He sank down on the bed like one whose knees had just given out, pondering what he had just said. He did not ponder long.

"No," he shouted, jumping to his feet, the anger returning to his eyes. "It was her doing; none of mine. I married her to have a son, someone to follow in my place; she gave me you – a daughter – instead. But I did not put her away, take another in her place, I didn't revenge myself for my disappointment. I let my love for her overrule my judgment. She was beautiful, more beautiful than any woman I had ever seen. When I looked at her I could feel the longing in my loins. It was the kind of beauty that makes you hurt, the kind that takes away your mind."

Suddenly, he turned to me. "Don't you ever say anything? All you do is sit there like some painted doll, your only function to remind me of a woman I hate! You're like that Sphinx they talk about in the Egyptian desert with that never changing expression hiding secrets no one can ever quite decipher. Is that what goes on behind that unearthly face of yours, something deep and mysterious – or, as I guess, nothing even slightly interesting?"

"You murdered my mother," I said without thinking. "Murdered her in this room, and now you bring me in here – for what purpose? To murder me because I remind you so much of the woman you say you hate?"

"There is something to you after all," he said, a sharp glitter in his eyes. "Good. Then maybe you can understand the story I'm going to tell you, why your mother deserved to die."

"You'll never convince me of that. You murdered her; she did nothing wrong!"

"Nothing wrong? Slept with another man in this very room, and then conspired to take both my life and my place as ruler. Nothing wrong? Not if you think treason and adultery are only minor amusements, a way to fight back boredom! You know nothing! But before this night is over you'll know everything, more than you might want!"

His rage spent itself and the passion of his hatred found refuge in the certainty of his own achievement, the evil he had accomplished, the sanctuary of his pride.

"You know they say that I have the power to become invisible. Some say that it is this ring I wear," he remarked, shaking his head at how gullible, how eager to believe were the great majority of men, how willing to explain what they did not understand by what defied belief. "This ring, this piece of gold and silver made by some Sicilian craftsman in the time of my father, given to me on my eighteenth birthday to symbolize that the succession would one day pass to me. The ring, they say, is the secret of my power; the ring allows me to pass among them silent and unseen, listening to everything they say."

A smile of contempt for the stupidity of others marched across his face, but just beneath it a kind of weary resignation; a sense of disappointment, if I understood correctly, at the part he had been forced to play. It was only there an instant, the wish that he could have held power with the willing, intelligent consent of those he ruled. A tyrant, he wished he were a king, but he had too much lawless passion, and too much fear, to try the hazard of that transition.

"What they say is true. I have that power: I can make myself invisible. You don't believe it. Why? Because you have seen that little trick of mine, that combustible I use to cloak my departure when I leave the throne, the way I use the sunlight and the golden armor to stop anyone looking at me? But what is that, if it isn't the power to achieve the very thing they think I have the power to do? What difference between one inanimate object – this ring – and the powder some seeker after nature's secrets made from his researches? What does it mean to be invisible if not to pass from one place to another unnoticed? Your mother thought no one could see what she was doing and now the world is invisible to her. Her lover, Lysias, thought no one would see what he had done and now he too is dead, his body left unburied for the dogs to tear apart. They did not have the power, only Hiero does!"

I looked at him as if entranced, the dutiful, the obedient, the willing slave, because it was what he wanted to see and then, seeing, would ignore. Cautiously, I sat up and slowly swung my legs over the side of the bed and put my bare naked feet on the marble floor, ready, if I needed to, to make my escape. He was roaring oaths to Zeus, to Eros and Aphrodite, to all the gods in heaven, swearing that what he was telling me was nothing but the truth.

"The most beautiful woman anywhere – not just her face, what everyone could see, but what she looked like here, in the bridal chamber, that first night I had her. She knew it, too – that she could make a man do anything, anything at all; promise to take his own life, if that's what it came to, for just one night with her. She was every dream of love any man has ever had, a poison in the blood, the kind that drives you mad. But when you had her, when you were finished, that's when you knew that life had changed, that from that night forward every day would be a torture. It was the look she had, worse than triumph, disappointment, that taunting silent glance as she walked naked to the bath, that glance that told me she had wanted more. That was what she gave me, that first night of ours, the mantic knowledge that I was second-best, second to whatever phantom lover had filled the empty depravity of her woman's evil mind. She did not have to sleep with other men; she slept with me and pretended I was someone else. She came to my bed a virgin and was unfaithful before she ever left it.

"Treated like this, made to suffer by a woman I knew I could not have each time I had her! Everyone thought I was the most fortunate man alive: the ruler not just of Syracuse but much of Sicily, anything I wanted at my fingertips. I ate whatever I wanted to eat, drank whatever I wanted to drink; I could have any woman or any boy that attracted my attention; and now I had a wife unlike any other, a young woman, almost still a girl, with a beauty men would die for. Die for? – Death would have been a pleasure after what she had done to me. I was the Tyrant of Syracuse, but she was the tyrant over me.

"Lysias, the fool – she had the same effect on him. Lysias,

brought in to become the commander of my guard, trained in all the habits of discipline and war, sworn by a sacred oath to protect me with his life. I knew he was ambitious, you could tell that at a glance, the eager way he carried out every order, the speed with which he would punish those who needed the lash. It was the way he looked at my wife that first taught me his weakness and my danger. There was too much reserve, achieved with too much conscious effort. I knew then that it was only a matter of time."

He turned toward the window and the silver moonlight dancing on the polished black surface of the sea, lost in a dream of what the gods of necessity had fated him do. I asked what he meant by 'a matter of time,' but he stood there as if turned to stone, the only sign that he had not lost all his senses, that he was still a living, breathing mortal being, the scorn, the hatred, that with each passing moment dug deeper into the twisted contours of his mouth.

"I am invisible!" he cried with such manic energy and force that what I had taken as a deathlike trance I thought now must have been the source of some new power. "The way my mind entered into all their secret thoughts, their cheap desires; the way I led them all unknowing into their criminal act of betrayal! That was my genius – do you understand the power I have: to know before the actor how the actor will act. Lysias wanted her – it was obvious from his forced indifference – wanted her with a hunger that nothing, neither loyalty nor fear, could stop. He would have her or die. Yes, well, I knew how that felt, didn't I?" A glint of malevolence, malevolence that was too proud not to love itself, a malevolence that had, whether you believe it or not, a kind of childlike innocence, danced unmolested in his eyes. "I wanted her like that; I had her like that, had her like that nearly every night for seven years and never really had her even once. I wonder ... I wonder if something like that happened when they ...."

He looked at me as if he thought I must know the answer, and in that moment I was not sure but that I did, had that knowledge, had it somewhere just below the surface of my conscious mind, waiting there for the time when it would be of use. He started again toward the window when, suddenly, he stopped, turned back and dropped into a gold cushioned chair an arm's length away from where I sat.

"You look just like she did, that night, that first night we spent together, that night ... You're even more beautiful ... I wonder if it would be the same, if ... "

6

I was my mother's daughter, but the product of his seed, and seeing me he knew what he had always known, that if everyone wanted the kinds of things he had, he alone had me; and now perhaps, if I read his eyes correctly, in a different way than as the father of the child he had first brought into being through his union with my mother. He saw the knowledge in my eyes, and seeing it, did not like what he saw, that he could not keep his secret thoughts secret from me, that I could see them as he thought them, and that I knew what he wanted, what he thought he had to have.

"Lysias!" he snorted, jumping to his feet. "He could not help himself; he had no choice but to do what he did."

"But nothing would have happened if you had stopped it, told him what you suspected, challenged him to deny it. He would not have dared try anything after that."

He shrugged with coarse indifference and shook his head.

"If it hadn't been Lysias, it would have been someone else. She would have found someone – there wasn't anyone she could not seduce – to murder me."

"You can't know that, you can't know she would have done that!"

He laughed, stopped, and then laughed again. "Can't know that? You think it's that difficult to see the future? I told you how she looked at me, how when she gave her body she held back her mind; how when she looked at me she was always thinking of something better than what she had. Can't know that? She was the same as me, nothing ever satisfies, nothing is enough; always this hungry need for what I haven't had."

"And that's why you killed them, murdered – why not just kill yourself!"

"They were executed because of their betrayal. They were planning my assassination while they copulated in this bed. Kill myself, instead of them? What for? Kill myself?" he continued with a flash of cruelty in his eyes. "When I still had you to raise, still had you to turn into a woman!"

"Turn me into a woman? Is that the next way you intend to disobey the gods, rape the daughter after you murder the mother?"

"Disobey the gods! You mean the ones invented by Homer, the ones whose endless generation Hesiod described – like Gaia and Ouranos, the mother and son who coupled together to bring forth other gods as children, including Kronos, who started time; Kronos who did what any loving child might do: lopped off the members of his own father and tossed them into the sea, so the sea could give birth to that 'modest lovely goddess called Aphrodite.' Are these the gods you mean? "

"There is a reason we believe in them," I shouted back. "They possess the virtues we would like to have; they set the pattern of what we could become: their strength, their wisdom – that's what those stories we're taught as children mean. That's how we learn – that's how I learned – to measure the difference between what has been done and what should be done, the difference between what justice calls for and what evil represents."

He laughed in my face, certain now that there was nothing more to me than the instincts of a woman.

"Justice! – The prayer of the weak, their insistence that the strong should do their bidding. I should limit myself – ?" he cried, scornful in his incredulity. "I should let anyone limit me – by the laws of others, by what others think? Why not just become a slave, let someone else be master, telling me what I can and cannot do. I rule here. Why should I not indulge myself, satisfy each appetite with what it desires? Wouldn't anyone let his desires become as strong as possible if he knew that when they reached their height he could take what he needed? Justice! A name invented by impotence to hide its weakness; a name invented by those who lack the power – and if they have the power, lack the will – to do what they want. It's like listening to a eunuch disparaging intercourse with a woman! The truth – and all the world knows it – is that luxury and the liberty from restraint are the only real virtues, the only source of happiness. All those other things, all the useless talk about the equal right to rule, stuff and nonsense, what someone called with justice the 'unnatural covenants of mankind.' If I've taught you nothing else, at least learn that!"

He stormed out, shouting orders as he left; so much the prisoner of his rage he did not notice there was no one there to listen and obey.

Thought races, not just far ahead of us, but retraces where we have been. So now Hesiod, whom my father had quoted with such disdain; Hesiod, the author of much of what we know about the gods, came clear speaking into my distracted, much worried mind, reminding me that the very passion, the limitless desire, Hiero bragged about was, and always would be, the source of his great weakness. I spoke out loud the lines, but heard them as from the voice of another, wiser counsel:

> "Eros, who breaks the limbs' strength,
> who in all gods, in all human beings
> overpowers the intelligence in the breast,
> and all their shrewd planning."

I would keep hold of my intelligence and not let Eros master me; I would make Eros help carry out my plans, plans that I would devise with all the shrewdness I could summon. No one would exercise a tyranny over me.

Plans? What plans could I make? I had to think, I had to reason. Night was coming, but I had to stay awake. Sleep was death's brother – isn't that what Hesiod wrote? – and despite the words with which I had challenged a tyrant's power I wanted almost more than anything to live, to stay alive, to see what the fates had waiting for me, to learn the reason, if there was a reason, why I had been born from an act of unrequited passion that might, for all my mother cared, have been a loveless rape. I ran to my room, put on a simple linen gown, the kind women in the city wore, and over that a dark hooded cape to cloak my face in shadows, and then left the palace.

For years I had practiced all the arts of concealment I could learn, compelled for my own protection to live a double, secret life, but I only noticed now that the place I lived was as much a riddle as any of the things I had learned to hide. The palace, Hiero's palace, was also like the face of Homer's Helen, the face my father bragged was no better than my own. It drew the envy and the admiration, the jealousy and desire, of everyone who saw it, and hid beneath its shiny brilliant surface a swirling self-absorption that knew no limits, and an endless ambition that recognized no measure but its own success. I wondered why I had not noticed it before, why I had not seen the parallel. There was not just one palace, there were several, each encircled by another, each inside a wall, a fortress built on a small island named Ortygia where no one could go without permission. There were two bridges, two bridges on or off, each of them at both ends protected by massive iron gates, each gate guarded every hour and every day, and all around, the surging relentless motion of the sea, the double harbor from which the city and its ruler could set to war two hundred ships, a navy that only Athens could threaten in a fight.

If the palace was impregnable, the vast interior, like Helen's mind, resisted all attempts to find an order. Rooms, like random thoughts, were impossible to number, some of them so difficult to find that if you found yourself lost in one of them no one would ever find you; rooms that glittered with every precious gem imaginable and some beyond imagining, not just gold and silver, not just emeralds and rubies, jewels of a common kind, but jewels so rare there were not enough to make a name for them. There was wealth enough inside these walls to purchase all the food that Sicily would ever need, but it went instead to satisfy the late night drunken dreams of a half-mad tyrant afraid that someone somewhere had something he could never get.

Helen's face, Helen's mind! All analogies are false, the use of something we do not know to explain something we do not understand. Helen's face, Helen's mind! A poet's legend, a made-up story, a light to follow through the twisted cruelties of a tyrant's will! If you cannot reason from one thing to another, seeing first what each thing is; if your only way of thinking is to see dead images in your head, the two-faced mask of Janus is a better and a simpler guide. That is what I told myself, angry that my mind still worked slower than my will. The Janus mask had at least the virtue of concentrating my attention. The double face of a divided soul, the nameless fear that was the mirror image of all his dauntless power, the late night terror that there were forces everywhere waiting to take away everything he had, his life included. Tyrants had their power, but honored above all other men were those who killed them.

The fear he felt was felt by everyone. He made sure of that. It spread through the city like a plague that came from nowhere and took more victims each day of the disease. The difference was that this contagion had a cause, the tyrant's belief that the only thing that would save him from his illness was to infect everyone with the same sickness. Trusting no one, Hiero took what security he could from the knowledge that in Syracuse trust had all but disappeared. Husbands, wives, close friends or relations, no one knew who might accuse them of being an enemy of the regime. There were spies everywhere, eager to report, and more than willing to invent, anything they heard. There was no privacy, no place where someone could speak his mind and not have to worry what might happen to him if he did. The chance to take revenge, to settle scores from some old quarrel, became more than irresistible, necessary, once it was understood that the informer had a better chance to live than those on whom he had informed. There were no impartial courts, no chance to prove your innocence. Hiero knew everything. He had the ring and with it the power to see unseen the hidden work of criminals and traitors, each new conspiracy against the city which he more than anyone had always protected.

He reminded them of that, staged twice each year in the amphitheater so all thirty thousand citizens could watch the battle in which the Sicilian Greeks defeated Carthage, and Syracuse became a power that no one now would think to threaten. No expense was spared, nothing could rival the production in which some of those who played the Carthaginians, slaves mainly, were killed by the swords of the brave soldiers of Syracuse. The crowd loved it, and when they cheered Hiero at the end their cheers were real. He made them in their victory feel their strength, made them know what it felt like to dominate their enemies. If he ruled them, it was only so that they could rule others. They loved that feeling, and they loved him because of it. It was only when things grew quiet, when there was nothing left to conquer and no one who could conquer them, when instead of motion there was only rest, that instead of triumph they remembered fear; only then that they found their enemy in the same men with whom they had once shared the sacrifice of battle.

I had watched for years the way Hiero played the crowd and the things he did to control their lives. He said that the only way to lead them was to follow what they wanted, but I had somehow always known that it was only his excuse, a way to blame others for his own degradation. He murdered my mother because he thought she might one day murder him; he had hundreds, maybe thousands, put to death on a mere suspicion that they harbored thoughts which, had they been free to find their voices, might have led to his expulsion. He murdered everyone, but always in a better cause. And now, I was certain, he was going to murder me.

I had to get away, go somewhere where no one would know me, where Hiero and his legion of paid-for spies could not find me. But where could I go, and what could I do when I got there? Strange, discordant possibilities danced before my eyes: distant places where I could live, places I had heard about, part of the adventures, the stories told of war; places where I could lead a different life, places where women had done more than take husbands and give them children, places where I could find someone who could teach me something of more than passing interest, something that had a timeless value. They were all fantasies, the dreams of inexperience, the soft indulgence of a will that had begun to falter. There was nowhere I could go. Staring out across the great harbor, I watched the cloudless sky grow darker in the scarlet light of dusk.

CHAPTER TWO

My beating heart kept threatening to betray me, the loud pounding of the fear I felt, the fear I did not know how long I could still control.

"You haven't said a word all evening," said my father after he took another long drink of wine. "It's because I lost my temper and shouted at you, but that's over now, all forgotten."

Pushing his gold wine cup first one way then another, Hiero's eyes grew brighter and the smile that cut across his cautious mouth became eager and enthusiastic, the certain signal that he had something to say about himself and could hardly wait to say it.

"The Persians, a play by Aeschylus, has just come from Athens, where it won first prize in last year's competition. I'm paying to have it done here. It wasn't cheap, but this Aeschylus knows what he's doing."

"It would be all right, I have your permission, to attend, when Aeschylus presents his play?" I asked as calmly as I could.

"You've been to every performance I have paid to have produced in the theater. You know your place. Why would you suddenly ask if I would allow it?"

"I understood what was expected of me, I knew what I was supposed to do, when I was Hiero's daughter. But since last night, after what you told me, I have to wonder: what am I – Hiero's daughter or his next victim?"

The blood rushed to his face as if I had stabbed him in the throat. His fingers tightened around the wine cup he held in his hand, crushing it slowly in his grip.

"Think of yourself anyway you like: daughter, victim; or better yet, call yourself what your mother was: call yourself a whore! You'll do what I tell you and you'll do it when I say!"

The crushed gold cup dangling in his hand, he rose from his chair and walked toward me with a slow, deliberate step.

"Stand up!"

No longer frightened by what I could not prevent, I looked straight at him. He slapped me hard across the face. He wanted me to cry, to scream, to show the pain I felt. I was not strong enough to fight him, but I was strong enough to fight myself: I made a slave of silence and stared at him in voiceless rage. He slapped my face the other side. My revenge was again to taunt him with a wordless stillness.

"That's another thing you have in common – you and that whore your mother – neither one of you is human."

He threw the cup hard on the floor, smashed it with his foot, picked up what was left of it and hurled it against the wall. Screaming dull obscenities, he left me to ponder what I had done and what might happen next. The outrage in his eyes when he hit me, the joy he took in violence, left little doubt that what he had done to me the night before was only the beginning, that tonight he would kill me or do something even worse. An hour later, full of wine and fantasy, he came to my room determined to prove himself the man he knew he was.

The door was locked, bolted from inside. He pounded in frustration, demanding that I let him in, that there were things he wanted to talk about, and when that had no effect, began to tell me that he was sorry for what he had done, that he had not meant to hurt me, that he would never hurt me again. I stood just the other side, a dagger in my hand, afraid to breathe. Convinced, finally, that I would not answer, that for that night at least there was nothing he could do, Hiero swore an oath that I would soon have cause to regret a daughter's disobedience and went away. With the dagger under my pillow, I tried to sleep; but all I could do was count the hours until the light of morning came and with it one more day in which to try to plan my escape.

I said I did not sleep that night, but I must have done so, because I know I dreamed, a dream that still stays with me, more powerful than any waking memory, the dream, the nightmare, of everything I feared. Instead of leaving, Hiero, my father, forced his way into my room, tore off my silk nightgown, forced my legs apart and drove himself inside me, and I understood at once, when he began to take me, that what he wanted more than anything, what he had to have, was the feeling of doing evil for the pleasure of doing it, of doing what he wanted to someone who had no power to resist. I knew, in this dream of mine, that no one would come to save me; no one who, if they heard my screams, would do anything but ignore them. I knew I could not stop the violent thrusts that were bringing so much pain; I knew that it was all but certain that I would be torn

14

to pieces and left to bleed to death, another new defilement of my parents' wedding bed, the bed on which I had been conceived. And then it came to me, a whispered message from the gods, my only hope to do more evil for the pleasure of doing it than he could do: instead of a forced submission, respond; instead of letting him have me, have him instead. If he wanted to make me feel the pain of what he was doing; I would make him start in astonishment at how much I seemed to like what he was doing. I screamed, not the scream of a victim being punished, the scream of false ecstasy at what it made me feel. And then, still screaming, I woke up.

The dream was too painful to remember, and it was only much later that it first began to come back to me, but I did not need a dream to tell me that my father would have me the way he had my mother, and that he would hide his crime by murdering me, the way he had murdered her. I did not need a dream to teach me fear; my fear was real, and my senses that much sharper because of it.

A traveler, a man who had visited many places and written about what he had heard and seen, had come at Hiero's invitation and, as Hiero's guest, was there to tell some of what he had discovered. His face was full of kindness and intelligence, the kind that, unlike a tyrant's soul, needs nothing more than what it learns.

Herodotus of Halicarnassus had seen the way that different people lived, not just among the Greeks, but among the Persians, with whom the Greeks had fought their greatest war, and the Egyptians, who taught the Greeks mathematics and even some of their own history. In a sign of his respect, my father sat on a chair facing him, a chair set on the same level. I was seated off to the side, close enough to be seen without suggesting that I might have anything to say. Herodotus would have none of it.

"Perhaps the child could draw closer. My voice isn't strong as it used to be."

Hiero, who with strangers wrapped his power in his charm, smiled as if he had only kept me back out of courtesy to his guest. A servant started to move my chair toward my father's side.

"Let me sit on this side," I remarked with quiet authority, "just between them. That way I won't miss anything that is said."

Hiero hid his anger, but left no doubt of his displeasure. Instead of waiting until the servant moved my chair he began the conversation while I was still standing.

"Is it really true, what you describe they did in Babylon: the way they arrange marriages, auctioning off the women until they run out of those the men are willing to pay for and then, changing things around, offer the women who are left, the ones no one wants, each of them, as they get uglier, bringing a bigger prize, a dowry that, if you take the ugliest one, almost makes you rich?"

They were sitting, as I said, at the same level, but there were times, and this was one of them, when I thought Herodotus looked down on him, or that Hiero, if not invisible, had shrunk in size.

"What I have written is either what I have learned through my own investigations, or what I learned from the testimony of others, what they have told me about what they believe is true. Those who read it carefully, who take the time to reason through it, will find inside it nothing that is false. You asked about that law of Babylon, the one they had before Babylon was destroyed. That was the law, and it was the best of all the laws they had."

His eyes had never left my father, but now, for a long moment, he looked at me, looked with such gentle benevolence that I felt the loss when his glance moved back to where it started.

"Your daughter, if I may say so, would have made the richest man in Babylon the poorest man in the city."

"I wondered when I read it," replied Hiero, "how long before those who bought the most beautiful women began to regret how much they had paid."

Herodotus could sense the tension in that remark; I do not imagine he could have guessed the cause. Perhaps he considered it the normal frustration of a parent with a willful daughter. I was of a mind to let him know the truth, give him another strange practice he could write about, but the way he smiled at me all I could think was to smile back.

"In the case of your daughter the richest man would also have become the proudest man in Babylon, the envy of all the others."

"You say this was the best law they had. What is the reason you believe that?"

With a cautious eye, Herodotus gazed around the rich furnishing of the room, the gilded chairs and couches, the painted vases and the shiny silver bowls, the sheer white silk draperies billowing gently in the air, fragrant with the scent of perfumes brought from Persia and other distant places. Hiero sensed his hesitation.

"Whatever it is, believe me when I tell you I am only interested in the truth. What works well in Babylon, what works well in Athens, may not work well everywhere – it may not work here – but I'm not offended by the difference. It's a strange custom you describe, anyone would say so; but you think it the best they had, and I would like to understand your reasons."

"It's right, of course – what you say. The laws, the customs, of one place may not always suit another; and what the Babylonians did, the way they married off their women, would be seen as not just strange, but abhorrent in many other places, but it was best for them because it kept Babylon one city instead of two."

Hiero bent forward, shook his head in confusion and then slapped his knee in frustration. "You speak in riddles. Two cities instead of one?"

"Every city is two cities, or in danger of becoming so: divided between rich and poor, each trying to dominate the other. But Babylon kept a balance; more than that, Babylon knit them both, rich and poor, together."

"By marriage?"

"By marriage, and by making them change places. Every year it happened: all the women of marriageable age, all the men at an age to marry. The rich got the women they desired, and the poor, who took the women the rich did not want, got their money. This reduced, if it did not eliminate, the disparity of what they had and removed the principle cause of dissention. They stayed one city instead of two. What happened later showed by contrast how sound their reasoning had been."

"What happened later?"

"After Babylon was conquered the daughters of the poor were forced into prostitution, plying their trade just outside the city gates."

Hiero was not interested in what was normal, what happened to people who lost a war; he was fascinated by what was novel, what was strange, and all of it for my benefit. For all his outward composure, his affable good manners to a guest, he was seething inside; angry at what I had done the night before, the way I had locked my door against him and deprived him of the sense of power that gave his life its meaning.

"Tell me about what you learned about the Libyans, that tribe that, like the Babylonians, has a marriage custom different than what others do. They don't auction off the brides to be; it's the way they treat the wedding guests."

Herodotus had described in his writings a great many things

with a candor some might think imprudent and even indecent, but he was not an ill-bred man interested in repeating obscenities for the amusement of an ill-bred audience. There were certain matters that should be discussed in private or not discussed at all; they were certainly not to be mentioned in the presence of a young girl, however exalted her position.

"Helen has read everything. There isn't anything she will find new or shocking. She isn't like other girls her age – I'll go farther: she isn't like other women. She's the only child I have and I spared no effort on her education. Your sense of what is right and proper, though it says much for your character, isn't needed here."

Herodotus did not like it. What did it mean – that a sense of what was right and proper was not needed here – except that precisely that was missing. He did what he was asked, but did it with reluctance.

"The custom, as you know, is to have the bride on her wedding night sleep with each invited guest, each of whom comes to her with a gift."

Now, finally, Hiero looked at me.

"Perhaps when you marry – when I marry you to whom I choose – I'll change the law and adopt the Libyan custom. But then, because of who I am there would have to be at least a thousand guests invited, each come to take their pleasure. Instead of a wedding night, there would have to be – what? – At least a week. You would do that, wouldn't you – be mounted by a thousand different lovers in exchange for all the gifts they'd bring? Or should I change the law the other way, have an auction like the Babylonians, restrict the number to the highest bidders and have you take not more than just a few dozen. You could probably do that in an hour's time!"

He was quick; I was quicker. He was hurtful; I was lethal.

"If they were all of your capacity, more like just a few minutes!"

Herodotus tried to disappear, vanish somewhere deep inside himself, but I called him back.

"In all your travels, in all your investigations, in all the courts and kingdoms you visited, did you ever find even one tyrant who, seizing the power to rule over others, had the power to rule himself?"

"You'll have to forgive my daughter," Hiero interposed. "I let her have a man's education and she lost a woman's virtue. She reads, and that alone was a mistake; reads things, hears things and worse yet, thinks about them. She has the face of Helen, but her mind works with the duplicity of the double-tongued Odysseus. She says things she does not mean and means what she does not say."

With a smile full of irony, Herodotus repeated what he had just been told. "A face like Helen and a mind like Odysseus. I knew when I first saw her that she had a depth men like you and I can only envy, and cannot really understand."

And then he was on his feet, and without another word just turned and walked away. Astounded by the daring, the sheer effrontery of it, Hiero did not even try to stop him.

That night I again slept with the door bolted and a knife beneath my pillow; and again, though I did not remember the dream until much later, what sleep I had was tortured by another nightmare of what, if I did not get away, my father was going to do. I reminded him too much of my mother, reminded him too much of what she had done, and even more than that, the look I had, the second face of Helen, burned too much inside his blood for him to think about restraint. The knowledge that incest was thought a greater crime than murder, hated by the gods, made the thought of rape all but irresistible.

Somehow, morning came, and then, late that same day, I was walking in procession, a single, measured step behind the great Hiero, ruler of the city, in his gold and scarlet robes of state, on our way to see the latest great play by Aeschylus. Herodotus, the tyrant's invited guest, was waiting for us in the middle seats of the middle row of the amphitheater. All the citizens of Syracuse rose as one body, trumpeting with a single voice their acknowledgement that Hiero, and only Hiero, was their leader. I hated and despised my father and all he stood for, but it was still impressive, the way he was idolized by the crowd, the way that he seemed somehow to embody all their hopes and dreams. He was a monster, a murderer, willing to kill anyone on a mere suspicion, but here, in public, he seemed to shine like the city, glowing in all the glory of the late day sun. I could see it in their eyes, the excitement, the emotion, the deep and intense satisfaction at being in proximity to Hiero's undoubted greatness. When, finally, the applause and clamor subsided and everyone resumed their places, the sound of all that movement like the soft refrain of distant thunder, Aeschylus came onto the stage below. He waited until the crowd went quiet, and then, in a clear deep voice gave a brief description of what the play was all about.

"It would not have been produced at all," explained Herodotus, leaning closer to my father, "if it had not been for the financial support of Pericles."

"Pericles? Should I know the name?"

"I suspect it's a name everyone will know soon enough. He comes from an old, distinguished family, and is already one of the leaders of the party in Athens that insists on a more equal distribution of power."

He said this as if he was only reporting a fact worth notice, but, as he knew as well as anyone, it was a fact that had a different meaning in Syracuse than it had in Athens. Hiero smiled with the shrewd cynicism with which he discovered the motives of other, lesser men.

"The leaders of the popular party always say that, and then, because they know so much better than anyone how to lead, take power for themselves."

He had such contempt for other men, judging them only by what he knew about himself, that my instinct – my young girl's hope, if you prefer – was to think that other men, free men, must be better, far better than what he claimed. The play, The Persians, made me see in ways I might not have seen before, the answer, or at least the beginning of an answer, to what my young mind had been forced to ponder.

It was a riddle, a sign of the irrationality in the world, a double irony that the play on which a tyrant had spent so much money, a play about the Persians and their unbearable defeat, had as its most serious message a warning against the rule of tyrants. The queen of Persia, Xerxes' mother, asks "who is the shepherd, master and commander of the Athenians the Persians have gone to fight?" The chorus tells her, "They are not called slaves or subjects to any man." But how then can they resist, how fight against an army as large as theirs. And the chorus tells her to remember what had happened to her dead husband when the Athenians "destroyed the large and splendid army of Darius."

I glanced across at Hiero to see his reaction, but, like all the others who sat watching, he was too dazzled by the defeat he knew was coming, all those Persian deaths, to think through the meaning of the lines.

The play was over; the actors and the chorus took their final bows. The heat of the Sicilian sun beat down on the thousand faces of the crowd, delirious with its own applause. The noise began to melt away and then started up again when Aeschylus came on stage to thank them for the reception that had been given and to make one last announcement. He wanted to thank Hiero for making it all possible, and, beckoning toward him, insisted he join him on stage to receive the tribute he was owed. The chorus, a dozen actors still wearing long robes and painted masks, came up the steps and closed us in their circle, Hiero's dramatic escort to the stage. Two of them passed behind me and suddenly I was covered in a robe and hidden in an actor's mask, part of Hiero's temporary guard. It happened quicker than the eye could see. Hiero was in front; no one paid attention to those who followed him; no one wondered where I was. Through the eye holes of the black mask, I watched, a prisoner, as Aeschylus, wearing makeup to accentuate his features for an audience some of whom sat at a great distance, with a sweeping gesture of his arm offered Hiero to the crowd. Hiero stepped forward, as if he could never get close enough to those who needed him, their love the constant object of his desire.

Everyone was on their feet giving the tribute of their applause. Hiero kept waving to the crowd, looking one way then the other, trying to make everyone think he was only there for them. I was in the back with the others, my arms held by two anonymous assailants, one on each side; and then, in the passing of a breath, I was gone, taken off the stage and behind the wall on which the room in the Persian palace had been painted, the background for all the action of the play. Someone helped me out of the robe and someone else took away the mask. They were both actors in the chorus. I never saw their faces, but when they saw mine they stopped what they were doing and for a moment could only stare.

"She needs something else to wear," one of them finally said. "And something – a wig, anything – to change the way she looks."

I was given the clothing of workman and a cover for my head, and then another member of the company, one of those who work behind the scenes, grabbed me by the arm and led me through a back entrance to the street outside. We walked quickly, keeping close to the buildings until we came to a narrow alleyway that took us down to the shore. A boat was waiting, a fisherman's one master with a sail. As if he had not a care in the world, and all the time there was, Herodotus smiled up at me and helped me get on board.

"Did you bring her clothing, what she was wearing at the play?"

The man who brought me handed him a canvas sack. My silk peplos, the garment that on the top third was folded over and then pinned on both shoulders, the thin scarlet mantel that fastened so delicately at my throat, the golden light sandals with the straps that wrapped around my ankles, had all been stuffed inside. Herodotus put the bulging sack down at his feet and gave the order to cast off.

"Where are you taking me?" I protested. "Why are you doing this? When my father …!" I caught myself, fought against my anger at the way I had been taken, made a captive, forced against my will to go – where? But did it matter where I was going, if I was going away from here, away from everything I hated, everything I feared? Whatever Herodotus intended, he only meant to help. That much I knew.

"You wanted someone to come and take you away – though I imagine you were thinking of another Paris come to take away another Helen. I saw it in your eyes, and something else as well: that these things that you keep hidden are things you wanted me to know."

The kindness in his fearless eyes, the strength of his intelligence, told me there was nothing I could conceal from him, nothing I needed to keep hidden. He could read the page that was not written.

"That is what you were thinking the other evening – was it not? – looking at the distant shore, dreaming of what might lie beyond it. That is what I did, years ago when I was young, wondered what was out there, what kind of people there might be; wondered whether there was something that might be worth knowing, something different from what, growing up, I had been taught to believe. Shall I tell you what I learned?" he asked with a gentleness I could only imagine was the way a father might talk to a daughter. He looked past me to the far horizon where the sinking sun had begun to leave behind a fading purple glow. "Every place I visited was different, and every place the same: madness and confusion everywhere and every place convinced it was the one exception."

His aging eyes came back to mine, the light within them brighter and more alive as he noticed with something close to amusement a strange coincidence of what he saw in front of him and what he knew.

"Your father was right about one thing. You have Helen's face, the face we have all been schooled about, the face that caused a war. The trouble is the story isn't true."

"Isn't true?" I asked, surprised at how quick I was to catch the suggestion that instead of common property, a shared remembrance, my face was more my own than that. "What part of it has been misinterpreted?"

Instead of answering, he reached into the canvas bag, he took out the clothing that I had worn that day and threw them overboard. I watched as they drifted back behind us, wondering how long before another boat, one of those sent to search for me, would find them; how long before it became known that Hiero's daughter had drowned; how long before Hiero thought of ways to use it to his best advantage.

"You can't go back," said Herodotus; "not while your father is still alive."

"Why would I want to? I was born there, and I lived there, but I've never been alive. How could I be, nothing but a dressed up doll, a showpiece, the way I looked something Hiero could brag about. My head could have been stuffed with sawdust for all anyone knew."

"No one who ever heard you speak," said Herodotus, gently and with a look of heartfelt sympathy.

How many other men would have felt sorry for a girl who looked like a second Helen and, as the daughter of a ruler with no limit to his power, had at her disposal everything the world prizes? I was beautiful and powerful and rich: what difference if I had any thoughts of my own? And if, because of that, I sometimes wished I were ugly, what was that if not proof of a frivolous intelligence that, like any woman, was and always would be a prisoner of appearances? But Herodotus saw everything.

The night was coming, chasing day to darkness. High up in the heavens, the evening star made its first appearance, waiting for the chance to signal the other stars to come and guard the sky. The wind stayed fresh, filling the boat's small sail, and the air felt cool against my skin as the wind raced past me. The rippled movement of the water reminded me of what he had said about that other Helen and how the story of her life was largely an invention. It seemed, as I thought about it, that the same thing could be said about the life I had lived so far: a fiction, a fiction that I had been forced to write. No one really knew me, including, especially, myself.

"Tell me what you were going to tell me, that the story told about Helen is not true. I asked you what part of it has been misinterpreted or misunderstood."

"All of it, or nearly so. Paris, guest of Helen's husband, took her to his bed, and then took her away. But Helen was not forced; she chose to go. They ran off together, but Helen never got to Troy. Their ship was blown off course and landed them in Egypt. They were brought to Memphis where Proteus, the Egyptian ruler, learning how Paris had betrayed the generosity of his host gave him three days to leave the country but made Helen stay behind. The Greeks sent all those ships, spent all those years, lost all those men, so that Troy could be destroyed, but Helen was not there. The Trojans did not have her; there was no Helen to give back. But Homer could not tell that story; the truth was not suitable for a poem of such epic proportions. And so Homer lied, and everyone still believes it."

He saw the question in my eyes, the only doubt I had.

"You think that telling this will change what the Greeks believe, telling them what the Egyptians, who keep better records and know more about the past than anyone else, told me themselves? It isn't that no one believes what I have written; people just ignore it. They listen, nod their agreement, and then continue to repeat as a truth too well-known to be questioned the legend just the way Homer wrote it. But never mind that, there are more important things to consider. Was I wrong in thinking that you are in some danger and need a place to hide?"

"Yes, but despite what others think, that thought they have from Homer, I wasn't thinking that another Paris might come to take me somewhere far away. If he did," I laughed, "I would tell him to take me straight to Egypt where I would ask asylum and that way avoid a war."

There was an irony in what I said, but I did not need to explain that to Herodotus who had seen it before I finished.

"And then some other poet would write an epic in which you never went to Egypt but were taken by an African so that the Sicilians could fight another, bigger war with Carthage." He smiled back at me, and then the smile vanished. "That still leaves the problem what can be done with you? Fortunately, I know a place, Agrigento, where there is someone who can help you, not just with a place to live, but to learn what, if I am not mistaken, you more than most others have the ability to grasp, a man of such great wisdom some think him a god." Something wonderful, the silent laughter of his mind, danced delighted through his deep-set eyes. "It is a belief my friend Empedocles does nothing to discourage."

We passed beyond the outer limits of the great harbor and were running with the shoreline on our right, starting on the course that would lead us first south and then west to Agrigento. The sun, going home to rest, had left the rose colored sky behind and changed the color of the endless sea from daylight blue to molten burnished brass.

A thin smile played on his lips as Herodotus thought about what might happen next, when we were far away, what Syracuse would be told, the kind of story that would explain my death and the legend it would doubtless soon create.

"Perhaps they'll say that, too beautiful for mortals, Poseidon took you for his own, promising the other gods that from that wedding match would be born another race of heroes, another generation to repeat the cycle of human triumph and defeat. It would fit with Hiero's purpose to have the children of the gods owe their lineage to him and that way live forever in the memories of men."

"He'll live forever in hell; it will take that long to count his crimes."

We sailed all night, steering by the stars, and then, in the fiery light of morning I saw them from the distance of the sea, shining in the scarlet glory of the sun, ten temples, ranged along the hillside, one below the other, stepping stones from heaven down to earth, the stately Doric columns carved from the yellow sandstone cut from the very hills on which they stood: Ten temples, several finished in just the last few years, each dedicated to a different god; the sacred life of the city, their offered tribute, expressed with a perfect sense of proportion and a perfect eye for beauty. More than a different place, Agrigento was a different world. Even Herodotus could think of nothing to rival the stunning splendor of what the citizens of Agrigento, living in their modest homes, sharing common walls with their neighbors and finding pleasure in the privacy of a sheltered garden and a few surrounding rooms, had done. Instead of spending their wealth on themselves they had spent it on places for their gods.

CHAPTER THREE

Still a prisoner of what I had heard from others: that I was Helen, with a face that, though the opposite of Medusa, could also drive men insane, I expected to have the same effect on anyone who met me, but Empedocles did not seem to notice me at all. Herodotus could only smile.

"This is the young woman I sent word about."

"The tyrant's daughter. Yes, I remember."

That was all. He barely glanced at me. We sat on stone benches ranged in a semi-circle at the edge of a rose-covered garden. Cypress trees towered high above us and in the distance, the ten stone temples looked down on the sea. Empedocles, the most respected man in Agrigento, lived a short distance from the city.

"It won't be a problem," he said before Herodotus had said anything. "The girl can stay here. We have room."

He was looking at Herodotus but I was not sure he saw him. When Herodotus talked to you, he held you captive not just with his eyes, but with his whole manner. He was animated, alive, eager to have you listen and, listening, understand what he was telling you, and just as eager, perhaps even more so, to hear your response. Empedocles was aloof, distant, and far more reserved. He had settled with a single sentence the prosaic question of what would happen to me, dismissed it as a matter of no great importance. I would stay there, a permanent guest in his home, a decision that for anyone else would have meant a major alteration in their life but for him seemed no different than if he had been asked if someone might pick a fig from his tree. The matter was settled. There was something more urgent he wanted to discuss.

"What difference does it make that Helen wasn't there?"

"Helen wasn't where?" asked Herodotus, a puzzled expression in his eyes. "In Syracuse, in Hiero's court – ?"

"Not that Helen," said Empedocles, showing some puzzlement of his own. It seemed impossible that Herodotus could not have known what he was talking about. "The real Helen, Homer's Helen."

Herodotus told me with his eyes that I should not take personally the strange eccentricities of the man under whose protection I was going to live. He looked at Empedocles and, unable to resist, told him that for all his attempts to see into the nature of things, he might do well to start with what was obvious.

"That Helen you have only heard about; this Helen you see with your own eyes. Or you could, if your mind was not so fixed on abstractions. She's the most beautiful young woman I have ever seen, the most beautiful woman anyone has ever seen, but she might as well be the ugliest for all you've seemed to notice."

Empedocles did not smile, and he did not look at me, but there was a subtle change in the way he now looked at Herodotus.

"Perhaps that's the reason I don't look at her: too much a reminder of the weakness, or I should say, the power, of the senses; what I had to overcome before I found the meaning of my life. It is not how she looks, but what you told me she might be that led me to agree to your request."

He looked at me with something in his eyes I had not seen before, the look a parent has for a child: a deep longing for what I might become.

"Do you know what he told me about you?" he asked, his voice a quiet warm whisper. "That you have the gift, not of prophecy, but of understanding. He said I should teach you what I know and that you would learn more than I can teach. You're welcome here, and you'll be safe here. That much I can promise."

Herodotus had charmed me with his friendship and with his daring, the bravery of what he had done, taking me away from Syracuse, saving me from Hiero's lethal vengeance; but I felt a sense of awe in the presence of Empedocles, a sense of something permanent and unchanging.

"But it is about that other Helen I wanted to speak," he said, immediately turning back to Herodotus. "What I asked you before: What difference that Helen was not there, that she was in Egypt and not in Troy. It was what the Greeks believed. Men act on what they believe; they don't investigate the truth; they don't look too closely into things."

Empedocles sat with his head bent at an angle. His elbow rested on the arm at the end of the stone bench. His thumb and fourth finger met together at the edge of his smooth shaven chin, while his second and third finger ran parallel along the side of his face to his temple. A sculptor would have envied the elegance of the line, the thoughtful solitude of a strange, uncanny self-sufficiency.

"Herodotus knows this," he said, turning slowly and quite deliberately to me. "He knows that Homer and Hesiod gave the Greeks their gods."

Their gods; not our gods. Whatever Empedocles thought about the gods – whether he believed in them or not – it was not what others believed.

"The gods they created weren't like the gods of the Egyptians or the Persians. They were gods of a different kind. Weren't they?" he asked, turning again to Herodotus. "They were gods in human shape or form. It is remarkable what these two poets, Hesiod and Homer, did, consciously and on purpose creating gods that because they are like human beings, separate us from all the other living things and give us a specific excellence. We are not just animals who live and die; we have gods we look up to, and that way can judge whether to despise or respect ourselves. The gods, these gods we created, established a sense of shame. This is more important than most of us imagine. The Egyptians, as you describe so well, gave their gods the shapes of animals, and because of that think themselves no better than their own subhuman part. The Persians, as you tell us, made their gods more than human, worshipping cosmic powers, and because of that have nothing, no specific excellence, to which they can aspire. It is the reason that among them, except for those who rule them, life has no more value than a speck of dust on the ground."

Herodotus replied with a smile that barely broke the long line of his mouth, the recognition of a kindred soul, a reader who could read, someone who with rare precision had understood exactly his intention. They spoke a while longer and then Herodotus said he had to leave. In just a few short days he had become the only real friend I had ever had. The dismal isolation in which I had lived my life, the mask my look had given me, all the habits of duplicity and double meaning, everything I had needed to survive, I had needed none of them with him. He protected me, and in the shelter of that protection I had, as it were, taken my first breath. He knew me better than I knew myself; he knew what I was thinking before the thought had reached my conscious mind.

"You'll be fine here," he said, as I walked him through the house to the door in front. "Now that you've met him, you can't be in any doubt about that. He's agreed to have you here as his ward, a responsibility he takes seriously. And you'll be one of his students.

He only has a few. We'll meet again, Helen; I'm sure of it."

And then he was gone. He told me he was going to Athens, but that there were a few other places he wanted to visit first, some other customs he wanted to learn more about.

Herodotus had been right when he said that Empedocles had the kind of intelligence that compels the assent of anyone not blinded by greed or ambition, but, as I had learned at the court of Hiero, greed and ambition are far more common than generosity or moderation. There had to be something more than his grave demeanor and obvious intelligence that explained the hold he had on the city. This became clear some weeks later when I was allowed to attend a dinner Empedocles put on for some of the city's most influential men. Their names had no meaning for me, but some of them reminded me of men I had known in Syracuse, men with money whose only interest was in getting more. I had watched the way they behaved in a tyrant's court: the cringing eagerness to do whatever they were asked, the willingness to submit to any indignity. Things were more civilized here, or so it seemed from the quiet way they discussed the common problems of the city. There were ten invited guests, three of whom, among the wealthiest men in the city, measured everything by its cost. Someone mentioned what a great achievement it had been to build the ten temples, that whatever happened in the future it would make the city last forever in the memories of men. Their eyes seemed to go into mourning at the memory of the expense. The others, if I judged them right, were more interested in making a name for themselves as men to watch. They understood the regard in which Empedocles was held and were quick to defer to him, but it was the deference paid to those we know we can never rival, someone whose hold on the first position is unassailable.

"You haven't introduced your new visitor," said Menedemus, a fat little man with moist lascivious lips and eyes full of cunning. "What is the boy's name?"

It had worked! I had changed sexes. My hair had been cut short and colored blonde instead of black. There was no more false shading around my eyes, none of the things the slave girls used to do to make my lips a deeper red. The girl who had captured the attention of every man who saw her was now a boy who captured – this? An aging reprobate, a pederast who had begun to sweat with pleasure at his fantasy of evil!

"The child," replied Empedocles in a voice that seemed to

underscore the innocence of my age, "has been entrusted to my care. I thought it good, part of an education I wish I had had, to listen to the conversation of serious men."

There was no change in Empedocles' voice, but Menedemus had a vague sense that there was a warning in his words. A tremor passed along his wet lips, a coward's indecision. Caught in the dilemma whether to take offense, or by his protest prove the implication, he took refuge in ambiguity.

"I thought he had the look of a young man interested in what he could be taught by those older. But I did not quite follow your remark, Empedocles. You wish you had had a different education than the one you had?" He looked around at the others to see if they agreed that this was more than strange. "You were a student of Pythagoras. What better education could you have had?"

"You forget, Menedemus – he was expelled." Sitting some distance away, Dion, one of the youngest men there, had difficulty restraining himself, his contempt for Menedemus was that obvious. "He published some of what he learned, the secret doctrines no one was supposed to talk about."

"That's a falsehood," insisted Cleanthes, who sat just below Empedocles. "A rumor started by those who opposed the democracy. Those," he added with a look that accused Dion of complicity, "who would like nothing better than to have everything run by just a few."

Dion may have been an enemy of freedom for others; he certainly felt free enough himself. He laughed at Cleanthes.

"Do you think we're better ruled now than we were when Theron was alive?" He fell silent for a moment, grappling with a thought that had just come to him. The open hostility passed away, replaced by what seemed almost a plea for understanding. "Do you think we'd be ruled at all, do you think there would be anything but chaos, if it weren't for Empedocles? We throw around the names of things – tyranny, democracy – as if they were always opposites; but let me tell you, the worst tyrant of all is the tyranny of a free people acting without constraint, free to change the laws at will, free to do whatever it happens to think best at the moment. It's a mob, this assembly of ours: no intelligence, only passion. It's all our worst impulses, without someone to guide it."

"Someone like you!" said Cleanthes, as unimpressed as he was unpersuaded.

Shaking his head in frustration, Dion reached for his wine cup but something changed his mind.

"What do you think, Empedocles?"

"What do I think?" There was a glow of mischief in his usually so solemn eyes. "About whether I was forbidden to return to the school of Pythagoras or left of my own accord?"

"No, not that; – well, yes, perhaps; if you care to. You did publish in one of your poems some of their teaching, did you not?"

Everyone was looking at him, waiting for him to answer, but for a long time Empedocles said nothing. Finally, his gaze, moving slowly, came to Dion, and then, to my surprise, instead of stopping, moved on to me.

"But you see, once you have learned something it belongs to you, your possession; something you are, or should be, free to share with others. No one owns the truth," he added as his eyes moved away and stopped briefly, but only briefly, at Menedemus who had not heard a word.

"I understand," said Dion, his voice filled with a new respect. "But I wanted – "

"Wanted to know what I think about the way we were ruled when Theron was still alive. But more than that, you want to know whether, like Cleanthes, I think democracy is always best. The best answer I can give you is yes and no."

There was laughter in the room. The tension that had been building disappeared. Several reached for their cups. Menedemus laughed along with the rest of them, but could not have told you why. Empedocles had done it all on purpose, known the effect his words would have. He was aware of everything, his senses like sentinels that kept coming back with new reports.

"Theron was called a tyrant because he ruled alone, but then the name lacks all definition. It was not just in birth and wealth that he surpassed all others. That is no achievement. Theron treated the people he ruled always with an eye toward their improvement. He cared more about them than he did about himself. That was the reason he surpassed not only all the other citizens – why he deserved to rule – but all the other Sicilian Greeks as well. Theron was not a tyrant; Theron was a king. But either way there is trouble. Better to be ruled by a king than a tyrant; better yet to be ruled by neither. We were not ruled by our own consent, and because of that, after Theron died, it was a question of succession. The king was dead and now his son, a tyrant of the worst description, took his place."

"How many guests last night at dinner?" asked Empedocles as if he was not sure, and as if the question had a significance of which I was not aware. We were walking in a shady grove a short distance from the house. The clean, clear sound of swift running water echoed through the trees from the creek just beyond a vine covered arbor. The hanging grapes were a dusty deep purple and almost ripe.

"How many – ? Ten," I answered without hesitation.

"How do you know?"

"How do I know there were ten? – I was there; I remember."

"You remember there were ten, but my question isn't whether you remember what you learned, but how you learned it."

"Learned that there were ten? I just saw it."

He stopped walking, folded his arms across his chest and stared down at the dust covered ground. "What did you see?"

"Everyone who was there."

He turned his head just far enough to see me. "Every one: They were each one?"

"Each one – yes, one person. There were ten of them."

"Ten ones?"

"Ten ones – ten men; isn't that what you asked?"

"Each one was a man?"

"Yes." Suddenly, remembering the pederast, Menedemus, I laughed. "Though there might be one exception."

He ignored my remark. There was something he was determined to teach me.

"Each one was a man, and there were ten of them. They each had that in common: that they were all men, human beings?"

"Yes, of course; I don't – "

"Who taught you that? How did you first learn it?"

"First learn it? No one taught me that."

"You knew the difference between a man and a horse. No one taught you that?" But before I could answer another question that seemed to make no sense, he brushed it aside. "No, never mind. The point I want to make – what I want you to see – is that we somehow know these things, know that there are differences that define each kind of being we see in the world. Without that there could be no mathematics."

He looked up at the sky and took a breath that seemed to flow through his whole body. Rising up on the balls of his feet he stretched his arms, took another deep breath, and then, once again, began to walk in the steady pace that never varied.

"You knew they were the same, that they were all human beings," he continued. "Suppose I had asked you just 'How many?' What would you do then? – Ask me 'how many what?' Isn't that correct? You see, there has to be a 'what,' we have to know what something is before we can know how many of them there are. So, again, how many guests last night at dinner?"

"Ten; but I said that at the beginning."

"And see how far we have advanced, how much progress we have made. You now know what you did not know before: that we can only count the things we know. That leads to another question, more difficult than the first. You say there were ten men. You mean a number like this?"

Bending down, he cleared the ground with the palm of his hand, and then, using white pebbles he made a line with four of them, and then, above that, a line of three, then a line of two, and finally, at the top, he placed just one. It was a perfect triangle, four pebbles on each of the three sides.

"Can you count them?"

"Of course," I said; eager to see where this was going to take us.

"And the reason you can count them?"

"Because they are all of one kind; or," I added as my mind began to grasp more of the meaning of his explanation, "all of the kind we have chosen to distinguish, to differentiate, from all other things."

"Very good; yes, exactly. How many pebbles are there?"

"Ten. The same number as your guests last night."

"What do you see, what do you learn, from the way the pebbles, the ten of them, have been arranged?"

But I saw nothing, nothing at all; a triangle with three equal sides.

"Keep looking."

Still nothing; ten pebbles, a triangle that looked the same whatever side you started from. Then, suddenly, I saw it; though, I confess, I did not know what it meant.

"The ten, it is the sum of the four numbers: four, three, two and one."

"It is called the tetraktys of the dekad. It represents the number

ten as the triangle of four. Ten is the first number that has in it an
equal number of prime and composite numbers. But never mind that
now; this is good enough for a start. This is extremely important, this
notion of number and counting. And of all the numbers, 'ten' may
turn out to be the most important; but, as I say, it will all become
clear later. There is plenty of time. For right now, let us leave it with
the observation that, according to our friend Herodotus, except for
a few backward people, the number 'ten' is used everywhere as the
basis of calculation."

He picked the pebbles from the ground and tossed them to the
side, and then nodded toward the empty space.

"What do you see now? Nothing. Which means?"

"Nothing left to count."

"Yes; exactly."

We walked some more, part of what, as I came to learn, was
his regular morning habit, the first thing he did. It cleared his mind,
he later told me; freed him from the dreams and vague half-thoughts
that disturbed his sleep.

"There were ten guests last night," he remarked. I thought he
was going to add more to his first lesson on the roots of mathematics,
but he did not want to know how I knew how or what to count, but
what I thought about them, the ones he had invited. "I have known
them all for years. I'm interested in your impression, how they struck
you on this, the first time, you had ever seen them. Which among
them did you find most interesting?"

"Dion," I replied immediately. "He more than any of the others
stood out."

"He usually does. What about him impressed you – what he
said, or the way he said it?"

The distinction was not new to me. I had learned to make it
almost with my first breath.

"Hiero has a way of saying things that makes at least some
people favor tyranny."

"Is that how Dion impresses you – someone who can persuade
others that he alone should rule?"

I stopped walking and said nothing until Empedocles, now two
steps ahead, turned and looked back at me.

"Yes, but the two things are not the same."

"Not the same? Because ...?"

"Hiero never persuaded anyone that he should have a tyrant's power; it was a power he was given, a gift from his brother. He did not need words to get what he has; he uses words to paint a better picture of what he does."

"Dion doesn't have that power, but you think that with his power of speech he could get it?"

"Yes, unless there are others who can speak just as well."

Empedocles studied me with a new intensity. "This is one of the things I try to teach, and the reason for it. If we are going to rule ourselves, we cannot afford to let one man, or even several, be more persuasive than all the others. But there are limits to what this or any other art can achieve. There will always be some men better than others; and, if you follow that out, always one man best among them. Dion thinks it is him."

I had seen enough, or thought I had, of the charm of men and their power. I was not nearly as interested in what Dion thought of himself as I was in numbers. That diagram, that simple triangle Empedocles had made with those small white pebbles, that strange relation of the first four numbers, the mystery of what those numbers might mean, worked a kind of magic in my mind. I could not stop thinking about it, wondering about it, and even, such was the nature of my obsession, dreaming about it. I saw triangles everywhere I looked; and not just triangles, but circles, squares and rectangles, every figure known and formed, every one of them, by the numbered pebbles of my sometimes fevered imagination. I counted everything, and tried to think through what it meant to count at all.

That question seemed the key to everything, the difference whether there was an order in the world or only chaos. I could count things; any child could do it. What I had not seen until Empedocles showed me was that the things that are countable have within them an order, something that holds them together and makes them, in principle, indistinguishable from each other. I could count the pebbles but only because I first knew they were pebbles and not something else. The things that were countable were all the same. But that was impossible. No two pebbles were exactly alike. Was this not to count as equal two unequal things?

I asked Empedocles, but instead of an answer, he dragged the point of a stick across the dirt and asked me to explain the meaning of the mark it left.

"It's a line."

"What kind of line – curved or straight?"

35

"Straight."

"Are you sure? Look at it again. Now, look at this." He drew another line in the dirt next to the first one. "If you stretched a string from a point at the top to a point at the bottom, which would be straighter?"

"The string, but ... " And suddenly, I knew. "The straight is different from the straight things we see. It isn't in the realm of sense – what we see, what we touch – it is what is straight and never varies, what it means in our mind."

"Now take it a step farther. What about the numbers themselves? We say 'two pebbles' plus 'four pebbles.' The pebbles, as we have seen, are objects of sense and can never be entirely equal with one another. But there is also a multitude in which each unit is equal, not in the least different, and has no parts. This is the realm of pure number in which the relation between them can be established. Pythagoras was among those who thought that numbers existed; more than that, that numbers make up the world."

That was all he would tell me, and I do not think I could have followed him had he tried to tell me more. I had understood, or thought I had, that implicit in the act of numbering or counting was the proof that there was an order in the world. But numbers were the things we used to count. In what way did it follow that numbers themselves somehow existed? And yet I had the feeling that it was true. The line drawn in the dirt was less a line than the one drawn perfectly in my mind. I could see the line in the dirt and I could not see the other. It seemed odd if only the one that could never be as good, as perfect, as the other, was the only one that was real. But for the present, I was content to have raised the question with myself. There were other things I had to learn, and other things I had to do.

Empedocles had told me that philosophy was not so much a subject as a way of life, but even that was something of a mystery. There seemed to be two parts to this: the way someone lived when they were just starting out, a student trying to learn, and the way someone lived when they no longer needed the help of others and could learn things on their own.

"In the school of Pythagoras, there was always a strict discipline; a strange discipline, if you want the truth," said Empedocles on one of the morning walks that had now become habitual. "But all for a purpose. All his students, his disciples, surrendered all their possession, which became common property. No one had anything they could call their own. And then, for five years, they were not allowed to speak. They had to keep their silence, listening only to Pythagoras, listening but never seeing him."

"Never seeing him?" I asked in astonishment. Then I remembered. "Hiero fooled people into believing he had the power to make himself invisible. Was that what Pythagoras was trying to do? – Make his disciples believe he had that kind of power."

"I have heard the story they tell about Hiero. It bears a likeness to the story of the ring of Gyges, told by Herodotus. Pythagoras claimed other powers. He gave his lectures at night, so everyone could concentrate on his words. You could not see him and no one else could speak; for five years, the only conversation the one you had with those remembered words of his in the silence of your mind. He knew what he was doing. There was nothing else, after you listened in the darkness to what he thought, but to think it through, over and over again, each time grasping another shade of meaning until, finally, if you were capable, you could see what he was saying almost as if you had seen it first."

Empedocles could sense my doubt, my hesitation. He knew that it was not because I did not believe what he was telling me, but that I could not yet quite understand what he meant.

"Let me give you a few examples. Pythagoras would offer various precepts, rules of conduct we should follow. They seem, on first impression, to be simple, even meaningless; what you might expect to hear from some half-demented child instead of a man honored for his wisdom.

"'Don't stir fire with a knife; don't step over the beam of a balance; don't sit down on your bushel; don't eat your heart' – ! What kind of nonsense is this? – you would be right to ask. But now, sit somewhere by yourself, sit there for days and try to think. What does it mean, what could it mean? Pythagoras will help you; he has helped you. He has given you other precepts, each as seemingly meaningless as these, but given you besides a commentary, an exegesis, on the deeper meaning hidden within.

"'Don't stir fire with a knife.' What does it mean? – Be careful not to stir up the passions, the pride and arrogance, of the great. 'Don't step over the beam of a balance' – Do not cross beyond the limit of what equity and justice require. 'Don't sit down on your bushel' – A 'bushel' refers to the ration, what you need to survive, for a single day. 'Don't sit down' means think about and take steps for the future. 'Don't eat your heart' – That may have had more meaning than any of the others, the best advice anyone could give: Do not waste your life troubling yourself with things you cannot control.

"This was all preliminary; a way to teach the habit of searching beyond the surface to what is irreducible."

"Irreducible?" I asked, puzzled and intrigued.

"Something that cannot be reduced to something else. Pythagoras thought that everything there is, the world, was derived from four elements: fire, water, earth and air; elements which interchange and turn into one another, and which in their combination produce a universe that is animate, intelligent and spherical, with the earth at its center."

"But how?" I asked in the pride of my youthful ignorance. "Who made the elements, and once they were made, who set them in order?"

"Who? You mean, which gods?"

Empedocles looked at me with knowing kindness, and I felt that I knew already what of course I did not know at all; a feeling that, as I later learned, was not nearly as strange as it seems. A blind man knows there are things he has not seen. He had asked me if I meant the gods, and I had; but as soon as he said it, I knew I had meant something else, though what I could not yet have imagined. And so I nodded my reply, but in the vague way that tells of one's uncertainty.

"If the elements had been made, they would not be irreducible. Anything created, anything that comes into being, perishes. The question was, is there such a thing as being simply, something that has always been and will always be, something permanent and unchanging. Pythagoras thought there were gods, but not the ones we claim to know. The sun, the moon, the other stars – those are the real gods. They have in them a preponderance of heat and heat is the cause of life. That was how he made the connection between gods and men: both partake of heat and that is the reason god takes thought for men and gives an order to things both as a whole and to each separately. Heat gives birth to life, but the soul is immortal. It lives forever, but never long in the same place. It follows a course from which no variance is possible. But be careful to make a distinction. It is not quite the same soul that continues on this endless cycle. The soul is divided into three parts: intelligence and passion, both of which are shared with the other animals, and reason. Only reason is immortal. Pythagoras was convinced of this, or so at least he said."

This suggested another possibility, that it was all a fiction designed for some other purpose, a way to hide or disguise the truth. I thought of what Empedocles had just told me, that the surface of things was not the place to finish but the place to start. The sun was almost overhead, our morning walk almost over. I listened even more intently as Empedocles explained what Pythagoras had done, or, for those who remain skeptical, said he had done.

"The soul – that part of it that is immortal, that part that at death survives the body – goes everywhere and sees everything. He said that he himself had lived in Hades for two hundred seven years before returning to live among mortal men. That was convenient, in a way: he could then speak with some authority about what had happened to the souls of certain other well-known men. He said – I did not hear it from his own lips, but I was told by someone who did – that he saw the soul of Hesiod bound fast to a brazen pillar gibbering nonsense, and the soul of Homer hung on a tree with serpents writhing all about it, the punishment, the fit punishment, they had been given for all the lies and falsehoods they had told about the gods."

It was a mark of how obsessed I had become with numbers and their meaning that I spent days trying to determine the significance of two hundred seven. If the soul was bound to the course fate had given it, if the soul of Pythagoras was bound to spend a certain definite allotted time in Hades before coming back to mortal life, nothing could be random in its journey. The number had to mean something, but all I could get with my poor powers was the senseless discovery that the number could be divided into several different numbers and that one of them, three times sixty nine, suggested the possibility of three lifetimes, but nothing more than that. Or could it refer to the three parts of the soul; that each had to spend a lifetime in Hades before it could emerge purified by punishment into a new and better form? The numbers made me crazy. If all the different permutations were somehow the cause of order in the world, they were also, as it seemed to me, likely to cause me to lose what little sanity I had. But there was something about this that would not let me stop, that drove me on, that made me think in ways I had never thought before, ways that before Empedocles began to teach me I had not known were possible.

Weeks went by, then months; autumn turned summer brown,

winter stole autumn's leaves and then spring again brought life back
to winter's dead. Other girls my age dreamed of boys and what their
life would be like when they were old enough to have their fathers
marry them to someone suitable; I dreamed – literally dreamed – of
elements and numbers and how without them nothing would exist.
I thought I was losing my mind; Empedocles thought I was only
just finding it. While other girls my age thought of the children they
would bring into the world, I thought, or tried to think, of how the
world itself had first come into being. What other girls, and not just
other girls, but men with their own boyish dreams, thought dry as
dust, boring and unimportant, I found compelling and exciting. I
was drawn to it, held captive by it, this strange desire to know, to
work out the mystery of existence, the meaning of all those elements
and numbers that kept dancing through my eager, delighted mind. It
was erotic; it was what eros meant: the desire for what, if you could
ever really have it, would make you whole and give you perfection. It
was a search for your own nature, what you were meant to be.

I was careful. My mind might be full of wild enthusiasms, but I
knew better than to betray with gushing impatience what I had only
half discovered. I asked questions, not very often and only when I
thought they might be questions that had not been asked before.

"There are four elements – fire, earth, air and water – but
these are not the principles of things. Numbers are. According to
Pythagoras everything in the beginning was one, what they call the
monad. Somehow, from this one or monad comes a two. This is the
beginning of division and multiplicity, the beginning of numbers,
both the odd and the even. These numbers are real, they exist, they
have bodily extension, as you explained. If each number is a pebble,
each number a point, then I can see how the line is formed, and from
the line a plane; and from the plane a solid figure, which means the
sensible bodies, the very ones that are supposed to be made up of the
four elements: fire, air, earth and water."

"Yes," replied Empedocles, stopping a few steps from the creek
just beyond the cedar grove. "I follow what you say, and what you
say is correct. That is what Pythagoras tried to teach."

"The numbers – what we use to count – each thing we see is
distinguished from the others by their different numbers. But the
one – the unit from which all other numbers are different in terms
of how many – would always be the same size. Instead of elements
– fire, earth, air and water – which themselves must be composed

of and differentiated by number, would it not be more correct to say that there is only one element out of which all the things that exist are composed; that number – the one that added together makes many – is the basic element out of which all other things are made?"

For a long time Empedocles said nothing. He stood there, staring into the distance, lost in a concentration so powerful that it almost seemed as if he had left his body. Then, slowly, he returned and, still silent, began to walk. We must have walked half a mile before he began to speak.

"Numbers, according to Pythagoras and those who follow him, are, as you describe, the way the world is ordered. Only things that are countable can form a kind. It is what we see when we look around, things that exist because of what each kind shares in common. Whatever these things are, whether, for example, we're talking about dogs or horses or human beings; whether we're talking about things that live and breathe or rocks on the ground, everything is reducible to one or more of those four elements, alone or in combination. The real problem is not whether these in turn can be reduced to something smaller, the simple number you refer to, but how those four elements work to produce the world we see. What makes them form in combination, what divides them and keeps them apart? Something is needed beyond the four elements themselves. What was missing – that was what I found, the thing that explains the nature of the world in which we live: love and strife, the two forces which through their constant motion make possible life and all existence."

Did they? I wondered. How could anything combine with any other unless there was something – some one thing – that held everything together? I was about to ask him about this when he told me something that made me forget everything but how much I had come to admire him.

"You have been here only a year, and already you're the best student I have had."

"But I know nothing," I protested behind a smile that had raced unbidden across my mouth. "Less than that, if that's possible."

"That by itself is a wisdom most men, no matter how long they live, never get. It is a wisdom that the man everyone seems to think my most brilliant student will never have. He knows everything, has an answer to every question and likes nothing better than to show you. He's here today, visiting from Leontini. You'll come with me.

He's going to lecture. There won't be an empty seat in the theater. You will be interested in this. He's going to prove that nothing Helen did – Homer's Helen – was Helen's fault. This is the sort of thing Gorgias does: argue absurdities in a way that seems to make it impossible to argue back. I tried to teach him how to persuade people to do the things they should. I didn't teach him very well. He gives speeches to show that, for a price, he can teach you how to make people do whatever is to your own advantage. I should have followed Pythagoras' example and made him keep his mouth shut for at least five years. But come and see for yourself, this new power in the world. Everyone wants to do it now, learn how to argue more effectively than those who argue on the other side, whichever side is right. The only question is how long before the people who have been persuaded to do things they shouldn't, will turn on those who tricked them into doing it."

CHAPTER FOUR

Gorgias was a fool. The wonder was that no one seemed to know it. Empedocles came dressed the way he did whenever he went out in public: a purple robe and a golden girdle, a Delphic laurel wreath in his thick hair and bronze slippers on his feet. He looked elegant and, with the grave demeanor that never left him, would have commanded respect among a crowd of strangers. It brought him something close to veneration from the free citizens of Agrigento.

Gorgias also wore a purple robe, but the better to make the long sweeping gestures with which he underscored the antitheses of his patterned speech, his hung loose around his waist. He wore rings on his fingers and bracelets on his arms, and his long, curled hair was tinted the color of the summer sun. Everything about him suggested a staged flamboyance. Every word, every gesture, was measured for effect. The smile that flashed across his prim and rather narrow mouth seemed false and artificial, without connection to any real feeling; and if he had learned through Empedocles what Pythagoras had taught of numbers, he used that knowledge only to count the interval between each change of expression. It was that precise, the words, the balanced sentences, the movement of his eyes from one side of the amphitheater to the other, the pause each time he finished one more step in the argument he had contrived with such painstaking calculation.

He was there, he said, to talk about Helen and why she had never been understood. I guessed there must have been nearly a thousand people crammed onto all the benches and hundreds more forced to stand. If Gorgias knew nothing else, he knew that a crowd, no matter how great a multitude, was, or could be, only one. I had spent years watching grown men, dozens, hundreds of them together, grovel before my father; this was the first time I had seen one man grovel before a thousand. And if grovel seems the wrong way to describe the way a master, a teacher, of the art of rhetoric speaks on a subject of his own choosing to an audience free to come or stay away, you should, like Odysseus, stuff your ears with cotton and watch what happens when the crowd around you goes crazy at what it hears.

It was all quite logical, a carefully prepared, well-ordered, presentation which, if you read it in the privacy of your study, would have seemed what you might expect from a clever schoolboy whose only purpose was to make sure you knew he was clever. And yet, were you able to read it over, think it through in all its implications, you would discover behind all that cleverness, all that attention to form, a much more serious design; a project, if you will, to make himself seem indispensable, this cheap talent of his the only one worth having. With a genius for self-promotion, he began by putting the question in a way that gave all the advantage to the other side:

"Helen is universally condemned and regarded as the symbol of disasters; I wish to subject her story to critical examination, and so rescue her from ignorant calumny."

Condemned out of ignorance! And that ignorance is universal. Only Gorgias knows better. The strutting arrogance of the man had to be seen to be believed. Two sentences into his speech and I was already annoyed.

"I shall not relate the story of who won Helen or how: to tell an audience what it knows wins belief but gives no pleasure. I shall pass over the period and come to the beginning of my defense, setting out the probable reasons for her journey to Troy."

We believe what we know, but there is no pleasure in that; we need to have something new, something we do not already have. I wondered whether anyone understood just how insidious this was. The new, the novel, what Gorgias promises, destroys all tradition, the foundation of what a people believes. Gorgias understood what he was doing. He was more than willing to tease you with certain doubts about the truth of what you believe, but he knew the danger of attacking it head on. He had too much prudence, or too much cowardice, to say what they could have read in the careful lines of Herodotus: that there was no journey, that Helen, instead of Troy, spent the war in Egypt.

And what is his defense? – a word, by the way, that reminded everyone of what happens in the law courts, how those who speak well have a better chance of prevailing – . Not that Helen did nothing wrong, but that she had had no choice. He was quite specific.

"She acted as she did either through Fate and the will of the gods and the decrees of Necessity, or because she was seized by force, or won over by persuasion or captivated by love. If the first, it is her accusers who deserve the blame; for no human foresight can hinder the will of god: the stronger cannot be hindered by the weaker, and God is stronger than man in every way. Therefore, if the cause was Fate, Helen cannot be blamed."

If, if, if – ! He did not say this is what happened; he did not say Helen was just the plaything of the gods; but if. If she was, then she is innocent of blame. But then what? – No one is responsible for anything except what has not been pre-ordained by Fate? What is Fate but the present's record of the past? But Gorgias is not finished.

"If she was carried off by force, clearly her abductor wronged her and she was unfortunate. He, a barbarian, committed an act of barbarism and should secure blame, disgrace and punishment, she being robbed of her country and her friends, deserves pity rather than obloquy."

Blame the barbarian? Well, what is a barbarian to do? Is he not as much the child of Necessity and Fate as Helen? A 'barbarian who committed an act of barbarism!' Isn't that what the word means?

Persuasion and love, the two other possible causes, are also both excuses. It was hard to believe that anyone believed this, but as I looked around in the booming silence at that gape-mouthed audience, waiting breathlessly for the conjuror's next trick, Gorgias had them, all of them, a thousand pair of eyes and a single willing mind. Beads of perspiration glistened on his face, the smooth slick skin of the panderer, one who trafficked not in women, but in words. His defense of Helen, absolving her of guilt, rested on proving himself the bigger whore.

"If it was speech that persuaded her and deceived her soul, her defense remains easy. Speech is a great power, which achieves the most divine works by means of the smallest and least visible form; for it can even put a stop to fear, remove grief, create joy, and increase pity. This I shall now prove."

And he did! It was incredible, the way in which he advertised himself, the way he put himself on sale for money.

Poetry – poetry! – is nothing but "speech in metre," that "sooths and persuades and transports by means of its wizardry." In whatever form speech works its magic, it is because "when men can neither remember the past nor observe the present nor prophecy the future, deception is easy." Not only easy, but complete. With oozing insincerity, Gorgias bragged that "persuasion by speech is equivalent to abduction by force." – Why bother to resist, why bother to try to think for yourself! – Poor Helen, persuaded by the honeyed words of Paris, "compelled to agree to what was said, and consent to what was done."

What need the rapist's knife or rope; what need had Hiero to force me to submit, when, had he only thought to speak, Helen would have forgotten that Helen had a will!

It gets better – or, rather, gets worse. Proof of how effective persuasive speech can be – "legal contests, in which a speech can sway and persuade a crowd, by the skill of its composition, not by the truth of its statements."

And what was the crowd's reaction to this admission, this proud confession, that they could so easily be deceived? – As eager to agree as a fool who has been called an idiot.

There was one more excuse, one more example of how, if you were quick enough, you could turn things upside down, make the simple appear complex and blame the victim for the crime. Lust, instead of a source of guilt, became mitigation.

"If Helen was persuaded by love, defense is equally easy. What we see has its own nature, not chosen by us; and the soul is impressed though sight." And? Helen saw him and had to have him and that is her defense? "If therefore Helen's eye, delighted with Paris's form, engendered the passion of love in her soul, this is not remarkable; for if a god is at work with divine power how can the weaker person resist him?"

There is no good and evil; pillage, rape and murder nothing more than the compulsions of a more than mortal power. Someone should murder Gorgias, just to try out his arguments.

There was thunderous applause when Gorgias finished; each member of the audience nodding to his neighbor their agreement that this day at least they had gotten their money's worth. That was when I began to understand that a crowd was a creature with two minds and, in a strange way, conscious of its own deficiencies. They applauded the performance, the skill he had with words, but they could not have done that had they not in some way known what he was doing. It was like watching someone applaud the dexterity of a thief, this one someone who stole the meaning out of words. They might not trust him with anything of their own, but if there was something they wanted, something that by all rights belonged to others, that would be a different matter. It was like watching the applause for an actor in the theater, the crowd delirious over how well he had played someone hounded by the furies into hell.

Those who lined up to shake hands with Gorgias and praise

his performance made way when Empedocles approached. It was a scene worth remembering. Slanting from an angle in the west, the sun bathed the amphitheater's yellow sandstone in a golden light. The eager bronzed faces of the crowd, their eyes full of approval, watched as the line of dignitaries waited their turn to exchange a few smiling words with the celebrated Gorgias of Leontini.

I was standing off to the side watching, not with the grinning stupidity of the crowd, but with a skepticism that changed immediately into suspicion. Gorgias had taken Empedocles by the hand and after a few words of greetings, pulled him close and whispered something in his ear. Empedocles made no answer, just a single, knowing nod.

I knew better than to ask what had been said; it was not my place to inquire about the details of a private conversation. I knew also that I did not need to, that my silence spoke my question more clearly than my words.

"He wants to see me. He is coming this evening for dinner."

We were on a hill just outside the city, less than a mile from home. It felt good to be out in the open air, away from the cloistered scent of the city and the closeness of the crowd. Palm trees towered along the borders of the road and gorgeous painted birds sang each their different song. It had become my favorite place to walk, that other city, the ten temples of the gods, shining in the distance down below and, far beyond it, the other side of Poseidon's silver sea, the coast of Africa and its nameless threat of danger.

A blue parrot, a frequent friend, landed on the shoulder of Empedocles, chattered his request and got the nut he wanted. The parrot took the hand Empedocles offered as a better perch, ate with his usual slow precision, and then, with an affectionate peck, flew off, back to all the other parrots where he could brag about what he had done.

"It was kind of you to invite him," I remarked, walking next to Empedocles with my light, practiced step. "It's more than I would have done."

"I did not invite him; he invited himself. He told me it was important, that he had to see me; that he was here on urgent business."

I suddenly started laughing. There was no reason, only that I felt too good, too full of energy, to hold back anything. I kicked at a stone, and when I caught up with it, kicked it again, harder this time, sent it flying, and for a half a second thought that if I wanted to I could go flying too. Empedocles plodded along, his steady gaze undisturbed by the strange exuberance of my antic ways.

"It's the only kind he knows," he went on. "If it was not urgent he might forget he was important. He thinks I don't know why he's here; that I don't know that he was sent from Leontini to seek our help."

"Help? He wasn't here to lecture, to show everyone how smart he is?"

Empedocles kept moving, but there was a brief, almost imperceptible hitch in his step, a momentary acknowledgment that there was a point to my remark.

"That is a chance he never misses. Rhetoric with him is a double-edged sword. He uses it to attract those willing to pay for what he can teach; but he also uses it in the interest of his city, Leontini, that now, because of that gift of his, often chooses him to represent them abroad. On the one hand, he'll teach you for a fee to argue in a way that will let you get any unjust result you desire, and, on the other, argue that what his city wants is what in the name of justice, in the name of all the gods, is the only decent choice you have. I try to comfort myself with the thought that the teacher is not responsible for what the student does with what he is taught. I hope you never have to learn how little comfort that really is. But, in any event, Gorgias will be our guest for dinner, and I think it would be good if you were there. This urgent business, the secret that he thinks is still a secret, has as much to do with you as anyone."

We reached the gray iron gate in the whitewashed wall at the entrance. He stopped and looked at me and something in the way he looked at me had changed.

"You're not a girl anymore; you've become a young woman. I think tonight, you can put off this disguise and become the woman you have been instead of the boy you never were."

The boy I never was! I had dressed the part, acted the part so long I had almost forgotten what I was. In a way, it had not mattered. My sex, what others thought it was, had not changed who I was, or, more importantly, and more precisely, what I was. A girl, a boy, a woman, a man – whatever sex my look, my sex changed nothing of what I saw, the looks of other things. My sex, what I looked like, belonged to others; my eyes belonged to me. For nearly two years I had turned the heads of both men and women for reasons exactly opposite of those with which I had had the same effect before; but now, a girl no longer, I could become a woman, and the change, though superficial, brought me pleasure. I liked adding blue color to my eyes and the blush of red to my lips. I liked letting down my hair and with the golden grasshopper, brought with me from Hiero's court, pinning back a part of it. I liked how smooth silk instead of linen felt against the contours of my skin. There was another effect which surprised me by how pronounced, how dominant, it was: I had a new sense of power; not power over others, but power over myself. It was more than confidence in what I could do; it was a sense that I was at the beginning of a new life, a second life, if you will, in which there was nothing I could not do.

I waited until Gorgias had been taken to the dining room before I made my appearance. Empedocles told me later that it was the first time Gorgias had been rendered speechless. It is true that for a moment he just stared at me in astonishment, but I am not sure it was so much the way I looked as his own surprise at realizing who I was.

"Helen!" he cried, certain he must be right. "The face I've heard so much about." He turned to Empedocles, reclining on the couch next to his. "I knew you had taken in a ward. I was told it was a boy. I knew that Helen, Hiero's daughter, had, at about the same time, disappeared; drowned in the sea, was the story; married to Poseidon was the favored interpretation. She's been here the whole time, two years?"

"My ward, and my student," replied Empedocles. "I haven't taught her rhetoric: she did not seem to have a need for it."

He meant it not so much as a tribute to my intelligence as my unwillingness to settle for the opinion of other people. It was a remark, he must have understood, Gorgias would not understand.

"The way she looks, what need would she have for words? All she has to do is look at someone to get them to do what she wants." He turned and studied me more closely. "You left Hiero of your own accord; ran away. You must have thought you were in danger. I have heard things, things I wouldn't want to believe, things that ... "

I sat down and with a distant, fearless smile tried to teach him that what he could do with a crowd he could not do with me.

"Do you want me to ask the question for you? Are you afraid you might offend me, make me think less of you, if you ask if the rumor you must have heard was true: that I was taken by the gods to save me from becoming instead of Hiero's daughter Hiero's wife?"

He was really speechless now. He looked at Empedocles

wondering if I were in my senses or gone insane. Empedocles raised an eyebrow and remarked as if the point were obvious, "If you're not careful, before the night is over you'll be paying her for lessons in how to speak."

It broke the tension, but only because Gorgias did not realize that Empedocles was serious.

The servants brought in platters of food and as we ate, Gorgias explained the urgent business that had brought him to Agrigento. Or rather, he started to, but then seemed to hesitate, uncertain whether to continue in my presence or wait until I had left.

"I wanted Helen here," said Empedocles. "You've come because of the situation in Syracuse. She knows how things are done there and may be able to help in the decisions that may have to be made here."

Gorgias hid his surprise behind a mask of seeming prior knowledge. He acted as if he would have been astonished if Empedocles had not known why he had come to Agrigento.

"Yes, of course; had I known she was here, it's the first thing I would have suggested. But let me start with the larger issue, not with what may happen in Syracuse, but the war that now seems all but inevitable."

After all the years that have passed, it is difficult to distinguish what I thought of Gorgias when I first met him from what I thought later. I had felt such contempt for what I thought the cheap theatrics of what he did that I may not have given sufficient credit for how quick and agile his mind could be. His range of comprehension for men and events, his grasp of the relations between the major powers, was almost without rival. He was far from the fool I wanted him to be. He had studied under Empedocles, and from everything I had heard had more than held his own, had in fact been considered superior to the other students at the time. It was not his ability that was ever in question. He was, within the limits of what he wanted, really quite brilliant. It was the obsequious, overeager sincerity he showed in the presence of those he wanted to impress and the insufferable conceit he showed to everyone else that made you want to hate him. But, as I say, when he talked of men and events he knew what he was doing.

"There is going to be a war, the biggest war we have ever seen. It will start with Athens and Sparta, but then it will spread. Everyone – every city in Greece and Sicily, and no doubt the Persians as well – will be drawn into it."

Empedocles, listening, showed no reaction of any kind. Gorgias laughed, but with a hint of anger in his eyes.

"I tell you that we are about to see a war bigger than any other and you look at me as if I had brought you news about this year's harvest!"

"Don't you remember what I taught you – or tried to teach you – about the nature of the world? That there is an endless cycle in which love and strife compete. Things are drawn to each other, and things are driven apart; drawn by love, repelled by strife or war."

"Yes, I remember; I understand," said Gorgias, trying to conceal his impatience. "But I am talking about what is happening now, here in Greece and Sicily."

"And do you think that what is happening now, here in Greece and Sicily, is somehow unconnected with the principles that rule the world? You have too much intelligence to settle for the perspective of the simple-minded. You of all people must understand that without first grasping the principles of things nothing can be understood; everything will remain in darkness and confusion. What I have said, what I have tried to teach, has often been misunderstood, but not, I would think, by you."

Gorgias started to interrupt, to move the conversation away from a discussion of first principles to the hard specifics of the current situation. Empedocles stopped him with a look.

"There are four elements – you remember that – everything that happens comes about because of their union, their coming together, or their disunion, their going apart. But there is something that too many miss: war is only another form of love, love of what is similar. If fire repels water it is because fire seeks its kindred, fire, and water also seeks its own. That means that love has two forms: love of the similar and love of the opposites. If it was just love of the similar, the elements would each come together, separate from the others, and the cosmos would disintegrate."

It was now the turn of Gorgias to show no reaction, to look as if nothing had been said that was either unexpected or of any particular interest. But what proved the depth and detachment of Empedocles' extraordinary mind, the long perspective of the philosopher, was in the case of his onetime pupil a confession that what he might have thought important as a boy he did not take seriously as a man. Empedocles refused to give up. Whether or not Gorgias, or anyone else, would listen, he did what he could to explain.

"If the similars always assembled in one place, there would be no cosmos: nothing would exist. That means that love of the opposites is identical with the formation of the cosmos; the formation – the creation, if you will – of beings which are composite. Take it a different way: love of similars leads to chaos, at least from the point of view of us mortals, and love of opposites leads to cosmos. What is heterosexuality but the love of opposites?

The love of opposites is the condition of human life. Love – Eros – makes possible everything; but that means that among the human beings there is an endless seeking, and that means war."

Gorgias smiled and nodded, and then smiled again.

"I remember what you taught, and I don't doubt that you're right: that these are the deepest causes of what we are and what we do; that this explains the fact, the repetition, of conflict and war. But we're forced now to deal with specifics: not war in general, but this war, the one that has not started yet, but will, sometime in the near future, a war that no one will be able to escape."

Empedocles had scarcely eaten anything. He beckoned for a servant to take away what was left.

"It is because of the causes of which I speak, causes I tried to teach, that the war you speak of, the war that is coming, will be even greater than you imagine. The Persians brought the largest army – more than a million men – an army that Xerxes had to stay seven days at the Hellespont to watch pass in front of him in review, and the Greeks defeated them. And what happened then? The Spartans went home and Athens, with its fleet, took the lead in a league of cities, including all the islands the Persians used to rule, and before anyone understood what was happening, it was not Athens the city anymore, it was Athens the empire, and nearly everyone was suddenly under an obligation to contribute men or money.

"Sparta, as always, wanted rest; Athens, never content with what it had, stayed in motion. The money that was contributed, the money that was supposed to go to a common cause, money stored at the temple at Delos, sanctified by the gods, was the money with which Athens began to build itself into a city that for power and beauty the world has never seen. The Athenians became an empire and when they saw what their city could do – the great gains from subjugating their weaker allies – every free citizen began to have the same ambition; striving, like the city of which they were each a part, to acquire more, always more, more riches and more power, for themselves. The city was free, and every citizen had now a tyrant in his soul, a desire that never slept and made them think the future always better than the past. You say a war is coming. It has been coming for years."

Gorgias, who had been listening with polite indifference, now turned to Empedocles with an eager eye.

"Yes, coming for years, and almost here. The city of Corinth is building up its fleet; the Spartans, always slow to react, are finally starting to worry that if they don't do something to stop Athenian expansion, Athens may get too strong to stop. The war has already started; they just don't know it yet. When the fighting does begin, when Athens launches its fleet and the Spartans send their army, the question will be what happens to us."

I sat watching as the teacher and his student, the teacher who still believed in what he taught and the student who, as near as I could tell, changed his beliefs with his audience, looked at the same thing and saw things that were anything but identical.

"What will happen to us? – You mean Leontini."

"Not just Leontini, but Sicily. The question is whether any of us will have the freedom to govern ourselves instead of being ruled by others. What the Athenians have done – what you said is correct: they have become an empire, but Athens is a free city, ruled by an assembly, and so are the cities that follow their lead. Agrigento rules itself and so do we in Leontini; but Syracuse is ruled by a tyrant, and the danger is that he will use the war between Athens and Sparta as an opportunity to destroy democracy everywhere in Sicily. There are men in Agrigento, men like Dion, just waiting for the chance to change the government, to seize the power they think they deserve."

"And that's why you are speaking tomorrow in the assembly: to convince us that we need to come to the assistance of Leontini because you are under threat of war from Syracuse?"

"The threat is real."

"To you perhaps, but not to us."

"Syracuse is a tyranny; Leontini is a democracy. Free people have to stand together."

"Is one form of government always that much better than the other?"

"If Syracuse takes Leontini, if Syracuse gets that much stronger, what makes you think Agrigento will be safe? It would be a mistake to rely on what Hiero might have done in the past. What was to his advantage may not be his advantage now. And, besides, there is something you do not know."

"There is a good deal I don't know, my friend. Everything, if you want the truth. But why don't you tell me what it is you think will change my mind."

"Hiero is dead. He died two days ago. It is still a secret. Thrasybulus, his brother, is taking steps to consolidate his power."

Hiero was dead! He was my father, I owed him my existence, but he had taken payment for that debt, more payment than was due. He had murdered my mother and he had murdered me; taken the life I should have had, that any child should have, and made me live another, double life that women twice my age would have found impossible to endure. He was dead, and my only wish was that his death had been slow and painful; my only regret that I was not there to watch him suffer.

"Thrasybulus!" I heard myself cry out. "Hiero was bad enough – greedy, violent, and depraved, a stranger to everything noble or decent in the world. But Thrasybulus! He'd murder you just for the pleasure of hearing you beg for mercy."

A war was coming, the greatest war that ever was; a war that, if Gorgias was right, would involve all the Greeks, here in Sicily as well as Greece itself; a war that, according to Empedocles, had been coming for a very long time. It would be a war that would bring death and destruction everywhere, set city against city and set cities against themselves. No one could know how it might end; the only certainty was that nothing would ever be the same. I knew all this, and I still did not care.

War was an abstraction, something that had happened before and would no doubt happen again, but had not happened yet. With Hiero's death I had been set free from the past; I was not about to become the slave of the future. There were more important things I wanted to understand. This was not some kind of adolescent obsession, a young girl's fantasy, a girl who had nothing better to do than daydream about the mystery of existence and the movement of the heavens. The questions that intrigued me as a girl still intrigue me. Whatever things I may have done, whatever others may have thought of me, this was how I lived: curious, always curious, more than curious, about the world.

We were on one of our morning walks. Empedocles had stopped to admire the horses galloping across a meadow toward the river on the other side. The clamor of their hooves raised an alarm among the birds nesting in the trees along the bank and the beat of their wings as they rose, thousands of them, a huge black cloud, made a drum-like chorus that buried every spoken word in silence and every silent thought in sound.

"How far off do you think those birds and horses are – two miles? Out here, away from the city, you can hear everything worth hearing. Sometimes, at night, I lay out under the stars and I can hear the sounds the heavens make, the rhythm of their movements. You have learned as much from me as I can teach; more about numbers than I was taught by Pythagoras, but there are things no one can teach you, things you have to learn on your own."

It was still a puzzle, but even deeper than before. He could hear the sound – the music, as he sometimes put it – of the heavens as the stars turned on their courses; and then that reminder that mathematics, number, was somehow the key to everything.

We walked along our usual route, high above the ten temples and the sea, and he did not speak or even once look at me again. He was lost in thought, whether about the nature of the universe or what he should advise the assembly to do about Leontini and the new aggression of Syracuse, I could not tell. I did not mind. I was used to his long silences and took pleasure in them, the strange, uncanny inner glow he had when he became so oblivious of his surroundings he might just as well have been alone.

There were flowers everywhere, all along the path, red and blue and yellow, and orange bougainvillea and purple wisteria and other nameless fragrant vines wrapped like serpents around the tall dark trees. I picked a red chrysanthemum and put it in my hair. A bumble bee settled on my nose and I laughed and looked cross-eyed at it and he slowly flew away. A dog, an old black mastiff who had early on befriended me, bounded up from behind and tossed his head against my hand. The long days of spring were getting longer; days, as I now remember, that seemed never long enough. All my fears were gone and, banished with them, all the need for hope. I lived in the moment and the moment was all I knew. How little did I know how much things would change, how those long idyllic days would be among the best, the very best, I would ever know.

We turned as the sun reached the zenith of its climb and made our way back to the villa with its red tile roof and whitewashed walls. Empedocles would usually sit beneath a fig tree in the courtyard and with his hands folded in his lap take a short nap. But, today he had me follow him into his study where, with the shutters closed against the midday heat, everything lay in shadows. He showed me to a chair just beside a window, opened the shutters to let in the light and then walked over to his desk. He picked up a manuscript written in his own hand and brought it over to me.

"I didn't write this for an audience; I wrote it to gain clarity in what I thought. I'll decide later whether others should read it. Take your time. I have to be away this afternoon. There is a meeting of the assembly I have to attend."

I changed positions so the light through the shutters behind me would fall directly on the page. Empedocles wrote in a hand that modeled the strict necessity of his mind, every word in exactly the right order, nothing that was needed left out. Two sentences into it and I could not put it down; three sentences into it and I knew it was unlike anything I had ever read. Every line, every word, has become part of my permanent memory, something I still carry with me, talking with it, the way I learned, part of a conversation that so long as I am alive will never end, asking questions of every answer I hear it give me.

"I go about you as an immortal god, no longer a mortal, held in honor by all, as I seem to them to deserve, crowned with flowers. And when I enter their flourishing towns and cities, men and women reverence me, follow me in thousands, asking how they can gain more than they have; some of them want me to act an oracle, telling what will happen; others, suffering the cruel pains of injury and disease, beg me to tell them the cure."

As I read this, I thought it was only a question of what others thought; then I read what he wrote next and was forced to a different conclusion.

"But why do I lay stress on these things, as if I had achieved something great by surpassing mortal men who will perish."

It isn't what others think; it is what he believes. He is a god, but a god in exile; a god banished from the company of all the other gods. There is an ancient ordinance of the gods that when one of the "divine spirits," those who were given the blessing of a long life, commits bloodshed or otherwise follows strife, he must by a law of necessity wander alone through thirty thousand seasons, forced to take every kind of mortal form, exchanging one difficult way of life for another. The air, the earth, the sea: all take him and throw him back. Empedocles is one of these, "an exile and a wanderer from the gods."

An exile, a wanderer from the gods through thirty thousand seasons of ever-changing life: Odysseus on a cosmic scale, his home not Ithaca or any other place, not even Olympus or any of the other oft spoken home of the gods, but everywhere and nowhere at once. He speaks of the "blessed gods" and the "wretched race of mortals," and says in no uncertain terms that, "Happy is he who has acquired the riches of divine thoughts, but wretched the man in whose mind dwells an obscure opinion about the gods." But he speaks not just of the gods, but God.

I did not notice this at first; I was too awestruck by what I read. But then, on reading it again, on second sight, if you will, I realized the enormous question this implied. There were gods, numbers of them, some of them capable of crimes, actions that could lead to banishment, divine spirits forced to experience all the different forms of life before their wandering was over; gods that were worshipped for their powers; gods whose appeasement was seen as the first condition of any earthbound achievement; but then there was God. One God – What did that mean?

Empedocles writes that, "It is not possible to bring God within reach of our eyes or grasp him with our hand." We cannot hear God, because God does not have a voice. He does not have a voice because God has no body. He is "Mind, holy and ineffable, and only Mind, which darts through the whole universe with its swift thoughts."

I began to see what he was saying, the hidden teaching in his meaning, although even now, after all this time, after all I have studied and learned, there is never more than a brief glimmer of recognition, a taunting sense that I can almost grasp the truth of what he wrote. He seemed to be sketching out the scale of our existence, the living creatures and their capabilities; their place, our place, in the world in which we have our being. Mortal man shares something of the intelligence of the gods, enough to allow some of them, men like Empedocles, to have a mind that can also "dart through the universe with its swift thoughts," something that takes thirty thousand seasons, the time between the first seeing, the forgotten memory of the soul's own intelligence, and its final return to the "company of the blessed."

Empedocles wrote about the way he was received, how thousands would come out to follow him, but it was because of what they thought he could do for them, showing them the way to more prosperity and healthier, longer lasting lives. He promised them that he could help them in ways no one else could do. But he wanted to make what he did, this quest for a wisdom that, if I understood him, only God could have, this thing called philosophy, more secure, immune somehow from the deathlike suspicion that it was a practice unfriendly to the gods. And so he promised that through his prudence and science, through his knowledge of the healing arts, he could teach them powers the like of which they had never dreamed.

It was astonishing what he promised. I had to read it three different times to convince myself that I had not read it wrong.

"You shall learn all the drugs that exist as a defense against illness and old age; for you alone I will accomplish all this. You shall check the violence of the unwearying winds that sweep the earth and waste the fields. And, if you wish, you shall bring the breezes back again. You shall be able to create a seasonable dryness after the dark rains have come, and after summer drought, bring back the streams that feed the trees. You shall bring back from Hades a dead man restored to strength."

What lesser god had ever promised this: the power to bring the dead back to the living? What was it that Empedocles thought he knew that no one else had ever known? This was strange enough, but what was stranger still was how he thought he could make a god of me.

Months had passed since Gorgias brought the news that Hiero was dead and his brother, my uncle Thrasybulus, had become the new tyrant of Syracuse. Everything I had prophesied had come true. Violent and murderous, Thrasybulus had engaged in wholesale executions, killing not just those he thought might prove a threat to his rule, but anyone whose wealth he wanted for himself. Each time I heard about another new murder, I remembered the look I had seen so often in my uncle's eyes, the hidden, excited regret that he could only watch and wait when Hiero had someone led out to slaughter. I have seen that same look on a thousand different faces, the blood lust of the crowd, the staring blank-eyed lust of men in heat; the look on Hiero's face the night he would have had me. Thrasybulus, like most men, was insane; unlike most men, he did not know how to hide it; unlike most men he did not think he had to. He was the Tyrant of Syracuse and there was, he believed, no limit to what a tyrant could do. With each new crime he gained more enemies until, finally, he found himself faced with a rebellion.

"You could go back," said Empedocles.

We were at dinner, just the two of us. I waited for him to explain.

"To Syracuse. An ambassador came today from the leaders of the rebellion. They want our help in defeating Thrasybulus. You could go back, take a position, and become the one everyone looks to for wisdom and advice."

"A woman? Worse yet, Hiero's daughter?"

"A woman … taken by Poseidon to be his wife. A tyrant's daughter rescued from the tyrant by the gods. What greater claim to power could the mind of man invent? "

With his strong fingers he beat a slow cadenced rhythm on the onyx table. Some thought had flown unsummoned to his mind, tantalizing in its implications.

"Helen, that other Helen – Homer's Helen – the story turns back on itself. Instead of half of Greece going to Troy to seek revenge, Helen comes to Syracuse to save Greece and Sicily from needless war. No more thousand ships: Helen's face saves us all from boundless strife."

He smiled at me with his eyes, and I knew that he believed it and that he knew it would never happen.

"Why would I want to go back to a life like that? Haven't you taught me how much better it is to seek the truth in the things that never change?"

"I have to leave Agrigento," he remarked suddenly.

"Are you going on a trip, traveling to another city?" I asked, hoping he would ask me to come along. Though I was free to go wherever I liked, I had not been anywhere farther than a half day's walk.

"A trip – yes, you could say so; or rather, a journey, one from which I will not be returning."

Something had happened and I did not know what it was. He sensed my uncertainty, my concern for his welfare, my eager desire to help.

"In the debate on whether we should become involved in the war in Syracuse, whether we should send ships and men to help defeat Thrasybulus, I argued against it. It is better if the people of Syracuse gain their freedom on their own. But there is another reason as well. If we send ships and an army, then we become like

Syracuse and Athens, a city that thinks in terms of power and what
it has the power to do. We give up our peaceful pursuits and start to
dream that with just a little more power – a hundred more ships, a
thousand more soldiers – we could in our turn become an empire and
rule over others."

"But you lost – to Dion and his friends?"

"Yes, to Dion and his friends and all those they persuaded with
the argument that the failure to go to the assistance of those who
fight for freedom, who want to rid themselves of tyranny, is worse
than cowardice, a basic distrust of the people and their right to rule
themselves."

"You lost a vote; one vote doesn't mean the loss of your
authority. There are other votes, other questions. When the war in
Syracuse is finished, when Thrasybulus is gone, everyone will look
to you again to lead."

"War – strife – changes everything; it changes what people
believe. If Thrasybulus is driven out, if the war is successful – and,
like you, I hope it is – Dion and his friends will claim all the credit.
When that happens, those who opposed them will be made to suffer
either banishment or death. That is why I am leaving."

The danger might be real; what he planned to do about it was
absurd.

"You fear banishment or death? I don't believe it."

He gave me a very strange look, and I had the feeling that
without any visible sign of it, he was laughing as if at some colossal
joke.

"It isn't death I fear, but dying in a way that gives no advantage.
But never mind that now. I want to talk to you about certain other
things, among them the provision I have made to make sure you
are never in need. I have no wife, no children; I mean for you to be
my sole heir. You will need this," he added when I began to protest
against this generosity. "I have to leave here, and so do you. It might
be safe for you here, but there is no one after me who can guarantee
that. More important is where you should go, where you can find
other people from whom you can learn. There is only one city where
you can be free to think and study; only one place where you can
expand your powers."

I knew the city he meant. He had told me how men from all
over had come there, drawn by the promise of its greatness.

"Athens; you want me to go to Athens."

"Yes, and I'll go with you, for part of your journey."

We did not leave right away; we did not leave for nearly a month. Empedocles never hurried; I do not think he knew how. It was simply who he was, his nature, part of that vast intelligence with which he put in proportion the relative importance of things.

The future unfolded almost exactly as Empedocles had predicted. With the help of Agrigento, the forces of Thrasybulus were defeated on both land and sea. Left with only the island of Ortygia and a small part of the mainland, Thrasybulus, as unwilling to die as he had been eager to murder, negotiated a truce under which he was allowed to leave Sicily. Syracuse became a free city and those in Agrigento who had led the military expedition proceeded to limit and restrict the freedom that, under Empedocles, the city had enjoyed.

Empedocles did not tell anyone we were leaving. He did not tell me until we were on our way into the city.

"There is something I have to do first," he said, when I asked why we were not going away from the city instead of toward it. "There is a dead woman I have to cure."

Yes, a dead woman; that is what he said. Her name was Panthea, a wealthy woman of Agrigento, who, according to the physicians who had been treating her, had stopped breathing and died. I do not know what happened, what Empedocles did, only that he was in the room alone with her dead body for more than an hour and that when he came out the dead woman was alive. Alive! She was sitting up and talking. Within a very short time, such is the speed of rumor, so was everyone in the city, convinced that they had been right in what they had always believed, that Empedocles, legislator and physician, teacher and philosopher, was somehow more than mortal. A crowd began to gather, shouting its praise for what Empedocles had done, brought the dead back from Hades. Empedocles ignored them and with the solemn announcement that he had now to offer sacrifice, we went out of the city and on our way.

He did what he said he would. In full view of the public, he made the burnt offering required by ritual, and then, taking me by the hand, told those close enough to listen that the time had come: he was going back to the gods from whose company he had long ago descended. And then, without further explanation, we made our way to Etna and the fire.

I should not reveal what happened next; I should let the legend of his death and resurrection serve the purpose he intended. But I am too old not to tell the truth, and I indulge myself in the hope that you will agree with me that what he did was more miraculous, more instructive, than what he was said to have done. There is a kind of genius in any great fiction, an ability to understand our limitations, how much most of what we think we think is only what we thoughtlessly believe. If Hesiod and Homer, two poets, could create all the gods of Olympus, gods with more than human excellences, but also more than human failings, what greater gift to human beings than a god to believe in that showed the greatness of the human mind? Empedocles had gone to the volcano, plunged into the fiery crater and was taken by the gods. One of his slippers, one of those made of bronze, was found on the slope, thrown up in the never ending flames, proof that it had happened, that he was now home among the gods.

He did go down into the volcano. I went with him. We watched the liquid fire jumping into the air, dazzling in its changing form, watched until our faces burned red with heat. We turned and started up, when suddenly, Empedocles took off his slippers, those bronze slippers that no one else wore, and threw them into the surging, dancing flames. One of them, thrown back by a sudden small eruption, sailed high above us; the one found later, proof that the gods had brought Empedocles back home.

You can say, if you wish, that the volcano, a natural force, caused that bronze slipper to fly where it did, but the real question is why that sudden small eruption happened at just that moment.

Careful to make sure no one would see us, traveling now only at night, we made our way to the sea and left Sicily for Greece. Empedocles made his way to somewhere in the Peloponnesus. I went straight for Athens.

CHAPTER FIVE

Aspasia motioned me to come closer. Under the noise of a dozen different conversations, I made my way across the crowded room to the blue cushioned chair where the leading woman in Athens was keeping watch on her guests.

"I'm glad you were able to come; I'm glad we are finally able to meet," she said in a voice as soft and lovely as any I had ever heard.

"I've been in Athens only a few weeks," I replied as I took a chair next to hers, the chair, as I noticed, reserved for whomever she wished to talk to next. "I was surprised, and delighted, at your invitation."

Somewhere in her late twenties or early thirties, and, it was obvious, as beautiful as she had ever been, she carried herself with the self-assurance of someone considerably older. Every movement, even the smallest gesture, came with the practiced ease of a woman who knew exactly what she was about. A mocking smile flew teasing across her lips.

"If we're going to be friends, you need to learn not to treat me like a fool."

My first thought was to protest, to argue, for politeness sake, that she was mistaken, but that would have been too conventional. And so instead I said nothing, and my silence told her all she needed.

"Or perhaps I should have said not to act like one yourself. Not invite you? You weren't in Athens three days before you were the only one anyone wanted to talk about. All you had to do was walk down the street and the rumors started flying. No one knows where you come from or why you're here. You must have noticed when you came in, how the room went silent and every eye turned to you. As we speak, they're all talking to each other, pretending they have other more important things to discuss, but you're the one who crowds out all their other thoughts."

I took it all in stride, as if I had expected nothing less. It always happened like this when I entered a room. The conversation stopped while everyone turned to look, and then that same nervous hesitation as one after another they forced themselves to turn away and try to remember what, a moment earlier, had seemed so important. I knew how I was looked at in the streets, I knew what was going through the minds of the men I passed; but this was Athens, and here, in the home of Pericles, were gathered some of the most interesting and influential people in the city. I could not be sure when I arrived exactly how I would be received.

"I don't think that's true in every case." I bent closer. "Those two, for example." I turned my head toward two men engrossed in a conversation so intense that it seemed that nothing, not even an earthquake, could have interrupted it.

Aspasia gave me a long look, searching, as it seemed, for some deeper meaning in what I thought a perfectly obvious remark. It would have been impossible not to notice those two, one of them, twenty years old at most, with long, flowing golden hair and eyes the color of the morning sky, and the other, twice his age, ugly beyond imagining, with strange, protruding eyes and the face of a satyr, and yet, somehow, with all its ugliness, so remarkable, so compelling, I found myself looking more at him. Perhaps it was those uncanny globe-like eyes of his, the way they seemed to look at everything from different depths and different angles, the way they seemed to see more than the human eye was made to see.

"Who are you? Where do you come from?" asked Aspasia with a new and, as it seemed, greater interest. "Well, never mind for now. Those two over there? You have an eye for what is significant. You really don't know who they are?"

"No, I'm afraid I don't. I've only just got here, and I don't know anyone."

"An interesting situation: you don't know anyone and everyone wants to know you." She put her hand in front of her mouth, stifling a laugh. "See that young man over there." A balding man with the sloping shoulders and round face of someone who spent much of his time indoors was holding forth among a small circle of eager-eyed admirers. "Aristophanes, an aspiring playwright; a comic poet who thinks the way to win the favor of an audience is to write with all the lewdness he can imagine to ridicule the leading men – and women – of the city. He told me, just before you arrived, that he has a new idea for a play: what happens when a city has to go to war and none of the men can fight because a woman of such remarkable beauty has come among them that they now have erections that never go away. He thinks it will be his first big hit. He says he'd like to call it 'Helen, the face that launched a thousand missiles.'"

As if on cue, Aristophanes turned toward us with a leering grin on his small, pudgy mouth. Swatting the air, Aspasia dismissed his charming impudence. With a brief smile and a slight, upward tilt of my chin, I let him know that, so far as I was concerned, his ribald suggestion was well within the realm of possibility. He seemed to enjoy that. Then, suddenly quite serious, he nodded and calmly smiled back.

Tugging at my sleeve, Aspasia bid me again to draw closer.

"Those two, talking over there – and they may go on like that, talking for hours. You're new to Athens; but still, the fact that you didn't know – and you pick them out right away. Well, perhaps that's not so strange. They must be just about the oddest looking couple in the history of the world. I mean, look at them! Alcibiades, my husband's ward, his brother's son, who he agreed to raise when his brother died; Alcibiades, given all the gifts the gods have to offer. And then, that other one – have you ever seen anywhere anyone who looks like that?"

Something almost electric took possession of her eyes. Excited by the memory of some exotic pleasure that had she not experienced it she would not have thought possible, the change in her expression was almost sexual.

"I can't explain it. Something happens when you are with him. You start to wish you were someone different, someone more like him with all that splendid ugliness and those astonishing all-seeing eyes. Once you listen to him talk, once you start trying to answer the questions he asks, you forget who you are – you forget everything! – Except how inadequate your own intelligence, your own understanding. And yet, somehow, you've never felt more alive, never felt more powerful. I've known him for a long time and I still don't think he is possible. Socrates is just a figment of my imagination. He does not exist."

The smile on her mouth slipped down at the left corner. Her eyes filled with more than irony, a kind of cheerful malice. She tossed her head and laughed.

"And look at him! – Alcibiades – how earnest he looks, almost boyish in his seeming innocence. Yes," she said sharply, her gaze coming back to mine. "'Seeming,' because young though he is, innocent he is not. How could he be, with everyone in Athens fawning all over him, telling him that there isn't anything he can't do, that all he has to do is step forward and everyone will follow. He believes it; he always has. And why shouldn't he? He knows what he is worth; he knows that he is better than all the others. He knows that all those honeyed words they throw at him, telling him how great he is, are only the coin of liars, cheats, and scoundrels trying to buy his favor. He treats them with the contempt they deserve. But he loves Socrates. And do you know why? – Because Socrates treats him like a fool!"

I darted another glance at the unlikely pair. The room could have been empty, everyone gone home, for all they would have noticed. Alcibiades, smiling and laughing, gestured with his hands, but then, at a word from Socrates, the smiling laughter stopped. With fascinated, solemn eyes he listened carefully to what he was told. I was so drawn to them and what they were doing that I did not hear Aspasia as she began to introduce me.

"No one can take their eyes off Alcibiades."

It was a voice of such soothing charm, such cultured confidence and rare intelligence, that I knew who it was before I turned to see him.

Pericles was considerably older than Aspasia, but handsome in the way of men of great achievement. His head was noticeably larger than normal, and his forehead more prominent. There were those who ridiculed him for this, but never to his face. When he walked into a room, or into the assembly, even mockery took on a certain dignity and became embarrassed.

"It is an honor to meet you," I said, beaming with unfeigned pleasure.

"I think it is really the other way round. You honor me with your presence. I knew when you first arrived, that for once the rumors running through the city did not exaggerate the truth. If anything, you're even more beautiful than what I had heard. And now that I see you closer, I realize there is much more to you than that." He threw a glance toward that private conversation that had drawn so much of my attention. "If Alcibiades had been born a woman, he would now know what it is like to be second-best."

Turning to Aspasia, his expression became more formal, more reserved, and yet, at the same time, more intimate. There was something they needed to discuss. Rising from her chair, she took me by the hand and thanked me for coming. She started to follow Pericles outside to the garden, but then stopped and made me promise to come again tomorrow when we could have a private talk.

It was true, what I had heard, that Aspasia was the only person Pericles trusted, the only one in whom he fully confided. The way he looked at her, the way he spoke, or did not need to speak, when they were together; they were like two different faces of the same person. I watched them standing in the garden in the shade of the olive trees, the Parthenon far off in the distance, shimmering bright and magnificent in the sun's remorseless heat. They were too far away for me to hear what they were saying, but suddenly her hand shot up to his shoulder and she buried her face against his chest. He stroked her hair and said something, some words of consolation as it appeared, and she looked up again, stroked the side of his face and braved a smile. This time it was her turn to talk, to say something that would comfort him.

"Aspasia," said a raspy voice from just behind me. "First the mistress, now the wife, of the great Pericles, ruler of a city that is supposed to rule itself!"

I turned and found myself under the loathsome gaze of a repellent rat-faced creature. His mouth, nearly as crooked as his teeth, was a broken shield against a breath so rancid I could scarcely bear to breathe. His eyes were black and bottomless; impenetrable, or perhaps, and this was the stronger suspicion, there was just nothing there to see.

"Aspasia," he went on, as if the sound of her name carried its own disparagement; "the woman who rules our ruler; the woman every intelligent man supposedly respects, the woman who everyone in Athens thinks a whore!"

"But surely not you," I replied with a cold smile. "Only someone who has to pay for sex would accept an invitation from a woman of the sort you describe, a woman who would sleep with anyone for money; although, unless she were really desperate, perhaps not someone with looks quite as unfortunate as yours."

He went white, he went red; smoke came out of his ears, his eyes darted everywhere at once. He opened his mouth to speak, but instead of speaking he could only sputter spit.

"I see you have met my friend Cleon," someone said. Before I could turn to see who said it, Cleon threw me a deathlike glance that wished me evil and stomped away.

I had watched Alcibiades, but I had seen him at a considerable distance and only in profile. Now I was looking straight at him, less than an arm's length away. My throat went dry and there was a hollow, empty feeling in the pit of my stomach. I was afraid to open my mouth, afraid that I would not remember how to speak. I had never seen anything like him. He was what Apollo, what Achilles, what all the gods and heroes were supposed to look like. Tall and perfectly proportioned, he had bright, flashing eyes that seemed as if they could see, not just everything around him, but all the way to tomorrow and all the days after that. His mouth had what in any other man would have been arrogance, but with him seemed almost modest, just the half-measure of what he could do. Everything about him, from the easy way he held his head to the catlike way he moved suggested a power that was all but irresistible. And that made me all the more determined to conceal the hot wild emotions that had begun tearing at my heart.

"Cleon hates everyone; that is his strength, the reason he has a following."

He did not bother to introduce himself; it would never occur to him that there might be anyone who did not know him. Nor did he ask for my name, because, as he told me later, he had heard it from Aspasia when I first arrived.

"He hates everyone, and that is his strength?" I asked, surprised I had not forgotten how to talk.

He started to explain why, in the case of a demagogue like Cleon, hatred could be a strength. Pretending an indifference that was far from what I felt, an indifference it took all my effort to invent, I smiled, and turned, and walked away.

People must have been watching, because the room went silent, everyone astonished at what they had just seen, that Alcibiades had been left alone. Then I heard his laughter, genuine, nothing forced; and I knew that instead of the end this was just the beginning, that the last thing Alcibiades could resist was a woman capable of resistance.

I lingered a while longer, watching how the Athenians behaved. They seemed less restrained by tradition or custom, less willing to acknowledge the superiority of others, than the people I had known in either Syracuse or Agrigento. Moving from one small group to another, they dropped one conversation and picked up another with all the ease of a change of expression. They loved to talk so much that from the excitement in their eyes you would have thought they had invented speech.

An hour later, the sky painted scarlet by the vanished sun, I left the house of Pericles and started on the long walk home. I had not gone half a block when someone took me by the arm.

"You shouldn't go through the city streets unescorted."

"Why, is it dangerous?"

Alcibiades twisted his fingers through the long ringlets of his hair. A look of vast amusement lit up the brilliant blue of his eyes.

"Walk alone in the streets and everyone will think streetwalking is what you do."

"Is that why you want my company: to protect your reputation?"

He did not understand. A woman with a tongue as quick, or quicker, than his own seemed a new experience. But then, an instant later, his eyes flew open, his gorgeous head flew back and his shoulders shook with laughter.

"Yes, I was hoping you would give me protection," he said, still laughing. "I seldom sleep at night, the way I worry about what others might think of me. Alcibiades – afraid of everyone and everything!" he shouted at the sky.

Suddenly, for no apparent reason, the laughter froze on his face. All the pride, the charming arrogance, the stunning self-assurance was pushed aside and he became, if not humble, embarrassed and seemingly contrite. Socrates was standing just a few feet away, on the corner of the cobblestone street. He was not laughing, but then, as I was to learn, he never did. Alcibiades had acted like an adolescent caught doing something he should not do, but there was nothing on the face of Socrates but kindness and good will, though I must confess he spoke to him in a way that on this, my first occasion to observe the two of them close up, seemed strange and uncanny, like nothing I had heard before.

Socrates was not quite as tall as Alcibiades, but his arms and shoulders were larger and more developed. He wore no sandals and there was a hard toughness about both his feet and legs. That is not a bad description of his mind. He began to talk as if the conversation they had been having earlier had not stopped.

"You insist you don't need anyone for anything, that what belongs to you, beginning with the body and ending with the soul – is so great that you need nothing. You have your looks, a distinguished family, a city that is the greatest in Greece, and best of all, the power that is available to you through your guardian, Pericles, a man who is able to act as he wishes not only in this city but in all of Greece and among many and great barbarian peoples."

Alcibiades lifted his chin in a show of defiance.

"Yes, and what of it? What if I had all those things? Shouldn't I use them?"

"If you learn how to use them well," Socrates fired back. "If I asked you – if one of the gods were to ask you – whether you would wish to live, having what you now have, or to die at once if it were not permitted you to acquire more, you would, it seems to me, choose to die. You believe that if you come before the people of Athens, and you think this will happen soon, that you will prove yourself more deserving of being honored than Pericles or anyone else who ever lived and that, having proved this, you will have very great power in the city and, if you are great here, be so as well among the other Greeks and not only among the Greeks, but among the barbarians who share the mainland with us. And if you were told that you must hold sway in Europe but will not be permitted to cross into Asia or to interest yourself in affairs there, it seems to me you would again be unwilling to live on those terms alone, without being able to fill with your name and your power all mankind, so to speak. And I suppose you believe that, apart from Cyrus and Xerxes, no one deserving of mention has ever existed. That this is the hope you have, then, I know very well – I am not guessing."

I stood there, astonished at what I had heard. Was it possible that Alcibiades, that anyone, could have so much ambition that he would think himself a failure if he did not rule the world? And how was it, if that were true, that Socrates had somehow come to penetrate his secret? There was no question but that he had. About that I had not the slightest doubt. Doubt? – The possibility never occurred to me. He meant every word he said and every word was true. And if I was surprised before, imagine what I felt when, after describing an ambition that the gods themselves might envy, he proceeded to tell Alcibiades that if that was what he wanted that he, Socrates, was the only one who could help him get it.

"It is not possible for all those things you have in mind to be brought to a completion without me. So great is the power I suppose myself to have regarding your affairs and you."

And then he added a remark that seemed to diminish the power, the ability to act as he pleased, not only in the city but everywhere in Greece and even among the barbarians that just a moment earlier he had attributed to Pericles.

"No guardian or relative or anyone else is capable of bestowing the power you desire apart from me."

Far from denying this, Alcibiades only asked how Socrates could help. The answer seemed ludicrous. If Alcibiades would only agree to answer the questions he wanted to ask, he would have all the help he needed!

For the next few minutes, Socrates fired questions and Alcibiades answered back; short questions and even shorter answers, all about the things we learn and who was best qualified to teach; everything from wrestling to building ships, a brief review of the various arts by which we train our bodies and our minds. And then, suddenly, the questions were about justice and what it means. This was when I learned how long Socrates had been watching Alcibiades, observing what from the very beginning had been his remarkable and perhaps unprecedented gifts.

"When you were a child," said Socrates with that gaze that seemed to look not through you but deep inside, "I often heard you, when you were throwing dice or playing at some other kind of play at your teachers' or elsewhere, instead of being at a loss about the just and the unjust things, speak in a very loud and confident way about one or another of the children being wicked and unjust and behaving unjustly. How did you know this?"

"How did I know? You think I didn't know when I was being treated unjustly?"

"But if you didn't just discover this by yourself – what justice means – from whom did you learn it?"

Alcibiades hesitated, seemed embarrassed by his hesitation, and then replied, "From the many, from the people."

Socrates gave him a scornful look. "They're not fit to teach skill at games. So the many agree with themselves or with another concerning just and unjust men and affairs?"

"Least of all, by Zeus, Socrates!"

"Have you ever heard of human beings differing so vehemently about which things are healthy and which things are not to fight and kill one another?"

"No indeed."

"But as far as the just and unjust things are concerned, you have heard about it from the many, and especially from Homer. For you have heard the Odyssey and the Iliad."

"Of course, Socrates."

"Aren't these poems about the just and the unjust?"

"Yes."

"It was on account of this difference there came to be battles and deaths? And those who died at Tanagra and later at Coronea, and among them your own father, Kleinias, the difference that led to the deaths and battles was about no other thing than the just and unjust. Is it not so?"

Alcibiades agreed and Socrates, as always, was ready with the next question: whether the men who fought and died over justice knew what justice meant. And when Alcibiades was forced to agree that they did not, Socrates asked, "Is it to such teachers that you refer, then, when you yourself agree they do not know?"

Socrates had now demolished any belief in the wisdom of not only Homer but all the famous men who had led the Greeks in war. They fought and died in the name of justice, a word they did not understand and could therefore never teach. With a few short questions he had taken away the very ground on which Alcibiades had a moment earlier stood so confident and brave.

I now understood why Socrates had taken so much trouble, watched over Alcibiades from such an early age. He had somehow read in the face of the child the future of the man, and knowing that thought it his duty to make him better than if left to the deplorable authority of the crowd. It was the strength, the power, the genius, if you will, of Alcibiades that it seemed at least to make him want to learn more.

Socrates was only just beginning. It was not enough to show Alcibiades that he knew nothing about the difference between just and unjust things; he forced him to admit that this was only what Alcibiades himself had said.

"Haven't I been the questioner throughout?"

"Yes."

"And you the answerer?"

"Very much so!"

"Now, then, which of us has said the things that were spoken?"

"From what has been agreed, Socrates, it appears to be I."

That was all it took, that was how he did it, how he brought Alcibiades to his knees. One more lethal sentence and there seemed nothing more anyone could say.

"And what was spoken was that Alcibiades, the son of Kleinias, does not have knowledge concerning just and unjust things but supposes he does, and is about to go to the assembly to advise Athenians on things he knows nothing about?" And then he added, in a sympathetic voice, "It is a mad thing you intend to undertake – to teach what you do not know, having taken no trouble to learn it."

This might have destroyed a lesser man, or at least reduced him to a vengeful silence; it only seemed to make Alcibiades more eager and determined. The phrase 'mad thing' had brought a spark of recognition to his eyes, a sudden insight into the way most people did things.

"I would suppose, Socrates, that the Athenians, and the other Greeks, rarely deliberate as to which things are more just or more unjust; for they believe such things are evident, and so they let these matters go and consider which things will be advantageous to those practicing them. For just and advantageous things are not, I suppose, the same, but many have profited from committing great injustices, and I suppose there are others who performed just acts that were not to their advantage."

I am still not sure what happened next. The question, though it took a different form, remained the same. If people do not know what is just, how do they know what is to their advantage? Alcibiades was compelled to admit first that at least some just things are advantageous, and then that all the just things are noble. And then it got interesting.

"Do you remember, then, what we agreed about the just things?"

"That, I suppose, those who practice the just things necessarily practice noble things."

"And those who practice the noble things necessarily practice good things?"

"Yes."

"And that the good things are advantageous?"

"So it seems," he replied reluctantly.

The eyes of Socrates, those globe-like eyes that seemed to see more than three dimensions, held Alcibiades tighter than if he had pinned his arms behind his back and forced him to the ground.

"If then someone gets up to advise the Athenians and, supposing he knows the just and unjust things, asserts that the just things are sometime bad, would you do anything else than laugh at him, since, you too happen to say that just and advantageous things are the same?"

And now Alcibiades made a stunning confession, one which I know with utter certainty he could never have been brought to make by any other human being.

"But by the gods, Socrates! I myself don't know what I am saying, and I seem like someone in an altogether strange condition; for at one time things seem a certain way as you question me but at another time another."

"Don't you think, that it is because you are like nearly everyone else, not only ignorant of the greatest things, but suppose you know them when you do not? I hesitate to use the term, but it is stupidity in its most extreme form, as the argument accuses you as well as you yourself. This is why you are rushing toward the political things before you have been educated. But you are not the only one in this condition – the many among those who practice the things of the city, except for a few at any rate, perhaps including your guardian Pericles."

Perhaps including Pericles! Alcibiades caught at once the implication, the subtle suggestion that the education of the city's leader had itself been in fundamental ways deficient. If he was too quick to miss it, he was quicker still to see the source of what had given Pericles the advantages he had.

"And in fact, Socrates, it is said he became wise not spontaneously but through keeping company with many wise men, including Pythokleides and Anaxagoras."

I thought Socrates was going to say something about Anaxagoras, one of the philosophers with whom I wanted to study, but he asked a question about Pericles instead.

"Now then, are you able to tell me whom Pericles has made wise, beginning with his own sons?"

I understood at once what he was doing. If Pericles had learned wisdom from Anaxagoras – if Anaxagoras had any wisdom to teach – then Pericles must have taught this same wisdom to others, especially his own sons. Alcibiades dismissed it with a laugh.

"What if the two sons of Pericles were born fools, Socrates?"

Socrates did not deny this, and in that way called attention to the limitations of what can be taught.

"But your brother Kleinias?"

"Why should you mention that madman Kleinias?"

"But if Kleinias is mad and the two sons of Pericles born fools," asked Socrates with painful directness, "how is it that he failed to see that you were in this condition?"

"I suppose it is my fault for not having paid attention. I

understand what you are saying. Apart from a few, those who practice the things of the city do seem to me to be uneducated."

"Well, what then?" asked Socrates, challenging him to speak his mind.

Watching Alcibiades was like watching two horses in harness, each willful and headstrong, fighting for the lead. One moment he seemed eager to admit his ignorance and anxious to learn the cause; the next moment, supremely confident of his powers, he dismissed any suggestion that he did not already know all that was needed.

"Well, what then?" repeated Socrates.

"If they were educated," he said, suddenly impatient, "then I might have to learn and practice to compete against them, but given what they are – ordinary men completely unprepared – why go to all the trouble? There isn't any question but that, where nature is concerned, I will easily get the better of them."

Throwing up his hands, Socrates stared at him with contempt and disbelief.

"What a thing to say! You thought the contest was against the men you find here?"

Alcibiades shook his head in confusion. "Then who?"

"The kings of the Persians and the kings of the Spartans, if you intend to lead this city. Those are your opponents, not the ones you suppose, and we will get the better of them by no other thing than by taking trouble and by art. If you fall short in these you will also fall short in becoming renowned among the Greeks and the barbarians – for which you have a greater love, it seems to me, than anyone has ever had for anything."

And he meant it! Alcibiades's love of glory was greater than the love anyone had ever had for anything! How often in the years that followed did I find myself wondering how Socrates, the most astonishing human being I would ever meet, had known all this when Alcibiades was only twenty? How many lives were changed, how many lives were lost or ruined, because of this love Alcibiades had for his own eternal glory? And yet, who but Alcibiades could have saved the city from itself?

Socrates was waiting with another question.

"What of this?" he asked. "As to what art makes us better, could we even know it if we were ignorant of what we are ourselves?"

"Impossible."

"Is it easy, then, to know oneself, and was the man who

inscribed this on the temple of the Pythian a mean sort, or is it difficult and something that does not belong to everyone?"

"It sometimes seems to me to belong to everyone, and sometimes to be very difficult."

"But whether it is easy or not, Alcibiades, this at any rate is the way the matter stands for us: if we know this, we can perhaps know what it is to take trouble over ourselves, but if we are ignorant, we never can."

"These things are so."

The street had grown quiet; the only sign of life the lamps in the windows from the nearby houses. A full moon cast a pale glow that caught the faces of Socrates and Alcibiades in a way that, concentrating my attention, seemed to make them the only two people in the world.

"Let me tell you what I fear the most, that having become a lover of the people, eager to win their applause, you will be corrupted. Many good men among the Athenians have already had this experience. For fair of face is 'the populace of great-hearted Erechtheus,'" he said, quoting Homer's Odyssey. "That is why you must learn what needs to be learned in order to approach the things of the city, and do not do it before, so that you have an antidote and suffer nothing terrible."

"What are the things I need to learn?" asked Alcibiades. His whole body tensed, ready to spring into action. His eyes burned in anticipation of the hard things he knew he must and would conquer.

"To be moderate and good. If you are going to practice the things of the city correctly and nobly, you must give the citizens a share of virtue, but you cannot give a share of something you do not have. It is not therefore personal license and rule that you must obtain in order to act as you wish for yourself and for the city but justice and moderation."

He stared hard at Alcibiades, a serious warning in those remarkable eyes of his. "But before one has virtue, it is better to be ruled, by one who is better, than to rule – for a man and not only for a child."

If I had not seen it with my own eyes I would not have believed it. Alcibiades had become not only willing, but eager to obey.

"We will probably be changing roles, Socrates, I taking yours and you mine, for from this day nothing can keep me from attending on you, and you from being attended by me. And I shall, beginning this moment, take trouble over justice."

He would have saluted, had Socrates commanded it; that was how willing he now was to serve. But instead of seeing what he had done as a victory, Socrates seemed more inclined to worry about defeat. He looked at Alcibiades with genuine affection.

"And I would wish you to continue doing so. Yet I stand in dread, not because I do not trust in your nature, but rather because, seeing the strength of the city, I fear it will overcome both you and me."

He could not have read the future better had he been talking about the past.

How long had I been standing there, a few steps away? An hour, even longer? I did not know and it did not matter. They could have talked until morning and I still would have felt a sense of loss when it was over, when Socrates said goodbye and went on his way. I had not said a word, and yet the voice inside my head, the one with which I talked so often to myself, began to ask me questions, the very questions Socrates had asked, in an endless dialogue of our own. I tried to answer, to see and feel what it must have been like for Alcibiades, until I finally realized that I had an advantage he did not have. I did not have his ambition to rule over others; I wanted something more than that. I wanted, like Socrates, to learn to rule myself. I wanted, like Socrates, to learn to know.

Chapter Six

I had taken rooms in the Piraeus, the harbor four miles southwest of Athens. Dozens of ships, some with two and even three banks of oars, sailed in and out every day; merchant ships that brought silks and spices from Persia and other distant places; warships with which Athens had conquered and now maintained its empire. Sailors called out to one another as they made ready to leave; slaves shuffled along the quay, bent beneath the burden of the cargo they had unloaded. I liked to watch from my window the constant comings and goings of broad muscled men and envied a little the loose freedom of the women who returned a sailor's laughing leer with a sultry, brazen look of their own. In Athens, as I was learning, everything was for sale.

I rose with the sun after a night's failed sleep in which I was not always sure if I were dreaming or thinking clearly, remembering or imagining what I had seen and heard in the stately home of Pericles and on that quiet city street where Alcibiades had taken me by the arm and Socrates, in a different sense, had taken hold of him. The two scenes seemed to merge, the brilliant crowd of famous artists and men of power, all that gaiety and thrilling laughter, fading into muted insignificance, the painted backdrop to a display of such concentrated intelligence that every word burned forever inside your mind.

Sitting alone at the table where I kept my ink and paper, I wrote down everything I had heard, all the questions, all the answers, that entire dialogue by which Socrates had humbled the overweening pride of Alcibiades and turned him into the willing student of what he was now convinced only Socrates could teach. My hand moved quickly; there was no need to stop to search my memory: I remembered everything, every quick flying word. I must have written for two or three hours, filled up at least a dozen pages, when there was a knock on the door.

A servant girl, young and quite pretty, handed me a white flower and in a calm, unhurried voice announced that her mistress, Aspasia, wished to see me.

"Yes, she asked if I would visit her today," I said, smiling back at her. "What time does she wish me to come?"

"She's waiting for you now, outside."

The servant girl waited while I dressed and then led me down the narrow stone stairs to a carriage parked across the street. A pair of gray horses with scarlet plumes just behind their ears pawed the ground in a hard brittle staccato that echoed above the harbor noise. The breath from their nostrils curled like smoke in the misty morning air. The driver, an old man with lanky shoulders and long black lashes, pulled gently on the reins to keep them still.

The door swung open and Aspasia greeted me from beneath a hooded cloak.

"Come, there are things I want to show you, things I think you'll like."

The door shut behind me and the carriage bolted forward.

"The Piraeus," she started to explain, and then realized that I would not know what she meant. Pulling the hood off her head, she looked at me with a smile full of what could have been either sympathy or irony. I was not sure. "This is the heart of the democracy, the Piraeus, where all the merchants, all the tradesmen, all the people for whom money measures everything, live and work. It is the place where men like Cleon start out, where they learn to tell everyone what they want to hear. It is the place where they learn to lie, the place where rumor starts. I never come here if I can avoid it."

Suddenly, the carriage stopped and I was thrown forward, crashing into Aspasia who caught me in her arms. The driver was swearing and men were swearing back. We looked out the window in time to see a pile of lumber go careening down the street, thrown off a cart that to avoid collision had turned on its side. Still shouting, the driver of our carriage pulled hard on the reigns and the horses galloped forward.

"The price of what Athens has become," remarked Aspasia as I fell back in my seat directly across from her. "More people all the time, always building, new houses – there are ten thousand houses here already – new buildings, all the monuments to how great we have become."

She pounded her hand against the ceiling of the carriage, instructing the driver to slow down.

"Three hundred fifty thousand people, the population of Athens by the last count. Half of them Athenians, men, women and children; about a tenth resident aliens, people who came here – like

I came here – from other places because Athens is the only place to
be if you want to become famous, or if you want to become rich, or
if you happen to be one of those rarest of all people, someone who
wants to study and learn. That was why I came here – or one of the
reasons," she added with a flashing eye and a smile that told me,
what it had taught me the day before, that Aspasia was a woman who
knew exactly what she was about. "As I was saying, half Athenian,
ten percent resident aliens, the rest slaves. Although, really, if you
think about things clearly – if you listen to your new friend, my old
friend, Socrates – you'll begin to wonder whether instead of forty
percent we ought to say a hundred. All of us are slaves; all of us
except him of course. He is the only one who is really free. Perhaps
you don't believe that, but, give it time, you will."

The carriage jolted over the pavement, the clatter of the wheels
a strident, broken rhythm that sometimes made it hard to hear.

"You didn't need to come get me," I said, almost shouting. "I
was going to come to you. You asked me to, last evening, just before
you and Pericles ... "

Both hands pressed against the seat, she braced herself against
the bumpy ride, laughing at the inconvenience.

"You walked to our place yesterday?"

"Yes, of course; I like walking. I like seeing new things."

"I'm not sure there is much worth seeing here," she remarked,
and then added brightly, "But there is where I'm taking you." Then
she remembered, and remembering, her expression changed, became
thoughtful and serious, the way of someone still struggling with a
dilemma. "When I asked you to come for a private talk, when we
were going into the garden – you saw us there?"

"Yes, I did; I saw ... "

"The way I reacted, my temporary despair."

The carriage seemed to slow down, though we had if anything
gained speed. The road had become smoother. We had left behind
the Piraeus and all its noise. Following the Long Walls that had been
built to make a single line of defense, we were drawing near to the
city.

"When he told me – I knew it was coming, knew it was only
a matter of time; but still, that isn't the same as knowing that it has
happened, that what you have feared more than anything is actually
about to start."

I did not know what she was talking about, only that it was

causing her great heartache and anguish; but then, suddenly, and quite unexpectedly, she laughed.

"It's one of the reasons why instead of waiting for you to come to see me, I came to see you. If you stay in Athens much longer, I'm sure they'll be coming after you as well."

"Come after ...? Who would be ...?"

"Can't you guess, after what you said to him last evening?"

I should not have been surprised, but I was. "You heard about that, what I said to ... How could you have – ?"

"I hear everything. At least three different people told me. I knew it moments after it happened. If Pericles liked you before, he's in love with you now."

"He knows – you know – what he said about – ?"

"'Aspasia, the woman every intelligent man is supposed to admire, and every one in Athens knows is a whore'? He says it all the time, thinks himself very clever. You think I should be outraged, upset – Why? He's right, in a stupid way at least. Intelligent men do admire me. They should. I've taught half of them how to speak. I don't mean speak words of love to women. I teach them, some of them, how to speak in public. I even, on occasion, write their speeches. Ask Socrates; he'll tell you."

"And Pericles – do you write speeches for him?"

Her gaze drew back on itself; the open, candid expression disappeared. She would talk about anything with this exception. Her loyalty to Pericles was absolute.

"I'm sorry; I shouldn't have asked," I quickly apologized.

She shook her head to let me know that it was not necessary, and went on as if my question had never been asked.

"And he is right, in that crude, unreflective way of his, to call me a whore, because for men like him, who know only buying and selling – he is a tanner, a trader who made his fortune in leather and hides – there are only two kinds of women: the ones they marry for their money and the children they can bring them, and the women they buy in the streets or the stews for their temporary pleasure. The idea of a woman of intelligence, a woman with whom a man might actually want to spend time, a woman from whom a man might learn something worth knowing – to men like Cleon that is worse than impossible, it is an absurdity. He despises me; he always has. And now, thanks to your quick wit, he hates you almost as much. It has already started."

"Already started? What do you mean?"

"Yesterday, when he left: 'Pericles now has two whores in his house instead of one.'"

"But as I told him yesterday," I laughed, "not anyone someone with his looks could ever buy!"

The carriage rattled to a halt. The driver jumped down and opened the door. I started to get up, but Aspasia held me by the wrist.

"Don't underestimate what he can do. He doesn't want to buy you; he wants to destroy you, the way he wants to destroy me. It's the only way he has to destroy Pericles and the hold he has on the city. He can't get to him yet, but he has another way to start. That is what Pericles told me yesterday; that, and what I'm going to show you now."

I got out of the carriage and found myself on the highest part of the Acropolis directly in front of the Parthenon. Seen from a distance, the Parthenon dominated not just the city but everything below; seen from a few steps away it drew you toward it in a way that banished every small-minded thought. The marble, brought from the quarries of Mt. Pentelicus, a few miles north-east of Athens, had an almost unearthly glow. There were eight Doric columns across the front and back, a width of one hundred and one feet, and seventeen along the two hundred twenty eight foot length of the building. The five doors of the grand entrance, not yet completed, led to a rectangular building divided by a wall into two porticoes. A blue coffered ceiling decorated with gold stars stretched like heaven itself over an enormous vestibule. Two wings, one of which housed a gallery of the finest art of Greece, flanked the main building. The Parthenon had taken fifteen years to build. The ten temples I had loved in Agrigento had been built to stand alone, a tribute to the gods; the Parthenon had been built to give shelter to a goddess, a forty foot gold and ivory statue of Athena, which had also taken fifteen years to make.

"There is nothing like it anywhere!" cried Aspasia in a voice that surprised me by its strangely bitter tone. "They talk about the Sphinx and the pyramids of Egypt – crude carvings, blocks of stone, in the arid desert. But this – look at her! She's alive! Forty feet high, covered all in gold, where else but Athens – who else but Pericles – could have brought something like this to completion? A thousand years from now, if the world remembers nothing else of us, they'll remember this! And what payment do they make him, what return for his far-sighted genius? – They're going to bring Phidias to trial, the sculptor who spent fifteen years – fifteen years! – doing this, creating in lifelike form the goddess all of Athens is supposed to worship. And the charge, the accusation some paid informer – some lying coward who will say whatever Cleon and that pack of braying asses want him to – will bring forward on his oath? – That Phidias is a thief; that the greatest sculptor in the world charged for gold that he did not use and that – though they have not yet the courage to say so directly – he got away with it because he paid Pericles for his connivance."

A shudder of rage and fury passed through her. She stamped her foot, threw back her head and laughed with indignation at the utter stupidity of it all.

"He should have charged twice what he did. He should have stolen, like they say he did; taken whatever he wanted – it would still have been a bargain! Make something like this! And these fools think they can quarrel about the price?"

Looking up at what Phidias had done, clothed immortality in the look of a mortal being, wrapped gold around sculpted stone and ivory and made a lifeless statue come alive, it was impossible to disagree. All the money in the world, if money were the measure, could not have paid for this. It was like asking the price of intelligence and genius.

"Do you know what they tried to do, all these self-proclaimed champions of the rights of the people to decide, these keepers of the public purse who made their fortunes stealing people blind? – They brought a bill of censure in the assembly, claiming that Pericles had acted without authority in spending public money on this and all the other buildings. Do you know how he defeated it?" She laughed with outsized pleasure at the memory of what Pericles had done. "He listened without expression to all their false complaints, listened without even the slightest reaction to the hooting and jeering of the crowd; and then, when they were finally finished, he stood up and – . You haven't heard him speak. He has a voice in public that warrants no comparison. – He stood up, waited until the assembly fell silent, and calmly announced that, given how they felt, he would pay for all of it – everything that had been built – out of his own private funds; and that because they did not wish to have anything to do with it, he would replace the monuments which declared that these things had been built by the people of Athens with ones that said that they had been built as a gift of Pericles, a citizen."

A smile of pride and triumph moved effortlessly across her straight, clean mouth.

"How quickly they changed their mind. It was one thing to scream about how the money that had been spent; it was quite another to have all the fame and glory go to him alone. He's better than they are, and they know it. They cannot come up to his level, so the ones like Cleon, who hunger after a power they would never know how to use, spend all their time trying to find ways to bring him down to theirs."

Her eyes turned toward the towering statue, comparing it, as it seemed, to the paltry ambitions of those who snapped at the heels of the man she worshipped as much as loved. There was something she wanted to tell me, but she hesitated, not sure that she should. I was still a stranger, new to the city. We walked the length of the Parthenon in a pensive silence. When we reached the end, she stood at the railing and with a sweeping gesture of her hand seemed to take in not just all of Athens, but what it meant, the hidden secret of the city.

"Shall I tell you why all this was done, the real reason for all this building, the reason why things everyone thought would take generations to complete were finished in such a short period of time?"

"To make the city beautiful and great," I replied, willing to chance the obvious in the hope of drawing her out. "To bring honor and glory, everlasting fame."

There was something about my utterly conventional answer that seemed to intrigue her.

"Yes, but ... " Her eyes narrowed into a gaze of astonishing intensity. Her mouth grew hard as her lips pressed tight together. "Yes, of course – glory, greatness, fame, all of that – but there is something deeper going on, something only Pericles understood. He gave it the form, he decided what the city ought to look like, but there were things at work here – an energy, a desire, a madness – an eros, if you will – that would have destroyed everything if he had not done what he did. Athens had become rich because of what happened after the war with Persia, when Athens took control of all the islands that the Persians used to rule. Everyone had been hard at work during the war – There was not any choice: survival was at stake! But with no more wars to fight, thousands of soldiers and sailors who had been paid from the public treasury were suddenly unemployed.

"It was a perfect recipe for endless trouble, the war of rich and poor that is always there, just below the surface, waiting for the spark that starts the conflagration. That is why Pericles built a city the likes of which no one has ever seen. Everyone was put to work. Men who by age and fitness were able to serve in the military abroad were paid with public funds; why not give public salaries to the undisciplined multitude, all those who practice the mechanical arts – the masons, the carpenters, the builders – here at home? Put them to work, instead of letting them sit around, brooding on their condition; put them to work on vast public projects, employing, and by that means perfecting, all the arts of construction and decoration; put them to work and that way keep the city not just employed, but proud of what they were doing. It would not just be those who took part in foreign expeditions, but those who stayed at home, who would have a share in the public greatness and the public money. From the admiral in the navy to the meanest artisan, everyone was now engaged in a competition to do things better than anyone had ever done them before. Pericles kept their minds on what they could do, and every day, right in front of them, they could see that he was right, that they could make the city great and that in doing that they could be great as well."

Aspasia's eyes flashed with sudden insight, the bitter recognition of a remedy that had become a greater danger than the problem it had been meant to solve.

"They learned to believe it, that there was nothing they could not do. And why would they need Pericles after he had taught them that?"

For the next hour or so, Aspasia gave me instruction in the recent history of Athens and the difference that Pericles had made in the life of the city and the people who lived there. She was nothing if not fiercely loyal, but it was a loyalty based as much on her own judgment of how things should be done as on the love and affection she obviously felt for her husband. She did not hesitate to admit that there had been occasions on which Pericles had made a mistake, but she would try to excuse it, or explain why the mistake had been unavoidable.

"With a man like Pericles, there is never any question but that he'll do whatever he has to do to excel. That is what drives him: what he thinks he has to be. That's how you tell the difference among men – the standard they set for themselves."

I suddenly found myself laughing. It sounded dismissive, and so I was forced to tell her the strange memory that her words had brought back to me.

"The standards are not always quite so noble. A man who thought I was a boy once reached up between my legs, and the look he had – what was driving him – and the look that followed when he discovered his mistake…!"

"A man who thought you were a boy! That scarcely seems possible."

"I think he still does," I added, mysteriously. "Thinks I'm a boy, I mean."

"Even without …? You'll have to tell me the whole story sometime." Her bright eyes sparkled with new mischief. "A boy, but one who will always be less than a man. That's a riddle we might try on someone." She gave me a long, searching look. "I'd suggest you try it on Alcibiades, but I think you have him quite worked up enough as it is."

"Really? He did not seem that interested last night. He walked me home and … "

"He walked you home, all the way to the Piraeus, and you don't think he was interested?"

"We ran into Socrates, just outside your house. They stood there talking for hours, and then, when he walked me home, all he talked about was how everyone was always telling him how great he was – "

"It's true; they do."

" – how he could do anything he wanted, but that whenever he talked to Socrates he knew they were all idiots and liars, and that Socrates, the ugliest man he had ever seen, was the only one who had the right look, the only one who spoke any sense."

A trace of disapproval darted through her beautiful, almond shaped eyes; a shadow of displeasure fell across the fine line of her marvelously sensitive mouth.

"It's good that Alcibiades listens to someone; he doesn't listen to his guardian."

I remembered what I had heard last night, the not so hidden reservations about Pericles that he and Socrates seemed to share.

"Alcibiades has all the arrogance of his brilliance. He's young – you're young, too; but you're a woman and a woman, especially at that age, is always wiser than a man. There were certain things

Pericles had to do to win support, things like making attendance in the assembly or jury service a public charge – paying people for doing their civic duty – that Alcibiades thinks went too far. He can afford to think that way: he hasn't had to fight for anything yet. Criticism is the prerogative of the inexperienced."

I wanted to ask her more about Alcibiades, but I did not want to seem overeager. I knew he would come to me, and that if he put it off, if he took his time, it would only be because, like me, he had too much pride. We were a double image, two people dancing the same dance in a double mirror.

"There is one other thing," said Aspasia when we were back in the carriage and on our way down to the Piraeus. "Pericles asked me to tell you that he will be very disappointed if you don't join us for dinner tomorrow night." She paused, quite on purpose, waiting to see, if only in my eyes, the question she was certain I wanted to ask. "Alcibiades said he hoped you would, though he was not sure whether he might not have made another commitment."

There was such joyful malice in her eyes that I could not help but burst out laughing.

"Tell Alcibiades that I could not think of a better way to spend an evening than to have dinner with you and Pericles alone."

The next night, when I went to have dinner, Alcibiades, just as I knew he would, made a point of being somewhere else. The only explanation offered by Aspasia when she greeted me at the door was a knowing smile and the whispered, sly remark that certain people had a way of reappearing when you least expected it, "or when they think you least expect it."

And he did, an hour after we had sat down, the three of us, to a dinner as rich in conversation as anything we ate; walked in as if he were keeping an appointment that Pericles had with him! He did not so much as say hello to Aspasia; he did not so much as look at me.

"Tell me, Pericles," he began at once, "can you tell me what a law is?"

Pericles took it all in good humor. "Of course," he replied in that sweet-tempered voice that had charmed a whole city. "But perhaps you might first like to say hello to our guest. You've met her before, if I'm not mistaken."

Alcibiades turned to me with forced civility, but we both knew his game: The bored indifference, the barely stifled yawn, the laughter I saw hidden deep in his eyes at the knowledge that I knew what he was doing and that in my own way I was laughing back.

"Yes," he said, turning back to Pericles; "if you're not mistaken, I have. Helen – I think that's her name. Fitting, don't you think, a name like that, given how she looks? Enough to break a man's heart, if he let her."

I could feel the glow begin to shine on my face, the warmth that raced through my body. Aspasia raised an eyebrow, and there was mocking laughter in her rich, clear voice.

"Something of course you would never do: let a woman – any woman – break that heart of yours!"

Alcibiades laughed, and then, quickly, as if to dare me to a danger for which he thought – or wanted me to think he thought – I lacked the courage, he looked at me.

"Take it, break it – it won't matter; I have as many hearts as I have lives. The only question is can you say the same?"

"I could, but that would only cheapen the prize. If I were to give my heart to anyone, it would not be because of what they might do with it; it would be because of what I felt and what I had to give."

Alcibiades, to my astonished pleasure, reddened with embarrassment, only slightly, and only for a moment, but long enough to establish a connection, something undeniable, that had taken place between us. Aspasia noticed and smiled like a cat. Pericles noticed Aspasia and, as always, was content with what he saw.

"Tell me," said Alcibiades, angry with himself, "what I asked before: What is a law?"

"I said I would, and I will," replied Pericles, enjoying his ward's discomfort.

But Alcibiades had more control than other men his age. He smiled with sudden confidence.

"Then by all means tell me. Because whenever I hear men praised for abiding by the laws, for protecting the laws, it occurs to me that no one really deserves that praise who doesn't know what a law really is."

"There is no great difficulty. You want to know what a law is. Laws are the rules approved and enacted by a majority in the assembly, by which they declare what should and should not be done."

"Do they suppose it is right to do good or evil?" Alcibiades immediately shot back.

Question, answer, question; suddenly, I realized what he was doing. He had even dressed the part, though perhaps without knowing it. Instead of the purple robe that trailed down behind his heels, he was wearing a plain white one of ordinary length. He wore his hair plain, without the ringlets and without any ornamentation, and instead of wearing sandals he was barefooted. He was doing what Socrates did, doing what had been done to him last night, asking what things were; questions that, pressed hard enough, raised a doubt about all our assumptions and made us wonder if we knew anything or if anything was true. I sat there, literally speechless, watching this strange transformation, wondering what Socrates would have thought, the student become the teacher to a man thought by everyone, except perhaps the two of them, to be the wisest man alive.

"Do they suppose it is right to do good or evil?" he repeated when Pericles hesitated, uncertain whether Alcibiades was really serious.

"Good, of course; certainly not evil."

"But if, instead of a democracy there is an oligarchy, and a minority, instead of a majority, enact rules of conduct, are those also laws?"

"Whatever the sovereign power enacts and directs to be done is law."

"If, then, a tyrant, being the sovereign power, enacts, whatever he decides the citizens are to do, that also is a law?"

"Yes, whatever a tyrant as ruler enacts is also known as law."

"But force, the negation of law, what is that, Pericles? Is it not the action of the stronger when he constrains the weaker to do whatever he chooses, not by persuasion, but by force?"

"That is my opinion."

Alcibiades' gaze never wavered. He had done this all before, done it in the elegant privacy of his mind; asked these same questions, heard these same answers. Nothing surprised him, nothing threw him off step. He was thirty years the junior and he was as much in charge, had the same control, as Socrates had last night of him. It was incredible, even more astonishing than what I had felt watching Socrates, because so much more unexpected. He had learned it all from Socrates, learned it with a power that was not just lightening quick, but capable of grasping and retaining in all its nuanced subtlety an argument that most men, even if they could read it on the written page, would not know how to follow. Now I began to understand how Socrates could claim that he had seen in the boy what the man would be, the ambition that could never be content with anything less than a world to rule. I stole a glance at Aspasia. Her face was ashen.

"Then whatever a tyrant by enactment constrains the citizens to do without persuasion, is the negation of law?"

"I think so," replied Pericles, seeming for the first time to be uncertain. "And I withdraw my answer that whatever a tyrant enacts without persuasion is a law."

Utterly remorseless, Alcibiades forced him back. "And when the minority passes enactments, not by persuading the majority, but through using its power, are we to call that force or not?"

"Everything, I think, that men constrain others to do 'without persuasion,' whether by enactment or not, is not law, but force."

"It follows then, that whatever the assembled majority, through using its power over the owners of property, enacts without persuasion is not law, but force?"

Pericles tried to cover defeat with the argument that is always used in the last resort against clear minded reason.

"Alcibiades, at your age, we, too, were very clever at this sort of thing. For the puzzles we thought about and exercised our wits on were just such as you seem to think about now."

"Ah, Pericles, if only I had known you better when you were at your cleverest in these things!"

Alcibiades was not smiling.

CHAPTER SEVEN

Anaxagoras, I had been told, was the first philosopher to settle in Athens. He had not come entirely of his own free will. He had been a soldier, one of those forced into the ranks of the Persian army, captured in the war. Had he been a Greek taken prisoner by the Persians he would have died a slave or been beaten to death the moment he opened his mouth to protest his treatment. It is one of the great ironies, an irony that like most great ironies passed unnoticed, that this man who became the teacher of not just both Pericles and Aspasia, but, for a time, Socrates as well, was in a way a gift, a wartime prize, of that other part of the world that we in our vanity and wisdom called barbarian. But if he was, as everyone seemed to insist, the first philosopher to come to Athens, he was very far from being the last; and, more to the point, he was not the one I wanted most to see.

I had heard something about what he had taught, that the world was somehow ruled by intelligence; but that, as it then seemed to me, was the kind of thing I wanted to avoid, those vague, amorphous suggestions that sounded so grand when you heard them but slipped through your fingers when you tried to figure out exactly what they meant. I was searching for something definite and precise. Empedocles had taught me that there were four basic elements that, combined with the twin forces of attraction and strife, provided the only rational explanation of the world, but it had never seemed quite right to me. Something was missing, something more basic that each of those elements must have in common; something that explained how they could combine with each other into all the things we see and touch. Aspasia had told me that there was a school in a place called Abdera, several days journey in Macedonia or Thrace, where they claimed to have discovered something like what I was looking for. She had even heard that one of their members, a leading exponent of what for some reason was called the atomic theory, was now living somewhere here in Athens. His name was Democritus and for weeks I had been trying to find him, but nothing had worked; no one seemed to have heard of him.

I had almost given up, decided that if he had ever been here he must have left and gone back to Abdera, when early one morning Aspasia's servant girl knocked on my door. Following her down to the street, I got into the waiting carriage.

"I've found Democritus, the one you've been looking for; but, first, come with me. I have to see Anaxagoras."

Her voice, normally so calm, had an anxious quality about it and there was a trace of impatience in her eyes. Slapping her hand against the ceiling of the carriage, she shouted at the driver to get moving.

"Trouble," she explained with a brief, distracted smile. "First Phidias and now this! They'll never stop, these people, Cleon and the rest of them."

"Phidias? The trial was a week ago and nothing was proved against him. What else are they ...?"

Aspasia's delicate chin came up, an unconscious act of defiance, and her fine, straight mouth twisted tight with high bred scorn. "Trial? – A trial is supposed to have an ending, supposed to bring things to a conclusion. There was a trial all right, but it was not to prove whether Phidias had done anything wrong!"

Her eyes were open wide; she was staring at me, but she was seeing someone else, someone she more than hated, despised. The carriage heaved wildly from side to side as the driver whipped the horses through the narrow, crooked streets, streets that, the farther we went, were in worse repair.

"Trial? They wanted to discover what kind of judges they would have to deal with if they ever had the chance – if they ever had the courage – to bring an accusation against Pericles himself. Trial? Hire your own witness, a villain named Menon, pay him for his perjury, but first have him stand in the marketplace with a petition asking for the protection of the public if he could prove that Phidias had cheated the city, charging for more than the gold he had really used on the statue of Athena."

Her eyes flashed with anger. She pounded on the carriage ceiling.

"Slow down! Are you trying to rattle the teeth out of my mouth! The trial! – Yes, the trial. A put up job from start to finish. They were there to test the jury – fifteen hundred members of the assembly, all those fine citizens who forgot how much they owe Pericles! Well, the prosecution had forgotten something as well; they had forgotten who they were dealing with. Phidias did not have to wait to see what those cheap demagogues could do, how far they could get the assembly to take leave of their senses; thanks to Pericles he had the means to prove his innocence."

She threw her head back and with a harsh and bitter laugh gave voice to her contempt; but also, if I read it right, her fear. Whatever had happened, if her enemies had been defeated, it was clear from her expression that it had only been the prelude to a greater threat and a greater danger.

"You see, Phidias had a way to prove beyond any doubt at all that the gold used on the statue was exactly the weight he said it was. Pericles had told him what to do, to wrap the gold in such a way that it could be taken off and weighed. When Pericles stood up in the assembly and challenged the prosecution, told them to take it off and weigh it, to prove themselves that Phidias was innocent, all the catcalls, all the jeers, all the shouted insults that had been directed at Phidias, and by reflection at Pericles himself, were now showered down on Cleon and his evil minded friends. That's one thing about the assembly: they love it every time someone is shown to be a liar or a fool!"

Folding her arms in front of her, Aspasia shook her head and sighed in seeming despair. For a long time she stared out the window as the carriage wheels clattered over the uneven, broken pavement.

"And do you know what happened then?" she asked finally. "After it was clear that nothing could be proved against Phidias, or, by implication, Pericles? It did not matter that Phidias was innocent of any crime; he was guilty of something worse. He had too much talent, he was too much the superior of all those lesser souls, and he did nothing to hide it. Hide it? He practically threw it in their faces. It would be comical if it weren't so tragic. On the shield of the goddess, where he represents the battle of the Amazons, he put in – unbelievable! – a likeness of himself, a bald old man holding up with both hands an enormous stone; and, as if that weren't bad enough, he added the image of Pericles fighting with an Amazon! It was a stupid thing to do. It gave Cleon and the others all they needed to work up resentment, easy enough to do among Athenians! They could not prove Phidias guilty of a crime, but they put him in prison anyway, punishment for his pride, what they called sacrilege, an offense against the gods."

"But they can't keep him there!" I protested. "Surely, Pericles …?"

"Pericles can't help him; no one can. He died in prison last night, poisoned."

"Poisoned? By whom? Cleon and that crowd?"

A thin smile of quiet anger moved with slow precision across her mouth. There was something remorseless in her eyes, an anticipation, if I can put it like this, of ultimate defeat, but defeat that brought with it honor instead of disgrace. I had seen that look before, though mainly on the faces of men about to die, the ones who had been brave enough to stand up to my father.

"The rumor – the slander – is that Pericles had it done, to protect himself from what Phidias, to secure his freedom, might have told. And to make sure that no one who helps them in their conspiracy of evil is ever punished for what they do, Glycon, one of Cleon's lieutenants, introduced, and the assembly approved, a proposal to make Menon, who brought the charges against Phidias, free from the payment of all taxes and customs, and ordered the generals to make sure no one does this false accuser any harm. There isn't anything they won't do to destroy Pericles. They murdered Phidias and reward his accuser; and now, because that was not enough, because Pericles still outwits them, they're going to murder me; and not just me, a woman they all think a whore, but an old man, Anaxagoras, who never had a harsh word for anyone in his life!"

The carriage slowed and gradually came to a stop. Despite all its wealth and beauty, there were neighborhoods in Athens still filled with poverty and destitution, and we were in one of the worst. A black crow with only one leg hopped among a horde of black flies buzzing around the garbage left in the street. The pack of small naked children splashing in the mud holes where sidewalks should have been did not seem to notice, or, more probably, were too used to it to mind. Halfway up the block of blighted tenements, a shaggy horse with sleepy eyes and ribs that stood out in bold relief waited in the worn out harness of a wooden cart with a broken wheel. Aspasia placed a silk handkerchief against her nose, slight protection against the corrosive, venomous smell.

We were standing in front of a small tumble down shack with an awning made of sticks. Sitting, or rather half-reclining on a window ledge, a bench in everything but name, an old man with scattered whiskers and long disheveled hair was talking quietly to a half dozen young men with pale, sometimes pockmarked, faces; students of an earnest disposition who thought to show contempt for the world by showing how little they thought about themselves.

"This is awful," muttered Aspasia, obviously grieved. "Worse than anything I imagined." But then, as we drew close enough to hear, she held me by the arm and a smile full of memory began to glow on her face. "Listen," she whispered; "just listen."

I did what she told me, listened to an old man's voice, as pure and melodic as any I had heard. We were less than twenty feet away, just the other side of a low brick wall that was all that separated the house and its porch from the street, but he was so intent on what he was saying, so concerned that his students understood what he was trying to explain, that though he must have seen us, it was as if we had made no impression.

"Mind is infinite and self-ruling, and is mixed with no other Thing, but is alone by itself." Pausing, he let them think about the meaning of what he had said, and then, with a gentle nod, as if he knew they understood, he continued. "If it were not by itself, but were mixed with anything else, it would have had a share of all Things, if it were mixed with anything; for in everything there is a portion of everything, as I have said before. And the things mixed with Mind would have prevented it, so that it could not rule over any Thing in the same way as it can being alone by itself."

I remembered what Empedocles had taught me. Love and Strife were the two competing forces that produced both rest and motion, that brought things together and drove them apart. Love and Strife, the twin forces of nature, and nature what things are. Mind, intelligence, had no part in any of it; mind, intelligence – that was how we understood, how we learned, what the world was made of and how it worked. What then this Mind the old man talked about? I listened with even more attention.

"For Mind is the finest of all Things, and the purest, and has complete understanding of everything, and has the greatest power. All things which have life, both the greater and the less, are ruled by Mind. Mind took command of the universal revolution, so as to make things revolve at the outset."

My curiosity, my sense of having until this moment failed to think clearly about anything, grew with every word that came from the mouth of this decrepit looking old man, lecturing patiently to a small group of adoring dull-eyed students who, whatever they might later remember, had no idea what he was really talking about. I wanted to chase them all away, and ask him all the questions that were now flooding through my mind. He must have sensed that, known with a clairvoyant's certainty the impatient eagerness that had taken possession of me, because his head, which had never moved, suddenly jolted up and he looked straight at me. That was all, nothing more; he just looked at me and somehow knew that there was someone who wanted more than anything to know, to learn, not what I could later tell others, but what I could keep inside me, my sole possession, the meaning of my life.

He went back to his lecture, describing how everything, "all the things that now exist, and whatever shall exist – all was arranged by Mind, as also the revolutions now followed by the stars, the sun and moon." The sun, he added, gives the moon its brilliance. And then, finally, he criticized "The Greeks who have an incorrect belief on Coming into Being and Passing Away. No Thing comes into being or passes away, but is mixed together or separated from existing Things. They would be correct if they called coming into being 'mixing,' and passing away 'separation-off.'"

He was finished, and with a wave of his hand dismissed his small class, telling them they could come back in a week, "if you still have an interest in learning, and I am still alive to teach."

He waited until they left and then motioned for us to come forward.

"Pericles will be distressed to learn that you live like this," said Aspasia, kissing him softly on the cheek.

"Pericles should be distressed to learn that he has forgotten his old friend and teacher," said Anaxagoras. There was shrewd glimmer in his eye. He was not complaining about how he had been treated; only stating a fact that, if unfortunate, was incontestable. "He is much too busy with Athens and the business of the world to remember me."

"A thing he does only because of what you taught him," replied Aspasia, gently turning what Pericles had done from base ingratitude to a teacher's pride. "There is a reason everyone calls you Nous or Mind. They mean the intelligence that first gave direction to your most famous student."

"I only tried to teach him rest instead of motion."

It seemed, even for a philosopher, a strange thing to say. As often happened when I was overtaken by a thought, at least when I knew it was safe to do so, I asked directly what he meant.

"And you are …?"

"A new friend of ours; Helen, only recently come to Athens, and already – "

"Loved by all the men and hated by all the women," said Anaxagoras, moving over so I could sit next to him. Smiling with his eyes, he placed his hand against my cheek, feeling with his fingers more than the shape, the inner structure, of my face. "Now I can die having known two women who were beautiful both inside and out. How long has it been, my dear Aspasia, since I saw you last?"

His fragile hand, still pressed against my skin, began to slide away. She started to answer, to make a guess at how much time had passed, but he had not forgotten what I had asked in my excitement.

"Rest instead of motion. Isn't that what you wanted to know? It's nothing difficult. If you study – no, more than study, take seriously – the basic principles of existence; if you grasp the being of things, the way that, instead of random chance, the world is ruled by intelligence, then you begin to see how unimportant, how contemptible, are the things that most men want, the way most men live their lives, the constant desire for more of what they never needed in the first place."

"And you taught him well; he learned that lesson," insisted Aspasia with sudden warmth. "That's why he has that composure that nothing can ever shake, that endless calmness that makes that mob in the assembly go quiet. It's why he speaks the way he does, with dignity and high purpose, nothing of the cheap theatrics, the strident breast-beating, the rampant dishonesty, the baboon eloquence, of all those other, lesser men. It's because of you, our old dear friend, that he has been able to make Athens great. And that's why you and I are now both in danger."

Anaxagoras leaned his bony shoulders against the wall behind him and thoughtfully stroked his narrow chin.

"There was danger in the days when I was wealthy, the danger that with that much money I would do something with it I should not do; but now, as poor as I am, what danger that I might do something wrong?"

Aspasia was not in the mood to be philosophic. She was not worried about the danger of doing an ignoble act; the danger she had come to warn him about was palpable and real.

"The enemies of Pericles mean to do you harm. They put Phidias on trial, and when they could not get a conviction threw him in prison anyway and had him poisoned. And now we're next, you

97

and me. You're going to be indicted for impiety, for not believing in the gods, and I'm going to be charged with that as well; that, and one thing more."

That was what she had meant, that having murdered Phidias they were going to murder her! A judicial murder, a trial on a charge against which, if you had so much as ever raised a question about the origin or nature of the world, if you had so much as listened to anyone who had, it was almost impossible to defend yourself. Impiety, a failure to believe in all the things the city believed, or, in the case of false minded men like Cleon, claimed that they did. There was a certain fatal genius in what they were doing; an instinct for what was most vulnerable. Their ambition, more sure footed than their intelligence, prevented them from seeing that what seemed weak and easy to destroy was the secret source of what, under Pericles, had been the city's strength. Like a pack of howling vicious dogs all they could think about was what they wanted now, not what might happen afterward when, having destroyed the very possibility of free thought, no one was left with the courage to speak his mind and point out their mistakes.

"One thing more?" I asked, thunderstruck by what Aspasia had said. "Impiety – not believing in the gods – and something else as well?"

Aspasia's chin came up that same defiant half inch it often did when there had been a challenge to her pride. Her mouth quivered in the first beginnings of scornful laughter, amused by what the enemies of Pericles had done, the lengths to which they had gone in their effort to infuriate the crowd.

"Impiety, and as a second, shall I say related, charge, procuring. I am accused of bringing freeborn women – notice that: not slaves or prostitutes, the kind of women on whom Cleon and the others like to spend their time and money – freeborn women into my house so that Pericles can sleep with them. I would not mind it so much – there isn't anything I wouldn't do for Pericles; though, if he wanted women he would scarcely need my help to get them – but they have such shrunken souls that they thought to insult me by having the charge brought by Hermippus, a comedian about whom the only thing laughable is his own disgusting appearance!"

She tried to put a brave face on it, to dismiss with contempt the idea that the choice of accuser was anything other than a mark of crude stupidity, but we both understood that it was as shrewd a thing as they could have done, forcing her to defend herself against the attack of someone who made his living in the arts of ridicule. The crowd would go crazy, listening to him banter charges of godless mockery in the house of Pericles' own kept madam.

"But I'm not worried about me," she said, turning to Anaxagoras. "I'm worried about you. They have all they need, what you wrote in that book of yours, what you tell everyone who comes to talk to you. Why do you do that, say things that can get you into trouble and say them so openly?"

"'In the beginning all things were mixed together; then reason came and introduced order,'" quoted Anaxagoras with a sly glance meant to remind Aspasia that she had heard these words before. If she had forgotten everything else he had taught her, she could not have forgotten that. "What difference would it have made if I had talked in parables or written more discreetly? Do you think that men like Cleon can only twist the truth; that they could not use to their own purposes, however we might try to conceal our meaning, anything you or I have ever said or written? I have heard it all before. Their minds are filled with confusion; they think that everything happens by chance, that their only hope of controlling what happens is to appeal to the gods who, they believe, have the power to make things turn out as they wish."

"They may be every bit as confused as you say they are," replied Aspasia; "but they are clear about what they intend to do. They're going to put you on trial and demand that you be killed!"

"Long ago nature condemned both my judges and myself to death," replied the aging Anaxagoras with an admirable shrug of indifference.

He got to his feet and went inside. I thought he was going to get us something to drink, but when he came back a minute later he had in his hands a book which he then gave me.

"You can read for yourself what I thought fit to write; read what I said about the sun, that it is a mass of red hot metal, larger than all of the Peloponnesus; read what I said about the firmament as a whole, that it is made of lifeless stones and that it would fall to pieces were it not for the speed of rotation that caused it in the first place to come together."

Moved beyond measure by this priceless gift, the work, I knew, of his lifetime, I mumbled a few inconsequential words of thanks, promising that I would not just read it, but study every word. He seemed profoundly grateful, and I realized, what I had not understood before, how for a man like this, someone who lived entirely in his mind, the promise of a common interest, another intelligence to take seriously what he had done, to share the insight he had with great diligence and effort achieved, was a greater gift than the one he had given. Anaxagoras took me by the hand and told me something strange and wonderful.

"Every moment is the culmination of everything that has gone before. When I see your face, such astonishing beauty, all the doubts I ever had are gone. I was right: the world is ruled by reason and intelligence. How else explain a being as lovely as you?"

Then he looked at Aspasia and flashed a smile of modest triumph.

"How can they accuse me of impiety, of not believing in the gods? She's a goddess, and I believe in her," he said as he bid us both goodbye.

Aspasia could not help but laugh. She sat across from me in the carriage, rolling her eyes in amazement.

"You know, none of this makes sense. I love Anaxagoras, that strange old man; but – do you see the irony? – We sit there talking about how 'reason came and introduced order' – Oh, yes, of course, by Zeus! I remember that passage, the key to everything he ever said or wrote – and at the very moment we're talking in such lofty tones about an intelligent order, we're about to be put to death by what seems to prove that there isn't any intelligence or reason in the world at all. It makes me angry, so angry I start to laugh – A world ruled by reason! There is nothing rational about it! And yet, in the middle of all this insanity, who would you rather be – Anaxagoras, with his supreme indifference to what the fates may have in store, or one of our fine citizens who believe that if you only ask in the right manner, the sun – or some other, lesser, god – will give you what you want and cheat death of its promised time? Anaxagoras or Cleon, the accused or the accuser; the one who will gladly take your life, the easy price of what he wants, or the one who, the moment they come to kill him, can look at them and laugh at their small, fly-bitten ambitions?"

The answer was obvious of course; easy, until it was a choice you yourself might actually have to make. Easy, in other words, for me, protected by my youth from the dismal possibility that death might come at any minute; but not easy at all for the grown woman

I was with, the wife of Pericles, about to go on trial for her life. What she was saying about Anaxagoras, the way he faced things, she was saying about herself; how she would like to feel, if only she could. And that was the point. She had, like Pericles, been a student of Anaxagoras; she had, like Pericles, a mind that allowed her – that forced her, really – to accept the rightness, the necessity, if you will, of rising superior to all the chance incidents of life; but she could not feel it, the way Anaxagoras could. She loved too much for that. Anaxagoras could live oblivious of all the dirt and flies, could look upward at the sheltered sky when asked where it was he lived; but Aspasia, wherever her mind might take her when she gave her mind to study, lived amidst all the splendor of the greatest city in the world. Beneath the easy laughter, the glowing pride at the way Anaxagoras had taken the news of his own impending trial and almost certain death, she was beset by a nervous agitation that led to long, brooding silences and frequent outbursts of sudden rage; but even then, because she remembered what she had learned and knew how she was supposed to act, never in terms of what might happen to her, but what it might mean for Pericles and Athens.

"If they ever succeed, if they ever drive Pericles from power, then – remember this; remember that I said it – there will be nothing but chaos. Everyone will be out for themselves and no one able to stop it. There won't be anyone who can convince them to put aside their private interests and sacrifice everything for the public good. No one will even ask what is good for the city; they'll just assume in their ignorance that the city will get on the way it always has, and that what happened here, the greatness we acquired, would have happened no matter who had been in charge. The only thing they will think about is how to show everyone else that they're the only one who can lead. They don't know how to stop themselves; they don't know the meaning, or the importance, of restraint. They'll kill us all and call it freedom while they fight among themselves to take our places."

Aspasia was not far wrong, if I were to judge from the frenzied faces I saw in the crowd the day that Anaxagoras was brought to trial. She had been right about a great many things. The indictment, the charge against Anaxagoras, was for impiety; the specific allegation that he had declared the sun to be a mass of red-hot metal. That proved impiety, because, as Cleon insisted with screeching insistence, everyone knew that the sun was "a living being, the greatest among the gods, the one who brings light and warmth to us, and will continue to do so, so long as we continue to offer Him sacrifice and prayers."

"We charge Anaxagoras," he announced with counterfeit outrage, "with impiety, because the law must be followed in all its forms. But Anaxagoras, and those who have been taught by him and have refused to renounce him," he added with an ominous glance toward that part of the amphitheater in which Pericles sat, patient and unmoved, "have done something worse than disbelief; they have by their nefarious teaching – telling everyone the sun is nothing but lifeless matter – insulted the god, and by so doing threatened his anger. Anaxagoras, by his words, has proven his impiety, his disbelief; Anaxagoras – as well as those who accept what he teaches – has proven that he cares nothing for the danger that his contempt for the gods has put our city. Anaxagoras is guilty, and the only fit punishment, the only way to appease the gods, to protect ourselves against their justice and their wrath, is to condemn him to the death he deserves!"

The crowd, including most of all the fifteen hundred chosen as jurors to hear the case, broke into wild applause. Shouts of anger, cries for vengeance, echoed from all directions. A hundred, a thousand, fists were pumped into the air; a hundred, a thousand faces were contorted into awful blue and purple shades of rage. Down at the bottom, on the front of the stage where the accused was forced to sit, Anaxagoras, bent with age, and weakened now with illness, held himself as straight as he could. I wondered what was passing through his mind, whether he was there in body only, his thought flying free through the outer world he loved; or whether, as a reminder of what, if death came, he would be leaving behind, he found another reason to talk indifference to his life.

The sun, that god-like mass of molten red metal, beat down on the proceedings, wringing perspiration from everyone; or nearly everyone, because, as I observed, Pericles, listening to Cleon's manic hate-filled words, had become as hard and cold as marble, proof, if proof were needed, how much above the others he really was. Cleon saw it, too: that nothing he said had had any effect; that not even the crowd's reaction, that roaring torrent of abuse, had made the slightest change in the look of noble reserve by which Pericles maintained his distance from the insanity raging all around him. It drove Cleon crazy. His voice began to break; his face, turned red by the burning sun, turned redder still with fury. He beat his arms in the air like someone trying to ward off an attack, repeating the same demand, death for Anaxagoras "and anyone else who neglects religion or teaches new doctrines about the things above!"

They would have given him what he wanted, the vast majority of those ill-chosen jurors with their wonder-struck eyes, mesmerized by Cleon's mindless demagoguery; not just found Anaxagoras guilty but had him executed on the spot, if anyone had tried to stop them. Pericles did nothing; he did not move; he did not change expression. He sat there, as still as any statue Phidias ever made; sat there, immobile and unyielding; sat there until, worn down by their own demented shouting, everyone, and especially the jurors, began to notice, and noticing, to pay attention. It was a tribute to the power he had, to the hold he had on their better instincts, their sense that however wild they were for something, however eager they were to do what someone else, someone like Cleon, told them would give them what they really wanted and what they deserved to have, that his presence alone was enough to hold them back; to pause, and if not to change their mind, at least listen to what he had to say.

Slowly, looking straight in front of him, Pericles rose from his seat and made his way unhurried down the aisle to the stage below where he put his hand on the frail shoulder of Anaxagoras and for a long moment studied the now puzzled faces of the crowd. The background noise, the talk that had gone on while he had come forward, had dissipated and finally disappeared. His own face, burnished bronze in the slanted light of the late afternoon, wore a solemn aspect, conveying a sense of both responsibility and deep regret.

"I have only one question." He stopped and waited while those few simple words, words which seemed to carry a warning that what they were about to decide was more important, had more significance, than they knew, echoed through the open theater. "Do you have any fault to find in my own public career, any fault with what I have tried to do to serve the city?"

Cleon and his friends, sitting together on the benches high up on the left, might think what they wanted; they knew better than to challenge Pericles directly. The same voices that had just minutes earlier formed the willing chorus to Cleon's demands for death to anyone thought guilty of impiety, now acknowledged their common debt to what Pericles had done. The difference was in the form it took. All the outrage, all the shouting, was gone, and in its place a long, sustained, and, as it seemed to me, thoughtful applause.

"Then, remember this: I am a pupil of Anaxagoras. He taught me much of what I know, all of which I have put at your disposal. Do not, if you value what I have done, let yourselves be carried away by these base slanders and put to death an honorable and decent man. Let me instead prevail upon you to release him."

I shot a glance at Cleon. Gnashing his teeth in frustration, he dug his nails so hard into the heel of his hand that he drew blood. I took more pleasure in that than perhaps I should have done. With a man like him, defeat taught nothing, except the need to do something worse. Pericles had saved Anaxagoras, the philosopher; it might not be quite so easy to save Aspasia, the woman he loved, the woman called behind her back the whore he had married.

CHAPTER EIGHT

I woke up to what I thought must be the sounds of an invasion, shouted voices everywhere and the clattered, harsh groaning noise of large moving ships. Jumping out of bed, I ran to the window. The harbor was full of warships, each with their three banks of oars. Armored men with shiny silver swords and bright sharpened spears were marching five abreast along the quay: soldiers, hoplites, from the city on their way to some invasion of their own. My eye was drawn to Alcibiades, looking straight ahead but smiling all the time; and next to him, a member of the same battalion, Socrates with a look just the opposite of the vast amusement with which Alcibiades seemed to view the future.

I dressed as quickly as I could, threw a cloak around my shoulder, and hurried outside. Half of Athens must have been there, women come to say goodbye to their sons and husbands; girls come to wave at the young men who, dressed as soldiers, were suddenly much more interesting. Laughing at how something like that same feeling had come over me, I caught up with Alcibiades. Dressed in the shining armor of an officer of rank, he looked like a god come down to earth. He turned his head when he heard my voice.

"You came to see me off, to wish me well, to tell me – " he started in that way he had that at the same time it bragged his advantages told you that it was all a game, a game he wanted you to enjoy. I ignored him and went straight to Socrates.

"You must be the best soldier Athens has, asked to meet the enemy in battle while watching out for someone so inexperienced," I said, nodding toward Alcibiades who, far from abashed, laughed even harder. "The enemy in front of you, while pulling this one after you so he won't turn and run away – You'll have to be a juggler to carry both your sword and shield in the same hand!"

"Why don't you come with us?" shouted Alcibiades over his shoulder. "The enemy won't have a chance – so long as they only fight with words!"

I would have gone with them, if there had been any way of doing it. I even asked Aspasia if I could.

"They were there this morning – Socrates, Alcibiades; I don't know how many others – getting ready to sail away. They're going to Potidaea, aren't they? I'm going there, too."

Aspasia had only just opened the door. She looked pale and drawn, but in my excitement I assumed it was because she had probably just gotten up.

"I'm serious," I insisted after we had settled into a couple of chairs on the veranda in back. "I need to go; I was going anyway, I was ... "

"You were going anyway? Where? Not to Potidaea; there is a war going on, whatever anyone wants to call it."

But I was too caught up in my own plans to pay attention. If she was talking about something else, it must be because she had forgotten what we had talked about before, when she told me that she had discovered the answer to the question I had asked weeks earlier.

"Democritus – remember? You told me, that day we went to see Anaxagoras, that you had found him, found out where he was; that he had left and gone back to Abdera. That is where I am going, where I was supposed to be going tomorrow in the morning."

This seemed only to deepen her confusion. She shook her head, trying, as it seemed, to clear her mind, frowned, and then blinked her eyes.

"Abdera? But you said you were going there anyway – Do you mean Potidaea, where there has been a revolt?"

"Yes," I said brightly. "I was going there anyway – to Abdera, which is not far from where the fleet is sailing. Why shouldn't I go? Wouldn't it be interesting to see what is going to happen; see with my own eyes, instead of waiting to hear what someone else – some man – reports?"

She made a listless gesture with her hand, and it was then that I realized how tired she was. It was not because she had just gotten up when I arrived, all eager and impatient, that she looked so dull and distracted; she had not slept, or, if she had, only the kind of fitful, abbreviated sleep that is worse than no sleep at all.

"The trial, the planning for the expedition – what you saw at dawn – all the other things that are going on; it's been hard to keep track of everything." She spoke slowly, staring into the middle distance, trying to collect her thoughts. "You can't go to Potidaea," she said suddenly. "That's quite impossible."

I could tell she meant it, that whatever she might think privately she would not offer any help. I understood that, but I still had to ask.

"You would go, though – wouldn't you – if you could? See what happens in a battle, instead of staying at home, as if what happens is too violent, too disturbing, for our eyes, the eyes of women?"

She did not answer, but there were traces of a smile that told me I was right, that given half a chance she would follow wherever the army went, no matter what the danger, and watch as they marched to victory or went down to defeat.

"I'm going!" I insisted.

"To Abdera, to find Democritus? You might still be able to do that. But Potidaea – that is out of the question. You can't go by land – there are too many hostile nations on the way. And you can't go by sea because of the blockade. Come with me. Let me show you something."

We went inside and on a map in the study Aspasia showed me why what had so much appealed to my imagination – to witness first-hand the sounds and sights of war, to learn what it was like to watch those you cared about and maybe even loved go in harm's way, face death and even die – had become all but impossible.

"There," she said, tracing with her finger a jagged line from Athens north along the coast then east to an isthmus of a small peninsula, the westernmost of three prongs of a much larger one. "It is called Pallene," she explained; "a third part of the greater Thracian peninsula called Chalkidike, between the Thermaic and the Strymonic Gulfs. The Thracians – if you don't already know this – are an evil, warlike race which, like their neighbors, the Macedonians, is always at each other's throats. The only thing you can ever know with certainty about them is that, no matter what they say, you can never trust them." She jabbed her finger at a point at the end of Pallene, the smallest of the three peninsulas. "The Dorian town of Potidaea – right there – is a tributary ally, one of the cities that pays for our protection and support. It was originally a colony of Corinth, and Corinth still sends magistrates each year, but despite that, Potidaea owes Athens its allegiance."

Aspasia looked at me to make sure I understood the significance of this, and then, moving her finger in an arc that took in nearly all of the Aegean, both the coastline and the islands, observed with clear-eyed realism, "This is what Athens has acquired: the empire that Athens now has to protect. You see how everything is dependent on control of the sea; but inland – places where our ships cannot reach – that is where the problem starts. Here," she said, pointing again at

Potidaea. "The other side, the inland territory, is ruled by Perdiccas, once a friend and ally, but now, because of a dispute with some other Macedonians who are themselves friends and allies of Athens, an active enemy. It is what I meant when I said you can never trust these people. His word means nothing. He wants to cause trouble, to start a war. All he is interested in is getting the advantage against his neighbors, getting a little more territory for himself. He sends envoys to Corinth to organize a revolt in Potidaea because he knows that will intensify the conflict Corinth has with Athens. But that was only half of what he did. He arranged an alliance with Sparta: a secret treaty – though Sparta had for fourteen years a treaty guaranteeing peace with Athens – in which Sparta promises to declare war, to invade Attica, if Athens attacks Potidaea.

"Perdiccas! Oh, well," she sighed, "if it hadn't been him, it would have been someone else. This war has been coming for a long time. That is why Pericles worries so much about what Cleon and the others like him are trying to do, these endless prosecutions, charges brought in an attempt to weaken his power, when if war comes Pericles is the only one with the strength of will to save us."

I wondered why, if war were that imminent, the Athenians would trigger it with an attack on Potidaea, why they did not pull back from the brink of all-out war and let Potidaea, an unimportant place, resume its independence. Why send an army to put down a revolt in a place that far away at the price of an invasion, an attack on everything that was close to home.

"Because we are now at the point where every sign of weakness becomes an invitation to another trial of strength," said another, different voice.

Startled, I turned to find Pericles standing just behind me. He had entered so quietly that I had not heard him. I began to apologize, to say that he had other, more important things to do, and that I had better go.

"No, please stay," he said, smiling past me at Aspasia who, suddenly, in his unexpected presence, lost the pallid, careworn look and became again the woman, eager and alive, he so obviously needed to see. "What you were saying," he said, looking now at me, "the question you were asking, goes to the very heart of our dilemma. If it were only Potidaea, a small city on the coast of the Aegean, if there were not dozens, hundreds, of other cities that pay us tribute and owe us their allegiance, if we did not have an empire to protect, we would have much more room to maneuver. But we are the prisoners of what we own. We have an empire and we are forced to rule it, not the way we rule ourselves, everyone equal and able to debate, but like a tyrant, insisting on what we are owed, money and supplies, to keep our navy as strong as it has to be. No one likes it, no one likes to be ruled like this; and so, in the same degree, and for the same reason, that we are respected, they hate us, these allies of ours, for the fear we inspire. You ask why Potidaea – because it is the weak link in the chain. Let it go – let any of them go – and all the others will follow. We are locked in a struggle that we cannot avoid; the only question is the timing: where and under what conditions war will start. That is the real reason why we are responding with as much force as we are: to forestall the Spartans, to get control of the situation in Potidaea before they have time to do anything about it. They always move with slow deliberation; and my hope is that this time at least the speed with which we have decided, the speed with which we act, will make them think better of their faithless promise of invasion."

"That is why I want to go, to see for myself what – "

"Want to go?" he asked, staring at me with a look of amused astonishment. "Where? – To Potidaea?"

"Yes. I was going to Abdera anyway," I began to explain. "And I ... " But before I could say another word, Pericles stopped me and looked at Aspasia.

"And why shouldn't she? – Go, I mean; to Potidaea, watch what happens, see things with her own eyes. That's what she wants, isn't it? That's what she came to see you about: to ask if you would help arrange it." He gave me a quick, sidelong glance that let me know that what I had done was more than all right, it had his approval. He liked the fact that I seemed to have courage. "But you told her it was out of the question, that a woman – especially a young woman – would never be allowed that close to a battle; told her it was dangerous, that she might get hurt. And the whole time you were telling her this – which was of course the proper, the expected, thing to do – you were secretly smiling to yourself, remembering how when I first met you, it was precisely the kind of thing you would have done; more than that, remembering how nothing would have stopped you, that you would have figured out a way to do it!"

He came up to where she was standing, next to the table on which the map she had been showing me lay open for inspection, and gently touched her cheek.

"I just saw off the fleet, forty triremes carrying two thousand hoplites, under Callias, his first command. Much as I would have missed you, I wanted to go, to be back on the field of battle, leading all those men. You should have seen Callias, how proud he looked. He is a young man of rare intelligence. Did you know that he once paid Zeno of Elea a great deal of money – a hundred minae, I was told – for instruction in rhetoric and philosophy?"

There was an irony in this, but was I the only one to see it? – Callias, who paid for lessons, in command; and Socrates, from whom he could have learned far more for nothing, marching under his orders. And what about Alcibiades, who paid more than that for the wine he drank; Alcibiades who had for the sheer fun of it given lessons to Pericles on the meaning of the law; Alcibiades who marched next in line to Socrates, his body, if not his mind, willing to be disciplined? The thought flew by me, left unexpressed except for a smile that barely flickered and then, the moment Pericles looked at me, vanished quickly from my mouth.

"If you want to go, I think you should."

"But Pericles, she can't! It's too dangerous, it's too ... "

The eyes of Pericles drew inward and his gaze became quite stern, not with anger or displeasure but with sympathy for what had happened.

"You came here from Agrigento, where you lived and studied with Empedocles; but you came to him from Syracuse, where your father was the tyrant, Hiero, who murdered your mother and might, from what I have been told, have one day murdered you."

"How long have you known?" I asked, not so much surprised that he knew as interested in how he had learned.

His response was vague, a slight movement of his head and a gesture with his hand, the suggestion that it did not matter, that my secret was safe with him, that the only people who would ever know the true story of my past were those I chose to tell myself. I wondered why I had not thought of it before; why I had not known that with all the sources of information he must have, sources from everywhere in which Athens had an interest, he would have made a point of finding out everything he could about a young woman who had become a friend of Aspasia and a frequent guest in his home. He could have kept it to himself, what he had learned, but he wanted to show that there was a reason why he had confidence that I could do what I said I wanted to do and do it without great risk of danger.

"She survived a tyrant's court; why should we assume she can't survive a battle, one which she will only witness from a distance?" His gaze became penetrating and shrewd. "We wouldn't hesitate to send a young man of her age to be our eyes and ears, to observe what happens and then report back to us. Do we deny her wish only because of her sex? And besides," he added as his eyes danced with a new amusement, "think how much harder everyone – especially my nephew, the ardent Alcibiades – will fight knowing they are under the careful watch of the beautiful young Helen!"

"She wants to go to Abdera," Aspasia reminded him. "She wants to see a philosopher, Democritus, who, like our late friend and teacher Anaxagoras, knows something about the nature of things; different, from what I have heard, than what others teach."

"Philosophy and war: a different trip than what most other men, or women, would want to take; but, then, when you think about it, the two things may not be that far apart. Isn't the nature of things, the forces that put all the things into motion, the same thing that drives us as well? What is the difference between the human beings and all the other beings if it isn't that we alone can understand, or try to understand, the world?"

Their son, the child they had together, the last of the three sons he had, the only one to carry his own name, came running, summoned, as it were, by the sound of his father's voice. In a single swift motion, Pericles swept him up in his arms, beaming with unfeigned pleasure at the young boy's eager, laughing face. In that same instant, I saw in Aspasia's large, dark eyes a burst of happiness and pride that I knew with all the certainty of intuition was a feeling that nothing else could rival. And I knew as well that I was an outsider and that it was time to leave.

"No," said Pericles, setting down the child and with a pat on his bottom sending him off to see his mother. "Not before we finish the business we have. If you are going to be my eyes and ears, you'll need some papers, signed by me, that will give your travels an official sanction; and, more important, not just to Aspasia, but to me as well, as much protection as the army can provide. And you'll need a ship."

"I have one," I said quickly, afraid that I had already become a burden. "One of the ships that bring corn from Abdera goes back tomorrow, and I have reserved a place."

Raising an eyebrow, Pericles stifled a laugh. He looked at me with the same cool kindness with which he listened to the half-demented reasoning of both friend and enemy alike, impenetrable and magnificent, the rare self-confidence of someone who has learned that the only real victory lies in mastering oneself.

"Which do you think the more ludicrous: that a woman with a face like yours should sail unescorted in an empty cargo ship that still smells of stale grain; or that an official envoy of Athens, carrying papers signed by Pericles, should proceed to her destination in the heaving hollow of some worm-holed vessel certain to sink the next time Neptune blows too hard upon the sea?"

"My God!" laughed Aspasia, holding young Pericles in her arms, "the effect you have on men! In your presence, even wise old Pericles becomes poetic – 'the heaving hollow of some worm-holed vessel!' – What next? Another Euripides; or another comic poet, the next Aristophanes, so you can ridicule in public the ones you now only ridicule in private, have the world as your audience instead of just your obedient, devoted wife?"

Pericles caught her mood and turned it to his advantage.

"Not another one of anyone – a new phenomenon!" he bragged to his own immense enjoyment. "I'll write a play – a drama – about this second Helen who, instead of war and heartbreak, brought the Greeks the triumph of seeing something that, more than anything we have built, more than anything anyone – even Phidias – can make out of marble, is closer to what is perfect than anything we have known. And I do not mean just how beautiful you are," he added as Aspasia came up and took him by the hand, "but that mind you have, that intelligence that made even Anaxagoras marvel at what he saw that day you met him. He told me all about it, that he thought you had more promise than anyone he had met; and believe me when I tell you that Anaxagoras was not just the wisest man I ever knew, but the only man who never lied."

He paused, and in the silence seemed to be remembering something, a warning or a prophecy of doom, because now when he looked at me his eyes were dark with danger. He grabbed me hard about the wrist.

"Be careful; the world turns on those who have too many of the things it prizes. They say that the gods curse those born with too many gifts. You're still young, and the young are forgiven many things; but when you're older – be careful not to let too many see how much you know." His eyes brightened, and he let go my wrist. "But go now, go to Abdera, learn what you can from this philosopher; and then – there will be time – join our forces at Potidaea. Come back safely and tell me everything – not the kind of report the generals make: what the troops did and the numbers engaged – but your impressions, why some did better than others, what makes an army fight instead of run; whatever you think important, whatever seems important to your mind."

I started to leave, but again he called me back.

"The ship, the one to take you there; it will be at the harbor, waiting in the morning. It is the fastest ship we have. Spend several days in Abdera if you need to; you'll be in Potidaea with time enough to spare."

There was thunder in the skies when I left the house of Pericles and it was raining, raining hard, when I got back to my house in the Piraeus, a rain as hard as any that had fallen since I first came to live here. It rained all night, but the next morning, when I woke up, the rain had gone and the wet streets were slick with sunshine as I made my way to the quay and the ship that Pericles had promised, the ship that would take me north to an adventure greater than any I had imagined.

At first I thought there must be some mistake. I stood at the dock, a blank expression on my face, wondering what I should do next, ask someone where the ship might be or wait until someone came to find me.

"If you're the one we're taking to Abdera," called a cheerful voice from the deck of the ship docked next to where I stood, "better come on board so we can get underway."

It was impossible, but true. When Pericles said he would provide a ship, that he would send me where I wanted to go, that I would be his envoy, his eyes and ears, I had not understood the way I should have precisely what he meant; I had not grasped the fact that when it came to his official duties there were no half-measures. He had not just sent a ship, some swift-sailing vessel; he had ordered the state ship, the Salaminia, the fastest ship in the fleet, the fastest ship afloat, to take me first to Abdera, then to Potidaea. The crew, all two hundred of them, stood waiting as I came aboard. The oarsmen, who sat three abreast on benches that slanted forward, allowing them to row together from three different heights above the water, held their long wooden oars like long-speared soldiers on parade. They were the pick of the navy, strong and lean and well-muscled, with the clear-eyed look of men who laughed at danger. The ship itself, unlike the bulky cargo vessels, was made for speed, a hundred twenty feet in length and barely twenty feet wide, with a shiny black hull and a prow that rose dramatically into a long hooked prow-post with a ram of solid wood and bronze fastened forward to sink any craft with which it came into collision. Two garish eyes, purple, red and green, were painted on the sides, to ward off bad luck or evil and protect it from all the misfortunes of the sea. A single mast with a large, square sail added the breath of wind to the power of the rowers' arms. The Salaminia, the pride of Athens and the fleet, seemed not so much to sail as to fly across the water.

We arrived in Abdera almost before we started; the voyage so quick the days seemed more like hours and the first sight of Abdera, seen from the sea, more like a reflection in the water of the Athens we had left. Distance did not matter, the time it took to go somewhere by land unimportant; the only question, and that one all decisive, who controlled the sea, because out here the world was smaller and there was nowhere you could hide. I began to grasp the reason why Themistocles was held in such high regard, the genius of the statesman who could see that the best, the only way to save the city was to abandon it to the enemy, leave Athens to the Persians and wage war upon the ocean. And I began to understand why Pericles was so insistent that Athens keep its allies, and with them the money tribute that made it possible to keep a fleet of three hundred ships in a constant state of readiness, prepared each day to do what was necessary to protect Athens and its power.

We had arrived late in the morning, three days after we left Athens; early that afternoon I stood at the door of the house where I had been told I could find Democritus, the man I had spent so much time trying to find in Athens. The house was not far from the harbor, less than half a mile, in a neighborhood that was anything but poor. A servant answered the door and when I told her that I was there to see Democritus and that I had come all the way from Athens, she asked with insolent indifference whether I was expected. I repeated what I had just told her: that I had come from Athens – I even pointed to the harbor and the black-hulled ship, thinking that might suggest a visit of more than ordinary importance – but she was obstinate in her insistence that Democritus did not see anyone he had not invited. I started to argue, to tell her that she could see for herself that I was no ordinary visitor, that I had come from Athens on the state owned vessel, that I had papers signed by Pericles himself; but it was no use, the more I said the more adamant she became. I could leave my name, and I would be sent for if her master wanted to see me. Leave my name! Sent for! This was outrageous. I began to protest, to repeat again, but in a far more angry tone, what I had said before, when a voice from somewhere inside told the servant that it was all right, that she could let me come in.

The room was dark, the windows all closed. I could barely make out the shape of a man sitting alone in one of four chairs that were arranged with what appeared geometrical precision at the four corners of a long, rectangular rug. He had his back to me and did not bother to turn around, much less get to his feet, when I entered, and when I took the chair to which he directed me by a careless wave of his hand, he did not say anything, not a word. He just sat there, tapping his fingers on his knee like someone forced to wait for an appointment he wished he had not made.

"I've come a long way to see you – "

"From Athens; I heard," he said abruptly, doing nothing to disguise his irritation. That was all, nothing else. He kept tapping his fingers in a slow, even rhythm, over and over again, making a sound that at any other time and place would have been inaudible, but now, in this oppressive silence, seemed almost unendurable. Finally, mercifully, he stopped. I thought he was going to say something, begin a conversation, ask me why I had come, ask me how he could help me; but instead he suddenly jumped to his feet and marched past me as if I were just a picture painted on the wall. He was at the door when he stopped, but only for a moment.

"You wanted to see me," he said without looking back. His voice was clear, crisp and to my astonishment not entirely free of annoyance. "Better come along if there is something you want to ask me."

I do not know why I followed him out into the street; why I did not stay where I was, treated with the contempt it deserved his impertinence, his rude self-importance. Part of it, of course, was that I had come too far to find him to turn away now; but part of it was an instinct, a belief, strange and uncanny, that what he had done, how he had behaved, the indifference he had shown, made him that much more mysterious, and that much more interesting.

I had not been able to see him clearly in the darkness, and when he marched out he had not once turned to look at me, with the consequence that I had not gotten a very good look at him. I could tell that he was of moderate height and rather thin, with a prominent forehead and short cropped hair. I guessed he was in his early forties, but he might have been even younger than that. His hands, smooth as marble and apparently well-cared for, were in constant motion, drumming his fingers on his knee when he sat in the chair in his living room, or, as he was doing now, opening and closing them as he walked along like someone clutching at an unseen fear; unseen, because on the surface at least he was boldly, even brazenly self-confident and assured. What struck me most about him, however, was his voice, the way it put a sharp edge on each word, creating an impression of almost stringent clarity. It was not a voice of command, the kind you hear in the law courts or the assembly – it was not loud enough for that – but the kind you sometimes hear in private conversation, the voice of someone who knows what he is talking about and never wastes a word. It was a voice in which things were measured exactly, the voice of someone who, whatever else he might dislike, hated imprecision.

"I lived in Athens for a while. I went there because it is the place to go if you want to meet other people who have serious interests like your own, but no one wanted to know me, so I left and came home, here, to Abdera. But you've come to see me. Why?"

The street was already crowded, people jostling against one another, everyone in a hurry to get where they were going. Someone stepped in front of me and I almost tripped, but Democritus did not stop or even seem to notice.

"Where are you going?" I fairly shouted.

He motioned with his hand for me to keep following, but I had had enough of his demanding bad manners. When he finally realized I was not coming, he slowed down and with a trailing hand beckoned for me to follow, a gesture that this time seemed more a plea than a command. Dodging my way through the surging crowd I caught up with him at the end of the block. We crossed the dirty, littered street and headed toward the long quay where the wide-beamed merchant ships waited their turn to be unloaded.

"I'm Democritus. You've been looking for me. Why?"

I began to laugh at how incongruous it all was, following him into the streets as if I were chasing after a thief. My laughter seemed to annoy him. He began to walk even faster.

"You come to my house unannounced and uninvited, tell my

servant that you ... Why are you here?"

He stopped abruptly and did something very curious. With his eyes on the ground, he changed position so that I was standing between him and the sea. The rising sun, red as molten metal, was now directly behind me. Slowly and of set purpose, he raised his eyes and looked straight at me, studying me with more detachment than I had ever been looked at before. The harsh, glaring light finally forced him to look away.

"It hurts even more than I thought it would."

"You did not think it would hurt to look straight into the sun!"

There was a flash of disapproval in his eyes, quick contempt for what he thought a deliberate falsification and, worse than that, an obvious, a too obvious attempt to elicit praise.

"I must have been wrong," he remarked with a quick, withering, glance. "I assumed that if you took the trouble to see me – if you knew who I was – you had to be intelligent."

I was quick, too quick, to take offense.

"Do you think I'm such a fool, that I know so little about myself, that I'm not aware of how I look and the effect it has on other people? Do you think that I don't notice what happens when I walk into a room; that I don't notice what happens – what happened just now – all those staring, gawking eyes, when I try to walk unmolested in the street?"

"No, I didn't mean to suggest that – "

"But you, Democritus, the man, the philosopher, I hoped could teach me something; all you can teach me is what I already know?"

"That's why you were looking for me – because you thought that I – ?"

"I was looking for you in Athens, where I had been told you were living. I knew that you came from Abdera, that you were taught by Leucippus, that you have a different theory of the elements, what the world is made of, than the others: Thales, or Heraclitus, or Pythagoras, or Empedocles, under whom I studied and whom I loved. So, yes, I thought – I hoped – I could learn from you things I did not already know, but I see I was wrong." I spun on my heel and started to walk away.

"Don't go," he cried in a voice turned soft and compelling. "I'll be glad to help you in any way I can."

CHAPTER NINE

Democritus wanted to know why Pericles had sent me, why I had come on the Salaminia.

"You're not here on an official mission to see me; there is something else going on."

I told him what had happened, the revolt in Potidaea and how I was going to observe the battle that would soon be fought there. He had heard about the revolt – Potidaea was not that far away – and he knew enough about the hatred felt toward Athens by the other Greeks to know that there must eventually be war, but he was far more interested in what I told him about what had been happening in Athens, especially what had happened in the trial of Anaxagoras.

"The verdict was right; he should have been convicted."

"You think that Anaxagoras got what he deserved?" I asked sharply, stunned that he – that anyone – could think that.

"I didn't say that he got what he deserved; I said that he should have been convicted. There is a difference."

"Should have been convicted – sentenced to death? One of the wisest – "

"Not wise; not in any sense," said Democritus. "That makes you angry? Then don't say you want to learn, if you only want to hear what pleases you. I don't say Anaxagoras deserved to be convicted for what he thinks – that the sun is a ball of burning metal, that it is as large, or larger, than the Peloponnesus; he deserved to be convicted because he was not smart enough to conceal what he thought from people who haven't the capacity to think for themselves, which means, if I have to spell it out for you, almost everyone! He wrote a book, told the world in plain language – plain language! – what he thought. Did he think that only people with minds of their own could read? Wrote a book and did not fill it with words with more than one meaning ... and you call him wise?"

On its own terms, without regard to the indignity, the ordeal, Anaxagoras, that wonderful old man, had been made to suffer, the argument was unassailable, but that only intensified my growing dislike for the man who had made it. "You would have him convicted for bravery, for saying, for writing, what he believed?"

And now Democritus did something for which I could easily have hated him. He stepped back, laughed with disdain, and, in a satire of decent behavior, slowly applauded.

"Oh, well done; well done, indeed! Called stupidity courage and made yourself feel better because of it!"

"Better, I think, than to call cowardice prudence and think yourself wiser for it!" I shot back with anger.

He did not seem to mind that; taking it, as far as I could see, as the beginning, instead of the end, of a quick-witted debate. But he also saw the need to adopt a more civil tone.

"I never met him, but I'm sure you're right when you say he was a decent and serious man. They all were, the ones you mentioned – Thales, Heraclitus, and all the others – It's just that none of them were right."

"And you are?"

A smile flashed first in his eyes, then on his mouth, as the thought he was now so eager to express flashed through his mind.

"Yes, of course; if I thought I was wrong, I would change, and then I would not be wrong any longer, but right once again. But, you're going to tell me, I could be wrong about being right, that thinking I'm right doesn't mean I'm not wrong."

That was exactly what I was going to tell him, and knowing that he knew that, I burst out laughing. The smile on his straight but querulous mouth became modest and withdrawn and the last trace of hostility and defiance disappeared. We began to walk, but at a normal, leisurely pace, along the quay. Fat white seagulls squawked among themselves, stabbing at the gutted remains of some fish left lying on the ground. A gigantic stevedore with glistening bronze skin and dazzling white teeth, a perfect figure of a man except for an arm that had been cut off just above the elbow, passed by us, carrying on his other, better shoulder an enormous bale of cotton, brought no doubt from somewhere far away in Egypt. A dwarf in a bright blue tunic walked next to him, carrying in his two pudgy arms a wicker basket filled with bread. Democritus lifted an eyebrow.

"Anaxagoras insists that the world is ordered by 'mind,' or 'intelligence'; but what kind of order is this? Where is the reason, the rationality, in what you just saw? A perfect example of the world's disorder: a man not a man at all, and a man permanently disfigured and partially disabled by – choose whatever motive or cause you wish: ambition, desire to dominate; whatever form insanity happens to take. Anaxagoras says that the elements – whichever of them you think are primary – need something else to provide the order in which they combine or dissolve. The problem is that he cannot account for the unreasonable, the irrational; which means, if you consider it carefully, he cannot account for anything."

I understood, or thought I understood, what Democritus was saying. Empedocles had taught me what the Pythagoreans had taught him about numbers, but I had not been able to grasp what it meant to say that numbers had their own existence. And if I could not see how numbers could exist apart from the things that they counted, how could I see that mind or intelligence could exist, much less be the cause of things that were not rational? Still, there seemed to be a problem.

"But there is an order in the world: the regular motion of the heavens, the repeating sequence of the seasons, the generation of beings – human beings, among others – in their endless cycle. And if what you say about Anaxagoras is true, even if 'mind' or 'intelligence' is not the cause that brought order, Empedocles agreed with him that there has to be something else that makes the elements combine into the things, the beings, that we know. Love and strife, a desire to combine and a need to separate, those for him were the twin principles that explained both the world and our own existence."

We had reached the end of the quay and sat on a wooden bench. The sounds of the harbor, the cries of men giving orders as the ships were unloaded, the shouted obscenities as someone struggled with a cargo net, all the eager, hard exuberance of strong men using their strength faded into the background the way each hour fades into the past. The soft breeze from the sea, falling cool and fresh against my skin, brought what seemed a new clarity to my mind.

"Love and strife," repeated Democritus in a tone close to derision. I say close, because it was not quite that. It would have been, I think, had he been talking to anyone else. We had reached the point where he showed me at least that much consideration. "Intelligence or mind," he went on, shaking his head in the manner of a school teacher forced to deal with truant children. "They're all like that, these so-called philosophers, these lovers of wisdom, of ours, each claiming to discover the secret of existence, the nature of the world. Everything is water, or everything is air, or everything is some unspecified changing combination of water and air, of earth and fire, and who knows what else. All their theories, just empty words that make people feel they know something when they don't know anything at all! Give them credit, Empedocles and Anaxagoras both understood this: that it isn't enough to say what things are made of, you have to explain how and why they were made. But to say that 'mind' or 'intelligence' ordered the world, or that 'love' and 'strife' explain the movement from order to disorder and back again ...! They all miss something basic: How does anything happen, how account for the fact that things exist? None of them have an answer for this; none of them seems to know there is even a question. You have to start from the beginning. Ask yourself this question: How is it possible for one thing to change into another; for water, for example, to change into steam when it is heated by fire? Because 'mind' or 'intelligence' has ordered it so; because 'love' or 'strife' or both of them together have through their conflict produced this result?"

Hunched over his knees, Democritus stared at the ground as he considered how best to turn his thought into words. His mind worked with rare precision, and his speech followed a strict logical order, but then, suddenly, some fugitive thought would break through and his eyes would flash with the recognition of a new idea.

"Take Anaxagoras, what happened to him: tried for impiety, put on trial for his life! Where was 'mind,' 'intelligence,' in that? 'Mind' orders everything? What mind, whose intelligence? – Some god? What is he talking about? He sees an order, what he thinks is an order, and then he looks for a cause. But what if there is no cause, what if everything happens by chance; what if in the infinity of time this world of ours just happened to come into existence because the parts, the atoms, just happened to take that form? Or Empedocles: He throws himself into a volcano to prove he is a god, or that he belongs among the gods? But then, if he believes in the gods, where does 'love' and 'strife' come in; what do they really explain?"

Despite my pledge of secrecy, despite what I had promised Empedocles, I had to say something that might give Democritus pause.

"Are you sure he threw himself into Etna; are you sure that isn't just legend? Are you sure," I went on, as I rose from the bench and walked to the railing at the edge of the quay, "that he did not leave a bronze slipper behind so the ignorant would have something to believe, someone whose life could serve as an example for how in their own way they might try to live?"

But Democritus was not listening. He was too caught up in his own thought, the distinction, the astonishing difference, between what he had discovered and what all the earlier thinkers had seemed to believe. His smile might be all sweetness and light, but something sinister had entered his eyes, the conviction, the utter certainty, that he alone knew the truth and that everyone else lived in error. The world was composed of atoms, a theory that seemed to turn the world into dust and not even dust you could see, and anyone who did not understand that was a fool. He spoke with perfect assurance, convinced, as it seemed, that only someone who did not listen could refuse to agree.

"There is nothing; nothing exists, except atoms and space. Everything else is an illusion, what we only think we can see and touch. The atoms are impassive and unalterable, unlimited in both size and number. They generate all the composite things – fire, water, air, earth – everything! The sun, the moon, all the things that are: nothing but masses of smooth and spherical atoms. There is nothing that is not, there is no nothing; because nothing can come into being from that which is not, nor pass away into that which is not."

"Do you see that building over there?" I asked, pointing to a warehouse under construction. "If I asked you what it was going to be, would you tell me it was a warehouse or a pile of bricks? These atoms that 'generate all the composite things' – you haven't told me how or why they do this. Why do those things, unlimited as they are in 'size' and 'number,' form themselves into one thing rather than another; why into that building over there, that pile of bricks, and not into a man or a woman; why into any building at all and not into a chicken or a horse? And if there is no nothing, if everything that exists is made out of these atoms of yours, how does space exist? And if space does not exist, there would be atoms everywhere and no room to move. Not only would 'nothing come into being from that which is not,' nothing would come into being from that which is."

I was rather pleased with myself, listening to what I was saying; pleased, not just that I could hold my own in the discussion, but that what I was saying seemed to make sense. Unlike Democritus, I had no theories of my own; but I at least knew some of the questions that had to be asked. How much time had I spent thinking about what I had learned, and, more importantly, all the things I still did not know? It was that, the effort itself, the attempt to understand, that somehow had begun to have an effect; enough, at least, to teach me the difference between ignorance and error, between knowing that I did not know and pretending that I did. Democritus cared nothing about that. He was too angry.

"No, no – you don't understand!" he sputtered, his face growing red not just with anger but with embarrassment, which seemed to make him angrier still. "Space is empty; it is a void in which the atoms move freely. There is no 'not-being;' everything is in process of becoming. Everything is composed of atoms which are mobile and invisible, whirling in the void."

"Then the void is a place within which this takes place, where all these invisible atoms are in – what did you say? – constant motion."

"Yes, precisely," he replied, relieved to discover that I was not quite the dunce he had begun to fear I was. "The atoms move inside space, inside the void, creating through their combination everything that is."

"Space, or void, then is not made up of atoms?"

"No, because then there would be no place for them to move, as you yourself just pointed out."

"I'm still not quite sure what you mean. Everything is in process of becoming – doesn't that mean that nothing is, that there is no being?"

"No, because everything is always changing; everything that comes into being passes away."

"But how can anything 'come into being,' if 'being' does not exist?"

"We define things, put them in categories, but nothing is exactly what the definition says it is."

I had the sense of sinking into sand, of drowning at sea; the more I struggled to grasp his meaning, the less I seemed to understand. There was no 'not-being' but it did not appear that there was any 'being' either. Still, the underlying thought, that something too small for the eye to see was the basic building block out of which everything was made, seemed to explain how one thing, even one of the elements, could change into another. But for all that, it did not answer the question both Empedocles and Anaxagoras had thought so important.

"These atoms, whirling inside the void – a place that somehow exists without the very things, the atoms, that make everything else real – why do they form themselves into one thing instead of another? What gives them direction?"

"Chance," replied Democritus.

He seemed to think that one word answer sufficient. I was incredulous.

"Chance? You mean there is no reason for anything, none? Existence, all the things that are, just an accident, something that might never have happened?"

"Everything that is, everything that exists, the fortuitous concurrence of these atoms, these invisible particles of matter, I have been trying to describe," he replied with irritating complacency.

"'Fortuitous concurrence,' 'chance' – ! There is more chance in this theory of yours than you know!"

"More chance than I ...?" he cried, bristling at my arrogance.

"What makes them form anything, form one thing instead of another; in other words, why do they form anything at all instead of remaining in some mindless pattern, chaos, no form at all: no order, no cosmos, no world of any kind? Chance? Fortuitous occurrence? Not very likely."

"Why not, in the infinity of time; why not many worlds, different worlds? The one we have – it came into being, it – "

"Why did it come into being – chance?"

"No, necessity."

"Necessity?"

"The vortex: all the atoms in the universe are borne along in a vortex and from this generate all composite things. The vortex is the cause of the creation of all things and this I call necessity. I see you're confused," he remarked with the indulgence of a wise man for an idiot. "It's my fault; I should have explained earlier. Yes, the vortex; all the atoms are carried along, and out of necessity they form themselves into that which comes into being, but it is merely by chance, the fortuitous occurrence of which I spoke, that they form themselves into one thing rather than another."

"Like generation?" I asked, picking up the thread of his changing argument. "It conforms to a necessity of our nature, but chance determines what we give birth to, what kind of child we have."

"Yes; that's not a bad analogy."

"But then it isn't true that everything is always coming into being, that everything is always changing." It was his turn to look puzzled and confused. "The atoms never change. Are they not the unchanging things that form the basis, the structure, of all the things that change? And if they never change, then in some sense at least the world never changes either, does it? If they never change, then they have no beginning; and that would mean – would it not? – that they and the world they make up are eternal. But that still leaves us with the question why chance, and not the mind or intelligence that Anaxagoras talked about? Is it more likely that order comes out of chaos by itself, or that the order was always there, and that these atoms of yours have the same, but no greater, importance than the bricks in that warehouse over there?"

His face went red again. He began to bluster, the words all jumbled up, convinced, perhaps more than ever, that he was right and that I was too young, and too stupid, to be capable of understanding what he was trying to explain.

"I'm talking about the facts of existence, what makes the world the way it is. If others speculate about why it is the way it is, you can – "

But I was not listening. Another question had come to my mind.

"What is the cause of this necessity of which you speak? Why is it necessary that atoms form themselves into things? Isn't that the same thing as saying what Anaxagoras said: that there is an intelligence that orders the world?"

Democritus would hear nothing of it. He insisted on what he knew, and nothing anyone could say would ever make him change his mind. He sat there, remote and majestic, his small eyes shining with the inner light of a certainty given only to zealots and other believers in what can never be proven, people full of an unshakeable faith that the question of existence, far from a riddle, is only their secret which they might or might not see fit to share. I had seen this look in the eyes of a great many men, and I would see it in the eyes of a great many more, but almost always in men for whom passion or ambition was the main driving force, men who thought in terms of victory, whether in politics or the harsher disciplines of war. Democritus was a serious thinker, a man who lived in his mind, and yet, there it was: the same rigid vanity, the same unyielding belief in his own infallibility, this strange sense that it was more important to be right than to discover where he was wrong. I wondered whether it might not be the consequence of the theoretical abstractions that formed the basis of his thought, building everything on what could not be seen but only imagined: atoms, particles so small they could not be touched. He was walking around with the world in his mind; one he could not so much prove as insist had to be there. It forced him to argue against what we grasped with our senses; it made him insufferably dogmatic. It also made him a little crazy, repeating the same thing over and over again as if there must be something wrong with my hearing if I did not immediately agree with what he said. It gave me a strange incentive.

"The void, space, where these atoms are free to move, it isn't made of atoms and therefore cannot exist," I said, taunting him with my obstinate refusal to grant him this necessary exception. "And the only way that the changing things can change, come and go out of being, is if there are all these other things, these atoms, which never change. Nothing exists except what, because it is always changing, does not exist; and everything exists because things no one can see or touch never come to rest but are always in motion. Let's start again," I said before he could again interrupt; "start again from the beginning, and perhaps this time you can make me understand how any of this is possible."

And then, before he could say anything, I turned and faced him and with all the charm I could summon, smiled at him in a way that, if I may speak without modesty, would have melted the heart of most other men. Democritus, who had risen from the bench as I walked toward him, went a little weak in the knees – he was at least that much a man of flesh and blood – but, gathering himself, lowered his gaze to the pavement and with what I am sure he thought admirable patience, began again to explain how the world began, all those whirling atoms, and why that was the only thing that did not depend on the inscrutable workings of chance.

And so we went, back and forth, back and forth for hours, back and forth over the same ground until there was nothing more to be said, nothing more to be repeated. I learned everything there was to know about the atomists and their school; everything that Democritus and his teacher, Leucippus, could teach. I learned enough to know that there was a great deal more I had to learn, that more than the answers, the questions were what were important; questions that none of them, not just Democritus, but Anaxagoras and Empedocles and all the others, men like Pythagoras and Heraclitus, had not thought to ask; questions which I could not yet formulate or even identify; questions that I could only feel were there, waiting for someone with eyes sharp enough to see them, ears sharp enough to hear them; someone for whom questioning was not so much a search for answers as a way of life.

Chapter Ten

It was nearly dark when I said goodbye to Democritus and walked the short distance to the Salaminia, waiting to take me away. There was still light enough for men to see where they were going, still light enough for them to work, loading the cargo ships that carried corn to Athens, the ships that could carry more than twelve hundred tons, the ships that took days to load. A long line of men stretched from the warehouse on the shore to the ship waiting at the end of the dock, their shoulders bent beneath the burden of the huge hemp sacks they carried. Next to them, a long line of torches were being lit so that the men could keep working after dark. Other, empty, ships formed a line of their own, waiting their turn to have their broad-beamed hulls filled with the cargo they would then carry to Athens where, this same night, thousands would sit down to dinner without a thought of how much time and trouble, how many broken bodies, it had taken to put that food on their table.

I had the feeling of watching the workings of some gigantic mechanism, a million finely calibrated parts, an intricate machine that never stopped, that like the world itself was always in motion, a motion so constant that it seemed itself a state of rest. Those atoms, too small for human vision, of which Democritus was so enamored; those changeless things that out of necessity formed all the other things by chance; were they really any different than what we did ourselves, the shifting patterns of our own behavior, drawn to do things by the necessity of our own nature, and the way we did them all the consequence of chance? In the dim half-light of evening I watched all these men with their strong backs and their hopeless eyes and wondered at the chance that had made some of us not much more than beasts of burden and some of us free to have others do our bidding. Democritus was right at least in this, that if there is an order in the world it is not, by any stretch of the imagination, all of it rational.

A few minutes after I was back on board, the Salaminia was again underway. The oars cut the water with such well-trained precision that we ran swift and silent as a leaf on the current, the only sound, unless even that was but an echo in my mind, the quiet revolution of the stars in heaven's high-vaulted dome. There were torches lit on the deck of the ship, and as with the men loading cargo on shore, I watched entranced the same constant motion of the sailors: the way they pulled in rhythm, the endless motion, the symmetrical design of four hundred hands, tied to the same beat, two hundred bodies with the same heart. In the quiet night the sail hung limp and lifeless on the mast, the man-made wind, the swift movement of that oar-driven ship, slipped warm and comforting across my bare skinned face. I took a long deep breath, feeling all the wonder of the purple sea. The night was everywhere; there was no horizon, no line to mark the difference between the solid earth and where it ended, nothing but the stars to mark a boundary between the dreams of men and the playground of the gods; and all around me, the measured movement of two hundred pairs of arms with two hundred oars, beating silent, always silent, against the sea. If I ever slept I did not sleep for long; I felt too alive to yield a moment to the oblivion of eyeless rest. If I ever slept, I woke before the dawn in time to see the sun's long pink fingers grasp again the edge of earth and climb back up the sky. And then, to my astonishment, I saw something else as well.

"Three ships! There, running right toward us!" cried the captain, who stood with his feet spread apart just a few feet away. His eyes, if not better, were more practiced than my own.

He knew immediately that the ships I had seen, three tiny dots in the distance, were ships of war and that they were the ships of an enemy. An officer in his mid-thirties with the steady gaze of a seasoned sailor, he had that look you seldom see on someone who spends their life on land, the look that told you that the only thing he feared was the possibility that through error or inadvertence he might fail to do his duty. There were three ships, enemy ships, bearing down on us and all he did was smile.

"Three to one," he said, raising an eyebrow that by its good-hearted arrogance almost made me laugh. "I'd say they were in a lot of trouble." And with that, he gave the order to face about and head directly for them

It was as if he had just announced shore leave for the crew. There was a sudden, and really quite extraordinary, burst of energy. Heads, bent down to the task, the slow, repetitive motion of hands and arms, shot up, and instead of silent running the ship seemed to come awake, the water all around us roaring with the sound of two hundred small explosions as the oars each struck their target and the sea, churning white water, was filled with foam. My hair, falling loose around my neck, flew out behind my shoulders.

We closed to within a quarter of a mile and then, to my astonishment, the three ships, three triremes flying the flag of Corinth, instead of forming a line of attack, formed a three-pointed circle, ready to defend themselves against a single ship of Athens. The captain had been right. The Corinthians could not match the speed, the quickness, the ability to maneuver and change direction; the Salaminia was like a sheepdog chasing sheep. They backed and filled until the captain, having shown he had the power to destroy any ship that dared to follow, gave the order to get back on course.

"They think that ships are all you need to have a navy," said the captain when we were safely away. "It's like saying all you need to be a soldier is a sword. It helps to know a little about how to use it, don't you think?"

No one came after us; no one dared. We sailed unmolested the remainder of the voyage, not a hostile sail in sight. Athens controlled the sea, and the only tactics learned by the Spartans or the Corinthians was how to avoid an engagement in which, no matter what their advantage in men or ships, the only question was the size of their defeat. More than confidence, the knowledge of their superiority bred a kind of exhilaration in the officers and sailors of the Salaminia and, from what I had heard, among the navy as a whole; a sense that each time they launched their ships, drove them back from the beach to the water, the sea, instead of a place of danger, became their own private lake. You could see it in their eyes, the eager daring, the utter certainty that there had never been men or ships to mark their equal, that they alone had achieved an excellence no one else would ever rival. They did not sleep, they did not rest; they sailed straight for Potidaea.

The forty triremes sent to aid in the attack on the city in revolt had joined thirty others that had been sent weeks earlier when the trouble first began. Together they patrolled the coast, preventing any more men or supplies coming to the aid of the rebellion. But the Corinthians had acted quickly and had managed to bring in reinforcements before the fleet arrived. Sixteen hundred hoplites, as well as four hundred light armed troops, had been added to the city's defenses. Not only was the enemy more numerous than anyone in Athens had expected, but they were better organized. Aristeus, son of Adeimantus, had been sent as general by the Corinthians and was such a popular commander that men, instead of being conscripted, had volunteered to serve.

Potidaea is on an isthmus at the northern end of the westernmost of three narrow, tear-shaped peninsulas that stretch from the Thracian mainland into the Aegean. The isthmus is less than two miles wide, giving the city the advantage of two different ways of access to the sea, one of the reasons why it had been among the richest cities allied with Athens. Walls had been built on all sides and at the beginning of the rebellion, and one of the causes of the revolt, Athens had demanded that Potidaea destroy the wall that faced the sea, the only use of which was protection against the seaborne might of Athens. Potidaea had refused. With the sure eye of a gifted commander, Aristeus took a position in front of the city facing west along the land.

He did more than that. Perdiccas, as if to underscore his duplicity and double-dealing, held the Thracian cavalry, two hundred well-trained horsemen under his command, seven miles away, north by northwest, in the town of Olynthus. When the Athenians began their attack on Potidaea and were fully engaged, he would attack them from the rear. Aristeus had set a trap, but Callias, the Athenian commander, had anticipated the enemy's plan of battle and made his own arrangements.

"We're camped here," he explained, showing me a rough outline of a map, drawn with his own hand. "This place is called Gigonus, twelve miles west of Potidaea. Now – up here – which will be on our left as we approach their position, and behind us as we get closer – Olynthus. They have had time to make their preparations. You can see Olynthus from Potidaea, clear enough so signals can be sent, which means it's possible to coordinate the movements of a force that has been divided."

Pausing, Callias looked down at the candle flickering next to the hand-drawn map on the table. The lines in his forehead deepening with worried doubt and, at the same time, a furtive grin raced across the corners of his straight angled mouth. He was handsome, though you might not have noticed it at a distance – there was nothing that remarkable about his features – but close up, when you became aware of the animation on his face, the clear, questioning intelligence in his still youthful eyes, when it was no longer what you saw but what you felt, that you understood the attraction.

"You find it strange that I'm here, that Pericles would have sent me instead of someone else; strange to have to explain to a woman what she should expect to see, what to look for when the fighting begins."

He looked at me with laughing kindness and with a rare generosity of spirit mocked himself for the admissions, as he told me, he would later have to make.

"Years from now, when I sit around a fire some winter night, the children born to the children I now have gathered all around, I will tell them that on the night before my first command, the battle for Potidaea, a beautiful young woman came unexpected and wrapped in mystery to my tent, and knowing I might face death the next day, that my eyes might be closed forever to the light, she did what every man hopes a woman, a beautiful woman, will do – questioned me about what I planned to do to gain victory on the field, and did it with more intelligence than any of the officers who now burden my existence!"

I loved him for that, more than even I knew until the next day and what I saw happen with my own eyes, what it became my responsibility – the burden of my existence – to report to Pericles in Athens. But now, when he finished saying that, he summoned two of the soldiers who stood guard outside and gave them strict instructions to see me safely to the tent where I would be quartered and that, in the morning, they were to stay with me and protect me with their lives, should the need arise. To make sure they understood that this was no idle, chance request, he informed them that the order came not from him but from Pericles himself.

As soon as I was settled, I told my two armed escorts that I had next to see Alcibiades, that I had brought a message from his guardian and uncle. The camp was laid out in parallel lines, with wide straight streets or pathways between the tents, and sentries stationed all along the perimeter. It was set on a low shelf of land that ran flat a half mile from the hills behind it to a jagged rocky cliff in front. Far below it was the narrow coastal valley through which the army would in the morning move east to Potidaea. I found Alcibiades outside his tent, polishing his sword.

In the light of a full moon I could see him as clearly as at midday, and I stood back a moment, watching at how intense was his concentration, how meticulous and careful he was, sharpening it to a lethal edge. Holding it upright, straight in front of him, he ran his thumb slowly down the blade, studying, as it seemed, the effect: how much pressure, how much force – or rather, how little – was required for this instrument of murder to do its deadly work. There was nothing of that look of eager triumph, none of the evil glitter seen in the eyes of someone who dreams of blood and loves to kill; there was nothing like that kind of male insanity. What I saw instead was something much more reasoned, and much more sober. For all his known extravagance, all his vaunted arrogance, his willingness to do anything – and the more outrageous the better – to attract attention and set himself apart, he was, with no one watching, astonishingly serious and single-minded. Watching him work on that sword, I remembered the look I had seen on the men of the Salaminia, that look that told you that they could never be defeated, that they knew every part of what they were doing, and that every, even the smallest, part was important.

Alcibiades had not seen me coming, he had not heard my approach; but when, suddenly, I spoke to him, he did not turn his eyes to look at me, but kept looking at the sword, turning it first one way then the other, examining the blade.

"I was just thinking about you," he said quietly, his eyes still fastened on what he was doing; "wondering if you would somehow figure out a way to come."

He turned and smiled as if he had somehow known all along that I would respond to those few taunting words of his; that laughing dare, shouted over his shoulder as he went marching off to the ships that were about to sail for Potidaea, that I should come with him; that dare that no one would have taken seriously and which for that reason had made him think I might. He had not known, of course; he could only guess, but guess with an instinct that went deeper than common knowledge, the sense he had that there was something between us that had already been written and that none of what happened would owe anything to chance.

"But I must have come to the wrong place," I said with defiant, straight-faced disappointment. "I was told this is where I might find Socrates."

He nodded knowingly and again started studying his sword, running his thumb down the edge of it as if looking for an imperfection.

"You were told right. This is where you can find him; or you could, if he were here."

"Then he isn't here? He's gone somewhere else?"

A strange, enigmatic look came into Alcibiades' shining eyes, a look that seemed an invitation to a game.

"Yes, you could say he has gone somewhere else."

Alcibiades put down the sword and folded his arms across the brass breastplate he wore. Tilting his head to the side, he studied me closely, as if the simple question I had asked contained within it a source of the greatest complexity and confusion. Finally, he shook his head and shrugged his shoulders.

"He hasn't gone anywhere; but when, if ever, he is coming back … only someone with a mind like his could answer. Come and see for yourself, if you don't believe me."

I followed him – followed him! – it was not more than three short steps, just around the front entrance to the tent he shared with Socrates; and there, on the other side, stood Socrates himself. He was not alone. There were at least a dozen other men, all of them sitting or kneeling on the ground, watching in a strange, eerie silence as Socrates did nothing at all, just stood there, still as night. I started to go up to him to say hello, but Alcibiades grabbed my arm.

"He hasn't moved since dinner more than four hours ago, has not taken a single step. Watch his eyes. They don't move. He's here; but then again, he isn't. Wouldn't you like to know what thought has hold of him; wouldn't you like to know what that must be like, to have a mind that powerful, a mind that free; so free you can leave your body and go somewhere only thought can go?"

The men around us would watch a while and then move off, and then others would come and without a word depart. It was astonishing, uncanny, as much because of the sudden realization how much we were ourselves always in a state of motion as because we had never seen anyone stay that motionless who was not dead.

"Are you just going to leave him like that?" I asked as Alcibiades took me gently by the arm and led me back to the other side of the tent where we could talk in private.

We sat on camp chairs with wooden backs and leather seats. A small fire cast shadows on the moonlit ground. Alcibiades tossed a few torn twigs on the fire and listened to the sudden crackle and hiss. The tent was open and I could see his helmet, the one he would wear tomorrow: the layered pounded brass that came wide across the cheekbones with a narrow strip that from the covered forehead came down the length of the nose. My eyes darted from the empty helmet to the shining sword. I could almost hear the harsh metallic striking sounds of battle; I could almost smell the blood.

"Don't be upset," said Alcibiades sympathetically, imagining a different cause for what he now saw in my eyes. "There's no reason. I've seen him like this before. Whatever happens to him when he is that far lost in thought, he comes out of it more rested and more alive. Strange, though, isn't it? I wanted to knock him on the head, just to see what would happen; but something would not let me, something held me back. Probably just that sense he gives you that when he isn't doing anything, he's doing something more important than you can possibly understand."

He laughed quietly at what he had just said, at how incongruous it all was: that he could somehow know that there was something, something important, that he did not know and might never know; that he – that any of us – could sense that someone else could know things more important than what we ourselves could ever comprehend.

"The reason – I think the reason – I did not bring him out of it is that it would show him how jealous I am that he can spend the night ignoring me, shutting me out from what must be this fascinating conversation he has only with himself. Well, let him have his privacy; let's go somewhere where we can have a conversation of our own." His voice grew quiet, distant, and determined. "This isn't a night I expect to get much sleep."

We made our way along a wooded path into the hills above the camp, and while we walked I told him what had happened, how I had become an official envoy, sent by Pericles, to observe tomorrow's battle and report on what I saw. I told him about my trip to Abdera and some of what Democritus had said. The more I talked, the more I wanted to say; things I had not thought about – minor, unimportant things: the way Democritus kept opening and closing his hands; the stevedore with the parrot that I now remembered had part of a wing missing, a forgotten parallel to its owner's partial arm – came spilling out of my mouth before I knew what I was saying, chattering like a friendless schoolgirl afraid that if she stopped her audience would disappear. Alcibiades might have done that already: he did not say anything, his only comment a silent smile as he walked ahead.

We came to a small clearing, a vantage point from which we could look down on the firelights of the camp and beyond it to the open water where the fire lamps on the ships made the sea look like a city sleeping fat and prosperous in the nighttime darkness.

"The parrot's wing was clipped," said Alcibiades as he sat on a moss-covered rock. He spread his legs wide apart and rested his tight-muscled arms on his knees. The moonlight was bright as day and the air warm as summer, and that may have been the reason why it was as if I were hearing his voice for the first time. There was something magical in that voice; more magical than any I had ever heard. It was the sound of every promise you had ever wanted to hear, and, more than that, the certainty that all those promised things would come true; the promise that life would always be the slow unfolding of everything you had ever thought you had wanted, every dream you had ever had.

"The parrot's wing was clipped," he said again, struck by some different meaning that he had now discovered. "That is one way to keep the loyalty of what you think belongs to you: clip its wing so it can't fly away. The better way of course is to train it in a way that it never wants to change; raise the bird from the time it leaves the nest, the way we do with human beings, teach them what they know. Isn't that what we do – especially the Athenians – teach them how they should live, tell them what will happen if they don't; tell them that the greatest enemy they have is change; tell them stories that make them think that anyone who wants to make them better than they are only wants to take power for himself; tell them that anyone who does not flatter them as having all the wisdom worth having is, no matter what he says, a tyrant in disguise."

"You mean Pericles?" I asked, watching closely each change in his expression, the way his eyes seemed the perfect mirror to the tone and sequence of his speech.

"Pericles?" he laughed. "No, not Pericles – Me! You've seen the way they throw themselves at me – men and women both – the way they tell me things, shameless things; you've seen the adulation in their eyes, as I were the answer to every desire they have ever had. Does this sound arrogant? It shouldn't – not to you, to whom the exact same thing has happened; happened far more often, if I am any judge, than it has happened to me. I've heard that at least three men have died already – suicide and heartbreak – when they finally realized that you not only did not love them, but did not even know that they existed!" he insisted with a quick, open and blatantly dishonest smile.

I laughed and shrugged and played indifference to the tragic fate of all the nameless lovers I had never known. But I was not at all indifferent to what he had said, the way he understood his own position.

"They love you because they want you," he said. "And then, when they discover that they can't have you, what is their reaction? They hate you because of what they cannot have. If you want to live in safety, be born with only normal talents."

The thought flashed through my mind that if we had both been born average we might have had a future; but I had no tolerance for pity, though I did not share the scorn of those who thought there was no hardship, no difficulty, in a life thought by those who did not have to live it the one that fortune favored. If those who wanted Alcibiades and could not have him ended up hating him, what feelings must he have, who wanted to rule not only Athens, but all of Greece and even more than that? What would the lover do when the world he loved did not love him back?

He stood a few steps away, his eyes shining, not like older men with their memories of ancient things, but with the memory of what had not yet happened, what his own life was certain to be, a life without precedent that would be remembered as long as there were men with memories of their own.

"Tomorrow, in the morning, when first light comes – you start for Potidaea and ... "

"Are you worried about me, afraid I might get hurt?" he asked in a gentle voice. All the false bravado, the face he showed the crowd, was gone; the only witness to what we said or did the stars.

I had a sudden impulse to tell him nothing but the truth, though that did not mean that I was going to be quite honest. "Yes; I don't want to have to come back when I'm an old woman and place flowers on your grave."

He seemed to think it almost funny. He looked at me as if he knew a secret in which, quite without my knowing, I was already involved.

"If I ever die, I'll arrange it so that no one can ever be quite sure I didn't escape whatever danger I was in, and am only waiting for the right time to let the world know I'm still alive. I won't leave a slipper on the slopes of Mt. Etna to convince the credulous that I have gone to live with the gods; I'll leave a sword buried in the throat of an enemy to convince the skeptical that I can never be defeated!"

And I believed him when he said it, that he would arrange a

death as large and unexampled as his life. It was as if he had the gift of prophecy and could see so far ahead that he could pause and look back, reflect on things that had not happened, and discover in each unwritten episode the cause of failure or success. There was that kind of certainty about him, strange, uncanny, as mysterious in its own way as the ability of Socrates to leave the world and disappear somewhere deep inside himself.

"I hope you'll wait a while," I remarked, smiling back at him. "At least until sometime after tomorrow."

His eyes brightened, his shoulders drew back, he thrust out his chin in an attitude of mock defiance; ready, for my benefit, to prove himself invulnerable to the slings and arrows of however many poor mortals were fool enough to challenge him in combat. Then, remembering that we were all alone, he relented, and for a time at least became quite serious about what tomorrow might bring.

"Callias is a decent man, and a brave one. He would be the first to come to your assistance if he saw you were in trouble; he would gladly give his own life to save the lives of those who serve under him. There is nothing wrong with his character, but he has not thought through his plan of battle. Like a lot of men responsible for the lives of others, he is not daring enough; he is too cautious."

"Too cautious? Why; what do you mean?"

Alcibiades pointed east, beyond the distant hills, to the muted glow of camp fires lighting up the sky.

"They're waiting for us – Aristeus and the Corinthians. They think to catch us in a trap: attack us in the rear with two hundred horses that Perdiccas has in Olynthus when we attack Potidaea."

"But the trap won't work: Callias has six hundred Macedonian horses to check their advance."

"What I mean by too cautious," he replied, his eyes flashing with the angry recognition of a chance gone begging. "We're going to hold them back, keep them in reserve, and in that way prevent Perdiccas coming down on us from the heights behind us at Olynthus. What we should be doing is taking the Macedonian cavalry with us, forming on our left wing as we advance, and that way not only keep Perdiccas at bay, but help cave in the Corinthian front. Aristeus has no horse with him, and we have six hundred, three times what Perdiccas could bring against us. This should be easy; now it will be difficult. Caution, instead of saving lives, will cost us dearly; it may even cost us Potidaea."

But he was not thinking of Potidaea and what might happen tomorrow when he went into battle. I could see it in his eyes, the way he was looking at me; I could feel it in myself, the sudden urge, the eager willingness to yield, the certain welcome knowledge of what I wanted as much as he. We did not speak, there was no need: speech was useless when there was between us only one thought, the chance necessity of what nothing now could stop. I was in his arms and my arms were around his neck, and then we were lying on the ground, and then he was deep inside me with his male force and power. I bit him on the shoulder, telling him I wanted more; I scratched him hard with my nails, telling him it would never be enough. I lost all sense of myself; I existed only in him. There was no separation, no point of distinction. It was not that I belonged to him, that he now possessed me – there was not anything left of me to have. My body disappeared, burned away by an eroticism I had never known, vanished in this thing, this new desire, that vanquished both of us and created in our two separate places one new being.

Then, suddenly, at the very moment when I reached the peak, when the world went white with the blinding light of ecstasy, I remembered – remembered that what I had dreamed, the awful nightmare that had come so often to me in my sleep, had not been a dream at all: the nightmare of what my father had done – raped me as a young girl, a child – had been true.

Tears ran down my face. Alcibiades, my new lover, the only man I ever loved, was mortified, believing that what he had done – yielding to what he felt, a burning, all-consuming desire – had, despite the way I had responded, done me unexpected harm.

"I'm sorry, I didn't mean... I didn't know; I shouldn't have... "

"No; it's all right. It isn't – it wasn't – you. It's just that ... "

But I could not tell him, I could not tell anyone, what had happened, what I had all this time kept hidden from myself: the degradation of what my father had done to me, the shame of what I felt. I could not tell Alcibiades why I was crying, and so, without another word, certain that he had done something I had not wanted, he picked me up in his arms and carried me back down the hill to the camp. I told him that it was all right, that I had wanted him as much as he had wanted me, but my tears told a different story, a story I could not bring myself to correct. I could not tell him – just remembering it had hurt almost more than I could bear – how my father had made me, his own daughter, another subject of his lawless will.

Alcibiades was kind and gentle, but I wished more than anything that he would take me again, let me be the woman I wanted to be and not the girl I remembered. But his desire had vanished with the onset of my tears, and he looked at me now with such anguish and regret that I knew that if we ever made love again it would not be the same; that instead of the white hot heat of passion there would be the gentler sentiments of love; that he would have too much respect for what he thought my feelings, too much concern for my well-being, to lose himself again in the blinding darkness in which for those few moments we had found in each other what was missing in ourselves.

Socrates was still there. He had not moved since we left; had not moved a muscle so far as I could see. It was late, well after midnight, dawn not more than two hours away. No one was watching anymore, everyone had left; but he was there, unmoved and unmovable, a being in a perfect state of rest, and yet, at the same time, if you could see inside him, inside the wondrous workings of his mind, a being in motion, a motion that seemed never quite so rapid as when his body stopped moving at all.

"He'll be ready, waiting, in the morning, when the rest of us awake," said Alcibiades, his eyes moving from Socrates to me and then back again for one last, final, glance.

I slept in the tent with Alcibiades. I slept on his fur covered cot, while he slept in Socrates' place on the cloth covered ground. I did not have the nightmare about my father and what he had done to me; I did not dream at all that night. But somehow in my dreamless sleep I decided that I owed it to Alcibiades, that I owed it to myself, to tell the truth about what had been done to me, and that far from doing me any harm, he had saved me from living longer with a lie. I was talking before I opened my eyes, and only then, when I opened them, did I discover that I was all alone. Alcibiades had gone, and so had Socrates. The army was breaking up camp, preparing for the march to Potidaea. My two erstwhile guards, the escort I had been given, were waiting for me. They had the horse I was to ride.

It was a four hour march to Potidaea. Safe on horseback with my two armed attendants, I followed a short distance behind the army. By mid-morning we were within sight of the walled city and the several thousand troops in battle array drawn up in front. On a signal from Callias, the Athenians formed themselves into order. While each unit took its position, I left my escort and rode off to the left, on the side of Olynthus where Perdiccas was waiting with his cavalry. He had been stationed there to attack the Athenians when they attacked Potidaea, but Callias had effectively prevented that by placing his own cavalry in position to attack them if they did. But if this meant that Perdiccas and the two hundred horse of his cavalry would not take part in the battle, neither would the six hundred horse cavalry that could have crushed the Corinthian troops that were now moving straight toward the troops of Callias. Alcibiades was right. Callias was too cautious by half. And the battle was very nearly lost because of it.

I had ridden nearly a mile, looking over the ground, seeing how easy it would have been to lead the cavalry between Olynthus and the battle lines of Potidaea, and then, with still overwhelming numbers, twice the size of what they had to deal with, four hundred to the two hundred they would fight, still have two hundred with which to turn the right flank of Aristeus and destroy his army. Instead, without cavalry engaged on either side, I watched in stunned amazement as Aristeus and his hand-picked men drove back the Athenians facing them on the very flank where the Athenian cavalry would have been decisive, drove them back with such slaughter that the Athenians broke and ran, Aristeus and the Corinthians following at their heels. I watched as soldier after soldier was cut down from behind; I watched men throw down their arms in abject surrender, men who were then run through with spears by an army that gave no quarter. I watched as heads rolled lifeless in the bloody dust; I listened as the screams of dying men became an awful, hellish chorus. I watched with such intensity of thought and feeling that at first I did not notice that my horse was pulling hard against my grip.

"Come here, you lucky whore! Whoever brought you here from Athens, you now belong to me!"

I looked into the evil, reddish eyes of a bearded soldier holding onto the reigns of my horse, brandishing a sword that still carried with it the entrails of his last helpless victim. Not content with murder, he wanted rape. I bent toward him with the most wanton, sultry smile that frenzied, feeble-minded Greek had ever dreamed of seeing.

"You want me? Come here! Let me have your mouth!"

My horse was still struggling, pulling hard to get away. The smell of battle, of blood and smoke, was everywhere. I bent closer, close enough to touch the side of his harsh wired face briefly with my hand; just long enough to make him think I meant it, that I was what he thought I was: the whore he wanted, the whore he had to have. He stared at me with stupid eyes and tried to pull me even closer. I kept smiling, looking straight at him, waiting, my heart beating like a drum, until, the moment he was certain he could have me, he lifted up his chin. Then I did it, grabbed the dagger I kept hidden on my saddle and with all the strength I had drove it through his throat. He grabbed at it, staring at me with mindless eyes, as if even now he could not believe that it had happened, that he had been bested by a woman and would soon be dead. I struck him hard across the face and, as he staggered back, pushed free of him with my foot and, shouting both strange obscenities and prayers of thanks, galloped off.

My hands were shaking; my eyes were filled with rage. I tried to get my bearings, to make sense of the confusion I saw all around me, what was happening in the battle, whether Aristeus and the Corinthians were everywhere successful, or whether what they had done to the left wing of the Athenians was only part of the story. Far away on the other side, where the right wing of the Athenian army was fighting, the Potidaeans and Peloponnesians began to give way, drawing back, as it seemed, to the city's walls. Circling around to a tree-covered knoll less than a quarter mile away, I had an unobstructed view of the action. I was just in time to see Alcibiades lead a charge, trying to breach the enemy's line and attack them from behind. He was fearless, calling on his men to follow him, and always far in advance. He had believed it when he said that death would never take him. But then, just as he seemed on the verge of breaking through, he dropped to his knees, wounded by the thrust of a sword on the back of his shoulder, just inches from his neck, a blow that left him without power either to get back on his feet or lift his own weapon. I wanted to turn away; I did not want to see what was going to happen next. His assailant raised his sword to strike another, this time lethal, blow from behind him, when, suddenly, it fell out of his hand and he tumbled, lifeless, to the ground. Socrates had killed him with a single, well-timed blow and now shielded with his body the injured Alcibiades from the assaults of at least a half dozen enemy soldiers. One after the other, Socrates drove them off, holding the ground until the Athenian attack surged forward and the last defenders were driven inside the walls.

There was no time to rest. Aristeus and the Corinthians had

gone so far in pursuit of the Athenians they had defeated that by the time they came back they found a victorious Athenian army between them and Potidaea. There were only two choices: flee and become themselves the pursued, or fight their way back into the city. Aristeus did not hesitate. He attacked at the far end of the Athenian flank, wading through the sea to the farthest reaches of the wall that cut across the isthmus where Potidaea remained still safe from invasion. The Potidaeans and their Corinthian allies lost the battle, but lost only three hundred men. Athens lost even less, perhaps only half that number, but one of them was their commander, the brilliant Callias who died both bravely and far too young.

There was at the end, the way there was at the conclusion of every battle in which the Athenians fought and were victorious, a ceremony honoring the one who had distinguished himself most for valor. It should have gone to Socrates, who, in the language used on such occasions, "had saved Alcibiades and his arms from the enemy by throwing himself in front of him to defend him." Both had behaved with what is called "signal bravery." The generals appeared eager to give the award to Alcibiades because of his family and his rank – generals are often moved by considerations of what might redound to their own future benefit – but no general was as insistent that the prize go to him as Socrates himself. He wanted, I suspected, to give Alcibiades yet another incentive to seek after glory of a nobler kind than the cheap adulation he was offered every day in Athens. And so he was the first to give evidence for him, and to demand that Alcibiades receive the crown of valor and the suit of armor that went with it. The courage, the virtue, of Socrates needed no incentive.

I left Potidaea, which was now in a state of siege, a blockade that would go on for years, and sailed back to Athens on the Salaminia. The ship did not seem quite the cheerful vessel I remembered; the sea, even in the burnished light of early evening, did not seem quite as new and miraculous. I had made love and watched a war. I had made love and remembered rape and incest. I had watched the bright flashing swords of men with golden helmets and heard the cries of agony of slaughtered blood red bodies. I had seen the lifeless eyes of the dead; I had killed a man who wanted me. In a single night and a single day, in less time than it takes the sun to go once around the world, I had lost what little innocence I had left, and lost it more often than I could count.

The ship sailed on, sailed on through the night, sailed without stop until we reached Athens where I would have to tell Pericles that Callias was dead, that Alcibiades had been wounded, and that Potidaea had not yet been taken.

CHAPTER ELEVEN

Aspasia wanted someone to talk to, someone she could trust, a woman who would understand the difficulty, and the danger, she was about to face defending herself on a charge of impiety in front of a jury made up entirely of men. The trial was just a few days off, the trial that, if the verdict went against her, could end in her execution; but whatever fear she might have felt had at least for the moment been buried away. She greeted me with a smile and then turned back to Socrates, taunting him with her bright, eager eyes, challenging him to explain himself.

"You often come to visit me, Socrates, sometimes with some of your acquaintances, some of whom sometime bring their wives; but you never do that, you never bring Xanthippe, not even once. Are you ashamed of me, ashamed of our friendship?"

It was a game she played, a game she enjoyed. She liked to turn things back around, to make Socrates, who loved to question others, answer what she asked; she liked the way he each time invented a different way to repeat the same unfortunate truth. He looked for a moment completely baffled.

"That's one of the reasons why I come to see you: in the hope that you can teach me what you teach others, how to speak with persuasion, – how to convince the woman I married to take an interest in the things I do."

Aspasia laughed, but with a pointed look that carried, as I thought, more than one meaning.

"There are some people who can never be persuaded, especially those who have the power to hurt us if they choose."

Seated at the edge of one of the scarlet colored couches in the spacious living room, Socrates bent forward and stared past us into the middle distance. His right hand, strong as any I had seen, stroked his chin.

"That is always the problem, how to persuade whoever has power to use it in the right way. It's more difficult, of course, when those who hold power, like that assembly of ours, are cowards and fools; merchants and traders, men who spend their lives buying and selling and think nothing more important than the money they make. The city is full of noise, everyone talking at once and scarcely anyone saying anything that makes sense."

Aspasia could read between the lines. She understood what he was saying, and the irony of what it meant.

"Yes, I know. Pericles made Athens great, greater than any empire on earth, and more beautiful than any city has ever been, more beautiful than any city will ever be again, but he could only do it because of the power he got by giving the people what they wanted. And what they wanted was more democracy, more power for themselves, and now that they have it, now that we are ruled by the kind of men you describe, what they want is to have me ... "

Her voice trailed off into a silent lament. She started to flash a brave smile, an apology for having briefly succumbed to self-pity. Socrates stopped her with a look.

"Have you convicted for impiety, for not believing in the gods? But that is only an excuse, a pretext."

"A way to embarrass Pericles; yes, I know that, but ... "

"You have done something worse than not believing in the gods. The proof that you do not believe in the gods is that you think yourself the equal of men." He turned suddenly to me. "More than an equal. Men and women are not equal. Women are better; they know things at which men can only guess."

Aspasia laughed with her eyes. She knew immediately the answer to what I was not yet sure was a riddle.

"A woman knows her own children; how many men can really know that?"

"Pericles, for one," replied Socrates. "Pericles knows Pericles."

Aspasia was quick, as quick as anyone I had known. The laughter in her eyes burst from her lips.

"Pericles knows Pericles, but that doesn't mean, does it, that Pericles knows himself?"

As if on command a boy of five or six, with sky blue eyes and a shock of unruly auburn hair, ran into the room and tumbled into Aspasia's waiting arms. It was the child she had had with Pericles, the child that had been given his father's name, the child that because his mother was a resident alien could never become a citizen. The boy clung to his mother's arm, laughing as she pulled his hair, but his gaze stayed fixed on Socrates, sitting on the couch a few feet away. Quiet and shy, he seemed fascinated. Finally, summoning all his courage, he walked over to him. Other men would have laughed and said something inconsequential, done something to put a young boy at his ease, but Socrates looked straight at him, peering into his eyes in a way that suggested there was some secret language, known only to themselves, that said more than speech. The boy's face glowed with pleasure.

"Thank you; I will," he said, inexplicably delighted, as he turned, waved once at his mother, and quite literally danced out of the room.

"What did you ...?" But Aspasia knew better than to ask; knew that the only answer would be an enigmatic gaze, a suggestion that there were things that could not be explained, or rather, could be, but only in a way that questioned the normal assumptions by which we lived our lives.

"We do that with dogs and horses – tell them things without speaking. That's what you do with young Pericles, don't you, each time you come? That's why he is always so excited when he learns you're here, why he always breaks in and runs up to you. He knows what you're saying, what you tell him with that look of yours, but unlike a dog or a horse he can talk, tell you that he understands. That's what it is, isn't it?" she asked, her eyes shining with the certainty that she was right, that her son, the child she had with Pericles, had the gift of swift intelligence.

"He still sees things through his own eyes, instead of the eyes of others," replied Socrates, nodding pensively. "He has not been corrupted by what he will later hear, what passes for wisdom among us. He has not been subjected to the flattery of people who will tell him that he is perfect as he is, that he does not have to work hard to become a better man. He has not been led to believe that the measure of success is the approval of the crowd."

"You mean like Alcibiades," I said, eager to hear his reply. I had not yet understood why Socrates took such an interest in him. Everyone seemed to want Alcibiades, wanted him with a need, an urgency, it would have been hard to credit if I had not known myself what it was like to be in his presence, to see how beautiful he was and feel this overwhelming sense of longing just to be with him. It was astonishing to watch, the way so many of these shameless lust-crazed Athenians, men and women both, slobbered all over themselves, telling him things that would have made the gods blush; telling him, some of them, that he was a god, come to give direction to lesser mortals. They gave him presents, they gave him money;

they would have given him their daughters, they might have given him their sons, if he had not laughed at the attempt. But not Socrates. I would never forget that night I first met them both, when Socrates spoke to Alcibiades, or rather questioned him, with such harsh severity and made him think himself a fool.

"Everyone wants Alcibiades," said Socrates, turning his full attention on me, "but Alcibiades seems only to want you." He said this with knowing kindness, as if instead of recent acquaintances we were already old friends. He got to his feet and came closer. "You have that in common with him: Everyone wants you both. It is an interesting question, isn't it?"

"Interesting …? I don't think I understand."

His eyes – it's almost absurd to use that word; as if the way he saw things had anything in common with how other, normal people see – seemed to take me out of myself, pull me closer, subject me to a kind of scrutiny that did not just penetrate, but destroyed all my defenses. Even had I wanted to, I could not have resisted, I could not have refused to become his partner in any conversation he chose to start.

"You understand perfectly. You're drawn to him, aren't you?"

"To Alcibiades? Yes," I heard myself admit. "In ways I didn't think possible."

"Not possible? Did you think that because everyone has always been drawn to you, you were immune from the same kind of attraction; that no one who could have the same power over you that you have over others?"

It was exactly what I had thought; that whoever I wanted would want me more; that I might love someone, but never as much as they loved me.

"You said I had something in common with Alcibiades: that everyone wanted us both. But don't you think that, when it comes to Alcibiades, I have more in common with you?"

"Are you now going to ask questions of me?"

"Yes, if you'll allow it. Will you answer?"

He exchanged a glance with Aspasia. "I'll be glad to try."

"Good. Everyone wants Alcibiades, but you don't, do you?"

"I will confess it, if I have to tell the truth: I do love Alcibiades."

"That's no answer."

"No answer? Do you think that I don't love Alcibiades?"

"No; but the question is do you want him the way others want him, to become his lover?"

"Does not a lover want what is best for his beloved?"

"No! He may say that; he may even believe it when he says it – he'll say a lot of things when he is trying to win him for himself – but what he really wants is possession; he wants the one he loves to love him back."

His eyes, those strange green goggle-like eyes that seemed to know everything about the future and about the past, everything that mattered, everything that was important, sparkled with delight. "Do you think Alcibiades could ever be made to love anyone as much as they love him?"

"Only someone he could not have," I replied, raising my chin in a way that announced my intention. "Someone who knew that what they lacked in themselves could not be made up by what they found in another; someone who ... "

"Someone who longed for something that had nothing to do with the body; someone who was driven by a longing for the truth – is that what you are trying to say?"

I felt a strange sensation, a vulnerability I had seldom known, a suspicion that what I had thought made me different, this fascination I had for the things of the mind, for learning, for understanding the world, was, if not a delusion, an error, caused by a false belief in my own importance. You had only to look at Socrates, at those remarkably contorted features, perhaps the ugliest face I had ever seen, to know that it was only a mask, a mask that was not real, because instead of hiding, it only seemed to underscore the astonishing god-like intelligence that held you in its grasp with such power that even the thought of resistance disappeared. And I wanted what he wanted! I had the temerity to believe that I could find the answers; that I could think of the same questions! It was madness, it was ...

"This longing, it is the reason why we love anything. Shall I tell you what someone, a woman, once told me: All human beings, male and female both, are pregnant, in terms of the body and in terms of the soul, and whenever we get to a certain age, our nature desires to give birth. This is eros, love of the beautiful; and that means, not just what is fair to look at, but noble and fair in the soul. Yes, I love Alcibiades: what is, or could be, noble in his soul; and in that sense all love is erotic. You love him, too, if I'm not mistaken. I saw it that first night I saw you, right here, when I was talking with

Alcibiades and you were with him. I saw the way you looked at him, how you were drawn to him; but I saw something else as well: how you held back, how you refused to let yourself follow what you might have felt. Like Alcibiades, you have never known what it was like to want someone who did not want you. That is what makes this so interesting. What is eros to do when the most beautiful young man and the most beautiful young woman meet and come together? It becomes more interesting still, when the young man wants nothing less than to rule, not just Athens, but everything Athens has and can ever possess, and the young woman wants something even more than the power to rule others, the power, the ability, to live with the gods."

Aspasia was watching intently; as much, I think, to see my reaction to the way in which Socrates could turn an argument into a new and unexpected direction as to follow what he said. This last remark of his brought her back to her own, immediate, situation. The issue, the issue that might cost her her life, was what she believed, or did not believe, about the gods. She wanted, desperately as it seemed to me, to know what Socrates thought about the gods, and implicit in that, what he thought she should do.

"Live with the gods, Socrates? What exactly do you mean?"

We were inside the house of Pericles, and the house of Pericles had many servants and servants had ears. Aspasia suggested that we go outside to enjoy the weather, and it was there, in the shadows of an ancient grove, that Socrates told us the secret teaching of the gods. It took me a long time to understand what I learned that day; a long time to understand just how important it was to keep secret what he said, to understand that in the wrong hands that secret meant death, and something worse than death: a long descent into the kind of ignorance from which rescue would be all but impossible.

He started by telling us what he had heard when he was still a young man.

"Parmenides was then quite old, but his mind was still powerful and clear. The question was what is, what can be, how does anything come into being? And Parmenides gave a very strange answer: Nothing can come into being; only unchangeable being is. But all the accounts given by the poets, Homer and Hesiod and the others, tell how the gods were created; and we know from these and other writings that every city has its own gods. Parmenides says that the gods having come into being cannot be. He replaces the gods by the unchangeable being. There cannot be a beginning, a genesis, because coming into being means a movement from nothing to being and nothing is not. What is there if the gods do not exist? – Intelligible principles. One of them is Eros, which Parmenides called the first and oldest of all the gods."

I thought I understood, but I was not sure; and let me confess that I was so much in awe of him that my usual self-confidence, what some no doubt thought my arrogance, had all but vanished and left me a stammering, tongue-tied fool. And he knew it, knew it probably before I did; knew it as easily, as completely, as I knew how to breathe.

"If the gods have not come into being," he said, "how then can anything, even these intelligible principles, come into being? They must, like the world itself, be eternal. But then, you wonder, is it possible for Parmenides, for anyone, to say that one of these principles, Eros, is the first and oldest."

He had read my mind, read it perfectly; read my thought before my thought came to me. It was more than that; the opposite of that, if you will permit what seems a contradiction, but is really only another, more essential element of the phenomena I am trying to describe. I said he could read my mind. I should have said that he had a power, a power I have never experienced with anyone else, to let you read his; bring you inside, let you see what he saw, feel what he felt, grasp, at least in passing, something of what he, and perhaps he alone, understood. The power was physical. I have already told you about his eyes, the way with their goggle-eyed stare he seemed to see in every direction at once, and not just in some passive sense, taking in what they observed, but always active, working, moving, that piercing gaze that, I swear, could see right through you, behind you, all around you, subjecting you to a search that nothing could stop and from which nothing could hide. I have not told you about his voice, a voice that seemed to come from everywhere at once, coming at you from all directions, as if he were standing in all four corners of a room and you were there, all alone, in the middle, standing still, the sound all around you, penetrating deep into your conscious mind. It was uncanny, it was inhuman, it was irresistible.

"If Parmenides is right, if there cannot be a beginning, a genesis; if nothing is not, if there cannot be a movement from nothing to being; if only unchangeable being exists, then time is infinite and immeasurable. And in all that immeasurable time, how many cities must have come into being and been destroyed – tens upon tens of thousands, don't you suppose?"

It was, like so much of what I heard from him, new to me. I had grasped what I had been taught by Empedocles about the nature of the world, the elements and the forces that gave them shape; I had followed, without quite agreeing, what Democritus had said about the way chance and necessity moved all those countless invisible atoms around; I had read in Herodotus about empires that had arisen and then fallen, gone from glory into dust; but the thought that this had gone on forever, back into an infinite, immeasurable past and, presumably, into an endless future, the birth and death of cities, of whole populations, no more significant, because no more permanent, than the passing of the seasons, had never entered my mind. I was a blind person who only thought she could see.

"And all these places, hasn't each of them been governed by every kind of regime, and haven't they grown in size or gotten smaller, and haven't they gone from better to worse and from worse to better?"

I agreed, but not because I knew this; I agreed because if he was right, if there were no limits on time, if there had been, and would be, countless cities, everything possible must have happened, and not just that, but happened over and over again. Then I remembered. Whatever may have happened in the past, whatever might happen in the future, what was happening here and now would change as well. Like every city, Athens would change; Athens would go from worse to better or better to worse.

"What is the cause of the change, the reason why these things happen?" I asked.

Socrates looked at me as if he was sure I must know the answer, and to my surprise I suddenly thought I might. I remembered the stories I had heard as a child.

"Floods and earthquakes, plagues … other things that happened that destroyed almost everyone."

"Of all the disasters which have left only a small remnant of the human race, let's consider one that occurred because of a flood. Those who escaped would almost all be herdsmen who lived on mountains, men with no knowledge of the arts, and none of the contrivances that city dwellers use against one another to achieve their ambitions, whether it be the desire of gain or the desire of victory. They were men who lived simple lives, and because they were neither poor nor rich they had no reason to quarrel with one another. They were good because of this, and because of their goodness and simplicity believed whenever they heard that something was noble or shameful that what they heard was the truth. No one had the wisdom, as they do now, to be on the lookout for lies. And so they believed that what they heard about the gods as well as about human beings was true, and they lived according to these things."

"What they heard? Heard from whom?" I asked, beginning to suspect that nothing Socrates said was quite as straightforward as it seemed; that whatever truth lay on the surface of what he said was nothing compared to what was hidden below.

He did not answer my question; he just looked at me, waiting, as if he had asked the question of me.

"Someone wiser than the rest who gave them whatever laws they had," I ventured; "someone who understood that the source of those laws had to be someone, some god, whose power could not be questioned, whose every word had to be obeyed?"

Again there was no answer, only another question, but this time one he asked.

"Has there ever been a city, could there be a city, could any city survive, that did not have gods in which all the citizens believed?"

"Then all the gods are made up fictions, invented by men as a way to maintain an order, a way of life, they themselves have created?"

"Do you think that because philosophers disagree about what wisdom is, that wisdom is impossible?"

"So there are gods, but not the ones described by the poets, Homer and Hesiod and the others?"

"The gods that Athens worships," interjected Aspasia, raising an eyebrow. "The gods that, whether or not they exist, can bring about the death of anyone accused of not believing in them."

Socrates lowered his gaze and stared at the ground, his expression serious and profound.

"How else could the city – any city – survive if everyone in it did not believe in the same things?"

"Or appear to believe in the same things; appear to believe in the gods?" I asked in reply. I was not an Athenian; I was a foreigner, a guest, come from a different place. "When you have been in several cities, witnessed their different beliefs, it isn't quite so easy to insist that all of them are false except the one you happen to have inherited."

We were both of us, Aspasia and I, come from different places; both of us born into cities under the tutelage and protection of different gods. That may have been one of the reasons Socrates was willing to talk to us, tell us things he would normally have kept to himself or spoken with only among a few trusted close friends. One of the reasons, because there was also the unusual relationship he had with Aspasia, a woman whose intelligence he admired, but whose main attraction, as I came to understand, was what he could learn from her about the nature of women. He said he loved Alcibiades, and in the sense of loving what someone could be I think that he did; but I believed he loved Aspasia as well, not because of what she could be, but because of what she was: a beautiful woman at the height of her powers. I am not certain exactly what he thought of Pericles. All I know is that he never came to see him.

"The gods we inherit are like the city we inherit, like the parents we have: they have given us life and taught us how to live. That is something to honor, not despise and treat with disrespect. We owe everything to the city, and nothing more than to make it better."

He did not need to say that there were limits: that making a city better was not the same thing as building a city from the beginning when you could give it the laws it needed instead of making slight changes in the laws it had; when you could give it gods that were responsible for the good things and none of the bad, gods that could not be bought off with the gifts of the unjust. He did not need to say that there were limits to what reason could do: that even in the best of cities it would always be a question of what people could be made to believe.

"You're familiar with certain writings of ours about the gods, some of them written as poetry, others written as prose. The most ancient discuss how first the heavens and then other things came into being and then, following that, how the gods came to exist. They say, some of them, that the finest things are produced by nature and chance, and that all the other, smaller, things are produced by art. Fire, water, earth and air are by nature and chance, and so are the things that come after them, the earth, sun, moon and stars, and that come into being through these elements which are themselves beings without soul. They claim, those that teach this, that each of these elements is carried about by chance, but that the mixing together of opposites according to chance arises out of necessity. The whole heaven and all the things in it, all the animals and all the plants have come into being, because the seasons came into being out of these things, all of it by nature and chance, not through intelligence, nor through some god, nor through some art.

"What does exist through art are the gods. The gods, in other words, exist not by nature but by certain legal conventions, conventions that differ from place to place, depending how each group agreed among themselves when they first laid down their laws. Those who say this insist that fire, water, earth and air are the first of all things and they name these things 'nature,' and beginning with that go on to say that soul or intelligence is not first at all, but comes later, somehow developing from those elements they describe and call 'nature.' This is the error they make, the reason why what they teach is wrong."

"The error they make?" I asked, trying hard to follow. "Are you saying that fire, water, earth and air are not the basic elements – are you saying that there is something they have in common, that they are, each of them, made up of the same element, so small we cannot see it? Or are you saying, like Anaxagoras, that whatever shape and form they might take, they cannot become the things we see and touch, the beings that exist, without an intelligence to guide them?"

"I read Anaxagoras; I was disappointed. He speaks of intelligence as a force outside the things it moves; he gives no account of intelligence within each of the beings, what gives each of the beings life. He says nothing about the soul. It is the soul that, not just Anaxagoras, but almost all of them have misunderstood: what kind of thing it is, what power it has, and how it comes into being. They do not understand how it is among the first things, coming into being before all the bodies; how it, more than anything else, is the ruling cause of their changes and all their re-orderings. They do not understand that the things belonging to the soul come into being before the things belonging to the body."

"The soul – intelligence – is the cause of all the beings, all the bodily things," I said, repeating what he had said to make certain I had it right. "That would mean that the soul – intelligence – is older than the elements, older than fire and water, earth and air; that soul – or intelligence – brought these things into being."

"Trace things back to their origins – what do you find?"

"I'm not sure I know what you mean."

"Generation, the coming into being of all things, occurs when what takes place? – When there is growth; but that means that things change, change in a way that makes them more of what they are. A child becomes a man, and the man becomes a father. Everything comes into being because of the action, the motion, of another being; but if every motion is caused by another motion, then there has to be one being that is capable of moving itself as well as others in coalescences and separations, growth and decline, generation and destruction. The motion which moves itself is the ruling cause of all motion; it is the first to have come into being. Anything that can move itself is alive. Only what can move itself is alive. The power of motion, of moving itself, the power of moving other things, is soul. It came before body, rules body, and causes all the changes; it drives all the things in heaven and on earth. When soul does this with the help of intelligence – god, in the correct sense – it guides all things toward what is correct and happy, while when it associates with lack of intelligence it produces all things just opposite to these."

God in the correct sense. The soul was not identical with intelligence; it was not identical with god. The soul could be guided by intelligence, or god; but it could also be guided by ignorance and error. Soul that came before body, that brought body – and that meant the elements from which everything else was made – into being; soul that moved everything, including itself, might or might not be under the direction of god or intelligence. That meant that the world, and everything in it, was a strange mixture of reason and unreason, sanity and madness – if Socrates was right, and if I really understood him.

"Remember what we agreed to at the beginning," he continued, though I could not remember that we had agreed about anything at all. "Remember what Parmenides once said, that Eros is the oldest god of all; remember what a woman once told me: that we are all of us, male and female, born to become pregnant. What does that mean if not that we are all driven to live, not just our own lives, but driven by Eros to bring others into being as well. Whatever else the city believes, the city believes that," he remarked, casting a glance at Aspasia who seemed to know at once what he meant. "Every house in Athens has in front of it a statue that represents Eros – a Hermae – the god who promises that death, instead of an end, is only the beginning of life."

Chapter Twelve

The Hermae, the god that everyone worshipped and was expected to worship, the satyr-faced statue with the permanent erection – the god with the permanent erection, the god in a constant state of arousal – that was the reason, the hidden, and not so hidden meaning, for this open exhibition; a penis in full view, the part that is capable of becoming aroused; the potential, the actual, the being of eros; a rigid erection if not eros incarnate, the mechanism of desire. It was a tribute, a mute offering, these stone statues that were everywhere in Athens, to the movement, the absence of rest; a prayer, if you will, for what desire can bring, desire for what the body and only the body in motion can create, the creation that lives beyond the death that each of us must face.

Eros is death, the desire for something more than the mortal, the desire to live beyond our own death in the lives of others; it is the prayer, the belief, that our own life is part of all the other lives that make the city what it is. The Hermae is the god that promises that Athens will live longer than death, all the deaths that make it possible for the city to live. The Hermae, this symbol of Eros, is easy to worship; the most philanthropic, the most generous of the gods, it gives pleasure, the pleasure that leads to the generation of others, the children who will take the place of their dead fathers; it brings pregnancy, it brings life.

But Eros is more than that. Eros is desire for possession, and possession of another's body brings about the generation of another mortal life and that way protects us all from death; but Eros at the highest, Eros properly understood, the oldest and greatest of the gods, is the desire for the possession of that which never comes into being; it is the knowledge of what never changes, knowledge of the whole. But Eros, as I dimly understood, was the desire for something that might never be achieved. Was that the meaning, the hidden meaning, the meaning almost no one else had grasped, the reason why that strange erection never went away, why this desire seen on the surface of all those same looking statues was always constant – because there could never be completion, never an end to the motion, the attempt to reach the end?

"You better be careful; they'll start to think you're trying to cast a spell, standing here all alone, moving your lips and not making a sound."

Startled, vaguely conscious that I had lost myself in thought, I looked around. The sun was in my eyes and I could not see more than the dark outline of someone's face, but that rich, laughing voice of his was unmistakable.

"I saw you from a distance," said Alcibiades, smiling down on me. "I thought you had fallen into a trance; all these people all around you and you just standing here, still as a statue."

"Like a Hermae?" I asked with eager impertinence.

It caught him off-guard. He was not sure whether to note the obvious difference, a difference which would equally apply to any woman, and risk offending me, or just dismiss it as a failed attempt at wit.

"Or would you prefer to see me as Athena: cold and distant and wrapped in the folds of a gown?"

"I said I saw you standing still as a statue; I didn't say I wanted to see you."

He turned and started to join the crowd that was headed toward the amphitheater where the trial of Aspasia was about to begin.

"Is that the best you can do? – Tell me that you didn't say you wanted to see me. How incisive, how much wit you have; you must stay up nights thinking of all the replies, all the rejoinders, you might make, all the – "

He turned and came back to me. Certain that my prattling sarcasm was the other side of an attraction; that if I were trying to wound him with words it was only because I wanted him and could not bring myself to admit it, he took me by the arm.

"Stop!" I shouted with such authority that though he did not let go of my arm, he stopped moving. He looked at me, surprised, I think, that I had as much will as that. He seemed actually to enjoy it, that someone could insist on something that he did not want. "You may not have wanted to see me, but once you did, you couldn't ... "

"Couldn't stop myself? Is that what you think? That because you're beautiful I lose all control; that I can't stop myself; that I'd do anything to be with you?"

I could feel the excitement surging through my body as I touched the side of his young barely bearded face and whispered in his ear so no one else could hear, "Yes, and we both know it!"

He laughed as I spun away; laughed as I gave him a last, taunting glance over my shoulder, daring him to deny it, daring him to follow. He laughed, and for perhaps the only time in his life, almost blushed when he drew close enough for me to whisper that neither one of us bore any close resemblance to the Hermae that were seen all over Athens. "Me, because I don't have the part that is needed; you, because, though I assume you have the part, theirs seem so much larger!"

He reached again for my wrist, but I was too quick; I raced ahead and wished immediately that I had waited. My mind was moving faster than my feet, filled with a dozen different thoughts, all of them unfinished, everything unsettled. I was angry at what they were doing to Pericles and Aspasia; angry at my own girlish weakness, the stupid things I had said to Alcibiades, the strange desire to deny what I felt, this need to challenge all his overweening confidence with all the unpleasant arrogance I could use. I was about to watch a trial that might end with the death of someone I admired and all I could think about was a young man that secretly I adored. I hated myself for that, and I hated him as well.

The crowd was enormous and kept growing larger, all the streets around the open air theater swelling with noise. Like a pebble in a rolling sea, I was swept along, bumped and jostled, until, passing through the narrow gate, there was suddenly room to breathe, though that itself was no great pleasure. In the stifling heat of a blood red sun, the air was full of dust and the sweated smell of bodies that clogged my nostrils and made my eyes begin to burn.

"This will help."

I felt a hand on my shoulder that, strange in this infernal heat, seemed to cool me. Standing barefoot as usual on ground you half-expected would at any moment burst into flames, Socrates handed me a wet cloth with which to wipe my eyes. I smiled in gratitude.

"I hadn't realized it was going to be this warm. When I left my house this morning, it did not seem unseasonable."

"Everything here is unseasonable," said he, with a quick, sideways glance. His thick lips, that ungainly mouth of his, quivered briefly with a silent irony that, had I not spent time with him before, would have passed undetected. He looked out over the crowd of people still waiting to get in. "The jury is already here, all of them are in their places. The trial will start in a few minutes. You can sit with the other spectators, or you can come with me."

"You're not one of the jurors? That isn't the reason you're here, but just to watch? Go with you where?"

"Far in the back, behind the benches; you can see and hear everything without being part of the crowd. It also has the advantage of being in the shade," he explained with a kindness I cannot begin to describe. It was different from the self-interested gestures of other men, men who want as much to be known for what they have done for you as whatever good effect their generosity might achieve. For a moment I was too astonished to know what to say.

"Yes, of course," I replied finally; "if you don't mind standing with a woman."

"Mind?" he asked, as his bulging eyes danced with glee. "Everyone will think it's because you find me irresistible, better looking than all the other men. Don't you think so?"

I would have chosen him over Alcibiades. We made our way into the tunnel that opened into the theater and stopped at the other end where the brick ceiling kept us enclosed within its shadows.

Down below, on the benches in the center closest to the stage, sat the jurors, fifteen hundred of them from what I had been told. Behind them, on both sides, separated by a half dozen empty benches, were the spectators, nearly everyone in Athens who was not a menial or a slave, come to see what would happen to the wife of Pericles, charged with grave offenses, more serious, in their way, than murder. Socrates took it all in with a glance.

"Each of them individually might be a fool, but when they meet together they are suddenly the last word in intelligence." His strong arms folded across his deep chest, he pawed the ground with his bare right foot. "It's like objecting that a coin is counterfeit but then assume that a whole pile of them must be genuine."

His eyes glittered with strange mischief, like someone seeing in a mirror their own face, but seeing it now in a way different, less familiar, than they had seen it before, forced to recognize the changes brought by some new knowledge of themselves.

"The charge is brought by Hermippus, the comic poet, the brother of Myrtilus, another comic poet. But Hermippus did not write this comedy himself; it was written by Cleon and other of his friends. There is sometimes irony in comedy, and there is irony in this, though neither Cleon nor Hermippus knows it. None of this would have been possible without Pericles. There would have been a different, a better, jury; a jury made up of a few of the best men,

men chosen for their judgment and intelligence, their ability to understand the evidence and render an impartial decision, instead of fifteen hundred men selected at random and paid for their service. Pericles did this, started the payment of jurors, appealed to their sense of greed; a system that has made the Athenians idle, cowardly, talkative and avaricious."

Whether it was out of loyalty to Aspasia, and what Aspasia loved, whether it was out of my own sense of the great things he had done for the city, I felt compelled to object.

"He is the greatest man in Athens, the greatest man in Greece; the greatest statesman Athens has ever known!"

"Greater than Themistocles, who saved Greece from the Persians; greater than Miltiades, the hero of Marathon; greater than Cimon who almost gave us Egypt? It would be good if you were right, given what happened to the others: Themistocles ostracized, sent into exile for ten years; Miltiades sentenced to be flung into the pit and left to die, a sentence that would have been carried out had it not been countermanded by the president of the council; and Cimon, like Themistocles, forced into exile, banished from Athens when he lost the political struggle with the man who turned his back on the few to win the favor of the many, the very man you now think the greatest statesman, Pericles, who, I admit, gave us all these walls and buildings, things we could easily, and far better, have done without."

I knew something of what had happened, how Themistocles, when the Persians came, convinced the Athenians to abandon Athens and save the city by winning victory at sea; and I knew of course how at a different time the battle of Marathon had been the difference between living free or slave; but all I had heard of Cimon was that he had favored Sparta and tried to keep Pericles in his place. But Socrates had a different point to make than whether banishment had been unfair, and, as was so often the case, he made it in a way that made you wonder if you understood quite all of what he meant.

"Every one of them – what do they have in common? That they had the power to lead the city in whatever direction they cared to take it, and in each case made the citizens worse instead of better."

The strange orbit of his eyes held me as fast as if he had placed his strong-fingered hand around my throat; his nostrils, facing sideways like a lover's quarrel, quivered with the sensitivity of a well-tuned lyre; and I understood, really for the first time, that hidden behind that prodigious ugliness, hidden, as it were, in plain view, was such an exquisite refinement of his senses that things were open to his mind that the rest of us could scarcely imagine. When I did not answer his question, when I let my eyes announce my ignorance, he seemed to approve of my reluctance to even guess at more than what I knew.

"Take Pericles alone," said Socrates. "When he came into power, after Cimon was banished, everyone would have followed wherever he led. But instead of making them more just, they have become more unjust; instead of making them tame, willing to listen to reason, they have become wilder; instead of forcing them into the strict discipline needed to have peace with each other, they are more than willing – eager – to tear the city and each other apart."

"He made the city great," I continued to protest, if without the same zeal or enthusiasm, without the same blind certainty, I had felt before.

A slight smile made a brief appearance on his lips; a smile that seemed to mirror some greater certainty of his own, a smile full of wistful sadness for a certainty he wished he did not have.

"That is not his failure; his failure is that he did not make the city good."

I was about to make some reply – put a mirror, I suppose, to my own perplexed confusion – when the earth beneath my feet began to shake and the air itself seemed to rush away, pushed aside by an enormous ear-splitting noise, the thunderous applause, the brazen, raucous laughter, the shouted clamor of a dozen thousand voices, echoing up to heaven, as Hermippus, the accuser, entered from the side of the stage down below, and Aspasia, the accused, entered from the other.

Aspasia came in what seemed the guise of a supplicant. Her dress was simple, nothing more than a servant girl might have worn; nothing in the way of jewelry, certainly nothing made of gold. Her hair was done with equal simplicity, or rather, done with great care to make it seem that way, as if she were a woman whose appearance had never been more than an afterthought, and even then only because she did not want to do anything, either by design or inadvertence, that might call attention to herself. The white lead favored by the fashionable women of Athens, eager to enhance their beauty, or pretend to what they had lost or perhaps had never had, the mixture they wore painted on their faces, had been scrupulously avoided.

She walked to the chair, not quite halfway across the front

circle of the stage, where the accused was required to sit. I wondered as I watched her whether I could have done it, walked with that same air of quiet confidence, what seemed almost casual indifference, in front of an audience that large and that menacing, the only support the tepid applause from those brave enough to show it, and that drowned out by the jeering catcalls of those who, taking sanctuary in the anonymity of the crowd, delighted in all the graphic insults of their obscene imagination.

"Stand naked to the charge!" shouted a fat, sweat-soaked man, his pudgy hands cupped round his mouth, his eager eyes waiting greedy for the prodding cheers of all his evil friends.

"Take it off – Show us you have nothing to hide!" screamed another, the line of wit lengthening of its own accord, each new mindless demand the basis of the next.

It went on like this, the theater echoing back and forth with the heated insults of a contest to settle once and for all the question who among them had the loudest mouth and the smallest mind. And like all such contests this one ended in a draw; or rather stopped unfinished when Hermippus, always jealous of a crowd and what it wanted, stepped forward and with an actor's presence produced a silence by a sudden upward thrust of his arm and such a look of harsh severity that those who did not know him might have thought he meant it.

If Aspasia had come with an air of modesty and sobriety, Hermippus had come to put on a show. He was not a handsome man to begin with, a fact which he tried to turn to his advantage by exaggerating his deficiencies to the point where they became, if not admirable, noteworthy for their difference from what was normal. The tendency toward corpulence, the sign of his gluttony, was made more pronounced by the tight fitting robe he wore, and his two spindly legs, skinny and misshapen, bowed beneath all the weight they had to carry, were shown in all their deformity by making sure that the robe in front came not much below his knees. It was the stage management of an actor who knew his craft, the painted backdrop of a one-man play in which he was, like you the audience, the spectator of his own achievement, the way he rose superior to the awkward misadventures of his body. Like you, the audience, he looked down on what he was, on how he looked, and made it all seem unimportant, and showed you, in the silent scornful way in which he held his head and narrowed his eyes, that you, his audience, had nothing to recommend yourself because you had, until he taught you better, thought too much of what was insignificant. It was right there, on his lips, the private withering contempt, the clinging bitterness that is always there, just below the surface, in everything the comic poet says or writes.

"Aspasia, wife of Pericles," he began in a deep, practiced voice, "you are accused of impiety, of not believing in the gods. And, as a second, separate offense against the laws of the city, of procuring women, of bringing into your house freeborn women for the use of your husband, Pericles!"

It was curious the way the crowd reacted. The only response elicited by the charge of impiety was a silence that seemed to deepen, become almost profound; what you might expect when an accusation went to the very being of the city. The charge of procuring women for Pericles brought a different response altogether: gross, derisive laughter from part of the crowd; but from a different part, the friends and allies of Pericles, a low rumble of discontent, a warning that patience might be running out, that there were those who would not forget what happened here today. You could almost smell the danger, the sense that it would not take much – a single gesture, one ill-chosen word – to start the violence.

"I understand what you have charged me with," said Aspasia, slowly getting to her feet. A faint smile creased the corners of her mouth. "And I also notice what you have not charged me with."

Hermippus had been about to throw back in her face some no doubt well-rehearsed remark, but this last and unexpected observation caused him some confusion.

"You haven't charged me with indulging Pericles in what, as we all know, would be your own besetting sin. I haven't been charged with procuring for the use of my husband any boys!"

The round fat face of the comic poet turned crimson. He stamped his foot in rage.

"Silence, woman! You're the one accused, no other."

"Accused of things that cannot be proven by a proven pederast!"

How many hours, how many days, must he have spent getting ready for this; how much time thinking through, memorizing, all his lines, all the wit-filled sayings, all the sharp-edged remarks; and now, barely finished with a statement of the charges, an object of ridicule to the crowd. I glanced at Socrates to see his reaction, but there was no change in his expression, nothing that would give away his thought. He stood there, watching with those strange eyes of his, penetrating every secret, but impenetrable themselves. There was nothing to show it, but I felt that he enjoyed it, this war of words that Aspasia seemed determined now to fight.

"Cannot be proved? Is that what you have to say in your defense? Not even a denial?" asked Hermippus with hatred in his eyes. "But you demand proof. We have all the proof we need."

He walked to the front of the stage where someone handed him a sheet of paper which he immediately flourished in the air as if it were a signed confession to every crime anyone could ever possibly commit.

"This is a list of names: women, freeborn women – "

"As opposed to the slaves, or the prostitutes in the streets you and your friends like to buy; the only kind of women you have ever known or ever had?"

His jaw clenched hard; his gaze became murderous and intense. " – freeborn women, women who are kept by you; women who live – "

"Let me see it!" she demanded; and such was the authority with which she said it, that Hermippus immediately complied. "Yes, I admit it; I know them all. And yes, they live under my protection. They provide companionship – intelligent conversation – to some of those who do me the honor of visiting my house."

"Who do you the honor …!" sputtered Hermippus with indignation. "So it isn't just Pericles who – ?"

"Pericles? Oh, no; he's almost never there. He has too much to do, looking out for the city, making Athens great. No, Pericles doesn't have the time, and what time he has," she added with a significant look, "he likes to spend with me. No, that is where you are wrong; that is where you have brought the wrong charge. I do not provide women – freeborn or otherwise – for Pericles; I do not provide them for anyone for immoral purposes. I provide – if you want to call it that – women of taste and intelligence, the way any matchmaker does. I introduce them to those men with whom I think they have most in common. There was one, though, who, as it turned out, though really quite nice was not as intelligent as the others. I think you know her. For a while at least, if I'm not mistaken, she became the mistress of the man whose bidding you so often do: Cleon, the man behind what you are trying to do today. They seemed to me a perfect match: a vacant face and an empty brain! There is an irony in this, don't you think," she shouted as Hermippus tried to interrupt. "That Cleon has you charge me with what some might call the skin trade, Cleon who made his fortune trading in skins!"

There were noise and bedlam everywhere, the crowd now become a laughing, jeering mob; even those come to condemn her ready to applaud the way she had put her accuser on the defense. Appalled at the stunning incompetence of Hermippus, Cleon took the stage himself.

"This is not some living room proceeding," he began in that scratchy voice of his, a voice that when he got angry became a high-pitched whine. "This is not some little dinner table conversation in which everyone – or I should say everyone in the circle in which the defendant lives her life of privilege – tries to show how smart and witty they are; one of those late night parties in which a bunch of drunken revelers entertain themselves with the sound of their own voices. This is a public court, a trial: judgment by the people whether someone has violated the laws that all of us have sworn oaths to obey.

"The defendant may joke about it, if she wishes; but there are some of us who believe that what we owe the gods is no laughing matter. She can, if she wishes, dismiss the charges brought against her as having no importance; but there are some of us who still believe that there is nothing more important to the future of our city – whether we continue to prosper, whether we continue to be the leading power in Greece and in the world – than the favor of the gods, and that nothing is more certain to endanger that than the impiety and the blatant immorality of which the defendant stands accused!

"She says there is no proof, but has already, in her scornful way, admitted it; admitted it without embarrassment or even reluctance, but with the kind of pride that tells you all you need to know about whether the heart that beats inside her is guilty or innocent. She admits – She announced it right here! – that she brings women, freeborn women, into her house. Some of them even live there, under her 'protection.' And what do these women do? – They're not there for her husband! No, he has too much else to do," cried Cleon with a garish, mocking grin. "No, they aren't there for her husband; they're there for other men, men who – What was it she said? – 'honor her with visiting her house'! And I was one of them. Well, if we are to include everyone who has ever been the guest of our exalted leader, the great Pericles, I am not sure I can think of anyone whose name would be left out. She says she supplies women for companionship, for 'intelligent conversation.' She says a great many things, all of them lies! She may pimp as many women as she likes; she may use them to gain the political support of whatever men among us are too weak to know their own duty, but I defy her to produce one witness who ever saw me do something I should not have done; one witness who can say something more substantial than this kind of empty slander with which she has, instead of a defense, answered the charges brought against her!"

I had thought Cleon an evil, small-minded man, incapable of arousing any emotion except the contempt of anyone with a minimum of intelligence. This was my mistake, not because I was wrong in that judgment but because it made me underestimate his abilities. What I had thought his weakness – the petty jealousies, the quick resentments – were, as it turned out, the source of his strength. He could appeal to the worst instincts of the crowd because those instincts were the only ones he had. There was nothing artificial, nothing contrived or rehearsed, in the things he said or in the way he said them. He might lie about the facts, twist them to his own advantage, but there was no dissembling in what he felt; the anger, the hatred, the rage – all of it was real.

I began to better understand what Socrates had said, that judgment I had thought so unfair, what Pericles had done, or rather failed to do, when he came to power. He had made the city greater than it had been before, but far from making the Athenians feel more modest in the light of that achievement, or more dependent on the wisdom of those who ruled them, they had come to believe that what had been done was proof of their own greatness. The crowd had become the ruling power, determined to bring down to their own level anyone who claimed to lead them.

Cleon worked on their envy and resentment, their feeling that the things they held sacred, the things they believed in, were objects of derision for those who claimed to want what was best for them but were only interested in themselves.

"They tell you one thing in their speeches," he insisted, his eyes become demonic in all the frustration of his rage; "they tell you what they think you want to hear, and then laugh at you behind your backs. They pray with you in public, raise their prayers to the gods, and then, safe behind the walls of their estates, talk as if the gods were nothing more than stories told to keep the rest of us from asking why they have so much and the rest of us so little, why we do all the work and they take all the credit!"

It was demagoguery, but there would not be that word if it did not point to something that had power. By the time he was finished, Cleon had the crowd demanding more than just conviction; driven crazy by what they had heard, they wanted blood. Aspasia challenged them to take it. Rising from the chair where she had waited without expression during Cleon's long harangue, she smiled and spread her arms wide open.

"Why not just proceed to execution; have Cleon stab me in the breast – why bother with anything irrelevant like a trial?"

"Yes, do it!" shouted several different voices, as hundreds more shouted their agreement. "Send her off to Hades where she can beg forgiveness of the gods!"

"Yes, but instead of forgiveness, I'll give thanks: first of all for saving me from having to listen anymore to the cruel stupidities of men like Cleon; but most of all to Hermes, that best, most gracious of the gods," said Aspasia, her voice growing quiet as the noise around her diminished and finally stopped. "Hermes who, after Zeus blessed us, Pericles and I, with our child, I pray to every night, giving thanks for what he did; Hermes, to whom, like most of you, we have dedicated a statue, a shrine, that stands guard over our home and happiness. And though it is true, as our friend Cleon has reminded us, that I was not born here; though it is true, as Cleon says – as if that fact is something of which I am to blame – that I live here only by the leave of the city; that also means that I can claim to worship the gods of the city, not by the accident of birth, like Cleon, but of my own volition.

"Despite what Cleon says, despite what they accuse me of – this charge of impiety they have invented – I not only believe in the gods, I know the gods are all-powerful. Do I need to remind you – someone should perhaps remind Cleon – of what we learn from Homer: how Hermes rescued Odysseus by showing him an herb that would protect him and his followers from the evil plans of Circe. And how would this be possible if the gods were not omnipotent, capable of doing everything, because, as Odysseus learned, Hermes and the other gods know the natures of all the things that are. You ask, do I believe in the gods? – You might as well ask if I believe that we can know anything, or in the life of my own child!"

There are few things that become as quiet as a great crowd

reduced to silence. No one said anything; no one stirred. An eagle's screech, as it tumbled down the sky, far away in the distance, made the stillness even more profound. Then, from just off stage, came the sounds of someone coming closer and a moment later Pericles appeared. He stood next to Aspasia, and with his arm around her shoulder appealed for her acquittal and her release. If he had ever done anything for Athens, he said, he wanted Athens to do this for him, to give him back the woman he loved and could not live without. And for the first time that anyone could remember, Pericles, the great Pericles, Pericles who was always in command of himself, shed tears.

I shed some myself as the jury, with a spontaneity that surprised everyone, voted acquittal by acclamation. Socrates, standing next to me, gave me a strange, ironic look.

"What she said about the gods, that they can do anything, that they are omnipotent because they know the nature of all things, means that they are not omnipotent at all. They know the natures of things which are wholly independent of them. The natures of things are immutable; there is nothing the gods can do to change them." His eyes danced delighted with what in that remarkable mind of his he had seen. "Do you think that Aspasia did not know that; that she did not know that the defense of her belief contained within it a more powerful attack on that belief than anything Cleon or the others could have done? But look, our friend Alcibiades is coming and he seems for some reason quite upset."

And it was true. Alcibiades was storming through the crowd, coming toward us, grim-faced with anger.

"They'll come after him directly now," he said, his voice hushed and strained. "They have to; there is no one left. And now, after what he had to do – show himself that vulnerable – he's weaker than he's ever been. And when they do, when Pericles is the one facing charges, there won't be anyone who will cry for him, no one whose tears can move the crowd. Something has to be done and someone has to do it."

I did not doubt who he had in mind, but what he planned to do, that I did not know; not at first, not until I understood all the other things that were going on, all the other reasons why Athens had to go to war.

CHAPTER THIRTEEN

My hand, as I begin to write this, begins to shake, perhaps because of age and infirmity, but more likely because of the memory of what I now have to record. The war came, the longest war there ever was, the war that killed, that murdered, everyone I loved; the war that destroyed what Athens was, the war that changed the world in ways that only someone in the future can ever know. No one knew how many years the war would last, or how much blood and treasure would be spent; no one knew how many lives would be lost, how many women would become widows, how many children would never know their fathers; but everyone knew that it was coming, that war had become inevitable. That did not mean that Pericles was eager to have it start.

"Are they crazy?" he asked, shaking his head. Aspasia looked up from the table in the kitchen where she had been talking to me. Pericles, who had just come across the courtyard from his study on the other side, was standing in the open doorway. "They decide they have to say something, and they say this! – That it is a rule of nature, a kind of requirement, that the strong rule the weaker and that everyone should be grateful because ...!" He shook his head again, a look of baffled indignation on his face. "It's impossible – we're impossible! The mindless arrogance of it, this false pride of ours that isn't content with what we have, but has to make sure everyone knows we have it; this hubris, this ... this insanity!"

"What has happened?" asked Aspasia calmly, as she got up from the table and went over to him. "Who decided they had to say something? What happened that makes whoever they are seem insane?"

He turned to her with a look of recognition that passes only between two people who have more than perfect love, perfect trust. Brushing a strand of hair from her forehead, he smiled gently.

"I'll tell you everything, what has happened, why I reacted the way I did."

He sat at the table while Aspasia brought wine.

"How are you, Helen?" he asked, when he noticed I was there. "The report you gave me about Potidaea – it was as if I were seeing everything myself. I wish you had been in Sparta, observing this other business."

"Start from the beginning," advised Aspasia, charming him into willing submission with her gentle, teasing laughter.

"From the beginning. We have Potidaea in a state of siege. The Corinthians are afraid of what may happen. They asked for a meeting with their allies at Sparta. They all had a chance to speak, to complain about the way they had been treated by us. The delegates from Megara insisted that we had excluded them not only from all the ports in our empire but from our own market here in Athens. But no one complained more than the Corinthians," he said, as a thin smile crossed his mouth. "They complained about the Spartans, blaming them for not doing anything to stop us from doing what we have done."

Pericles glanced at the scroll of paper he had brought with him from his study. The smile on his mouth became shrewd and calculating.

"It was the Spartans who 'allowed the Athenians to fortify their city and build the Long Walls after the Persian war;' the Spartans who failed to understand what sort of people these Athenians are, how 'an Athenian is always an innovator, quick to form a resolution and quick at carrying it out.'" Pericles picked up the scroll and began to read. "'You, on the other hand, are good at keeping things as they are; you never originate an idea, and your action tends to stop short of its aim.'"

His eyes raced ahead to the next assertion he wanted to read out loud. He started, but then stopped and looked at both of us.

"In matters that affect them directly, the Corinthians never hesitate to lie; but in what they say about us, on the difference between the way we do things and the Spartans, I do not find anything with which I disagree. You need to hear this in full.

"'While you are hanging back, they never hesitate; while you stay at home, they are always going places; for they think that the farther they go the more they will get, while you think that any movement will endanger what you have already. If they win a victory, they follow it up at once, and if they suffer a defeat, they scarcely fall back at all. As for their bodies, they regard them as expendable for their city's sake, as though they were not their own; but each man cultivates his own intelligence, again with a view of doing something notable for his city. If they aim at something and do not get it, they think that they have been deprived of what belonged to them already; but if their enterprise is successful, they regard it as nothing compared to what they will do next. Suppose they fail in some undertaking; they make good the loss immediately by setting their hopes in some other direction. Of them alone it may be said that they possess a thing almost as soon as they have begun to desire it, so quickly with them does action follow upon decision. And so they go on, working away in hardship and danger all the days of their lives, seldom enjoying their possessions because they are always adding to them. Their view of a holiday is to do what needs doing; they prefer hardship and activity to peace and quiet. In a word, they are by nature incapable of either living a quiet life themselves or allowing anyone else to do so.'"

Pericles put down the scroll and looked at Aspasia.

"That is rather well put, isn't it? Athens, restless and ambitious, daring and adventurous, eager for what it does not have, always wanting more; Sparta, slow and cautious, afraid of change. Motion and rest, those two conditions, the way they interact, explain, or at least helps us understand, the world we live in. Sparta, slow to move, wants nothing to change, and because of that has lasted now four hundred years, the oldest Greek regime, their simple militant equality the guarantee against disorder. Athens, never satisfied, always searching for new sources of wealth and power; willing, as we did in the war against the Persians, to abandon everything – our country, our homes – to save the freedom which allows us to live the way we want; driven by our fear of living under the control of others – the Persians, then the Spartans – to establish an empire and keep increasing it, and driven now, for the same reason, to go to war. It is the eternal, universal conflict between motion and rest, the principles of nature that form the basis of the human condition."

Raising the wine cup Aspasia had placed on the table in front of him, Pericles admired the elegant shape and the colorful painting of a scene from Homer, a warrior with his spear and shield taking leave of his young wife and child.

"We make beautiful things out of the memories of war and slaughter. Or, rather, out of the tragic beauty of what men and women feel when the only thought is victory and what victory will achieve, before anyone has had to read the list of the wounded and the dead."

The thought seemed to deepen his expression and increase the worry in his eyes. He drank from the cup, but slowly and with reluctance, as if the taste of what he liked had become a guilty pleasure, a form of self-indulgence that by suggesting better times betrayed an unwillingness to face directly what was coming, a change bigger than anything anyone had ever known.

"There might still be a chance," he mused, stroking his chin. Then, remembering why he had been so agitated before, he tapped the side of his head twice with his finger as if he blamed himself for what had happened. "Someone should have told them – I should have made it clear – that when we send anyone on state business – in this case to discuss certain commercial questions – they are expected to restrict themselves to what they are there to do. So what happens instead? They are sitting there, spectators, listening to what the Corinthians are saying in the assembly and decide they have to say something in reply, that they have to show the world that the Corinthians are wrong."

A look of disgust swept across his mouth. Then, with a helpless laugh, he shrugged his shoulders as if to underscore the futility of trying to teach prudence to people who did not know the meaning of the word.

"They were Athenians – of course they had to speak!"

Pericles lifted the cup and studied it again, this time with a calmer, more balanced gaze, seeing, as it were, both sides of what had gone into its production: the ancient war between the Trojans and the Greeks, and the sheer genius of an artist who had captured in his mind's eye the nobility, which is to say the beauty, of the cause, and had then, with the talent of his hand, given a picture of what he had seen. It seemed to teach a lesson, that look I saw, that part, and no unimportant one, of what it means to be a human being is the capacity to grasp the deeper, unchanging meaning in the motion that swirls all around us, even, or perhaps especially, in that awful motion known as war.

"What did they say?" asked Aspasia. "How much harm did they do?"

"Harm?" Pericles tilted his head to the side, a rueful, thoughtful smile on his lips. "They told the truth, or at least one version of it. How much more harmful could it have been?"

"As bad as that?" she asked, with a wistful smile that for a moment forced from his mind every thought except the one he had of her.

"Yes, as bad as that. They started out well enough, saying that they were not going to respond to any of the specific charges that had been made against Athens, that they only wished to make a general statement. As I say, they started out well enough; and it was all right – it did no harm – to remind the Spartans and the others what we did first at Marathon, and then, when the Persians came a second time, how we left the city, took to our ships, and joined in the battle at Salamis, and in that way stopped the Persians from invading the Peloponnesus and destroying all their cities; reminding them how our navy saved Hellas, how two-thirds of the four hundred ships that fought and defeated the Persians were ours, and that the commander was Themistocles, an Athenian. It probably did no harm to remind the Spartans and the others that the empire we have did not come through force, that our allies came to us of their own accord at a time when the Spartans were unwilling to fight beyond the necessities of their own defense and we were left to remove the Persians as a threat. All of that was all right. It was when they moved from how we came to have an empire to whether we should keep it that they lost their senses and, in the eyes of those who believe that injustice never goes unpunished, lost the favor of the gods."

Pericles reached for the scroll he had moments earlier put aside.

"Here is what they had to say, a defense that is not just unconvincing but a provocation:

"'We have done nothing extraordinary, nothing contrary to human nature in accepting an empire when it was offered to us and then in refusing to give it up. Three very powerful motives prevent us from doing so – security, honor, and self-interest. And we were not the first to act in this way. Far from it. It has always been the rule that the weak should be subject to the strong; and besides, we consider that we are worthy of our power.'"

Pericles slammed his hand on the table. "'The weak should be subject to the strong!' What purpose served by that – except to make them even more determined to combine their strength?" His eyes darted all around, as if searching for a point of sanity in a world gone mad; and then, coming back to Aspasia and me, shone with the triumph of a sarcasm proved right. "And then they tell these delegates from all these hostile cities that they should be grateful that we have not used the power of the stronger in all the ways we could have!

"'... we consider that we are worthy of our power. Up till the present moment you, too, used to think that we were, but now, after calculating your own interest, you are beginning to talk in terms of right and wrong. Considerations of this kind have never yet turned people aside from the opportunities of aggrandizement offered by superior strength. Those who really deserve praise are people who, while human enough to enjoy power, nevertheless pay more attention to justice than they were compelled to do by their situation.'

"They warned of the danger of going to war, of how it was impossible to predict what would happen once war started; they urged the Spartans not to break the peace and to settle through arbitration any differences that still remained between us. But what they had said about our power, how they should all be grateful for the restraint with which we used it – the insistence that justice was nothing more than the last refuge of the weak – left an impression that nothing could efface. Archidamus, the Spartan king, a man of moderation and intelligence, tried to stop it, this rush to war, warning the Spartans that they needed more time, that they were not ready, that they did not understand what they were getting into, that, in his words, 'it is impossible to calculate accurately events that are determined by chance.' His words had no effect. The vote to go to war was not even close."

And so it started. Sparta and its allies, all those cities like Corinth and Megara with their anger and their grievances, had decided that war was imperative, that they had to stop Athens before Athens, with its growing power, became unstoppable. But the Spartans needed time to prepare, and they also wanted to make the war seem the fault of Athens. Insisting first on one demand then another, they announced finally that if only Athens would change its attitude toward Megara and allow them entry to all the ports under their control, allow them access to the market in Athens, all their other differences could be settled peaceably. Finally, the Spartans came, three chosen representatives, and with laconic brevity announced that, "Sparta wants peace. Peace is still possible if you will give the Hellenes their freedom."

This from the Spartans, who had kept their own peace on the slavery of thousands of Helots whose territory they had taken hundreds of years before. Pericles would have none of it.

"Athenians," he began in a speech he gave in the assembly called to debate the question; "my views are the same as they have always been: I am against making any concessions to the Peloponnesians, even though I am aware that the enthusiastic state of mind in which people are persuaded to enter upon a war is not retained when it comes to action, and that people's minds are altered by the course of events. I call upon those of you who are persuaded by my words," he went on, driving home the point, "to give your full support to these resolutions we are making all together, and to abide by them even if in some respect or other we find ourselves in difficulty; for, unless you do so, you will be able to claim no credit for intelligence when things go well with us."

Standing at the back of the assembly, watching the crowd's reaction – a crowd that was more than twenty, and may have been as large, as thirty thousand – I was caught by how his voice carried, as if instead of speaking down below from the stage of the amphitheater, he was somewhere just a few rows ahead, speaking in the normal tones of conversation. He held his audience that close; everyone bent forward, listening carefully to every word.

"Let none of you think that we should be going to war for a trifle if we refuse to revoke the Megarian Decree." His eyes narrowed into a piercing stare, and his shoulders hunched forward as he jabbed his finger in the air. "If you give in, you will immediately be confronted with some other greater demand, since they will think that you only gave way on this point through fear."

Others might at this point have tried to work the crowd into a fury, appealing to the bloodlust that drives men mad with thoughts of violence; Pericles insisted they reason through it, try to understand where their advantage lie, how they could achieve victory and not suffer defeat. The Spartans lacked financial resources; they and their allies – different nations with different interests – had no central authority to make decisions; and, most important of all, they did not have a navy. They could do harm to Athens by land, but they could do nothing to prevent Athens retaliating by sea. Moreover, Athens knew how to fight on land.

"We have acquired more experience of land fighting through our naval operations than they have of sea fighting through their operations on land. And as for seamanship, they will find that a difficult lesson to learn. You yourselves have been studying it ever since the end of the Persian wars, and have still not entirely mastered the subject. How, then, can it be supposed that they could ever make such progress? It is not something that can be picked up and studied in one's spare time; indeed it allows one no spare time for anything else."

Pericles was emphatic: Nothing was as important as naval supremacy, that and understanding how to use it. It was extraordinary how well he could explain things, how clearly he could see what had to be done.

"Look at it this way," he said with the patience of a teacher. "Suppose we were an island, would we not be absolutely secure from attack? We must try to think of ourselves as islanders, willing to abandon our land and our houses and safeguard the city and the sea. We must not, through anger at losing lands and homes, join battle with the greatly superior forces of the Peloponnesians. If we won a victory, we should still have to fight them again in the same numbers, and if we suffered a defeat, our allies, on whom our strength depends, would immediately revolt, knowing that we did not have sufficient troops to send against them."

Pausing, he looked around, deciding, as it seemed, whether to say what he really thought, whether this vast audience had the courage and the force of will to undertake the kind of sacrifice on which their survival might depend.

"We should not lament the loss of our houses or our land; but the loss of men's lives. Men come first; everything else is the result of what they do. And if I thought I could persuade you to do it," he exclaimed in words meant to challenge not just their revolve but their attachment to their city, the memory of their fathers and what their fathers had done, "I would urge you to go out and destroy your property with your own hands and show the Peloponnesians that it is not for the sake of this that you are likely to give in to them."

I shudder now when I recall what he said next, the words, the warning that, quite without his knowing, became a prophecy of doom, the urgent need for restraint by a people who knew only deeds of daring. One sentence, the next sentence he spoke, told the whole history of a war that had not yet started.

"I could give you many other reasons why you should feel confident in ultimate victory, if only you will make up your minds not to add to your empire while the war is in progress, and not to go out of your way to involve yourselves in new perils."

I wonder now, looking back, if anyone paid attention; whether the advice that would turn out to have been so prescient and, because of the failure to follow it, productive of more evil than even Pericles could have imagined, was remembered five minutes after it was uttered. There were nearly thirty thousand people listening as intently as any audience ever did, but they were there to decide on war. They listened, and they heard, but they heard what they wanted, that the war could be won, that they were better than their adversaries, that they had more daring and more courage, that they controlled the sea with their navy and could strike anywhere at will. For all his talk of caution and restraint, the message the Athenians wanted to hear was that if war was necessary, victory was not only inevitable but would be complete. They cheered him, all thirty thousand, when he reminded them of their greatness and what they owed to those who had made the city the empire that it was.

"This war is being forced upon us. The more readily we accept the challenge the less eager to attack us will our opponents be. We must realize, too, that, both for cities and for individuals, it is from the greatest dangers that the greatest glory is to be won. When our fathers stood against the Persians they had no such resources as we have now; indeed, they abandoned even what they had, and then it was by wisdom rather than by good fortune, by daring rather than by material power, that they drove back the foreign invader and made our city what it is today. We must live up to the standard they set; we must resist our enemies in any and every way, and try to leave to those who come after us an Athens that is as great as ever."

The Athenians did not destroy their own land and houses as Pericles would have had them do, what he knew he could not persuade them to do, but he did convince them to bring their wives and children, as well as all their moveable goods, out of the country and into the city. The sheep and cattle, the livestock from their farms, were sent north to Euobea and the islands close to the coast. The towns and villages of Attica, where most of the Athenians lived, might be ravaged by the Peloponnesians, but the city would be protected by twenty nine thousand hoplites drawn from the oldest and the youngest citizens in the army together with qualified resident aliens. This was a force more than adequate to defend the wall of Phalerum which ran four miles from the sea, the nearly five mile wall that surrounded the city, and the Long Walls that extended four and a half miles to the harbor at Piraeus. In addition to all this, there was another seven and a half miles of fortifications surrounding the harbor, half of which was guarded. So long as Athens had a navy, the city was impregnable.

But Athens was now crowded as it had never been before, people everywhere, living in places no one was supposed to live, anywhere they could find space. A few of those who moved in from the country had houses of their own, and there were others who had friends or relatives with whom they could stay, but most of those who came had to find shelter wherever they could, whether camped in vacant fields where nothing yet had been built or in the public shrines and temples in which, other than the Acropolis, it was not prohibited. Every part of the city was affected, every neighborhood was changed, but nowhere was there more crowding than Piraeus where I lived. It became the home to a teeming mass of refugees, the Long Walls a new kind of tenement where thousand of families now slept and cooked their meals, and prayed the gods that the war would not last more than one season.

The market where I went several times each week, the covered stalls where I bantered with the vendors about the price and quality of what they sold, the vendors with their lying eyes that laughed as their practiced mouths rattled off the endless virtues of their goods, the market where I could wander unmolested in the morning sun, became overnight a place to be avoided. The lines were a labyrinth without start or finish, the noise of shouted voices a strident chorus of complaint, the pushing and shoving, the hot impatience, the angry swearing at rising prices, had changed everyday life out of all recognition.

"It isn't the crowding; it's the uncertainty about what is going to happen."

I was standing at the corner, a block from my house, across the street from the market. Distracted by all the movement, the surging bustle of the crowd, I had not noticed Alcibiades come up next to me. I tried to hide both my surprise and my pleasure.

"What are you doing here? Took pity on how common people have to live, come to confer a benefit on we poor mortals by your presence? Decided that ...?"

He was laughing at me, shaking his head against the pure imposture of my mantic indictment of his reputation. He took me by the hand and, still laughing, led me into the marketplace across the street.

It was astonishing, the effect he had, the way everything seemed to come to a stop when he suddenly appeared. I had seen it before, on other days, when we tried to go somewhere together. There was a kind of magic about it, as if some god, Hermes, quick as thought, whispered news of his coming, causing heads to turn before eyes had seen him. The noise, the bedlam, the crowded, shouted voices, lost their capacity for complaint and changed into a single instant observation: Alcibiades was there. He did not once change his step, did not once even by an inch change his direction; a path opened in front of us and we walked a gauntlet of a thousand eager eyes. The shadowed light turned the golden, ribboned hair that fell over his shoulders a shade more bronze than yellow. An easy smile of nonchalance played effortlessly on his handsome mouth. He bought two oranges and when the peddler gestured that payment was not necessary, gave him twice the normal price.

We emerged on the other side of the market like two swimmers from the sea; the crowd, like the water, closed behind us and for a few moments we were finally all alone. He found a stone bench on the palisade that overlooked the harbor and peeled me an orange. He took a boyish pride in how he did it, cutting his way in with his thumb and then, with a constant, twisting motion of his finger, taking off the peel in a single, unbroken spiral, so that when he had finished he could make a show.

"Here are two oranges instead of one; one that has everything you need," he said as he handed me the orange's naked juicy body. "And this one," he added, holding up for closer inspection the peel cupped into a hollow sphere. "The one that, seeing it, is the one everyone wants." A strange, cryptic glance, deep and unearthly, seemed to take possession of his eyes, reminding him of some uncertainty, some doubt about his fate. "They see me, they hear me; they think they know me." He turned to look at me, his gaze now much softer. "And I know they don't, but I still want their applause and their approval. There is something wrong with that, isn't there?"

He watched while I ate two pieces of the orange. I had not eaten anything all morning and the blood orange, brought from far away in Sicily, tasted good.

"We should go. There is something I have to do, something you should see."

"You didn't come to see me?"

"I come to see you almost every day. You saved my life; you helped take care of me when I was recovering from my wounds. You ..."

"You come to see me out of gratitude?" I asked more sharply than I intended. It wounded me to think that; it hurt even more to know that it was not that at all. He still thought – he would always think – that he had taken me that night against my will, that my desire had been nothing like as furious as his own. I had cried like a girl, and he could only think that it was because I was not yet a woman.

"I didn't save your life; Socrates did that. And if I helped a little while you recovered," I added with pretended pride, "I learned a little of the physician's art in the years I lived as the ward of Empedocles in Agrigento."

"Your face, the way you look, was all the medicine I needed," he said with such ardent and unexpected kindness that I had to look away.

"Where is it you want to go? What is it you think I should see?" I asked as I got to my feet and began to dry on the folds of my silk robe my fingers, still wet from the orange I had eaten.

"I want you to see why everyone is angry at Pericles, and what we're going to do about it."

"They're angry at Pericles because the Spartans are in Attica, at Acharnae, only seven miles from Athens, and he refuses to fight."

"Yes, but come and see for yourself," said Alcibiades with a grim, determined look.

We went back to where I had met him, but not the way we had come, through the marketplace full of noise and people, but through some side streets where, moving quickly, we passed unnoticed. He had come on horseback and had for some reason brought his armor, his sword and shield, which lay against the wall where the horse had been tied. The shield was new, richly gilded and instead of the ensigns found on the shields of other Athenians had one of his own design, a cupid holding a thunderbolt in his hand, an announcement, as if one were needed, that Alcibiades was protected both by Eros and the force of his own power.

He caught me looking. His eyes flashed with a kind of triumph, the shared knowledge of a secret, which then changed into something close to irony.

"It is a way to write the story of the future. Tell everyone what is going to happen, and then, when everyone believes it – it will!"

"Why are you …?" I asked as he buckled the bronze greaves on his lower legs and hoisted the shield onto his arm.

"You'll see," he replied, as he mounted the horse. He gave me his hand and swung me up behind him.

We rode to the city, out to the walls that looked west to Attica and Acharnae. Gathered together just inside the gate, forty other men on horses were waiting for Alcibiades to join them. The wall was crowded with spectators, hundreds, perhaps thousands, come to watch in angry disbelief as the Spartans methodically ravished Attica, burning houses, destroying orchards, trampling under the crops that had been planted months before and would now lie rotting in the summer heat. I stood with the others, looking out across the plains to Acharnae and the swift-paced devastation, all around me cries of anguish, cries of rage, oaths of vengeance sworn to heaven, oaths of hatred sworn to Hades. Eager to draw the Athenians into a pitched battle, to fight on land with their superior numbers, a detachment of Spartan cavalry rode close enough to shout with brazen insult the scorn they felt for walled up cowards who refused even to go to the protection of their own homes.

They were close enough to see their faces, twisted in derision; close enough to see the contempt in their narrowed eyes; close enough for the dust from the hooves of their horses to fill the nostrils of those of us who stood watching in the shadow of the rising sun. I understood at once what was going to happen; the only question was when. How long would Alcibiades wait, how long before the gate would open and this raucous band of Spartans who did not expect to fight at all would suddenly be attacked?

I looked down inside and saw Alcibiades struggling with the reins of a horse that had thrown its rider. Dazed and angry, the man got to his feet, grabbed the reins away from Alcibiades and began to strike the horse with his fist. The horse circled around, pulling harder to get free; the man, his face red with rage, beat it again with his fist and, when that did not work, reached for his sword, ready, as it appeared, to cut the animal's throat if that was the only way to establish his own idiotic control. Before I knew what I was doing, I was off the wall, down on the ground, and then, as Alcibiades grabbed the reins away, on the back of the horse and suddenly flying ahead of all the others out the wooden gate that had finally been shoved open.

Everything went too fast, there was no time to think, no time to do anything but react and let my instincts take over. As I shot through the gate I reached for the spear of a startled guard who had been standing sentry just inside. The horse, which one moment had been wild and uncontrollable, now went straight as an arrow, devoted to my touch. The Spartans, when they finally realized that the gate had been open and someone was bearing down on them, a rider leading an armed force more than equal to their own, lost at first all composure. Separated as they were one from the other, they were not sure what to do, whether to turn and run or stand and fight and take their chances. That instant of indecision saved me. I was moving so fast, that it was only at the last second that the mounted Spartan right in front of me realized that he was only threatened by a woman. The laughter in his eyes moved quickly to his mouth, laughter stopped by the spear point that shattered his teeth in pieces and, full of blood and brains, burst through the back of his splintered skull. Blood shot through his nose and ears; his eyes rolled back, all white and then all black as the light left him forever and he went down to the darkness that never changes.

The head of my horse made a sudden, abrupt movement back and I nearly fell as he jolted to a stop.

"Get back!" cried Alcibiades, slapping the hindquarters of the horse. "Get back inside the walls!"

And then, with a shout of triumph, he led the attack.

The Spartans were routed, a dozen dead left on the field, but Athens, though it continued to control the sea, was still confined within its walls on land and, with the exception of an occasional small battle in front of the city, could only watch as Attica was destroyed. I had now killed two men in battle, but each time I watched what the Spartans did, how they burned and pillaged what had been built by generations of hard labor, my only regret was that I had not killed more.

The Athenians stayed within their walls while the Spartans destroyed the land and the houses abandoned in Attica, but when the Spartans finally left the entire Athenian army joined forces with the fleet of a hundred ships that had done damage to some of the Peloponnesian cities and launched an attack on Megara. This was no small venture. It was designed to show that not only did Athens control the sea, but that Athens could fight on land. With more than ten thousand hoplites drawn from the citizens, and at least another three thousand from the population of resident aliens, it was the largest army Athens had ever sent into the field. Like the Spartans in Attica, they met little resistance and were content to ravage the land. There were other actions, other efforts to achieve advantage, but at the end of the summer the situation was essentially unchanged from what it had been at the beginning: Athens would not fight Sparta on land, and Sparta could not fight Athens at sea.

"This war may last forever," remarked Alcibiades with a rueful expression. "Last forever, if we go on like this, staying within the limits of what we have, instead of changing the aim of what we are fighting for."

"Change the policy, go against the advice of Pericles and try to expand the empire, and that way expand the war?"

We were walking together, on our way to the ceremony to commemorate the sacrifices of those who had fallen in this, the first year of the war. The funeral took place in a public burial ground in the most beautiful part of Athens outside the city walls. It was warm and pleasant, as if instead of winter, autumn was just beginning. The road was filled with people, as far as the eye could see, an endless procession, the whole city come to gather around the graves of the dead and listen as someone chosen for his great gifts and reputation gives a speech to praise the fallen and what they did. It was an ancient custom which, like all such customs, bound the city to its past and by doing that promised that while the lives of its citizens were mortal, the city itself, the city that gave those lives their meaning, would never die. The funeral oration was to be given, as only seemed appropriate, by Pericles himself.

"We can't survive that way. We're not like the Spartans who want to live always in the same orbit, where nothing ever changes. We have to keep growing, keeping making new acquisitions, becoming larger and more powerful, or we'll perish. And besides," he added with a sharp, sideways glance, "we're better than anyone else, and the better always rules the worse." He caught the reaction in my eyes before I knew I had one. "You doubt that? – You think that every city, every nation, is the equal of the others? You think there is no difference between the way of life of the Spartans – taught from birth to live like soldiers in camp – and the life we live here? No difference between the life that we are free to live and under the Persian king, where the king alone is the only one not a slave? Where else besides Athens would you ever find someone like Socrates? The Spartans would not allow him to speak; the Persians would not allow him to live."

"How long do you think the Athenians would allow him to live if someone like Cleon ever came to power?" I asked with a sharpness of my own.

"Not as long as I'm in a position to do anything about it," said

Alcibiades with a determined look that made his still youthful face seem even younger.

"Do you know why you are so drawn to him?"

"Why I'm so ...?" He stopped walking and then stepped off the road to let others pass. "You ask that? You've spent time with him; you've talked to him, listened to him. How could anyone not be drawn to him?"

"That's no answer. What do you see in him you don't see in yourself?"

The question seemed to take him by surprise; or rather, not the question, but the need to answer it, answer it out loud, tell it to another human being when the answer cannot be avoided, put aside, the way we do with questions we only have to ask ourselves. He seemed almost embarrassed.

"Because he makes me realize just how imperfect I really am; because he makes me see that what I want – what I have to have – is nothing like as important as what the world thinks; that unlike his, my life will always be insufficient. He makes me see that, glimpse it for a moment, but then, when I'm left alone, when I am with other people, I go back to what I am. The truth is that, much as I love him, I sometimes hate him for that."

I smiled at Alcibiades. I knew what he was trying to say. He could not see what Socrates could see – none of us could do that – but he could see enough to know that what Socrates could see was the only thing worth seeing, the only thing that was real. It made him a little crazy, that knowledge that there was something he might not be able to do, something he might not be able to conquer; something that, no matter how much he wanted it and loved it, might not love him back. It was not hard to understand what they had in common, and how that was at the same time the great difference between them. They both wanted everything, all of it. Socrates wanted the knowledge of the whole, what everything meant; Alcibiades – well, I remembered what Socrates had said that night I first met them both, that first night Aspasia had invited me to the home of Pericles, the night Socrates told Alcibiades that he wanted to rule not just Athens, not just all the Greeks, but all the world besides. In all the time I had known him since Alcibiades had never once denied it.

"To live forever in the minds and memories of men, like Achilles – is that what you want?" I asked, feeling suddenly with the thought of Socrates the futility of everything that depended on the judgment, the opinion, of others.

"No, of course not," replied Alcibiades, smiling with all the confidence of a fate foretold. "Achilles lost. That could never happen to me."

"But still he lives forever," I reminded him, "because he had a Homer."

"And why would I need a blind poet to make up stories, when I have you to tell the truth about all the things I am going to do. I've seen you writing. I know what you can do."

"Play the scribe to the great victories you have not yet won?" I laughed. "You've seen me writing, but you haven't seen what I write."

"And you've never offered to show me. So tell me, what do you write that is so important you keep it private?"

I studied him for a moment, and then looked away.

"Tell me," he insisted, gently taking me by the arm and leading me back onto the road where the funeral procession continued along like some vast river that flowed on forever and never changed. "Tell me what you spend hours every day writing at your desk."

The winter sun glowed bright on my cheek. We were on our way to honor the dead and I felt, strangely, more alive than I had ever felt. It was the sense, I think, of being in the only place I wanted to be, walking next to the young man I adored, talking about things that I would have talked about with no one else. I looked straight at him, straight into those piercing sky blue eyes of his.

"Everything I remember, everything I've heard from the mouth of Socrates; everything I have heard and seen worth remembering; everything that someone who has never heard or seen them might want to know; everything that might help them understand what happened here and, not what rumor said, but what it really meant."

There were people, mourners, all around us. The smile that now appeared in the wonderful all-seeing eyes of Alcibiades stayed hidden from his lips.

"I said you would be writing about me. But, really, you're writing down what Socrates says, the conversations you have heard?" Grabbing hold of my wrist, he squeezed it with a strange urgency. "It's a good thing; someone should. Just don't tell anyone. And never let anyone – anyone but me – see what you have written." He read the question in my eyes. "After what happened to Anaxagoras, what they tried to do to Aspasia – what do you think they would do to him? But, good; write it all down, let them hear in future years what we did. Think of how jealous everyone will be, knowing that there once were people like us, people who knew what it meant to be alive! But, come on, we can't keep everyone waiting."

And they were waiting, waiting for us to pass, waiting for Alcibiades to take his rightful place among those who had come to listen to Pericles praise Athens and what Athens had done, brought civilization to the world.

Two days earlier the bones of those killed in the war had been brought to a tent where the relatives of the fallen could make their own offerings. In the funeral procession itself coffins of cypress wood were carried on wagons, along with an empty bier, decorated and covered with flowers, for those whose bodies could not be recovered. All the dead are buried in the same, common tomb. When everyone who had joined the procession had arrived, Pericles came out from the tomb onto a high platform from which he could be seen and heard clearly by a crowd which must have numbered more than fifty thousand, including as it did not only all the citizens but foreigners of every rank and description. The size of the audience meant nothing; his voice, as I have said before, seemed to come from somewhere just in front of you, and those who stood the farthest away could hear him just as plainly as those who were barely an arm's length from where he spoke.

It was more than a speech to honor the dead; it was a speech to honor Athens. He did not want to make a long speech on things with which everyone was already familiar; he was not going to say anything "about the warlike deeds by which we acquired our power or the battles in which we or our fathers gallantly resisted our enemies, Greek or foreign." He wanted instead, "to discuss the spirit in which we faced our trials and also our constitution and the way of life that has made us great."

I knew something of what Pericles was going to say. Aspasia had helped him write it, and had told me that he wanted to impress upon all the citizens of Athens what they were fighting for and why the war was necessary. He wanted them to understand that Athens represented the light, and Sparta the darkness, in the world. I listened as Pericles reminded the Athenians what they were.

"Our form of government does not copy the laws of neighboring states. It is more the case of being a model to others, than of our imitating anyone else. Because power is in the hands of the whole people and not just the few, it is called a democracy. Everyone is equal before the law in their private disputes, while in conferring positions of public responsibility one man is preferred before another not because of the reputation of his family but because of his virtue and ability. No one who can be of service to the city is kept in obscurity because of poverty. Our political life is free and open, and so is our life with each other. We do not get angry with our neighbor if he enjoys himself in his own way, nor do we give him the kind of black looks which, though they do no real harm, hurt their feelings. We are free and tolerant in our private lives; but in public matters we follow the law, obedient to those whom we put in positions of authority, obedient to the laws themselves, especially those which are for the protection of the oppressed and those unwritten laws which bring undeniable shame to those who transgress them."

Pericles was not speaking in private to a few gifted friends with whom he could explore both the strengths and weaknesses of the Athenian democracy, the virtues and the vices of their restless way of life; he was talking to an audience that by its nature required that he speak about what they had in common, what they together considered good. And so he would at different times stop, as he did now, to remind them of how it was only because of their city that they could enjoy their private pleasures. He reminded them that they had "various kinds of contests and sacrifices regularly throughout the year," and that in their own homes "we find a beauty and good taste which delight us every day and which drive away our cares," and told them, in case they should forget it, that "the greatness of the city brings from all over the world things they can enjoy as easily as the goods they have at home."

He then drew certain, pointed, distinctions between their way of life and that of the Spartans, who "from their earliest childhood are given the most laborious training in courage. We pass our lives without all these restrictions, and yet are just as ready to face the same danger as they are. Here is proof of this: When the Spartans invade our land, they do not come by themselves, but bring all their allies with them; when we launch an attack abroad we do the job ourselves and, though fighting on foreign soil do not often fail to defeat our opponents." And then, a moment later, he added, "There are certain advantages, I think, in our way of meeting danger voluntarily, with an easy mind, instead of with a laborious training, with natural rather than with indoctrinated courage. We do not have to spend all our time practicing to meet sufferings which are still in the future; and when they are actually upon us we show ourselves just as brave as those others who are always in strict training."

Had I ever doubted Pericles' genius, I doubted it no longer. If he understood the limitations of his audience, what he could talk to them about, he also knew that sometimes the only way to tell the truth is not to tell the truth in its entirety. Everyone knew that the Spartans were a city of soldiers, an armed camp in a constant state of high alert, where children were trained to march and not to think. The problem for Pericles was how to make what seemed a source of Spartan strength a guarantee of their defeat; how to neutralize the advantage they had on land with their strict, regimented lives. His answer was to pass over in silence, to ignore, what he had just the year before told the Athenians was their own guarantee of victory, their long and unremitting practice in the art of war, not on land but on sea. He had told them then, in words I still remembered, words that everyone else had now forgotten, that seamanship was not something that could be learned in one's spare time, but was instead something that left no spare time for anything else. It was fascinating to watch the subtle way in which he connected courage, the kind that counted, with the freedom of the Athenian regime.

"We weigh what we undertake and apprehend it perfectly in our minds; we do not believe that words are a hindrance to action but that it is rather a hindrance to action to fail adequately to debate what we propose to do. For also in this do we excel others, daring to undertake as much as any and yet examining what we undertake, while others dare through ignorance and become cowards when they begin to think of what they are doing. They are truly brave who understand both what is difficult and what is easy and then meet whatever danger comes."

Then he said something that I shall never forget, what some might thing arrogance but was really only proper pride, a brief summary of what Athens had become and, more importantly, because nothing in this mortal world of ours ever lasts, what Athens meant.

"This is no empty boasting, but a real tangible fact. Consider the power our city possesses, won by the very qualities I mentioned. It is the only power now found greater in proof than in fame, the only power greater than what was imagined of her. In her case, and in her case alone, no invading army is ashamed of being defeated, and no city subjected to us can complain of being governed by men unfit for their responsibilities. Mighty indeed are the marks and monuments of the empire we have left. Future ages will wonder at us as the present age wonders at us now. We do not need the praises of a Homer, or of anyone else whose words may delight us for the moment, but whose estimation of what we have done will fall short of what is really true. For our courage and our daring has forced an entry into every sea and into every land; and everywhere we have left behind us everlasting memorials to the evil we have done our enemies and the good we have done our friends. This, then, is the kind of city for which these men, who could not bear the thought of losing her, nobly fought and nobly died."

He spoke now of the men who had died in battle, of their courage and gallantry, of how "they thought it more honorable to stand their ground and suffer death than to give in and save their lives," adding that those who remained behind, "may hope to be spared their fate, but must resolve to keep the same daring spirit against the enemy."

And then he paused, waiting, as it seemed in the deathlike silence of that enormous crowd, for some god to come, swift-flying Hermes, bringing words of inspiration that would speak clear and true to their hearts what they knew, deep down, they really wanted.

"What I want more than anything," said Pericles finally, "is that every day you fix your eyes on the greatness of Athens, see her as she really is, and that every day you fall in love with her again. When you realize her greatness, realize as well that what made her great were men with daring, men who knew their duty, men who understood the need for honor. They gave their lives, to her and all of us, and won the kind of praise that never ages, the most splendid of sepulchers – not the sepulchers in which their bodies are laid, but where their glory remains forever in the minds of men, always there on the right occasion to stir others to speech and action. For famous men have the whole earth as their memorial."

There were a few more words, counseling the parents and the loved ones of the dead how to mourn their losses, words about the importance of propriety and honor, words reminding them that whatever their private grief they still had their duty to the city and the living. And then it was over, the speech that no one who heard it would ever forget, the speech that, though none of us yet knew it, marked the beginning of the end of the greatness it described.

CHAPTER FOURTEEN

It happened the following summer, the invasion that left Athens a scene of death and devastation the like of which no one had ever seen or imagined, an invasion that changed my life forever. The Peloponnesians and their allies had invaded Attica again and with the same ruthless efficiency had begun to destroy whatever they had left standing the year before. While we watched from the walls, shouting words of scorn and swearing oaths of revenge, and even, when a Spartan rode too close, striking out with arrows aimed from strong bent bows, we were being attacked from the other side by an enemy that, starting out somewhere far away in Ethiopia, passed first through Egypt and then through the country of the Persian king to arrive unmolested on ships that entered at the seaport of Piraeus. The invasion came on quiet feet, passed blind before our eyes, and was discovered only when it was too late to resist. I lived so close to where they landed that I was one of the first to fall victim to an all too deadly assault that, before it was over, would take the lives of as many as a third of everyone who lived in Athens, and not just men and women, but children, too.

It was strange that it happened when it did, at a time when I had never felt better in my life. I was strong and healthy, never sick, and I was happier than I had ever been. Though I often stayed in the background, content to listen, I was at the very center of things; or perhaps I should say part of two circles that touched and on occasion overlapped. As a frequent guest in the home of Pericles and Aspasia, I heard all about the plans for war and the political problems that had to be dealt with here at home; but I also spent whatever time I could listening, a silent participant, if you will, in those astonishing conversations in which Socrates sometimes called into question nearly everything I had ever thought or believed.

It was like this everywhere in Athens. I do not mean this small double circle I was just describing, but, rather, that everyone had more than one pursuit. The same men who built ships in daytime listened to someone recite Homer at night; the men who, when those ships were finished, sailed off to war, came home and gathered in the thousands to see the latest tragedy of Euripides or laugh until their laughter hurt at one of the obscene productions of the comic poet Aristophanes. The Athenians were more vibrant and alive, more daring and more driven, more willing to risk everything on chance, than any people I had ever heard or read about, and I was one of them. Each night when I put my head on the pillow I did not think of what I had done that day; I thought about what was I going to do the next day and the day after that, what I could learn about the art of war from Pericles or what Socrates might teach me. I thought about what I might do with Alcibiades the next time we made love.

We did that, made love; we had never really stopped. Though he was still, in his surprisingly gentle soul, more kind and considerate, more concerned with what he thought I felt than what, had he only known the truth, I wanted, he had gradually become more aggressive, less inhibited by the fear that he might take me with too much violence. The physical pleasure we gave one another was now close to perfect; we learned together not just how to begin, but how to end, together. He had been there, in my bed, the night before the morning that I discovered that the invasion had begun.

As soon as I woke up, as soon as I opened my eyes, I had to close them again. The rising sun had just begun to paint the sky in the soft pink light of morning, but it was still more than I could take. My temples throbbed with sharp, stabbing pain and my head was burning as if my brain had been set on fire. I tried to get out of bed, but before I could take two steps the room began to spin and everything seemed to go upside down, the ceiling where the floor had been and the floor gone missing altogether. Stumbling blind and dizzy I fell back on the bed and must have lain there for hours, maybe longer, falling in and out of consciousness, one moment dreaming that I was back in Syracuse, certain the next that I was laying under the stars on a mountain miles away from that next day's battle at Potidaea in the arms of Alcibiades; or someone I thought was Alcibiades, because when he suddenly turned to look at me all I saw was a grinning death's head that wore the dreaded face of my hated father. Hours – longer – I lay delirious, calling out in my feverish confusion the names of a long parade of heroes and villains from my half-remembered and now distorted past.

I might have lain there all day, shouting muffled screams of agony, if the servant girl I employed had not finally found me. That she found me at all was nothing more than chance. Or was it? This was the one day of the week she did not work, the only day when she did not arrive at dawn to make my breakfast and help me dress, but she came because, as she later told me, she had forgotten what day it was and only remembered when she was almost to my house. She thought that as long as she was here anyway, she might as well look in on me and see if there were anything she could do. It would have been better for her, though neither of us could have known it at the time, if her memory had been better and she had never come at all; not that day, or any day after that.

I remember that she cried out when she saw me; I remember – I saw it all as through a dense fog – that her first reaction was to cover her face with her hands. But after that, she did not hesitate. The next thing I knew she was sitting next to me, pressing a cold, damp cloth against my forehead, telling me that I was going to be all right.

"You have a fever. It will pass. We'll keep cold compresses on your forehead until it does."

The cool, soft feel of it, the calm, soothing tone of her voice, seemed to clear my head and bring my mind back into focus. After a few minutes, she removed the compress from my forehead and put another, fresh one in its place. With another damp cloth she rubbed my chest and cleaned my arms. I opened my eyes and saw the worried look on the girl's face.

"What is it?" I asked; my voice so weak I had to struggle just to whisper.

"Nothing," she replied, shaking her head in that exaggerated way someone does when for your own good they want to hide the truth. "Nothing," she repeated reluctantly, when by my persistent look I gave her no choice but to tell me. "You're eyes – they're just a little red, inflamed from the fever. That's all."

'That's all.' There was something final, something deathlike in the way she said it; as if those two words were a summary of what was happening to me, what nothing could now prevent. I wanted to protest, to cry out that it was all too stupid, that I was fine, that there was nothing wrong; a little harmless illness, nothing that would not pass. More than anything, I wanted to laugh, to show her that all these worried looks of hers were an overreaction, that there was nothing to worry about, that I would be all right, that I was fine.

"I'm not really ill; I'm only - ." I had to stop; my mouth was too full for words. But full of what, I wondered. I had not eaten; I had not ... Then it started, the blood that had filled my mouth shot through my lips, covering my chin. I began to gag. If she had not been there, if she had not bent me forward over my knees, slapped me on the back until all the blood from my throat and tongue had all gone out, I might not have been able to breathe. Before I could gain my breath to thank her, she was running out the door, promising that she would be back in a few minutes, as soon as she could find a physician.

She did not come back for hours, and when she did the physician she brought with her looked himself as if he were ready to fall down. He explained as he examined me that he had been up all night, treating other patients in Piraeus with symptoms similar to my own. He sat on the bed next to me, pulled down the lower lids of my eyes with a gentle, practiced movement of his thumb and asked me to look first in one direction and then another. Nodding to himself, as if what he had seen confirmed the suspicion he already had, he held my left wrist with two of his fingers, checking my pulse.

"It's a fever; something that is going around," he remarked in a voice trained to give comfort. "You passed some blood. It's a common symptom; nothing to worry about."

The physician, Acumenus, had an excellent reputation, a man highly skilled in his profession. I felt better listening to what he told me, certain now that the sickness I had was nothing more than a temporary condition and that with a few days rest I would be back on my feet without any lingering complaints.

"I'll come tomorrow," he promised, patting me on the forehead. "Try to sleep. Don't drink any wine; only water."

I had not said anything, I did not have energy even for something as simple as speech, but now that he was leaving, I tried to whisper my thanks. I opened my mouth, but nothing came out, only my breath, a breath that had become not just labored and dry but noxious and vile. The reaction of the physician was immediate, instinctive, a quick grimace of disgust, as he pulled back, and then, just as quickly, in a gesture of apology and compassion, he put his hand on my bare, naked arm, braving a smile at the stinking, deathlike smell which had come from some infection deep inside my body. It was then, in that moment, that I knew that I was not just sick, but in serious danger. With all the strength I could summon, which was little enough, I grasped his wrist and stared up into his kind, considerate eyes.

"You'll be all right," he assured me. "I won't let anything happen to you."

Almost as soon as he was gone, I got worse. I began to sneeze, not the way you do on a lazy springtime day when the trees are all in flower, but violently, repeatedly, until my throat was so raw I could barely swallow. I tried to drink water, but even when I could get it down it provided no more than a moment's relief. From my throat, the pain moved to my chest and instead of sneezing I began to cough. Cough! It was more like an explosion, a harsh revolt against any attempt to breathe; pain so awful my face turned red as I tried not to breathe at all. Tears ran down my face; clots of blood thickened around my lips. I kept telling myself that this must be the end of it, the point at which, just before the body starts to recover, the worst symptoms are experienced and the worst pain is felt, but I knew it was not true; I knew that instead of getting better I was only going to get worse. I do not know how I knew this; how I knew that I was at the beginning, and not the end, of an endless torment, that something was inside me tearing me apart, and that before it was over the pain and suffering would be so great that I would look upon death as the only friend I had.

I tried to think of other things, to rise above myself, but it was more than I could do. Each time I thought I could, each time my mind started to clear, each time I thought I could at least for a few brief, merciful, moments concentrate on something other than what I felt, I was attacked from another, different direction. Then, all at once, I stopped coughing and my chest was clear. I could breathe without discomfort; I could rest. A smile came slowly to my mouth, a smile of gratitude and relief, a smile that died still-born on my lips as I suddenly doubled over in the most excruciating pain I had ever experienced. It was as if a dog and a serpent were trying to bite and claw their way through my stomach at the same time they tried to kill each other. I had seen men on the battlefield, their bodies hacked to pieces, left dying disemboweled, a scene that now took on a meaning personal to myself. Writhing in agony on my bed, I clutched at my stomach, searching for the sword that had killed me, driven crazy by the knowledge that it was not there, that there was nothing there, nothing I could see, the hand of some demonic god twisting, crushing, the life slowly out of me. My eyes shot wide open, my head flew forward; I was half out of my bed and then, my mouth open, I began to wretch, vomiting every kind of bile, every kind of disgusting substance. I kept doing it until there was nothing left, and still the retching, violent, painful and automatic, kept going, on and on, for what seemed an eternity. And then, finally, there was nothing left of me and I fell back on the bed and lay there, my eyes wide open, seeing nothing.

The physician came the next day, as he had promised, and the next day after that. The lines in his forehead that had given him a solemn, distinguished countenance had become noticeably deeper, and his large brown eyes, which had been filled with such confidence, now seemed less certain and even confused.

"There are hundreds of cases now," I heard him tell the servant girl as she poured him a cup of water. "I've heard of outbreaks in other places – Lemnos, for example – but never anything like it here. It's because of all the overcrowding, and perhaps also because here, in Piraeus, there are no wells, no sources of fresh water. It is brought from the reservoirs. There are rumors that the Peloponnesians poisoned them, but I don't believe it. This sickness was transmitted another way, brought by ships from other places. But it spreads by contact, and when you have this many people in such close quarters ..."

He heard me moaning as I tried to change position. He came over and sat next to me. A green amulet he wore around his neck on a gold chain seemed to shine with some internal fire and was so enchanting that for a moment I could not take my eyes off it. Was it possible, I asked myself, that there was life in even lifeless things?

"It hurts when you move? The touch of anything against your skin, even silk or linen, is unbearable?" he asked.

I still could not speak above a whisper. I tried to nod, but even that was a torture.

"Don't. It's all right; I understand."

There was such great comfort in his rich, cultured voice, and such great sadness, but there was something else as well, something strange that seemed to give everything a new and deeper meaning. Then, suddenly, I knew. I looked at him with alarm. It was his breath, dirty and vile, the stench of the disease that had now claimed him as another victim.

"Yes, I have it, too; but don't worry," he said with as brave a smile as I have ever seen. "What better way for a physician to know what he is treating than to experience all the symptoms himself?"

He knew when he told me that the disease was fatal; he knew that this was not some random illness, that the plague had come to Athens and that once you had it there was very little chance you would not die. He knew all that, but he promised that he would come the next day and he did; and he came a few more days after that, and then he did not come, and shortly after that I learned that he was dead.

I did not die, though I did not count that to my advantage; for a while I thought, when I could think at all, that I was being left alive as an act of malice. The gods, if they existed, were playing a demented game in which the object was to see how long a victim of all the cruelty they could devise could stay alive. It was, if you have a mind to analyze it, surprising how much I could take. My skin turned red and livid and then broke out in small pustules and ulcers until my body was covered with open wounds. The sickness that had begun with violent headaches, which had descended through first my throat and chest and then my stomach, settled finally at the end of a week in my bowels. What happened then is unspeakable, the constant eruptions of excrescence, the endless diarrhea that left me too weak to move even if every movement had not been itself an unbearable torture. My only solace was the sometimes sleep I had when I fell victim to complete exhaustion. Then, and only then, I could dream that I was still alive.

They were strange dreams, bizarre dreams, dreams that were one moment completely innocent, the dreams of my childhood, things I had done, or wished I had done, as a girl; dreams that at another moment were more brazenly erotic than anything I had ever imagined as a woman. They were all of them dreams of life, dreams so vivid, so real, that I was not always sure they were dreams at all, that they were not instead what my soul, freed from the shackles of my body by the racking pain of my disease, had been allowed to see, a new reality that had lain hidden behind the veil of our mortal nature. In the frenzy of my disordered mind I saw things with a kind of clarity I had never known before.

I lived a child again in the castle fortress of my father, wandering on the seaborne shore of Syracuse, watching from the rocks the dolphins swim round the island of Ortygia. The cloudless sky was azure blue; the air warm and gentle against my eager, laughing face. On the far side of the great harbor, I could see the low ridge of hills and, behind them, the white cliffs from where I would sometimes look out at the trackless sea and the flat, straight line of the horizon and await the arrival of the morning sun. I dreamed, I saw, the chalk white cliffs and the emerald green water, saw them with the eyes of the child I had once been and felt again the same sense of wonder, the utter joy, at everything I experienced. The soaring flight of an eagle, the silent movement of the wind, the distant cracking sound as someone somewhere began to fell a tree, the sudden croaking of a frog, the vibrant color of a new flower, the soft, steady hum of a friendly swarm of bees, the certain knowledge that each thing had a meaning of its own, the knowledge that the world lay open and needed only eyes to see it, the wisdom of a child the only wisdom needed.

That was one dream, there were others; dreams of incest and murder, dreams of things so awful they had of their own accord vanished from my conscious mind. Faced with an illness that more than threatened, promised, death, they now came rushing forward as if, having been hidden from my memory, they had now to make one last appearance, bring with them one last torment, before they also were, like the rest of my mind and body, lost forever beyond the power of anyone to call them back. There are those who claim that dreams have meaning, that they contain messages from the gods; that they tell us, if we know the secret of interpretation, what will happen in the future. It would have taken more than the normal art of the diviner to find the meaning, the real meaning, of these forbidden dreams of mine.

I dreamed – I lived again – what had happened the night my father took me, the night he made a wife of his own daughter. I could feel him force himself between my thighs; I could feel inside my vagina how much it hurt. But I could also feel – I could see myself – what happened next, the decision I made, that I had to make if I was going to stay alive, that instead of letting him make me the victim, I would rape him instead. I could see myself, after it was over, walking naked to the bath, and I could feel again the effort of my defiance, feel the hatred of my scorn as I taunted him with words I was certain mirrored what I hoped my mother said the night she had first been taken in his bed, that far from satisfied I had expected something more. I could feel again the howling emptiness of bleak despair, as I sat on the marble floor, my arms wrapped tight around my knees, as I cried bitter tears for everything I had lost.

And then, in other dreams, I forgot the pain and remembered only pleasure, the mounting intensity at the hard fire driven deep inside me by a man I did not hate, the sudden, violent rapture, the utter joy in living, how erotic was my nature when I was with a man like Alcibiades. There were no trembling hesitations, no remembered fears, in these erotic dreams of mine. I was moving underneath him, digging my nails hard into his back, biting at his shoulder until, in that final moment of ecstasy, we both exploded.

"I don't want to die!" I screamed as I woke up.

I was soaking wet as were the sheets on the bed. I looked around the darkened room, but no one had come when I cried out. I called for the servant girl, surprised that I had the strength. She did not answer and I assumed she had gone to fetch a physician if she could find one, or perhaps to get more food. I swung my legs out of bed and without thinking got to my feet. A little dizzy, I took hold of a chair, but then I realized that I was not delirious, that my mind was working. The fever had broken, the disease had passed. I was safe, I was alive, or, rather, I was alive, which meant I was safe because no one who had the disease got it twice. Survival meant immunity, a reward for all the pain and suffering, or perhaps instead a few were left alive only as a reminder of what the disease could do. If it did not kill you, it always left its mark. It left its mark on me.

The plague was everywhere, ravaging Athens in a way that no one who was there will ever forget, and no one who was not there can ever fully understand. There was no cure, no reason why it affected some and not others, or why it seemed to make no difference whether those affected had been strong and healthy before they got it. Other diseases disappeared; there were no other illnesses while the plague ran rampant. People died in agony and alone, because, as it was quickly discovered, those who visited the sick and tried to nurse them were the soonest to fall victim. Those with the greatest sense of honor, who refused to put their own safety ahead of the comfort and well-being of others, perished in greater numbers than those whose only thought was of themselves. There was only one class, a very small one, which could safely visit the sick, one class who could feel pity instead of fear in the presence of those about to die, those who, like me, had had the plague and recovered. You knew what it was like to undergo the torture and the torment, the excruciating pain, the hopeless despair at the all too slow approach of death. There was another side to this, another perhaps less generous feeling, a feeling of elation at having somehow escaped, of having been given a second chance, and, even more than that, a sense that because the plague had not killed you, nothing ever could; that you were not just a lucky survivor, a victim who had somehow cheated death, but that nothing else could ever kill you, that you had cheated death forever.

I had that feeling, I knew what it was like; and if I was not quite as grateful for my good fortune as some others, it was because, though death had not taken me away, the plague had done another kind of damage and turned me into something I had not been before. The ulceration, the boils, the gross disfigurement that had made my once silk smooth skin so sensitive to the touch and so hideous to the eye, had healed. I was unmarked by any permanent scars, but the youthful bloom that had given me my beauty, the rose colored glow that had given life to my cheek, had vanished and would not return. My vision had not been affected, I had not gone blind the way some less fortunate people had, but my left eye now remained always half-closed and my eyes, no longer bright and lovely, seemed sinister and evil instead. I could see the world as clearly as I had before, but the world did not want to see me. The face that so many had stared at in astonishment, the face that had made men forget everything but the face they were looking at, had become a face no one now noticed, or, if they did, one they glanced at with repugnance.

There was more. Many of those who survived lost the use of their extremities: fingers, toes, even genitals. My left hand had become partially paralyzed. The three middle fingers were folded into a useless grip; the thumb and little finger the only ones that still worked. The hand had the look of a claw, not a hand any man would ever want to hold. In a weird kind of symmetry, the same thing had happened to the middle three toes of my left foot. I could not walk, only limp, and that destroyed all grace of movement. The plague had changed me out of all recognition. From a beautiful young woman, I had become a plain looking creature without any of the features that attract, and hold, the attention of the world. Though it may seem strange to say it, there was a kind of elation that came with that as well, the knowledge that I could watch what went on around me, what people said and did, and pass among them unobserved. My presence made no difference; instead of one of the players in life's small game, I had now become part of that vast audience that watches, silent and unseen.

I did not realize this right away. When I was well enough to leave my bed, when I began to experience that rush of energy, that sudden, overwhelming sense of having once and forever triumphed over death, I could not wait to see again the people I knew, to tell them, share with them, my own good fortune in what had happened. In a curtained, horse-drawn carriage, I left Piraeus and went toward town, eager to see Aspasia and hear about everything I had missed.

The wheels of the carriage bumped hard against the jagged stone street, but instead of irritation and discomfort, the jolting movement had the strange effect of making me feel only more alive. And then I saw it, or rather, smelled it, the smoke from a funeral pyre, or what I thought was one, because when I pushed aside the curtain I saw something that was just the opposite of what it was supposed to be. It was a pyre all right, the dead, all victims of the plague, were being burned in flames, but there was no one there to mourn their passing or perform the rituals or obsequies by which the dead were consecrated. It was, I quickly realized, a random, desperate act. The dead, instead of being honored, were now looked on as the first thing to be avoided, a source not of sadness for those who survived them, but of the same disease that had killed them. No one dared give anyone a proper burial; there was too much risk involved. No one took the time to start a funeral pyre of their own; bodies were thrown on any fire still burning with someone else's dead father or mother, husband, wife or child. The city had become a smoking cauldron, an endless burning funeral on what seemed every street. The stench of death was everywhere. My eyes began to smart from the ever-present smoke; my nostrils tightened in rebellion at the constant, putrid smell.

The carriage clattered on. The smoke began to dissipate and the smell of death to disappear. It did not seem nearly as bad in the city as it had in Piraeus. I remembered what the physician had told my servant girl before they both had died, that there were more victims in crowded places without good water than in the more established neighborhoods farther from the harbor. But whether or not more died in one part of Athens than another, no one anywhere was safe. Everyone lived in fear of death. Passing beneath the Acropolis, unchanged and as majestic as ever, I saw something I had never seen before, a couple fornicating openly on the walkway next to the street, and, just beyond them, another couple, their clothing soaked with the cheap wine they were drinking, doing the same thing. Men were sitting on the ground, blank stares on their faces; women shrieked and pulled their hair; children with dirty faces ran around aimless and unattended. The whole of Athens was now engaged in a dismal dance of death.

"They've all given up," said the driver when he dropped me at the house of Pericles. "They're all afraid of the disease; certain, all of them, that they're going to die. Shows you what they really believed in," he added with contempt.

He had the short legs and powerful shoulders of a man who works mainly with his hands, but he had honest eyes and what I thought unflinching courage. The scars on his shoulders told me that he had once been a soldier.

"You would think no one had ever told them that there hasn't been a man born who was not going to die soon enough. They act like they have just discovered it, and that because they don't know whether, or how soon, it might happen to them – how quickly they might fall victim to the plague – all they can think about is getting what they can." He shook his head in something more than regret, something close to remorse, embarrassed at what the city had become. "Honor, dignity, and pride: those words lost all meaning. This life we have now isn't even human."

I wondered, as I watched him start to drive away, whether he would survive it, whether he might also become a victim of the plague. But if there was no way to know what would happen, who would get it and who would not, there was at least the certainty that there were some, like him, who, whatever happened, would not become in death the coward they had never been in life. On a sudden impulse, I called him back.

"Here," I said, as I gave him all the money I had on me. "Keep this for your retirement, and enjoy your old age."

He took two coins of only modest value and gave back the remainder. He thanked me for what he had taken and smiled at what he returned.

"I might get too full of myself if I had that much money." And then, with a high-pitched whistle at his horses, he drove away.

Aspasia did not know I was coming, and when she saw me was not sure who I was.

"It's me – Helen," I said, a little shaken by her lack of response. "I was sick, but I've recovered. I wanted to – "

"Helen! Yes, of course; we were all worried. Come in, come in," she said as she stepped aside and then shut the door behind us.

It was the middle of the afternoon, but the room was dark, all the windows shuttered, and the air was stale and close. Nothing had changed. The couches were all in the same places, none of the tables had been moved, but there was something – a cramped feeling, a sense of withdrawal – for which the darkness alone could not account.

The laughter, the noise, the exuberance of a room filled with people, the leading lights of the city, that I had seen gathered here on my first visit, came back into my mind, the memory a counterpoint to what I can only describe as a bleak scene of depression. I had come in my innocence eager to tell my relief and found myself in the presence of a woman filled with despair. What I had thought the effect of my changed appearance had not been the reason for Aspasia's initial absence of recognition. She was too distracted by sorrows of her own to notice what had happened to me.

"Pericles ... " She sat straight on a chair, her oval eyes wide open, seeing nothing. "His sister, both his sons ... "

Rich, poor, the most famous families, the anonymous slave, the plague made no distinctions.

"Both his sons, one after the other; his only son left, the one he has with me, young Pericles, who because I am not Athenian can never become a citizen and can never take his father's place. When the first one died, Pericles endured it; showed no emotion, went through the funeral with all his dignity intact. He set the example he wanted others to follow, the example we have to follow if the city is to recover. And when others of his relations – there were more than his sister – he was always unwavering in his devotion to duty; but when the other son died, his favorite, he could not do it anymore. Overcome with grief, he broke down in tears at the funeral and when I finally got him home he wept all night."

"But you ... and Pericles himself? You haven't been ...?"

"Afflicted with the disease? No, but there have been times when I've wondered whether living through all this has not been worse. To lose both sons ... If young Pericles had ... No, I wouldn't want to live beyond the life of my child. He saved us both; young Pericles, I mean. I kept reminding his father that there was one child left. I did not have to remind him that the city, or what was left of it, needed him as well."

I left Aspasia in the grieving, dark seclusion of her home without any clear idea where I was going next. My feeling of elation at having found myself free from disease and the imminent danger of death had given way to an oppressive sense of sadness that bordered on depression. The world seemed a madhouse, devoid of all purpose. It was what Democritus had said it was, everything that happened the necessity of chance, the collision of things too small to see and far too numerous to count. Where was the reason, the intelligence, in any of this; where the order in which everything had its place?

"I'm glad you're all right, glad you survived."

It was Alcibiades, and when I turned around to see him I forgot for a moment how my looks had changed and remembered only how much I had missed him, but I saw in his expression the kindness that only comes with pity and became suddenly self-conscious and even, strangely enough, a little afraid.

"I was just there," I said, nodding down the street toward the villa and its darkened rooms. "Poor Pericles, losing both sons."

"But we did not lose you. That's what we need to think about, all the things we still have left."

There was no mistaking his meaning, no doubt that he was talking about me, telling me to be grateful that I had not died, that I was still alive. He put his arm around my shoulder and pulled me close, and with that gesture taught me that there was a depth to him, a sensibility, that none of his many enemies would ever have guessed was there.

CHAPTER FIFTEEN

Helen, the name I had been given, the name my father had bragged about when Helen's famous face had only suffered in comparison with mine, had now the sound of a twice-told story of tragedy and loss, my face become a double mirror, the present made more intolerable by the memory of the past. I have been told that a blind man sees more clearly the things that are important, that Homer, a blind poet, had made Helen come alive. I do not know how much of this is true; I only know that I began to see things more clearly when I became invisible, when the world became blind to me. I began to understand that all of us live inside a double mirror, watching, as it were, both ways at once, seeing the present through the past, flush with past victories, angry and disheartened at what we have lost. But if none of us can escape the past, there is still the question what we do about it: whether we go on with our lives, take what fate has given us, and make the best of what we have. The temptation to feel sorry for myself, to feel a victim because instead of a source of rapture and enchantment, a light that brightened the eyes of others, my face now wore a disfigurement I kept hidden behind a veil, died a victim to the stunning power of Pericles and the words I heard him speak.

Everyone in Athens knew what had happened; they had all seen him at the funeral of his favorite son. Through all his private suffering and grief, through the death of his sister and so many of his relatives, even through the death of the first son who died, Pericles had set an example of courage and restraint that was beyond what most would have thought possible. It was a mark of how much this had cost him, the effort that it had taken, that when he began to place a garland of flowers on his dead son's head he suddenly became so overcome with emotion that he began to scream with all his deep-felt agony and shed tears he could not stop. In a strange way, what happened that day, instead of diminishing, only heightened the city's anger and resentment. It reminded people that nothing had come from the war into which Pericles had led them but suffering and death; that even Pericles himself, that great master of self-command, could not endure it any longer, and that something had to be done.

Knowing what they felt and what he had to say, Pericles

summoned an assembly. It was a study in something more than human nature, it was a study in human art and science, watching how, instead of telling them what they wanted to hear, he told them what they needed to know. No one else could have done what he did that day. The words themselves might be repeated, it might even be possible to imitate the way he phrased them, but the major part of persuasion is not what the speaker says, but who the speaker is. Pericles was not just a politician, a man who lived for the adulation of the crowd; he was a general who had fought for Athens in every major battle and a statesman respected everywhere in Greece. More than anything, however – and this no one could dispute – he had always put the interest of Athens and its people above any interest of his own. When the war broke out, it was Pericles who had his own property destroyed to make sure that the Spartans, whose king, Archidamus, had been his friend, would not leave it, alone among the estates in Attica, untouched. The moment he stood up, the crowd went silent. He began by reminding them that nothing had changed but themselves.

"I am the same as I was; I have not altered. It is you that has changed. You are angry with me and I understand the reason. You took my advice when you were still untouched by misfortune, and repented of your action when things went badly; it is because your own resolution is weak that you think my policy mistaken. It is a policy which entails suffering and all of you have suffered, but the ultimate benefits of that policy are still far away and not yet clear for all of you to see. A great and sudden disaster has fallen on you, a plague that no one could foresee, but you must not let that take the heart out of you. Despite what you have suffered, remember that you are citizens of a great city and that you were brought up in a way of life suited to her greatness; you must be willing to face the greatest disasters and be determined never to sacrifice the glory that is yours. Each of us must try to stifle our own sorrow and join together with the rest in working for the safety of us all."

The silence of the crowd became profound, a solemn meditation on what each of them had suffered and what the city had lost, men and women who had once sat among them, now joined together in death's embrace. I watched how with lowered eyes they lowered their heads, how some of them clutched at their slow heaving breasts, remembering the faces they would never see again, hearing in the solitude of their minds the voices that would never speak again.

The anger at what had happened, the anger directed at Pericles because they could not bear the burden of such great responsibility alone, had turned to a deep mournful sadness. Pericles tried to give them assurances that what they had suffered was no reason for discouragement, that the greatness of Athens would continue unimpaired.

"You think that your empire consists simply of your allies, but I have something else to tell you. The whole world is divided into two parts, the land and the sea. You are in control of all of one of these two parts – not only what is at present in your power, but elsewhere too, if you want to go further. With your navy as it is today no power on earth – not the King of Persia nor any people under the sun – can stop you from sailing where you wish. This power of yours is in a different category from all the advantages of houses or of cultivated land. You may think that when you lose them you have suffered a great loss, but weigh them in the balance with the real source of your power and see that, in comparison, they are no more to be valued than gardens and other elegances that go with wealth. Remember, too, that freedom, if we preserve it with our own efforts, will easily restore us to our old position; but to submit to the will of others means to lose even what we still have. You must not fall below the standard of your fathers, who not only won an empire by their own toil and sweat, but kept it safe so they could hand it down to you."

It was almost palpable, the new sense of resolution that swept through the assembled citizens of Athens. Their heads were up, their eyes were focused and alert, as they listened to what seemed the promise of a second chance. They had suffered, but they had not been defeated. In a few short sentences, Pericles had made them believe again that they were, or could be, the rulers of the world. There was danger in that, danger that they might one day exceed the limits of what they or anyone could do; but the greater danger, because it threatened immediate ruin, was to let them think the only way out of the present difficulty was to give up, let the empire crumble, and live out their days in the long twilight of weakness and inconsequence.

"It is right and proper to support the imperial dignity of Athens. This is something in which you all take pride, and you cannot continue to enjoy the privilege unless you also shoulder the burden of empire. And do not imagine that what we are fighting for is simply the question of freedom or slavery: there is also involved the loss of our empire and the dangers arising from the hatred which we have incurred in administering it. It is no longer possible for you to give up this empire, though there may be some people who think this would be a fine and noble thing. Your empire is now like a tyranny: it may have been wrong to take it; it is certainly dangerous to let it go."

Caught up as much as anyone in what Pericles was saying, forced to the same conclusion that Athens without its empire would be Athens destroyed, I did not fully grasp the significance of what he said next, that when he turned to those who did not agree, who thought it would be a 'fine and noble thing' to let the empire slip away, that among those who Pericles thought mistaken was Socrates himself.

"The kind of people who talk of doing this and persuade others to adopt their point of view would very soon bring the state to ruin, and would still do so even if they lived by themselves in isolation. For those who are politically apathetic can only survive if they are supported by people who are capable of taking action. They have no value in a city which controls an empire, though they would be safe slaves in a city that was controlled by others."

The question, which, as I say, I did not immediately grasp, was whether you could just keep an empire, whether the same thing that led you to acquire it in the first place, that ruthless energy, the endless desire for something new, that erotic need to use your strength, would not compel you to keep acquiring more. The choice was not between keeping and giving up what you had; the choice was between recognizing a limit, a point at which to come to rest, and an endless struggle for power after power that ended only in the loss of everything, including your own identity. Underneath all the encouragement to go forward and not look back, Pericles seemed to sense this, an acknowledgement, no less poignant for being brief, that nothing mortal lasts.

"It is right to endure with resignation what the gods send, and to face one's enemies with courage. This was the old Athenian way; do not let any act of yours prevent it from still being so. Remember, too, that the reason why Athens has the greatest name in all the world is because she has never given in to adversity, but has spent more life and labor in warfare than any other city, thus winning the greatest power that has ever existed, such a power that will be remembered for ever by posterity, even if now, since all things are born to decay, there should come a time when we were forced to yield: yet still it will be remembered that of all Hellenic powers we held the widest sway over the Hellenes, that we stood firm in the greatest wars against their combined forces and against individual states, that we lived in a city which had been perfectly equipped in every direction and which was the greatest in Hellas.

"All this may be disparaged by people who hold back from politics, but those who prefer a life of action will try to imitate us, and, if they fail to secure what we have secured, will envy us. All who have taken it upon themselves to rule over others have incurred hatred and unpopularity for a time; but if one has a great aim to pursue, the burden of envy must be accepted, and it is wise to accept it. Hatred does not last for long; but the brilliance of the present is the glory of the future stored up forever in the memory of man."

It seemed an echo of what Socrates had taught me, that eros was the desire for immortality, that the same impulse that led some to live beyond themselves in the children they left behind, led others to want fame. That was the secret of Pericles' appeal, why he had the hold he had on Athens, how he had been able all these years to teach them restraint, convince them to put aside what they wanted for what they needed to do. It was the promise of immortality, the certain knowledge that if they never gave in, if they persevered, even if they ultimately suffered defeat, the memory of what they had done would live forever in the minds of men. Their children might turn out everything they had hoped for or everything they feared, their children might die too early and never have children of their own, the line that ran through their fathers might end with them, but what Athens had done would last as long as there were human beings on earth. You could see it in their eyes, the glowing pride, the half-crazed look of triumph in the way future generations would look back at them. It was no wonder the Athenians worshipped Hermes with such devotion. They believed that they alone were the favorites of the gods, the greatest nation in the long history of the world. Anyone who doubted that had only to look around at the city they had built and the empire over which they ruled.

Dragging my bad foot after me, my claw-like hand hidden inside my robe, I limped away, surrounded by the solemn voices of the crowd that, now that Pericles had finished, had begun to disperse. There had been no applause, none of the wild cheering that often accompanies public speeches: what they had heard from Pericles had been too serious for that. When he finished, they rose as one and stood in silent tribute until he left the stage, and then, quietly, without commotion of any kind, they filed out of the great amphitheater a different people than when they entered. Their terrible pent-up anger had been released, transformed, by a catharsis built not on emotion but on reason. They had come in with the shuffling steps of people distracted by their grievances; they left with the slow, measured step of people determined and resolute. They had come ready to sue for peace on any terms; they left ready once again for war.

The plague still took its victims, but the worst of it seemed over, though that may perhaps have been as much the result of what Pericles had said that day as any real decline in the number of new cases. I could still smell smoke when I made my way along the streets, but the funeral pyres I passed were now treated with more respect. Bodies were no longer simply thrown onto the first fire someone found burning. There were not the same signs of frightened despair: no more random couplings, no more disregard for everything but the pleasure of the moment; no more women's mindless shrieking, no more the abject cowardice of men. The disease might still affect their bodies, but thanks to Pericles, his words and his example, it did not any longer so much affect their minds. Whatever fear they might still feel, whatever late night terror at the approach of what might be the first, fatal symptoms of the plague, they held up, they did not yield: they waited without complaint for what fate might bring them. Pericles might try to make a clear distinction between words and action, but that belied his own achievement. Without his words there would have been no action, Athens would have relapsed into a lethargy that made motion impossible; without his words, Athens could not act. Without his words, Athens would have died. And if Pericles did not understand that, Alcibiades did.

"He was not going to give that speech; he was not going to do anything. It took everything I had to convince him that he had to do something; that he could not just stay at home, mourning over what he had lost."

We were sitting on the steps outside the temple of Athena on the Acropolis, high above the city, looking southward to the harbor and the sea. The air was clean and fresh, not dank and stale the way it was now in the dark confines of Piraeus filled with make-shift tenements and alleys full of garbage. I sat on his left so he would not see my wounded eye. The veil I now always wore was pulled back just the other side of my mouth and nose. I had almost forgotten – or had I ever noticed? – how powerful and well-made were his thighs and legs; strong, not like those of a wrestler, but of a well-trained athlete, someone who could run with deer-like speed or hold the reins with perfect balance as he steered a chariot through the hairpin turns of a race. Wearing a long purple robe and with a golden grasshopper in his long, curling hair, he kept his eyes on the far horizon in a way that reminded how much his own ambition had no known limit.

"I had to convince him that he could not wait, that things would only get worse; that Cleon and others like him were only too eager to take advantage of what had happened, eager to blame him for everything that had gone wrong."

The sun felt good against my face, and there was comfort in the warmth of his body next to mine. I remembered the nights we had spent together, the joy and pleasure of our bodies intermingled, nights I knew we would never share again. But I knew something else as well, something that made what I felt for him deeper than it had been before: I knew that in that part of his soul that remained untouched by eros and ambition, that part of his soul that made him sometimes regret that he had not been born with less of this drive for fame and glory, in that part of his soul that made him so much greater than all those who loved and hated him, he would always love me. It was, I know, ironic, that what had first drawn him toward me, the face that Helen had, had by its absence, by the change it had undergone, drawn him closer. He spoke to me now without reserve or inhibition, as if we were different sides of the same person sharing the same inner dialogue that we had alone with ourselves.

"He had good reason to be in mourning, to want to stay out of the public eye."

"Yes, I know that; I know what he lost, what happens when death takes place outside the order of time."

"The son before his father."

"Even though the son will never measure up to what the father is. One of them always wanted more money; the other one, the one he shed tears over, was honest but inordinately slow. The little one – Aspasia's child – better that he was the one who survived. He'll be someone worth knowing. But, whatever the nature, the causes, of his grief, Pericles has obligations."

"He knows that; it was only a matter of time."

"It's always a matter of time, and there was not any. He could not wait; he had to act now."

"And you convinced him of that; which means he knew it already. He knew what he had to do; you reminded him of it."

The sunlight, slanting off his cheek, gave it the color of bronze as he turned to me and smiled.

"Isn't that how persuasion works: remind people of what they are supposed to do, even if they don't know it?"

"That reminds me of what I wanted to ask you. Do you remember when he warned in his speech against listening to those who would tell them that giving up the empire would be a 'fine and noble thing' to do, against listening to those who do not take an active part in politics, who are 'quite without value in a city which controls an empire.' Was he talking about Socrates?"

As a strange, enigmatic smile started across his mouth, the lashes on his eyes seemed to hood his intentions.

"Not Socrates – someone else?" I persisted.

"Socrates, yes; though that isn't who he had in mind."

The answer made no sense; then, again, it did.

"Someone influenced by what Socrates has said."

The eyes of Alcibiades danced with cheerful eagerness at the secret he was going to share, though not before he had had some fun with it, played a game in which he made me guess.

"Perhaps not what he said, but ... "

"He thinks the empire is a mistake, a fatal flaw – doesn't he? That it starts in motion things that can't be stopped; that it turns everyone's mind to thoughts of acquisition; that – "

"Whatever he thinks, have you ever heard him say it to anyone in public?"

"Is that what Pericles meant when he said that even if someone 'lived by themselves in isolation'? That just by saying this kind of thing to a few people in private, those people will repeat it, and if enough people listen to them then everyone will be in danger?"

"Forget Socrates for a moment. Which dramatic poet writes plays about the way things were; which one tries to show how much better we were in the days before we acquired an empire?"

"Euripides? Is that who you mean?"

The smile on his mouth became shrewd and cunning and yet charged with mirth, like someone full of admiration for a conspiracy they had only just discovered.

"You know who the oracle said was the wisest man alive?"

"Socrates."

"Yes, and of course he denied it; but do you know who the oracle said was the second wisest? – Euripides. There is a story that the oracle explained that the reason was that Euripides was wise enough to know that he was not as wise as Socrates. There is a rumor, which I have reason to believe, that at least part of what Euripides is supposed to write, is written by Socrates himself, and that what he writes is precisely those lines that directly or indirectly tell us that this empire we have acquired is a mistake."

"Is that the reason that Socrates never goes to see a tragic drama unless it is a new production by Euripides?"

Alcibiades laughed. "And probably only listens to the parts he wrote."

"Whether or not Socrates helps write the plays of Euripides, why is Pericles so concerned with those who think the empire is not a good thing, that Athens should give it up?"

"He gave the reason. Remember the line: 'it may have been wrong to take it, it is certainly dangerous to let it go.' I don't know how many times I have listened to him worry about what might happen if we ever start to lose our grasp on what we have, what will happen if these so-called allies of ours decide they have a chance to break free and become independent of our power. We tell them that democracy is the only decent regime, we proclaim everywhere our devotion to the freedom to make our own decisions, we tell them that we only want to protect them from those like the Persians or the Spartans who would enslave them, but then we insist that they follow our lead and pay us for the privilege."

A sudden light flashed through his eyes and his mouth pulled back sharply at the corners. It was the look of someone who knows what needs to be done, but knows as well that no one will listen.

"Before Pericles, when Cimon could get the assembly to do whatever he wanted it to do, we invaded Egypt and very nearly destroyed the Persian King. There was a time when no one loyal to the King would come within a hundred miles of the sea we controlled. Cimon lacked the forces to make victory in Egypt complete, but he was right about something Pericles does not understand: the only way to keep the Greeks from warring with each other is to have them war against someone else. And what is true of the Greeks is doubly true for us: Athens cannot sit immobile, her empire in a state of rest; Athens needs constant motion, the empire needs expansion, or Athens turns against itself. It would not be dangerous to let the empire go, it would be suicidal."

"Dangerous, suicidal, whatever you want to call it, haven't you, like Pericles, left something out? Athens could be in a state of rest, remain content within its borders, if it used its navy to protect itself instead of using it to control the seas and dominate those who live near it. What kind of people do you want the Athenians to be: always grasping for more than what they have, always after something new, a people driven half-mad by dreams of future glory, a people who die gruesome deaths from disease and this endless slaughter; or a people civilized by what the arts and sciences can teach, who compete to become as good as they can be, a people who practice all the virtues? I was there, I heard the call for greatness, and I have no doubt it is true: that the 'brilliance of the present is the glory of the future stored up forever in the memory of man.' But what is that brilliance if it isn't what Athens has built, not this empire you think always needs expanding, not all the beautiful buildings that make the city so magnificent to see; it is what in this place alone the human mind was able to achieve. What was that speech of Pericles if not a work of art; what those conversations of Socrates if not the dialogues of genius? This war, who will remember anything except what it destroyed? Glory? – Yes, perhaps, because there is nobility in courage; but there are always wars – read Homer and Herodotus – and in them always acts of courage. Glory? – Homer and Herodotus, what they pass down to future generations; what gets remembered, if anyone should make a record, of how Pericles spoke and what Socrates said. And yes, you may be remembered, because I have a feeling you won't let anyone forget. But is it enough to be remembered; is it not more important to remember instead what you are and what you could be?"

He looked at me for a moment with what I thought was new respect, and then with laughing eyes told me that he knew I was right but that there was nothing he could do: he was who he was and his life was foreordained.

"Can you imagine me, barefoot like Socrates, thinking, thinking all the time? Can you imagine me so indifferent to the world?"

He laughed at the thought of it, but I could see in his eyes a doubt, a kind of dissatisfaction that he was not different, that he could not do those things. Socrates had something he knew he could not have, and that bothered him a good deal more than he would admit, perhaps more than he even knew. Socrates had the same effect on me. You were drawn to him the way we are drawn to anyone who has a gift more perfect than our own: we somehow know that they know more than us, another way of saying, I suppose, that we all know our own ignorance.

"I wanted to see you to tell you goodbye, and to tell you that I have made arrangements for you to have another place to live."

"Arrangements for me to …?"

"Piraeus is dangerous, and it's getting worse; it's – "

"It isn't dangerous to me. I've had the plague," I cried in a voice suddenly angry and bitter. "I'm sorry; I didn't mean …, only there is nothing that can happen to me now."

"The plague hasn't gone away; no one knows what will happen. Even if you can't get it again yourself, others have and others will. The crowding down there keeps getting worse; there is sickness all around. It isn't good for you; it isn't good for your mind. I have property on the other side of the city, not more than a mile from where Pericles and Aspasia live. It is high in the hills with a wonderful view, and the house itself, though small, is big enough.

"You'll have fresh air and all the privacy you could want. You won't have to push your way through crowded streets; you won't have to … "

"Hide my face from view?"

I had not meant to say it. I could not have said it to anyone but him; it was only when I was near him that I remembered what I had lost. He gave me the stern glance he might have given a soldier tempted by cowardice.

"You're not disfigured; there is nothing wrong with how you look. You have an eye that does not open quite as wide as the other. You aren't blind, you can still see; if anything you see better than you did before. And if some of those demented fools that could not take their eyes off you before don't look at you in the same way, where exactly is the loss in that?"

"You don't look at me in the same way, and there is a loss in that," I replied with equal honesty.

He bent toward me, drawing me even closer with the stunning generosity in his wonderfully warm-hearted gaze.

"Perhaps we both see each other more clearly than we did before, see things we did not see at all before." He smiled and took my hand and held it gently in his own. "We know this, don't we? –

Whatever happens you and I will last forever." Laughing softly, he added: "'The brilliance of the present is the glory of the future stored up for ever in the memory of man.' Our memory, what I learn from you, what you teach me about myself – better than all the glory, what those who will never know me may remember of what I have done."

My disfigurement, this mark of my survival, vanished with his words. He brought me back from my vanity and self-absorption, and gave me what I needed more than anything: the knowledge that the eros that bound us together was deeper and more enduring than a moment's passion, the attraction of a mask.

"To say goodbye? Why? Where are you – ?"

"The war goes on. Pericles sails with a hundred ships against the Peloponnese. He takes a force of four thousand hoplites and three hundred cavalry. Another fifty ships from Chios and Lesbos will join him. While the Peloponnesians are destroying what they can of Attica, we will be doing something worse to them. I'll tell you all about it when I get back and you can write the record of it in that journal you keep. The new house, the one in the hills I want you to have, has a perfect room in which to work. There is a window from which you can look out to the Acropolis and, beyond it, out to the sea."

I began to protest, insisting that I had all my things in the house in Piraeus, and that I had grown used to my life there, that it would be too difficult to learn my way around another place, and that it was in any event too generous a gift for me to accept. He paid no attention to anything I said. Once he had decided upon something, he would keep talking until, even if you had not been convinced, you became too tired to resist. But this argument was over before it started.

"Your home in Piraeus was sold this morning. All your belongings have been moved. Don't worry," he laughed when he saw the look of anger and bewilderment on my face; "I got you more than you paid for it. And everything in the new house is ready for you. Come along, I'll show you."

It was more a cottage than a house, five small rooms and a vine-covered porch, but with a view even better than what he had described. From my desk, which, as he had promised, was already in place, I could see all of Athens and the sea beyond it, and in the evening watch the dark red sun slip down the side of the sky. I liked the house; I loved the garden.

There were fig trees, olive trees, orange, lemon, pomegranate, several towering palms; there were flowers of every kind and color from the chrysanthemums growing next to the small pond to the pink roses that climbed along the whitewashed walls to the edge of the red tile roof. With boyish enthusiasm, Alcibiades was rattling off the names of trees and flowers like a practiced horticulturalist and then, a moment later, began to describe with the precision of a second generation mason the way each of the stones had been made to fit together in the tall surrounding wall. There seemed to be no detail he did not know about, nothing so small that it passed his notice.

"You thought I only liked to play at war, that I had no interest in how things were built?" he laughed. "What do you think I was doing, a small boy, while my uncle was pouring over plans for the city he wanted Athens to become? All those discussions he had with Phidias – do you think I was not listening, trying to learn? I might have become an architect if I had been someone different than who I am!"

I laughed back, teasing him with what I knew.

"And you would not have been content until you had built the biggest building anyone had ever seen."

He smiled in vindication.

"Bigger than the pyramids, bigger than the world; I'd build something higher than the sun."

It was getting late. He started to go, but then seemed to hesitate.

"Do you think it will be better here? Do you think I did the right thing? I wanted you to have – "

"I love the house. And, yes; it will be better for me here, above the city. I won't go down to Piraeus again."

"I leave in the morning. I'll see you when I get back."

"Don't go," I said, taking his hand. "I might not look the same woman, but I'm still a woman, and I still ... No, I'm sorry," I said, letting go. "For a moment I forgot how much I've changed, forgot that I'm not Helen anymore."

Whether it was lust or mercy, the erotic impulse of the moment or a deeper, lasting love, we forgot the way I had changed and remembered only what we wanted. In a moment I was naked; a moment later we were making love, thrusting hard against each other as he drove himself deep inside me, an arrow shot by eros that penetrated not just my body but my heart as well. I do not know how many times we made love that night, the numbers did not matter, nothing more than fractions of a single endless unity. There was no becoming, only being; changeless motion, changing rest; eros leading finally to a blinding recognition that the secret of existence was found inside ourselves.

Alcibiades left before dawn to join the expedition that Pericles was leading against the Peloponnese. I watched from the window of my new house the hundred ship armada sail out of the harbor, wondering what would happen when the Spartans and their allies discovered that instead of sinking under the burden of the plague, Athens was launching an attack; that instead of wasting away under the onslaught of a debilitating disease, Athens was still alive. And if they were at first surprised, how long would it take them to realize that this was just what they should have expected, that what the Corinthians had said at Sparta was true: that the Athenians were incapable of rest, that they did not know the meaning of defeat. In the evening, when I sat down, alone, to dinner, I tried to imagine what Alcibiades was doing, whether as his ship sailed through the darkened sea he remembered what we had done together in the night, or whether, being Alcibiades, his only thought was for the future. But then, suddenly, that question was shoved aside, forgotten, at the discovery that Alcibiades was not on a ship; Alcibiades was here.

"What are you – ?" I asked, astonished that he was standing right in front of me.

In that languid way he had, he tilted his head to the side, smiled briefly and helped himself to a grape. He dropped into a chair the other side of the small table.

"I decided it was much more fun to spend the night in bed with you instead of in a hammock somewhere on a ship, so I deserted. They'll come for me in the morning," he remarked with bragging indifference, "and no doubt execute me in the afternoon; but why worry about tomorrow when the night is ours?"

I knew he was lying, but before I could think to say anything, he was back on his feet, his expression quite serious.

"There was a change at the last minute. After the attack on the Peloponnese, after Pericles has done as much damage as he can, there is going to be another assault on Potidaea. I have to help get things ready for that. There is a lot to do and not much time to do it, but I wanted to tell you what has happened. And I wanted to make sure you were all right, that after last night ... "

He left the thought unfinished, a note of apology in his voice, a trace of regret that we were not any longer two people that would turn the heads of everyone they passed, the only looks those of sympathy and confusion, the only question why the most beautiful man alive was with a woman nothing like his equal. There was no pity in Alcibiades; I would not have loved him if there were. What some might think cruelty, I thought honesty, and, to tell the whole brutal truth, good judgment and intelligence. The public, on whose ever changing opinion everything depended, would begin to think less of him if he was seen too often with a woman who looked like me. Everything he did was for effect; every gesture, every word he uttered, designed to attract the attention, and the envy, of the crowd. He could no more afford to incur their doubt or disapproval than I could think of talking to a dunce. We understood each other; we understood what each of us had to do.

"Don't worry about me. I have things to do myself."

He stayed a short while longer and then he left and I did not see him again for a very long time, until, following the return of Pericles, he had sailed with an even larger force to the siege at Potidaea. It did not go well. I have tried to write it all down, everything that happened, but I did not see things with my own eyes and can only report what others told me. There is a difference seeing things through the eyes of someone else, seeing things only in description. When they arrived – the generals in charge were Hagnon and Cleopompus, colleagues of Pericles – they brought up siege engines and used all their ingenuity to capture Potidaea, but nothing worked. It was not because there were greater numbers on the other side, or the strength of their defenses; it was not for any of the reasons usually associated with defeat. The Athenians were defeated by the plague. They brought it with them; some among the soldiers must have had it before they started. Even those who had been there before, the ones involved in the siege itself, strong and healthy when the fleet arrived, became victims of the disease. In forty days, more than a quarter of the four thousand hoplites brought from Athens had perished in the same tortuous way that countless others had died at home, a death that made a mockery of all their dreams of a glory that, in that phrase that I could never forget, would live forever in the memories of man.

When the fleet came home and I saw Alcibiades again, he seemed older, much older, than when he had left. He had not been sick for so much as a day, but if his body had been free of the disease, the plague had still changed him and made him even more impatient.

The knowledge that death could come at any moment, come unseen and without warning, made him more determined than ever to take what life had to offer as quickly as he could. And then something happened that forced the issue and left him no choice but to do whatever he had to do to lead. Pericles died.

CHAPTER SIXTEEN

Gorgias, Gorgias of Leontini, Gorgias with his smiling insincerity, his smug self-assurance, his monumental conceit; Gorgias, whom I had despised and distrusted the moment I first saw him that day, years ago, when Empedocles took me to see his former student speak in Agrigento, was here, in Athens, come as an ambassador to seek assistance for his city in another one of Sicily's many wars. Nothing could have given a clearer demonstration of how much had changed, how much things had gotten worse, since Pericles had died. Gorgias, with all his preening self-confidence, giving set-piece speeches filled with antitheses, full of balanced clauses, designed as much to show his practiced eloquence, his power as a speaker, as to prove that Athens should help defend Leontini against the imperial ambitions of Syracuse. And his audiences could not get enough of it!

Gorgias did more than speak; he could teach, and nearly everyone in Athens was now desperate to learn. With the death of Pericles there was no one who could oppose the multitude and act as a restraint; no one who represented rest in the motion that swirled all around him, no one who had acquired that kind of knowledge. After Pericles, no one had the kind of obvious superiority that made everyone else hold back; after Pericles, the path to power was open to anyone who could persuade the people that he could give them what they wanted and thought they deserved to have. It was no wonder Gorgias had become so famous, no wonder everyone with ambition flocked to hear the speeches he gave in public, no wonder they thought themselves honored by an invitation to any home where Gorgias was the featured guest. Gorgias was in Athens, and Athens talked of little else.

"Come with me. It will be interesting."

Alcibiades was standing in my doorway, leaning against it, one foot crossed over the other, a lazy smile on his lips. I had been writing at my desk when he knocked. It was cool inside the house; the last thing I felt like doing was to venture out into the searing heat of an August afternoon.

"No, really; you won't regret it," he persisted when I laughed at the suggestion. "It's a little warm outside," he said, shrugging with indifference. "What would you like in summer – snow and ice?"

"Yes," I replied; "I wouldn't wish for them in winter."

"Take the seasons as they come. Why rush the future?" he said, with a sense of expectation. He raised his eyes, waiting for approval at this turn of phrase.

I gave him a jaundiced look. "Have you joined all the others and gone to school with that garrulous fraud, Gorgias?"

He fairly glowed as he tried to mimic indignation. "If I went to school with him, he would be the one who learned, not me." His eyes flashed with confidence as his manner became secretive. A teasing smile played on his mouth. "Come with me, if you don't believe me."

"Why? Are you going to teach Gorgias a lesson?"

"Someone is, and I don't want to miss it."

"What do you mean? A lesson about what? – How to speak?"

"Teach rhetoric to a famous teacher of rhetoric, give a lesson in persuasion to one who does it for a living, and do it all for free. Who do you imagine could do that?"

I could think of only one person.

"Socrates? He's going to see Gorgias? He's going to sit, part of an audience, while Gorgias speaks? That does not sound like the Socrates I know."

"No, Gorgias already gave his speech today. He must have just finished it. He's staying at the house of Callicles. It is not far from here. There is a small gathering, a few dozen people, invited to listen as the great Gorgias answers any questions they care to ask."

"And Socrates was invited? Does Gorgias have any idea what he can do?"

"Socrates invited himself. He asked Chaerephon to take him. I was talking to Socrates when Chaerephon came to get him. But, don't worry: we'll get there before Socrates. Chaerephon is so desperate to have everyone like him that he'll stop and talk to everyone in the marketplace. That's what they're all trying to do these days, since my uncle's death, become a 'friend of the people.' They don't understand that you have to keep a distance if you want to lead." He gave me a sudden, sharp look full of significance. It was a measure of his enormous self-confidence that he spoke of his fellow citizens as if they were a different people against whom he was planning a campaign. "What the Athenians want more than anything is to be astonished. That's why they will let me lead. Because no one has ever astonished them the way I have. No one."

We left my house and walked along the shadowed, twisting streets toward the stately home of the rich and influential Callicles. I did not ask Alcibiades if he had been invited. He did not need an invitation. No one had ever turned him away. When Callicles saw him, his face flushed with excitement.

"Let me get Gorgias! I know he wants to meet you," he said, clapping his hands together like a young girl thrilled at the sight of the man she secretly, and hopelessly, adores.

Alcibiades raised an eyebrow, and stopped him cold.

"I came to see Socrates. Isn't he here yet?"

His tone was so peremptory, so controlling, that Callicles could barely stutter a response.

"No, he hasn't arrived. Are you sure he's coming? I don't really know if ... "

"He's coming with Chaerephon. Do you have something to eat and drink?" he asked, as he started toward a table laden with food and wine. Callicles was left to stare in amazement as his young, uninvited guest assumed a preeminence that no one, including Callicles himself, so much as thought to challenge.

"Meet Gorgias! Why would I want to do that?" laughed Alcibiades as we stood together at the end of the long marble entryway. "Look at them, standing there with their eager eyes, panting breathless, listening to the great man talk. They think that if they could just talk like him, everyone else would listen to them with the same kind of stupid adulation. He wears his hair in ringlets, even braids some of it with jewels; dresses like some kind of sexless whore, all that gauzy, flowing silk." he said, his eyes narrowing into a glance of shrewd appraisal. "He does it all on purpose to show what he can afford. He advertises his success: tells everyone that he knows what he is doing, that he has gotten rich through his ability to speak."

"It's hard to believe he ever studied under Empedocles," I remarked.

"Don't blame Empedocles. Think of some of those who have studied under Socrates." He gave me a strange look, as if he had just thought of something that put things in a different perspective. "Think of me. Do you think no one will ever think to blame him for what I might one day do? Do you think they would never put him on trial – these good, god-fearing Athenians – if things went wrong? Do you think they would never do to him what they did to Anaxagoras?"

His eyes suddenly brightened and he looked past my shoulder. Socrates had just arrived.

"To join in a fight or fray, as the saying goes, Socrates. You have chosen your time well enough," said Callicles, with a trace of condescension in his voice.

Socrates glanced at the small crowd that had turned to see who had just come in, and then looked back at Callicles.

"Do you mean, according to the proverb, 'we have come too late for a feast'?"

"A most elegant one. Gorgias has just given us a fine display of what he can do."

"Chaerephon is to blame. He forced us to spend our time in the marketplace."

Alcibiades took me by the hand and moved off to the side where we could see everything more clearly.

"Notice that," he whispered. "Chaerephon forced him to stay in the marketplace. He did not want to be there. But, then, why did he allow himself to be forced? Why didn't he insist on getting here on time, unless he did not want to listen to this?"

"Gorgias is a friend of mine, Socrates," said Chaerephon, "so he will give us a display now, if you think fit."

Callicles seized on the suggestion. "I'm sure he would be glad to do exactly that, give you a display, the way he just did now."

But that was not what Socrates wanted.

"Thank you, but would he agree to have a discussion with us? I want to discover what is the function of his art, what it is that he professes and teaches – as for the rest of his performance, he can do that some other time."

"The best thing is to ask our friend himself. Only this moment he was telling us he would answer any questions anyone might like to ask."

Gorgias was tired after the long discourse he had given, and Socrates knew it. There was more truth than what Callicles had known in the line he had quoted about joining in a 'fight or a fray.' This was to be a contest in which, like war itself, Socrates would give no quarter. Something important was at stake, something Socrates thought vital. He never smiled, he never laughed; I had never seen anyone so serious.

"What is the art, Gorgias, in which you are skilled?"

"Rhetoric, Socrates."

"So we should call you a rhetorician?"

"Yes, and a good one, if you are pleased to call me what – to use Homer's phrase – 'I vaunt myself to be.'"

That was Gorgias; he had not changed, quoting verses from the Iliad he had written out and memorized, ready on a moment's notice, the way he had once done with Homer's Helen, to twist the meaning out of all recognition to gain popular applause. Socrates ignored him.

"Are you able to make others like yourself?"

"Yes, that is what I profess to do," he replied. And then, because he had always to remind everyone of how famous he had become, he added with a smile of satisfaction, "Not only here, but elsewhere also."

"Then would you be willing to continue this discussion by way of alternate question and answer, and leave to some other time the lengthy speeches that rhetoric often uses?"

"I will try to be as brief as possible. It is one of my claims that no one could express the same thing in briefer terms than myself."

Socrates jumped on it. "That is just what I want, Gorgias: give me a display of this very skill – in brevity of speech; your lengthy style will do another time."

"I will do that, and you will admit that you have never heard anyone speak more briefly."

"Come then; since you claim to be skilled in rhetorical art, and to be able to make anyone else a rhetorician, tell me with what particular thing rhetoric is concerned: as, for example, weaving is concerned with clothing, is it not?"

"Yes."

"And music, likewise, with the making of tunes?"

"Yes."

"Upon my word, Gorgias, I do admire your answers! You make them as brief as they well can be. But now, answer me: with what particular thing is rhetoric concerned?"

"With speech."

"What kind of speech? The kind that shows sick people how to get well?"

"No."

"Then rhetoric is not concerned with all kinds of speech."

"No, as I say."

"Yet it does make men able to speak and to understand the things about which they speak."

"Of course."

"Does the medical art make men able to understand and speak about the sick?"

"Yes."

Socrates then asked about other arts, and got the same kind of answer. Socrates kept pressing, demanding to know not what rhetoric did, but what rhetoric was.

"Tell us, what is this thing you say is the greatest good for men and that you, more than anyone, claim to produce?"

Gorgias looked at him as if he were an innocent, someone who knew nothing of the world.

"It is the greatest good, the cause of freedom to mankind at large, and the source of domination in their cities to those individuals who learn how to use it."

"Well, and what do you call it?" asked Socrates, unimpressed.

"The ability to persuade in speeches judges in the law courts, statesmen in the council chambers, the people in the assembly – any audience at any meeting held on public matters," replied Gorgias, becoming with each word more intense. "And I tell you that by virtue of this power you will have the doctor as your slave, and the trainer as your slave, and the money-maker will make money not for himself, but for you, you who are able to speak and persuade the multitude."

His arms folded across his chest, Socrates stared at the ground, considering, as it seemed, what he wanted to ask next. He raised his eyes and looked at Gorgias with a glance even more penetrating than it had been before, measuring in advance the response he would receive, not just to the next question but who knows how many after that. It was uncanny, but I somehow knew that he had had this same conversation by himself, asked each question, given each answer, as close to word for word as if, like one of the plays of Euripides, he had written all the lines himself. That was the reason his eyes blazed with such astonishing enthusiasm, such incredible confidence, each time he waited to hear an answer that somewhere in the depths of his mind he had heard before.

"When a man teaches anything, does he persuade in his teaching? Or do you think not?"

"No, to be sure, Socrates, I think he most certainly does

persuade."

"All the arts, then, are producers of persuasion?"

"Yes."

"Rhetoric, then, is not the only producer of persuasion."

"You are right."

"Then of what kind of persuasion, and of persuasion dealing with what, is rhetoric the art?"

"The kind of persuasion you find in the law-courts and in any public gatherings, as I just now said. It deals with the just and the unjust."

"Is there something you call 'having learned'?"

"There is."

"And again, 'having come to belief'?"

"Yes."

"Then do you think that having learned and having believed, or learning and faith, are the same thing, or different?"

"In my opinion, Socrates, they are different."

"And your opinion is right, as you can prove in this way: if someone asked you – is there, Gorgias, a false and a true belief – you would say, yes, I believe."

"I should."

"But now, is there a false and a true knowledge?"

"Surely not."

"So it is evident now that they are not the same."

"You are right."

"But yet those who have learned have been persuaded, as well as those who have believed."

"That is so."

"Then would you have us assume two forms of persuasion – one providing belief without knowledge, and the other sure knowledge?"

"Certainly."

"Now which kind of persuasion is it that rhetoric creates in law courts or any public meeting on matters of justice and injustice? The kind from which we get belief without knowledge, or that from which we get knowledge?"

"Obviously, I presume, Socrates, that from which we get belief."

"Then rhetoric, it seems, is a producer of persuasion for belief, not for instruction in the matter of the just and the unjust."

"Yes."

"And so the rhetorician's business is not to teach a law court or a public meeting in matters of justice and injustice, but only to make them believe; since, I take it, he could not in a short while teach such a multitude in matters so important."

"No, to be sure."

Socrates looked around at the people who had crowded close, waiting to see what would happen next, whether Socrates or Gorgias would prove more capable in arguing their case. Like everything else he did, there was a reason – a method, if you will – in this brief pause.

"You claim to be an orator yourself and to make orators of others. It is proper, therefore, to ask you to explain what you do, and you should believe me when I tell you that I am only furthering your own interest."

An elbow pushed against my ribs. Alcibiades was muffling a laugh.

"Watch this! Watch the way he puts him on the defensive."

"It is likely, isn't it," continued Socrates, now become Gorgias' sudden friend, "that more than a few of those standing here would like to become your pupil, but are perhaps too embarrassed to ask you any questions of their own – "

"You'll notice he isn't embarrassed, he isn't intimidated," whispered Alcibiades loud enough that several standing near us turned to look.

" – so, when you are being pressed with questions of mine, imagine that you are being questioned by them as well, and more than any other questions, this is one to which they would like an answer: what shall we get, Gorgias, by coming to hear you? On what matters shall we be enabled to give advice to the city? Will it be only on the just and the unjust, or on other things as well?"

"Everything. The power of rhetoric has no limit. It comprises within itself practically all powers at once. If a rhetorician and a doctor were to contest in speech before the Assembly as to which of the two should be appointed physician, the physician would be nowhere. Whatever the profession, the rhetorician would persuade the meeting to appoint him before anyone else. There is no subject on which the rhetorician could not speak more persuasively than a member of any other profession whatsoever, before a multitude. So great, so strange, is the power of this art."

Though Gorgias did not know it, this was the turning point,

the point at which everything he said would show him for the fool he was, at least to those who cared more for the truth than their own ambition. Because, as I was about to learn again, the truth was the last thing some men wanted. But Socrates never cared for what others found inconvenient. He was back at Gorgias with all the force of his own form of rhetoric.

"You say you are able to make a rhetorician of any one who chooses to learn from you?" he asked with a strange insistence.

"Yes, I do."

"Now, do you mean, to make him carry conviction to the crowd on all subjects, not by teaching them, but by persuading?"

"Certainly, I do," replied Gorgias, bristling with indignation.

"You said that even on the question of health the orator would be more convincing than the doctor."

"Yes – I meant, to the crowd."

"And 'to the crowd' means 'to the ignorant'? For surely, to those who know, he will not be more convincing than the doctor."

"Yes, you're right," said Gorgias with reluctance.

"And if he becomes more convincing than the doctor, he becomes more convincing than he who knows?"

"Certainly."

"Though not himself a doctor?"

"Yes."

"But he who is not a doctor is without knowledge of that whereof the doctor has knowledge."

"Certainly."

"So he who does not know will be more convincing to those who do not know than he who knows, supposing the orator to be more convincing than the doctor. Is that, or something else, the consequence?"

"In this case it does follow."

"Then the case is the same in all the other arts for the orator and his rhetoric: there is no need to know the truth of actual matters, but one merely needs to have discovered some device of persuasion which will make one appear to those who do not know to know better than those who know."

"Well, and is it not a great convenience, Socrates, to make oneself a match for the professionals by learning just this single art and omitting all the others?"

Socrates stared at him with a show of disbelief. I say show, because it was exactly what he had expected from Gorgias. The reaction was for the crowd, those who had thought that Gorgias could teach them something worth knowing, a power by which to win public approval and advance their own ambitions. He wanted to show the emptiness of the claim, to show how easily this false rhetoric could be defeated, and perhaps show some few among those watching that there was something better than what they had thought they wanted to be.

Alcibiades told me with a glance that it was time to go. We moved around the circle that surrounded the continuing debate, left the house of Callicles and started down the street.

"How long did that take? – Half an hour, if that. Who would believe it? The famous Gorgias, the man some even claim invented rhetoric, the great Gorgias – "

"The blowhard Gorgias; the only thing great about him his overweening vanity," I interjected. I would have danced in the streets, had my foot been willing, at how much joy I felt on what I had just witnessed.

" – the great Gorgias, defeated – no, destroyed – in less than thirty minutes. He could not have known what he was getting into, could not have known what Socrates was like. Even if someone had tried to tell him, if you haven't seen it yourself, seen that power of his, nothing could prepare you. They probably told him that Socrates liked to pester people with questions, that he managed somehow to turn an argument in directions you had not expected – about as helpful as telling an athlete that some other runner is fast. How explain a difference that isn't one of degree but of kind? Gorgias would have listened to what they told him and in his mind dismissed it as beneath his notice. A man who asks questions, a man who likes to argue, a man who can catch a contradiction where you did not know one existed! – What was that but an invitation to a challenge he had won a thousand times before. Every time I see him do it, every time I watch him do his work – you know what I feel? – Glad I was not born earlier or later, glad to be living in the middle of the greatest war there has ever been and in the presence of the greatest mind that will ever be."

"The greatest motion and the greatest rest," I remarked, thinking back over what I had seen and what I had learned. "Is it just a coincidence that these two things are happening at the same time? Or is there some connection between the violent uncertainty of the times we live in and this astonishing intelligence, this strange gift of Socrates?"

"When things begin to fall apart, things begin to look different. That is when you start to question what you have always believed. Think what the plague had done: made some people forget everything they had been taught about right and wrong and live for nothing more than pleasure, and made others even more religious, certain that what was happening was a punishment from the gods because we had not worshipped them in the ways we should have. The greatest motion, this war we're in – you're right to call it that – but there is a double war: the one with the Peloponnesians and the one we fight among ourselves. And if it were not for that, this constant conflict over what we believe, if we were like the Spartans or the Persians and everyone believed, or pretended to believe – the same thing, there could not be a Socrates. He would have to think alone. As it is, he has to be careful, because for all our disagreements, there are some things no Athenian can safely say in public." With a knowing look, he added, "We all believe in the gods, don't we? We all believe that the only fit punishment for impiety is death. Although," he remarked, with a quick, sideways glance that seemed a warning of things about to happen, "if the gods exist, it is hard to believe that they could believe in us."

"Why? What has happened? You don't mean what we just saw, do you? The way everyone fawns over Gorgias, eager to learn how to lie their way to power. It is a question, though, isn't it, why the gods would take any interest in what happens to anyone who thinks in such small-minded terms?"

The streets were silent and empty, as if the city had been deserted, abandoned to the ravages of the brutal midday heat. It did not seem to bother Alcibiades, and, caught up in our conversation, listening to the way he lisped his words, it did not bother me.

"The plague, the death of Pericles – it is the end of all restraint. Everything now goes to extremes. What did Socrates just prove? – That what Gorgias teaches – what all those second rate orators of ours, Cleon and the rest of those baying jackals, are so anxious to learn – is that power is its own defense; that the only thing worth knowing is how to tell the kind of lies that people will believe. They won't even do decency the favor of hypocrisy; they brag about their commitment to dishonor. Witness what Paches has just done; witness what, I can almost guarantee it, all of Athens is about to do."

"Paches? The one sent to put down the revolt on Lesbos?"

Mytilene, a city on Lesbos, an ally of Athens since the Persian war, had revolted. Athens, determined to show that their power had not been diminished and that they still controlled the seas, had put two hundred fifty ships into action. A hundred sailed against the Peloponnese, a hundred guarded the coast around Athens, and fifty more were at various other places. Paches, with a thousand hoplites, invaded Mytilene. The siege lasted half a year, until, with their food running out and the promised help from Sparta still not there, Mytilene was forced to surrender. Paches agreed to do nothing against the people of Mytilene, but to let them make their case to the Athenians. But that was not all that Paches had done, as Alcibiades now explained.

"The Peloponnesians sent forty ships to Mytilene, but they never got there. They sailed around the cities of Ionia, and Paches went after them. By chance, he put in at a place called Notium, the harbor of Colophon, a city split into two opposing parties, one of which had called in Arcadian mercenaries. The other party asked Paches for help. This is how honorable we have become. Paches invites the general of the Arcadians, Hippias, to negotiate, and promises that if he leaves his fortification and no agreement is reached he will personally make sure that Hippias gets back safely. Hippias takes him at his word and comes to negotiate. But there is no negotiation. Paches has him arrested and makes a surprise attack on the fortification. All of the troops inside are put to death."

"And Hippias – what happened to him?"

"Paches kept his promise. He had him taken back to the fortification where he was then shot down with arrows and became the last casualty of this war of duplicity and infamy. And now Paches has sent to Athens a thousand prisoners from Mytilene whom he claims were part of the insurrection."

Alcibiades stopped walking, placed his left hand against the wall of a dark stone building, and gathered his thoughts. In a square a block ahead, a fountain gurgled and the sound alone made me remember, and for a moment feel, the cool sensation of water splashing against my skin.

"I'm still too young. I'm almost old enough, but still too young to speak in the Assembly. Cleon rules it now with the same control as Pericles, but with a different effect: Pericles appealed to what was best in them; Cleon to what is worst. Pericles made them want to be like him; Cleon makes them think they have nothing to aspire to, and that anyone who pretends to be different than they are only wants to use them for his own advantage. What Cleon did yesterday ... Did you see the faces of some of those clustered close to Gorgias – how they hung on every word? They had just seen Cleon do what Gorgias claims to teach! Power, power, nothing ever but that – how to get it, how to keep it, how to use it for your own purposes. Cleon worked them into a fever pitch, telling them that Mytilene had revolted though it was not a subject state and therefore had nothing to complain about, and that not only had they revolted but that because of them a Peloponnesian fleet had for the first time dared to challenge our supremacy at sea by crossing over to Ionia to lend support to the rebels. He had them so angry, so ready to do anything, that they voted to put to death not only the thousand men sent here by Paches as responsible for the revolt, but the entire male population of Mytilene and to sell into slavery all the women and children.

"That was the reason, the real reason, why Socrates was late; why Chaerephon spent so much time in the marketplace. Chaerephon always has his ear to the ground, listening to what people say. Whichever way he voted yesterday, he'll vote tomorrow in favor of a change."

"A change?" I asked, stunned and deeply shocked by what he had told me. Kill all the men, make slaves of everyone else, no matter whether they took an active part in the revolt; no matter, even, if they opposed it? Wipe out a people for the crime of wanting to live free and independent? "A change in what?"

"Once it was done, once it was over, once the decision had been made, there was a reaction, a sense of revulsion. It was cruel, unprecedented, and indefensible: punishing the innocent and the guilty alike. They want a chance to reconsider. Another assembly has been called for tomorrow."

So it had come to this, rampant insanity followed by regret, a last trace of conscience, a second debate on a question that should never have been raised, much less decided; a sudden concern that the extermination of a whole people might have been a mistake.

"'The brilliance of the present is the glory of the future stored up for ever in the memory of man.' I don't imagine even Cleon had the temerity to quote that line!"

"Or the wit to remember it," remarked Alcibiades with a grim expression. "Come tomorrow. See what happens. Cleon won't back down, won't change his mind. He'll see it as a challenge to his influence. That is the only thing that matters to him. He would have all the women and children killed, too, if he thought he could carry a majority."

I remembered those words, and the scorn with which Alcibiades had spoken them, as I stood the next day watching from the back of the amphitheater as Cleon attacked those who wanted to stop the wholesale execution he had convinced the Assembly to approve. His speech, the way he phrased things, the use he made of antitheses and other standard tricks of what now passed for rhetoric, bore at times an uncanny similarity to the speeches that Gorgias gave. Would that have been the only similarity, that there had not been the same blind insistence on immediate advantage instead of the long term best interest of the city, the kind of conduct required of any nation with a claim to greatness.

Cleon liked to brag that he had a more realistic understanding of what people wanted and how they behaved, that better than anyone he knew how to cut through all the cant and hypocrisy and get right to the heart of the matter. He did not hesitate to tell everyone that compassion was a weakness which would do great and perhaps irreversible damage. If Cleon knew anything, he knew how to appeal to fear.

"What you do not realize is that your empire is a tyranny exercised over subjects who do not like it and who are always plotting against you; you will not make them obey you by ignoring your own interests to do them a favor; your leadership depends on superior strength and not on any good will of theirs."

With his head cocked to the side, and his small, pointed chin jutted out, he waved a clenched fist in the air and shouted that they were fools to change their minds, to decide to revisit a decision once it had been taken.

"It is the worst thing we could do, pass measures and then ignore them. Better to have bad laws, than to have good ones that are always being altered. And you know that, but you let yourselves be deceived by people who want to appear wiser than anyone else, who want to show how well they can speak. These are not the people you should be guided by. A lack of learning combined with sound common sense is more helpful than the kind of cleverness that gets out of hand. It is better to be governed by the man in the street than by intellectuals; better to be governed by people who do not think themselves wiser than the laws, people who are willing to be unbiased judges instead of competitors in a contest to see who can give the better speech.

"It's your fault that things have come to this. You like nothing more than to hear people talk; if something is to be done in the future you estimate the possibilities by hearing a good speech on the subject, and as for the past you rely not so much on the facts which you have seen with your own eyes as on what you have heard about them in some clever piece of verbal criticism. Any novelty in an argument deceives you at once, but when the argument is tried and proved you become unwilling to follow it; you look with suspicion on what is normal and are the slaves of every paradox that comes your way. Each of you would like to make a speech himself, and if you cannot do that, you think the next best thing is to look as though you followed everything in the speeches given by others by applauding a good point even before it is made, and by being as quick at seeing how an argument is going to be developed as you are slow at understanding what it will lead to in the end."

There was a kind of genius in the way Cleon attacked his audience, the very people on whose approval his own power depended. The first time I heard him lecture a crowd on its deficiencies, I thought for a moment that I had been mistaken, that he was not the ruthless demagogue I had believed he was; that he was, in his own way, as willing to teach restraint as Pericles had been. Then, as I looked at the faces in the crowd, when I saw how quick, how eager, they were to agree, I realized that everyone thought he was talking about all the others and that those harsh criticisms were deserved. They might all applaud together, raise their voices in a common shout of praise or condemnation, but they had, each of them, their own, separate identity, this strange belief that they had each time acted independently and of their own accord and that what the crowd decided had nothing to do with them. Slaves to the impulse of the moment, they rejected any suggestion that they might not be free.

Cleon listed the reasons why the revolt of Mytilene had been so harmful, and what should be done about it.

"What we should have done long ago with the Mytilenians was to treat them exactly the same way as all the rest; then they would never have grown so arrogant; for it is a general rule of human nature that people despise those who treat them well and look up to those who make no concessions. Let them now therefore have the punishment which their crime deserves."

A 'general rule of human nature' to despise those who treat us well! That said everything about Cleon's nature. He could only look up or look down, be a master or a slave; he could treat no one as an equal, perhaps because the only people who were his equal would have to be treated with contempt.

"Let no hope be held out to the Mytilenes. They knew what they were doing, they planned it; and one only forgives actions that were not deliberate. To feel pity, to be carried away by clever argument, to listen to the claims of decency, are three things that are entirely against the interests of an imperial power. As for compassion, feel it for people like ourselves, not for our enemies. As for clever speeches, let those who give them argue among themselves on matters that are not so vital for our survival. And as for decency, feel it toward those who are going to be our friends in the future, not those who will remain as much our enemies as they have ever been. As for the Mytilenes, punish them as they deserve and make an example of them to your other allies, show that revolt will be punished by death."

Cleon's speech was greeted with thunderous applause that seemed to deepen and grow stronger the longer it continued. There seemed little chance now that Mytilene would be spared. The next speaker, Diodotus, a man I had never met, and, from what I later gathered, someone who had seldom taken an active part in public debate but had opposed the motion to put the Mytilenes to death, waited until the audience, which must have numbered more than twenty thousand, finally fell silent. And then he waited longer, waited until his silence became the subject of attention and the audience began to wonder what he was going to say, instead of still thinking about what Cleon had done. Two sentences into his speech and it was as if Cleon had not spoken at all.

"I do not blame those who have proposed a new debate on the subject of Mytilene, and I do not share the view which we have heard expressed, that it is a bad thing to have frequent discussions on matters of importance. Haste and anger are, to my mind, the two greatest obstacles to wise counsel – haste, that usually goes with folly, anger, that is the mark of primitive and narrow minds. And anyone who maintains that words cannot be a guide to action must be a fool. It is impossible to deal with the uncertainties of the future by any other medium."

Where else but in Athens could anything like this have happened? Someone who had passed unnoticed, a man without any known ambition, suddenly rises from the crowd and before he has finished the first paragraph of his speech has attacked and destroyed the premise of the argument that the most forceful advocate in the assembly had spent nearly an hour trying to make. I had the feeling that Diodotus was one of those good citizens of Athens who had learned from Pericles how to speak and what it was important to say. More than a great statesman, Pericles had been a public teacher, teaching those who listened to his speeches that intelligence and honor, and not the cheap verbal tricks taught by men like Gorgias, were the secrets of persuasion. Diodotus did not speak as long as Cleon, but he said a great deal more.

"One of Cleon's chief points is that to inflict the death penalty will be useful to us in the future as a means for deterring other cities from revolt, but I, who am just as concerned with the future, am quite convinced that this is not so. Cities and individuals alike, are all disposed to do wrong, and there is no law that will prevent it. Men have tried every kind of punishment, yet even with the death penalty, the laws are still broken. We must not come to the wrong conclusion by having too much confidence in the effectiveness of capital punishment, and we must not make the condition of those who revolt desperate by depriving them of the possibility of repentance. If a city revolts and then realizes that the revolt cannot succeed, it will come to terms if it can pay an indemnity and continue to pay tribute afterwards. But if Cleon's method is adopted, every city will not only make more careful preparations for revolt, but will hold out until the very end because they know that the only alternative is death.

"There is only one way to deal with a free people, and that is not to inflict tremendous punishment on them after they have revolted, but to take tremendous care of them before this point is reached. And if we do have to use force with them, to hold as few as possible responsible for this. If you destroy the democratic party in Mytilene, who never took any part in the revolt and who, as soon as they got arms, surrendered the city, you will be guilty of killing those who helped you and helping your enemies. From now on, when the oligarchies start a revolt, they will have the people on their side because you have made it clear that the same punishment is laid down for both the guilty and the innocent. But even if they were guilty, you should pretend that they were not, and in that way keep on your side that part of the population that is still not opposed to you. It is far more useful to us, in preserving our empire, to put up with injustice than justly put to death the wrong people."

I watched breathless as the issue was decided by a show of hands. My eyes searched the crowd below, until I found where Alcibiades was sitting. He was involved in what seemed a heated conversation with someone sitting next to him in the front row, closest to the stage where the speakers had stood. Farther back, sitting with Chaerephon and several other young men I had seen gathered around Gorgias in the luxurious home of Callicles, Socrates tapped his bare foot, keeping time to some thought of his own.

The vote was so close that a second show of hands was called to confirm the result. By the narrowest of margins, the motion to reconsider passed and Mytilene was saved. Cleon's face flushed with rage as he stormed out, shoving aside anyone who stood in his way. Alcibiades watched without expression. Socrates nodded silently and with what appeared to be infinite sadness. I could not understand why. He was the last man who would have wanted the senseless slaughter that Cleon had been demanding. Then I realized what had happened. They were not going to kill the entire male population of Mytilene; they were only going to kill a thousand, all the prisoners brought from Mytilene, all those that Patches thought responsible for the revolt, would now be led out and executed one by one. Where, I wondered, was the glory in that?

CHAPTER SEVENTEEN

Aspasia came to see me. I was not expecting it. She seldom left her house after the death of Pericles, and had, for the first month or so, even refused to leave her room, her grief so great that it was feared she had lost the desire to live. I had never believed it; the woman I knew was too strong and independent to give up, and too intelligent. She had a child to raise, young Pericles, and nothing would have stopped her doing that. When I saw her standing at my door, she seemed not to have changed at all; or rather to have changed for the better from the last time I had seen her when, with all the euphoria of my recovery, I had gone to tell her that I was still alive. The sad distraction, the burden of the deaths of Pericles' two sons and so many of his other, close relations, had vanished from her face. Perhaps it was the finality of what had happened, the knowledge that if, now that he was gone, things would never be quite so good again at least the worst was over.

"What a pretty house you have," she said with a sweet smile as I invited her inside.

She wore a white tunic and a white silk scarf around her head. The days of mourning had now passed. I offered her something to drink, but she was too busy admiring my room to want anything.

"This is where you work." Pausing next to the desk piled high with papers, she ran her finger down the margin of an uncompleted sheet still damp with ink. There was a flash of recognition, or, rather, I should say recollection, in her large almond-shaped eyes. "It's been a long time since I've written anything. I should start again. It's the only way to think." She turned to look at me. "Don't you find that's true? I listen – I used to listen – to Pericles talking with other people, but I only really understood things when I wrote them down. It concentrates the mind; makes you get down to the essentials. Don't you find that's true?"

I started to agree, but something else caught her attention.

"What a lovely garden!" she exclaimed. Her eyes were wide with wonder as she looked out the door I had left open. Aspasia had a way of making the most ordinary things seem like something just discovered. "Could we sit out there?"

It was not yet noon and the garden was full of music, birds singing defiance to all the laws of property as they stole every fig they could reach. The air mixed the scent of a dozen different flowers in a different kind of harmony. This menagerie of sights and smells and sounds had become so much a part of the background of the secluded life I led that I scarcely noticed until someone mentioned it, or I had to be away from it.

"Alcibiades found this house for you. I think that is what he told me." She said this with a vague gesture suggesting that there were a great many things she was not sure she had not forgotten.

"After I recovered – that bitter pestilence that left so many dead – he thought I should have a place where the air was cleaner and there were not so many people crowded together, the way they are in Piraeus."

She sat at an angle on a stone bench, her hands folded in her lap, looking out toward the Acropolis and the sea beyond. A smile full of wisdom and nostalgia moved slowly across her lips.

"Alcibiades …! He knows nothing of the small gesture. He wanted to build a house for Socrates on a plot of land he owns, but Socrates told him he did not need anything more than what he had. What else would Socrates have said? The games are coming up, a chance for everyone who wants to make an impression to show how wealthy they are by entering a chariot in the races. Alcibiades is entering seven, a thing no one has ever done; all to prove by a show of extravagance that he has no rivals, that he can never be defeated. He has no choice, I suppose, now that the only thing anyone thinks about is what is profitable and expedient."

A bumble bee landed on Aspasia's milk colored hand. She put her finger next to its wings, waited until the bee wobbled onto it, then slowly raised it into the air and watched him fly away. A wistful smile told her own regret that she could not fly off as well.

"Alcibiades loves no one like he loves himself; no one, except, I think, Socrates, and you. He would have married you, if it had not been for … "

A sudden look of self-reproach darkened her expression, a silent apology for what, she realized, I must be thinking. I told her that it was not necessary, that she was wrong, or almost wrong, in what she thought.

"I know the way I have changed; I know I am not Helen anymore, the Helen that everyone wanted and everyone talked about.

I know I don't look the same way, that I am slightly disabled and somewhat disfigured, that if people stop and stare it is now for all the wrong reasons. But they don't – stop and stare, I mean – I am no longer beautiful and I am not ugly enough for that, especially if I am careful where I go and how I dress. But Alcibiades – no, marriage was never possible, however strong the feeling we might have had for one another. I would have been his mistress – "

"I was that to Pericles before he married me."

"But I was not that to Alcibiades, only friends who a few times slept together. Or perhaps, in a deeper sense, we were lovers, forced to stay apart because we were, each of us, more in love with something else: Alcibiades, with his astonishing ambition; I, with this strange longing to know more than just what my body tells me. But none of that matters now. Helen is what Helen is, not what Helen was."

With eyes full of hope and kindness, Aspasia politely disagreed.

"The Helen I knew and loved has not changed at all; if anything, she is better than she was: wiser with experience, more forgiving in her judgments."

I felt a tear come to my eye and tried to fight it with a laugh.

"Less forgiving in some judgments: Cleon, for example, who I now regard as nothing short of despicable."

Aspasia bobbed her head from side to side, weighing in the balance her own judgment in the matter.

"No, you're wrong in that. To call Cleon despicable is to be not just forgiving, but generous to a fault. But let's not talk of him. Come with me down to Pireaus. There is something you need to see."

We went down to Pireaus and found the harbor swarming with men and ships. There were at least a dozen new ones under construction, and several dozen more in for refitting. There was always a good deal of commotion in the harbor, especially since the beginning of the war, but there was something different about this. You could almost hear it, the sense of something extraordinary about to happen, something so ambitious and far-reaching it would change everything. You could see it on the faces of all the men at work, the eager certainty shining in their eyes, the feeling that they were part of something as great, or greater, than anything that the Athenians, or perhaps anyone, had ever tried before, a venture, a challenge, that if they were willing to dare it, might change the world.

"I wanted to see it; I wanted you to see it with me. Look at this, how astonishing it is: all the parts of a great enterprise, the way they start to fit together; the hundred ships, or whatever the number when you count up all the ones needed for supplies and equipment – a thousand sailors, ten thousand soldiers, all the men those ships will carry – the proudest fleet ever assembled, a force more powerful than any we have ever sent to foreign shores, the Sicilian expedition, the very thing that Pericles once warned would be the one way to lose the war." A wistful smile cut through her eyes; a trace of bitter regret lingered afterward on her lip. "It is magnificent to see, though, isn't it? All these ships, these strange dreams of conquest. We're told that Sicily is paradise, wide deep rivers and green forests everywhere, and air as sweet as nectar. We always dream of things we have never seen, and think our happiness depends on what we have never had. Alcibiades has been waiting for this moment all his life."

She turned to me with a look that was almost frightening in its intensity, the product of some inner struggle, a choice between telling the truth of what she felt or continuing to honor unquestioned the memory of the only man she would ever love.

"Alcibiades thinks he can do this, conquer Sicily and Carthage after that, make Athens the greatest empire the world has ever known, make everyone forget Pericles and remember only him. And the awful truth is that I believe it, too; not that what he is so intent on doing will be good for Athens, not because I think Pericles was wrong, but because, once Alcibiades has decided what he wants no one can stop him from getting it. And there is nothing – nothing – that he doesn't want. He is the most driven man I have ever known; more driven, I think, than anyone who ever lived. There are no limits to his ambition. He loves Athens the way a man loves a woman, because she is beautiful and because she can love him back. There is no one like him; he is what Hesiod and Homer had in mind when they invented the gods."

"Eros," I added, with a wistful look of my own. "Eros, in every meaning of the word."

I woke up early, the morning light cold and sinister, still bothered by a dream only parts of which I could remember. It was about my father, Hiero – that much I was sure of – and a play I had seen; or a play that had not yet been written – I was not certain. All I had were bits and pieces, the fragments of what might have been several different dreams instead of only one. I lay in bed, staring at the ceiling, trying to recall what had seemed so vivid when

I saw it in my sleep. Gradually it began to come back, to make a second appearance. It was not a play, it was the idea of one, or, more precisely, the idea of what every play, every human work of art was in its nature all about. Like every tyrant who had done unspeakable things, Hiero wanted to have himself immortalized. He had paid the poet Pindar a small fortune to write words that would capture forever the glory of his achievements, but Pindar, with a poet's license, had played a double-game, extolling the triumphs of the tyrant with what only seemed a passing comment on the honesty of other writers. The dream had brought back to memory lines that had lain forgotten in the deep recesses of my mind, lines where the poet spoke of how "stories starting from mortals somehow stretch truth to deception woven cunningly on the loom of lies." That was the meaning of the dream – I knew it now. We see nothing clearly, and if we did, if there are some of us who see the truth of things, the words we use, the spoken symbols of the things we grasp, carry with them so many other shades of meaning – so many combinations of what are half-truths at best – that the light is always mingled with the darkness. And that – those feeble words of worn-out meaning – becomes in turn the only standard against which to measure all the lies we tell on purpose.

Out my window I could see dawn's first gray light. In protest against the need to start another day, I pulled the covers up to my chin and tried to lie myself back to sleep, insisting that for all I knew this was just another dream and that I might as well enjoy it. But my conscience had an arsenal of punishments. My lame foot began to throb and that wretched claw-like hand of mine began to ache, the way they now did almost every time I woke up in the chill morning cold. I threw a shawl around my shoulders and, laughing oaths of vengeance against the sun come too early, crossed over the hard tile floor to the washstand in the corner.

An old line of Pindar, remembered in the dream, echoed in my mind like the voice of a lost lover, telling me over and over again how stories, the things we say, "somehow stretch truth to deception woven cunningly on the loom of lies." It seemed as much a prophecy as a chronicle of the past, a history of the future written by an author who knows that tomorrow is nothing more than yesterday unrecorded, that what has not happened yet is just as real as anything that has already taken place. The Athenians were about to meet in assembly to decide, once and for all, whether to launch the attack on

Sicily and begin another war of conquest. But it seemed to me that it was all inevitable, that it had long since been written – written, if I dare say it, the day that Alcibiades was born – that Sicily would seize on Athens like a madness and that Alcibiades would be there to turn that frenzy into lust; written that he would promise them the world and that in the single most erotic thing Athens, or any city, had ever done, would rush headlong into either victory or destruction without even stopping to calculate the odds, or rather become more ardent by the danger.

I was not sure I would go; or so I told myself as I sat down to a meager breakfast of figs and nectar. I knew I would, of course; that I would not miss it, that what happened in today's debate would change everything: that whatever happened, nothing would ever be the same. It was a mistake, the greatest mistake they could make, but no one was going to listen. The empire was a mistake, but no one now was going to say so. We were all driven by forces we did not understand; or rather that most of us did not understand. Athens was great, and what had made her great – this endless desire for acquisition, this endless need for something new – made her want to be greater than she was. It was restless motion that knows no rest; constant change that never changes. Athens, which ruled over so many cities, was too much the slave of what it wanted to rule itself. And that was what made it so exciting: the sheer uncertainty of daring more than anyone had ever dared before. They might be the slaves of their impulses, the prisoners of their desires, but they dreamed of greatness and there was something not just astonishing but worth honoring in that.

The morning chill vanished with the morning mist. It was a windless day, the trees speechless without a breeze to start the talking of their leaves. There was not a sound anywhere. Dogs prowled silent in the streets; even the birds, perched high on branches, were mute witnesses of the scene below. People on their way to the Assembly moved quietly, lost in thought, all of them thinking the same thing: whether they would really do it, leave behind the fetters of the past, what they had been told since Pericles, fight one opponent at a time, or venture everything on a new and different war. Nicias insisted it would be the biggest mistake they would ever make.

Nicias was conservative, pious, and unwilling to take any chance at all. As I listened to him speak, he seemed to have the kind of humble arrogance seen in members of old, established families:

nothing specifically to be proud of, but a general appreciation of his own self-worth. He understood his own limitations, but instead of seeing them as a weakness he seemed to think them a strength. Limits were like rules, fixed and unalterable, never under any circumstances to be ignored. He was in that the mirror image of Alcibiades, which was perhaps the reason he hated him as much as he did; hated him the way someone who believes nothing should be questioned hates someone who questions everything. More than anything, he hated, he despised, what Alcibiades represented: the eager daring of the Athenians. He as much as admitted it at the very beginning of his speech.

"I know that no speech of mine would be powerful enough to alter your character, and it would be useless to advise you to safeguard what you have and not to risk what is yours already for doubtful prospects in the future."

Nevertheless, he urged them not to do what they plainly wanted to do.

"This is not the time for running risks or for grasping at a new empire before we have secured the one we have already. Even if we did conquer the Sicilians, there are so many of them and Sicily so far away that it would be almost impossible to govern them. It makes no sense to go to war against a people who, even if conquered, could not be controlled, while if we fail we would be in a much worse situation than if we had never made the attempt."

There was some applause at this, but there was a louder demonstration on the other side: cat-calls, cries of derision, angry demands that he should take his seat and let someone with the courage to lead speak instead. The noise became deafening, and what started as a debate threatened to end in riot. Nicias stood his ground, waiting, silent and unmoved, until finally, tired of hearing its own voices, the crowd relented. But though he had not shown it, Nicias had become incensed. He gave up any thought of strategic advice and went after Alcibiades directly. His iron-gray eyebrows were knit together in a tantrum of indignation; his voice, usually so calm and soothing, had an edge of heavy sarcasm.

"No doubt there is someone sitting here who is delighted at having been chosen for the command and who, entirely for his own selfish reasons, will urge you to make the expedition – and all the more so because he is still too young for his post."

This was greeted with boos and hisses. Nicias threw his head back and smiled his scorn.

"He wants to be admired for the horses he keeps, and because these things are expensive, wants to make profit from his appointment. Beware of him; he will endanger everything you have acquired in order to live a brilliant life of his own. You are here to decide an important matter, not something that can, or should, be left to the decision of a young man in a hurry to make a name for himself."

The reaction was immediate, and intense. The friends of Alcibiades, for the most part young men themselves, were enraged, shouting insults as Nicias, undeterred, continued his attack.

"I see that he has brought with him a party of his own, young men who think that all they have to do to win a victory is to wish for it, and that opposition to this Sicilian expedition of theirs must be based on cowardice instead of on the recognition that it constitutes the greatest danger we have ever known."

Alcibiades was on his feet, demanding to be heard.

"Athenians, since Nicias has made this attack on me, let me say at the beginning that I have a better right than others to hold the command and that I am quite worthy of the position. As for all the talk against me, it is about things which have brought honor to myself and to our city. When everyone thought our city had been ruined by the war, I did something no one had ever done before, entered seven chariots in the Olympic Games and took first, second, and fourth places, and by that made everyone believe that Athens was even greater than she was. And again, though my fellow citizens may envy me for the magnificence with which I have done things in Athens, providing choruses and other public benefits, to the outside world this also is evidence of our strength. And it is perfectly reasonable, when a man has a high opinion of himself, and that opinion is warranted, not to be put on a level with everyone else. Anyone whose brilliance has made them prominent are unpopular while they live, but in future time people claim relationship with them, even where none exist, and their cities boast of them, not as strangers or disreputable characters, but as fellow citizens and doers of great deeds. This is what I aim at myself, and because of this my private life is criticized; but the question is whether you have anyone who deals with public affairs better than I do."

This was stunning, not so much for what he said, though that was astonishing enough, but the way he said it, as if it were nothing more than an observable fact, one with which no one in their senses could possible disagree. It was incredible! He had told them in effect that he was the greatest man alive and that that was the reason why others would try to find fault with what he did. I smiled to myself, wondering if anyone had ever dared be so honest. And then, showing his mastery of the situation, the conditions with which the Athenians would have to deal, he proceeded to argue the case against Nicias and his call for restraint, and did it as if he were the one who did not want to break with tradition.

"They talk about the enemies we shall leave behind us if we sail, but our fathers left behind them these same enemies when they had the Persians on their hands as well, and so founded our empire, relying solely on their superiority in sea power. The Peloponnesians have never had so little hope of success against us as they have now. It is true that if they had the confidence they could invade us by land, but they could do this whether we sailed to Sicily or not. They can do us no harm at all with their fleet, since we shall leave behind us a fleet of our own more than capable of dealing with theirs."

He had them in the palm of his hand. They were ready to do anything he asked. He might be young, but there was no one of any age – surely not Nicias – who had a better grasp of political and military realities, no one who could marshal facts into a more convincing argument.

"The fact is that we have reached a stage where we are forced to plan new conquests and forced to hold on to what we have got, because there is a danger that we ourselves may fall under the power of others unless others are in our power. And you cannot look upon this idea of a quiet life in quite the same way as others do – not unless you are going to change your whole way of living. This voyage will have a depressing effect on the Peloponnesians when they see that we despise the quiet life we are living now and have taken on the expedition to Sicily. At the same time, we shall either, as is quite likely, become the rulers of all Hellas by using what we gain in Sicily, or, in any case, we shall do harm to the Syracusans, and so do good to ourselves and our allies.

"Do not be put off by Nicias' arguments. Instead, keep to the old ways of our fathers who joined together, young and old alike, and raised our city to the position it now holds. Make it your endeavor to raise this city to even greater heights, and remember that, like everything else, the city will wear out of its own accord if it remains at rest. Its skill in everything will grow out of date. It is not at rest, but in conflict that it will gain new experiences and grow used to defend itself not by speeches but in action. A city which is active by nature will ruin itself if it changes its nature and tries to become idle."

Alcibiades! They loved him, they hated him, they did not know what to do with him, and so they did what he told them and hoped against hope that it would all somehow turn out for the best. He was a force of nature, their own nature writ large, and when they looked too closely at what he was they discovered that they were looking at themselves, what they would have wanted to be if they had not lacked his daring and his genius. They were in love with what he made them think they could become.

"He is everything I said he was," whispered a voice from just behind my shoulder. I turned to find Socrates standing idle, looking at me from under lowered eyes. "This will not go well," he remarked. But he was not talking to me, he was thinking out loud. "This won't go well at all. Pericles was right – it is a mistake to try for more than what we have – but the fault was his: He started this expansion and nothing now except defeat can stop it. The only hope is that Alcibiades is left alive to see it through. The others – Nicias and those like him – are too worried about what will happen if they lose. The only way to win a battle is to think of nothing but the honor of your death." He pointed past the crowd to where Alcibiades stood waving to his admirers. "He was born for this. You could see it when he was still a child. All the other children gave way to him; they let him take the lead in all the games they played. He was born to do great things, another Achilles; the only question whether he would bring the city glory or hasten its destruction. Nicias thinks the expedition is doomed, that it cannot possibly succeed. That is why he spoke against it, and why, when he could not stop it, he agreed to go along as one of three commanders. Nicias is a fool if he thinks he can stop Alcibiades from doing what he wishes. No good will come of this. It will be the beginning of the end for us. What happened here today will one day be remembered as the day we lost the war."

I was not sure that he was right. It was difficult, after what I had seen, to believe that Alcibiades could ever be defeated. He had spoken with all the certainty of someone who could not just read the future, but bend it to his will. When I listened to him I forgot the search for order in the world and remembered that in all

248

the important things in life chance, not necessity, played the larger part, and that chance seldom favored the cautious or the timid.

I stayed up late that night, recording my impressions, writing out in my slow longhand everything I thought worth remembering in that speech Alcibiades had given, trying to capture at least some of what I had felt and how that differed from the way the crowd had reacted when he made the argument for a new, Sicilian, war. I tried to paint an honest picture of the deep deception by which he had turned the respect for the ancestral, the obedience owed to the memory of what their fathers had done, into a reason for a break with the past; I tried to describe the growing fervor of the crowd, the slow built-up frenzy as someone thought too young to lead insisted that innovation was the one tradition that more than any other had to be conserved. I tried to describe the look of stunned and angry amazement with which Nicias had heard those words. I tried to describe everything I had heard and seen, but the more I wrote the less I liked of what I had written.

I started over with, unfortunately, the same result. A third, and then a fourth draft, and it was still no better, my desk a wasteland of ink stained paper. It was easy enough to write down what I remembered of what I had heard, but the way the crowd reacted, even my own thoughts, how much of that was accurate, what really happened at the time, and how much only what I thought later, after I had thought it all through again? How much of what I remembered was what I had wanted to hear, how much of what I read in all those eager eyes thoughts they really had and not what I imagined those looks must mean? I remembered what Democritus had told me about the prosecution of Anaxagoras: that only a fool would ever put down on paper what he really thought without concealing it in lies. I remembered it and laughed, laughed so hard that the flame in my candle wavered and went out. Why worry about whether someone might discover what you really thought in something you had written when you did not know the truth yourself?

With a sigh, I relit the candle and tried again, and this time, finally, the words seemed to come of their own accord, writing with more exact precision than I had known before all the thoughts and memories I wanted to preserve. My hand, my good hand, sailed across the page. Everything I wrote was true. I could see a picture of it in my mind, and yet, as I began to realize, the whole of it, taken together, still seemed false and misleading. How describe the way a crowd suddenly becomes a single being, driven by a single feeling, a common urge to express itself in some single act of daring? How give an adequate account, one that would make a reader really know what it had been like to be there, part of this great sweating mass of humanity, with their frenzied eyes and twisted mouths, driven mad by thoughts of glory promised by the magic tongue of Alcibiades? Laying aside my pen, I laughed at my own, tongue-tied, incompetence, my inability to bring to the surface what lay hidden in my mind.

I sat there, staring at my shadow cast in candlelight, remembering that it did not matter, that the only purpose I had in writing was to try to gain some clarity myself and give some permanence to things that, time's prisoner, would otherwise vanish into a forgotten past. If we were not time's creatures, it was only memory that made us whole. I sat and pondered, slid the chair back from the table and sat some more, silent and alone, listening to the quiet beating of my heart and my own slow, measured, breath, repeating in my mind what I had seen and heard and did not want to lose.

There was a sudden, tremendous racket. Someone was shouting my name, hammering at my door. I had not been asleep, I was sure of that, but I must have fallen into some kind of trance. I staggered out of the chair.

"Who is it?" I demanded. The door was still bolted and the only reply was loud, drunken laughter, but I knew right away who it was. "You're drunk!" I shouted gleefully, as I opened the door. "And with such a stupid smile on your face that you can't even hide it! You thought you would just drop by, pay a short visit, at this hour – too early for breakfast and too late for dinner – or did you forget where you lived and thought you were home?"

"I'm not drunk," said Alcibiades, with a bashful grin. He took a step inside and began to wobble. "It's all right," he insisted, as I started to help him. "I'm fine. Really. I was drunk – that's true – but that was hours ago. All you see now are the residual effects, a little fatigue. I've had a long night."

"I'll bet you have. Look at the way you're dressed: ribbons in your hair, long flowing robes, and that wreath around your head ...! Wherever you have been, I imagine you were, as always, the center of attention."

He laughed, but not like before, drunken and haphazard, but with something remarkably close to detachment. His face was still flushed with cheerful enthusiasm, and he was none too steady when he lowered himself into the chair I offered him, but his gaze when he looked up at me was cool and decisive.

"I had a lot to drink, early in the evening. Some of us were out celebrating, and then I remembered that there was a dinner at Agathon's – he won the prize for tragic poetry at the Linaean Festival yesterday – or was it the day before? and I decided to go."

I could not help myself; I had to ask why.

"Because you had been invited – or because you had not been?"

He liked the question, liked that I knew enough about him to discover at least some of the things that moved him. Drawing his eyes close together, he pretended confusion, mocking what the world thought significant. Invited, not invited, what conceivable difference could that make to him?

"I don't remember," he lied with such a theatrical show of indifference that I had to laugh. "But, listen, none of that is important. I was drunk, that is true; drunk in the way that loosens restraint. I was drunk, and I did something I try never to do."

He waited, daring me to ask, which meant I never would. I sat in a chair facing him and waited for him to tell me.

"I told the truth."

"It must have been difficult to do something you had never done before."

His chin came up a short fraction of an inch. A smile moved hidden like a fugitive across his mouth.

"I never lied to you."

"You were always intoxicated."

"Yes, whenever I saw you – I always was."

There was a long, wistful silence as we remembered how things had been before, when the future still seemed a straight road ahead that we could take at our leisure.

"I was quite drunk, and completely lucid. I knew exactly what I was doing," he said, starting over from the beginning. "The wine did what it always does: gave an excuse for saying what I wanted. I did not go there with that intention; I just went there to see what would happen. I walked in, unannounced, making every kind of noise. Aristophanes – "

"He was there? Aristophanes, who – "

" – He had just started to talk. It was his turn, or maybe he had already had his turn and wanted to reply to something that ... They were all making speeches, telling what they believed was the real nature of the god Eros. Socrates had apparently just finished and – "

"You knew he was going to be there? Is that the reason you – ?"

"No, I didn't know anything. I didn't even see him at first. But when I did, it all came out, everything I wanted to say, about Socrates and who and what he really is."

For the next hour or so, until it was almost dawn, I listened to what may have been the most remarkable thing I had ever heard, the truth about Socrates, that most enigmatic of human beings, from someone who, though not his equal, was in his own way superior to all other men.

"I told him at the beginning that I would only tell the truth, and that he should stop me if I told a lie, and he never stopped me, not once." Alcibiades emitted a deep-throated laugh. "I told him that he was like those silenuses – the woodland god, an old man with the ears of a horse, often drunk, usually riding a wine jar or an ass – that sit in the shops of the sculptors who make the Hermes: if you slit them open, you find an image of the gods. And I meant it. What is inside him seems so opposite to the strange way he looks. I told the truth. I told him – I told them all – that when I heard Pericles and other good speakers, I thought they spoke well, but they did not affect me the way he did: they did not make me troubled and distressed at the slavish condition in which I live. He is the only man who makes me feel shame. For I know that I am incapable of contradicting him or of saying what he commands should not be done; and whenever I go away, I know that I am doing it because I still want the honor I get from the crowd, all the popular applause. So I run away to avoid him, and whenever I see him, I am ashamed of what we have agreed I would do and I have not done. And there are times, more than I care to admit, when I should be glad if he were no longer alive and could not trouble me; and yet, if this should happen – if he should ever die – my only wish would be that I could have died in his place. I do not know what to do with this human being!"

I looked at Alcibiades with genuine sympathy.

"There is a kind of symmetry in this: You don't know what to do with Socrates, and Athens does not know what to do with you. No one really understands Socrates, and no one understands you. How could it be any different? Neither one of you believes what the city believes, and when either of you tells the truth you tells it wrapped in lies."

"He sees things I could never see, and, seeing them, makes me think I am blind. But what you just said – the truth wrapped in lies – that is what I said, what I told them about what he really is. It happened almost without my knowing it. I was trying to describe the power he has. I told them that despite what they thought, not one of them really knew him. I told them that he did not care at all if someone was beautiful – that he holds this in such great contempt that no one would believe it – any more than if someone is rich or has any other honor of those praised by the multitude. He believes that all these possessions are worth nothing and that we are nothing; that all his life he keeps on being ironical and playful to human beings. And when he is in earnest and, like a silenus, opened up, I do not know if anyone has seen those imagines within; but I once saw them and they were so divine, golden, and altogether beautiful that I knew that I would do anything to hear from Socrates everything he knew. That was when I decided to give myself to him, to let him become my lover."

He had never spoken of this before, never told me that he had been willing to go as far as that. He did not need to tell me anything. I knew enough about them both to know what happened.

"You told them that: that you were willing to sleep with Socrates? Did you then tell them how it felt to be rejected?"

Staring past me, his chest heaved with silent laughter as he considered what might have been the effect of his performance.

"Some of them – Pausanias in particular, who used to follow me around – were astonished; others, like Aristophanes, who is ridiculous and wants to be, did not know what to think. I did not care what anyone thought. I wanted Socrates to know the truth, and to tell you the truth, I actually took some pride in my rejection. What did it mean, if it was not to show me, what I should have known from the beginning, that Socrates was not interested in my body, that his interest went much deeper than that?"

"Yes, I know. He thought you could save Athens, make it better than it is, and more, importantly, make yourself better than you are. He does not think he can save all of humanity by what he tries to teach, but that he might, perhaps, help a few, those that have your kind of gift."

"A gift you have more than I," he replied with a sharp glance. "But Socrates – I told him that what deserves wonder is that respect in which he is like no other human being, neither the ancients nor those of the present day. In his strangeness, both in himself and in his speeches, there is no one with whom he can be compared, unless, again, to no human being, but to silenuses and satyrs. For if one were willing to hear his speeches, they would look at first altogether laughable. The words and phrases that they wrap around themselves on the outside are like that, the very hide of a hybristic satyr. For he talks of pack asses, blacksmiths, shoemakers and tanners, and it looks as if he is always saying the same things through the same things; and hence every inexperienced and foolish human being would laugh at his speeches. But if one sees them opened up and gets oneself inside them, one will find first, that they alone of speeches have sense inside, and second, that they are most divine and have the largest numbers of images of virtue in them; and that they apply to the largest area, indeed to the whole area that it is proper to examine for one who is going to be beautiful and good."

A sudden look of self-deprecation came into his eyes, and I had the feeling that he was questioning what he had done, whether he had come any closer than anyone else at getting hold of precisely what made Socrates so different, so unlike any other human being.

"I haven't seen what you have seen," I told him, trying to encourage him; "but I have seen enough to know that you're right: the hidden meaning of his words, the great nobility, the great beauty, inside of all those commonplace allusions – No, you were right, right about everything. There has never been anyone like him; there will never be anyone like him again. But does he really have that effect on you? Does he really make you so dissatisfied with yourself that you almost wish him dead?"

Alcibiades shook his head, laughed quietly, paused, and then, with a rueful and slightly puzzled expression, pronounced what seemed a final judgment on himself.

"No. I know myself too well for that. I can't be what he is, and I could never just follow him. It was true what I said – that I would have given anything, myself included, to hear from Socrates everything he knows – but that would not make me Socrates. He does not need anyone to tell him what they know. That is the difference. I can understand the things he tells me; he can understand them on his own. You do that, too; not as well as he does yet, but you do it, grasp things by themselves. I have at least that much understanding: I know that you see things I can see only darkly or cannot see at all. What makes me sometimes wish him dead is that I then might not feel quite so caught between what I know is better and what I know is worse, that world that you and Socrates live inside of and the world out there, all those fools and madmen whose approval I have to win, because without them there is nothing I can do."

"Conquer Sicily, then Carthage and Libya and how much else?"

A smile marched triumphant through his eyes, a smile that glittered like the sun and made me forget everything except how much I wanted him to succeed.

"Nicias thinks Sicily is the end of everything; Sicily is only the beginning. You were there; you saw how they responded, how much the Athenians are in love with the idea, how much they want it, how much they have to have it." He began to get excited, remembering what had happened and what it meant. "Nicias will keep trying to stop it; he'll invent excuses, reasons for delay. He will insist on consulting oracles, on reading omens, on searching meaning in the stars, but it is too late. Nothing can stop it now. You saw what happened when he tried to turn everyone against it by telling them how many more ships and men would be needed. – They wanted to send even more! Nothing can stop me, nothing! We sail in six days, and – "

There was a clatter outside, a harsh scraping noise and the sounds of men, what seemed dozens of them, running down the street, some drunken mob of revelers doing mischief in what was left of the night. Alcibiades bolted out the door, following in pursuit. A few minutes later, he was back, moving slowly, his eyes fixed on the ground, pondering, as it seemed, the meaning of something strange and unexpected he had just seen.

"What is it?" I asked, worried by the look of deep concern that now furrowed his brow. "What has happened?"

"The Hermae – the statues – all of them, up and down the street – destroyed, hit with hammers, broken into pieces."

CHAPTER EIGHTEEN

The Hermae had been destroyed, their square faces cut and disfigured, but it had not been a random act of vandalism by a few misguided youths too drunk to know what they were doing; it had happened all over Athens, thousands of Hermae defaced, and not just those on private porches but those in the public temples as well. It had been an organized attack, a conspiracy to put the city in a state of fear, and in this the conspirators, whoever they were, had succeeded beyond anything they could have imagined. No one knew who was responsible; no one knew who was behind this attempt to bring down the wrath of the gods. Rewards were offered to anyone who could provide information, and because whoever had committed such an unprecedented act of sacrilege might have done something like it before, immunity was promised to anyone who came forward, even if guilty themselves.

This had an immediate and calamitous effect. Slaves, aliens, people who would not have been listened to, much less taken seriously, were now considered reliable witnesses when they reported that they had seen other, earlier cases, of statues broken by young men who had had too much to drink. And then one of them insisted that something even more serious had happened, that he had seen with his own eyes a mock celebration of the mysteries in a private home and that the part of the chief priest had been played by Alcibiades himself.

In the terror-stricken atmosphere of the city there was a willing audience for any accusation that had even the slightest connection to what seemed possible. Everyone knew that Alcibiades thought himself somehow outside the rules that others followed, that he flouted convention and ignored tradition. There must have been a hundred people who had seen him drunk that night, and a hundred different rumors about where he had gone and what he had said. And who besides a man of uncommon ambition, a man who many suspected of wanting to rule Athens alone, would conspire to throw the people into such confusion that they would look to some one man to save them from their enemies? That was the argument taken up by those who wanted him out of the way so that they could, in their turn, taking the leading place in the affairs of the city. They pounded away on the same theme, that all anyone had to do was look at the way Alcibiades lived his life, the undemocratic character of everything he did, to know that what had been done to the Hermae was part of a plot by which he sought to overthrow the democracy and take power himself.

"Six days before I sail to Sicily?" he replied. "Six days before I lead the greatest expedition this or any other city has ever launched? If I am guilty of that, kill me twice, once for what I have done, and once more for criminal stupidity!"

He stood on stage, thousands watching him, come to see whether he or his accusers would prevail. If they thought he had come to ask for sympathy, to offer some explanation for what it was said he had done, to speak in mitigation, he quickly disabused them. He issued a flat denial, and followed it with a demand.

"Put me on trial, if you think I did this; put me on trial here, today. If I am found guilty, put me to death; but if I am acquitted let me take up my command and get on with the city's business. Now, put me on trial. I am not about to lead this expedition with a charge like this hanging over my head!"

The effect of his defense was dramatic. No one seemed quite sure what to do. And then, just before they were about to decide to have a trial, a trial in which it was almost certain he would be absolved of any responsibility for what had happened, one of those who hated him most, Androcles, as young as Alcibiades and equally ambitious, organized a small conspiracy of his own. He got some of those who hated Alcibiades, but who had not been so public about it, to speak as if they were his friends, arguing that it would be unthinkable to delay the departure of the fleet while the things necessary for a trial were being arranged; that Alcibiades, who had been given absolute power over the army, should be free to exercise it for the benefit of the city and the empire; and that there would be time enough for him to make his defense against the charges that had been brought against him after he had achieved victory in the war in Sicily.

It was an evil, insidious thing to do, and Alcibiades knew it. He protested that it was impossible to leave without an end to this campaign of defamation and repeated his demand that they should kill him if he could not clear himself of the false accusations that had been brought against him. After he had proven his innocence, he could then wage war without the fear of being stabbed in the back at home. But they would not do it; they refused to give him the trial he wanted. He was ordered to sail on schedule.

"Watch out," he warned later that same day. "Be careful what you say and what you do. We're now the slaves of informers; words can kill. People hear what they want to hear, and they don't understand even that. The story that I played a priest, that the mysteries were mocked – do you know how that started? It was what happened at Agathon's, when they had that dinner party and gave their own account of what the god Eros really was. Aristophanes knows what happened, but he is the last person to tell the truth – though in this case it is better that he doesn't. The mysteries were divulged, all right; but they were not our mysteries, the mysteries of Eleusis, but mysteries told by a priestess from Mantineia. Socrates described them. I only heard about it later; I did not arrive, did not make my drunken appearance, until sometime after he finished. Never mention this to anyone. It is better if people think it was me. I know how to deal with these cheap demagogues of ours."

I did not see Alcibiades again until the day he sailed, and then only from a distance when, like everyone else in Athens, I went down to Piraeus to watch the greatest force ever assembled start its long voyage across the sea. Everywhere I looked I saw the same mixture of emotions on the faces of the friends and relations of those about to leave: pride at the sheer power that had been marshaled and at the daring of the adventure, and fear at what, now that it was starting, they knew might be the result. And everywhere I heard voices, quiet and insistent, raising questions, encouraging doubts, whether, after what had happened to the Hermae, the gods might punish all of them for the crimes committed by a few. Beneath those voices I could hear the whispers of Alcibiades' many enemies, whispers about new rumors, words, not yet spoken, like bow-strings just pulled back, waiting for the moment, soon to come, when they would with lethal force be sent flying straight to their target.

But for now, every eye was on the bright-colored fleet and the thousands of bronze covered men that lined the decks. A hundred ships stood waiting while a trumpet ordered silence. A herald, with a voice as clear and pure as crystal, gave the prayer, each word repeated by all the ships in unison, a sound so full of promise, so profound in its meaning, that it was as if all of Hellas were shouting to the gods in heaven. Everyone on board the ships made their libations from cups shining gold and silver in the orange and scarlet light of morning, and then, when the prayers were finished and the last song sung, the ships, with banners flying, raced the rising sun.

After the fleet had sailed, it was not long before the attention of the Athenians turned once again to the destruction of the Hermae and the defilement of their religion. Every rumor fed suspicion, and every informer, however dishonest, was believed. Dozens, hundreds, were arrested on the strength of nothing more than an accusation, and, despite the absence of evidence, put to death. Each new arrest, each new execution, each new addition to the number of those held responsible for what had happened, confirmed people in their fear that this was a broad-based conspiracy, a war against democracy itself. There was only one person who could have organized it, only one man who could have set it in motion. The Salaminia, the fastest ship in the fleet – the ship in which I had once sailed to Abdera to meet Democritus and then to Potidaea where I first made love with Alcibiades, where I saw Socrates spend a night in silent contemplation, where I saw him, the next day, put himself between Alcibiades and almost certain death – the Salaminia was now sent to bring him back from Sicily to stand trial for sacrilege and treason. But even that did not stop the arrests and the executions.

I kept to myself even more than usual, and when I had to go somewhere I was careful not to draw attention to myself. This was not difficult. Ever since the plague had left its mark on me, ever since I had, like the Hermae, suffered disfigurement, I had been able to pass unnoticed, left free to observe the changes I saw everywhere. It was astonishing how complete those changes seemed, the eagerness with which people who just weeks before would have followed Alcibiades to Sicily and anywhere beyond now looked forward to his trial and execution. No one doubted that he would be convicted; few seemed to doubt that he should. The strangest thing of all was how quickly everyone had forgotten how convinced they had been that without Alcibiades, without his skill and daring, the expedition to Sicily would almost certainly fail. They had just sent off to war the greatest force in their history, and now, without a second thought, were going to execute the only man fit to lead it. I wondered what Alcibiades would do, whether he would submit to the indignity of being recalled or try in some way to resist. Unless he was willing to lead a mutiny of his own men and declare war on Athens, what choice did he have but to come back and try to prove his innocence to a jury already convinced of his guilt? Then I remembered that it was Alcibiades, and that he would find in what others thought a weakness and a danger a source of strength and a way to triumph. I remembered what he could do, the power he had with the crowd, and, remembering, felt better than I had. I went to bed at a decent hour and fell almost immediately into the long and dreamless sleep I needed.

Or was it dreamless? When I opened my eyes, it was still quite dark, so dark that my eyes played tricks on me. Two luminous circles were moving parallel to one another at the foot of my bed, jumping up and down and from side to side like two bright colored birds that had flown in through the window and were busy exploring everything at once. Mesmerized by this strange apparition, I began to think I must be still asleep, dreaming what I was seeing, or, only half-awake, unable to distinguish reality from my own imaginings. And then I saw that between those two floating globes were two large black holes, two voids in space, which opened in opposite directions.

"Socrates!" I cried, as I sat up. "What are you ...?"

"I did not mean to alarm you," he said, coming closer so I could see him clearly. "I would have knocked, but in order to wake you I might have woken someone down the street. I did not want to take the chance."

"Take the chance?"

"That someone would know I had come – or that someone would find out that you were leaving."

"Leaving? Why would I ...?" But I knew, knew it from the tone of his voice, knew it from the fact that he had come here, surreptitiously, in the night. "You mean ...?"

"Yes, exactly; they're coming for you in the morning. The order has been signed. You've been named as one of the conspirators, one of those who had agreed to help Alcibiades take power."

I swung my legs out of bed and threw a robe around my shoulders. I lit a candle and led Socrates into the kitchen where we could sit down and I could decide what to do. He quickly informed me that there was nothing to decide: I had to leave Athens and I had to leave tonight.

"Hundreds have been killed, anyone who has been accused. You're a friend of Alcibiades: that is sufficient proof of guilt. And you are a resident alien, not a citizen; they won't even bother with the formalities of a trial. But there is nothing to fear. Arrangements have been made. There is a boat waiting in the harbor."

"A boat? Where am I supposed to go?"

Suddenly, I realized that if I was in danger so was he. I remembered what Alcibiades had told me about what had really happened that night at Agathon's: that it had been Socrates who had talked about the mysteries, which, though they were not the ones held sacred in Athens, would have been enough in present circumstances to get him killed. Even if no one found out about that, he was known to be someone Alcibiades had trusted, which was tantamount to guilt. Socrates dismissed the possibility as not worth discussion.

"Perhaps Aristophanes did me a favor after all when he wrote The Clouds. After that play was performed everyone thinks I spend all my time in a basket up in the air, studying the stars, that I live in 'cloud-cuckoo land' to use his phrase. How could I be involved in a political conspiracy? – I don't even know where Athens is! Now, grab a few things – just what you need to wear, just what you can carry. If we leave now, we won't be seen, and before morning you will be safe at sea."

I gathered up the few things I would need for the journey, a journey to a destination I did not know, remembered to put the manuscript in which I had written my strange musings on what I had seen and learned in a leather pouch, and in a few short minutes was ready to leave. I wondered if I would ever see Athens again, whether I would ever sleep another night in this house, the gift of Alcibiades, that I had come so much to love, the only real home I had ever had. I locked the door, but kept the key, and that way promised myself that I was not really leaving at all, that when it was safe again, when Athens remembered what Athens was, I would come back to this, the only home I wanted.

We had an hour's walk ahead of us, and to pass the time we talked; or rather, after I asked one question, Socrates talked and I listened. It was, I admit, not the kind of question people normally ask to relieve the tedium of a journey

"The way Aristophanes described you in The Clouds – always studying the things either below the earth or in the heavens, oblivious of all the things around you – it seemed to me to describe almost anyone but you. It seemed to describe what those like Thales and Anaximander, or Heraclitus, or even my own teacher, Empedocles, thought, the world defined by the various elements of which it is composed or as held together by forces like love and strife. Or do you think I am wrong about that?"

"When I was young I was what Aristophanes tried to say about me. I had a great passion for natural science. I wanted to know the causes for which each thing comes to be and then ceases to be. It was always a puzzle. Was it with the blood that courses through our veins that we think, or with the air and fire that is within us? Or is it instead the brain that gives us our sense of hearing and our ability to see and smell. And is it from these that memory and opinion arise, and is knowledge then the result? Then I wondered how these faculties, these abilities are lost, and I studied celestial and terrestrial phenomenon – the things in heaven and the things beneath the earth – until, finally, I became convinced that I was uniquely unqualified for this kind of inquiry. And then one day I heard someone reading from a book and what I heard seemed to answer everything."

The city was dark and silent, our footsteps echoing softly in the night. The voice of Socrates seemed to come from everywhere at once, a voice so comforting, so reassuring, so certain of itself, that though I was fleeing danger, running for my life, I never had a thought that there was any place I would rather be, or anyone else I would rather be with.

"The book?" I asked, as we hurried along. "What book was it?"

"Something Anaxagoras had written."

I stopped dead in my tracks. A book by Anaxagoras, who would have been convicted of impiety and punished with death if it had not been for Pericles and his plea to spare his teacher. The accusation brought against him had been based on what he had, perhaps foolishly, put in writing.

"The book that nearly got him killed?"

"Yes, probably. The only thing you can be sure of when you put anything in writing is that most people won't understand it. But I understood it, or thought I did, when I heard someone reading from it. You cannot imagine how eager I was to read it for myself. Here was someone insisting that mind produces order, that mind is the cause of everything. It made perfect sense. And it seemed to me when I first heard it that if mind is the cause of everything that it must set everything in order and arrange each individual thing in a way that is best for it. And it followed from this that if anyone wanted to discover the reasons why any given thing came into being he had to find out how it was best for that thing to be, to discover, in other words, the best and highest good. These reflections made me suppose that I had found in Anaxagoras an authority on causation who would begin by telling me whether the earth is flat or round and would then explain the reason and the largest meaning for this by stating how and why it was better that it should be so. It never occurred to me that a man who asserted that the ordering of things is due to mind would offer any explanation for them than that it is best for them to be as they are. I thought that by assigning a cause to each phenomenon separately – the sun, and moon, other heavenly bodies, their relative velocities and orbits, all such phenomenon – and to the universe as a whole he would make clear what is best for each and what is the universal good. I got the books he had written and read them as quickly as I could. I wanted to know as soon as possible all about the best and the less good."

Socrates fell into a long silence. Far ahead in the distance, I began to make out the shadowed outline of the harbor. Suddenly, I tripped and almost fell. Someone let out a moan. I had stepped on the foot of a drunk who lay sprawled at the entrance to an alley. I caught my balance and we moved on. I wanted Socrates to keep talking; I wanted to keep my mind occupied. I did not want to think about what was going to happen when, in a few more minutes, I would have to leave.

"What happened – when you read Anaxagoras? It wasn't what you hoped, was it?"

His eyes flashed with light; his head shuddered with more than disappointment, contempt, for what he had read in those long forgotten pages.

"It was supposed to be about mind, how mind had ordered the world, but mind was never used. The causes he talked about were the usual absurdities, things like air and aether and water. Everything about it was inconsistent. It was as if someone said that the cause of everything Socrates does is mind – and then, in trying to account for my actions, said that the reason that I am walking along this street is that my body is made up of bones and sinews, that the bones are rigid and separated, but the sinews are capable of contraction and relaxation and make it possible for the bones to move freely in their joints and that is the cause of my moving now the way I am – and the same thing about you – and never thought to mention that the real reason is that we are determined to get you out of harm's way to a place of safety. It is true that without these bones and sinews we could not move, but to say that it is because of them that we are doing what we are doing, and not through having made a choice of what we thought best is not something that should be taken seriously. Our actions are controlled by what our minds tell us is best to do. There is a difference between the cause of a thing and the conditions without which it could not be a cause! But Anaxagoras, and a number of those other so-called philosophers, never seem to grasp that simple fact, and by that failure do nothing but breed confusion. There is a power that keeps things disposed at any given moment in the best possible way, but they never look for it or even believe that it exists. They think one day they will find some mighty and immortal all-sustaining god and do not understand that everything is really bound and held together by this thing I call the good, what is best in its nature."

We were almost there, another hundred yards before we reached the wharf and the boat that was waiting to take me away. I did not want to go. There were so many questions crowding together in my mind, questions no one else could answer, questions I would keep asking until the day I died. He knew what I was thinking, understood what I was going through, the deep uncertainty I had begun to feel.

"I turned away from all that – the movement of the heavens, the elements out of which things are made – when I realized that we are all parts of a whole, and that the order of the whole can be found in each of its parts. The order of the universe, in other words, can be found in each of us. If you want to know the world, know yourself. Now, you have to go."

Dawn was just about to break. Socrates helped me into the small fishing boat with its single sail. The captain was an old friend of his, who, like all his other friends, was only too willing to do any favor he asked.

"Where am I taking her?" he asked, as he pushed away.

Socrates seemed to think about it. He stood there for a moment, his hands behind his back, pacing first in one direction and then another.

"Sicily," he finally called out. "To Syracuse, where her journey started." Then he looked one last time at me. "Remember what I told you. And remember also this: there is more of beauty in you than anything that other Helen ever had."

And then he turned away, and a moment later disappeared.

I was going back to where I had come from, but that place was no longer home to me. I had left Syracuse a young girl and I was now a woman. I had left Syracuse the daughter of a tyrant who ruled the city with an iron hand; I came back a stranger to a place in which the people ruled themselves, or rather, like Athens, were ruled by whoever at any given moment had the power to persuade them what to do. I came back just in time to witness the greatest single battle of the war, a war from which the man most needed, Alcibiades, had by an act of collective madness been removed.

Within days of my arrival in Sicily I had learned what had happened, how the state ship Salaminia had come to bring Alcibiades back to Athens, how Alcibiades had agreed to follow in his own ship and then, as soon as they were out to sea, made his escape. It was said that he had promised that it would not be long before he would teach Athens a lesson it would never forget. When I heard that he had escaped, that he was free, that he was not going to be put to death by those demagogues in Athens who cared only for their own power, I did not wonder that he would one day take his revenge, my only doubt the way he would do it. He loved Athens too much to bear the thought that anyone else might have her.

With Alcibiades now a fugitive, Nicias, who had never thought Sicily anything but a mistake, was left in charge, which meant that nothing would happen without delay. Convinced that the expedition could not possibly succeed and certain that he would be blamed for defeat, he would not dare the kind of chances that for Alcibiades were second nature, but neither would he agree to cut his losses and leave the island. And then, finally, when it became apparent that there was no choice, that the only alternative was destruction or withdrawal, when time meant everything and they were, at long last, ready to sail, something happened that proved that the fear and anger that swept through the city when the Hermae were defaced had not been some temporary aberration, the affliction of disordered minds, but the result of a deeply held religious belief. Nicias and all those thousands of men, almost the entire Athenian army, their last clear chance to make their escape stopped by a simple eclipse, a dark shadow covering the moon which instead of a phenomenon of nature was taken as a sign from the gods that nothing could be done until, as the soothsayers on whom Nicias, that most pious of men, relied, insisted, three times nine days had passed. If these priests had known their business, if they had really any knowledge of the future – or if Nicias had possessed even a modicum of common sense and strategic judgment – they would have known that this was nothing less than a prophecy of doom.

And I was there to see it, the way the Syracusans and their Spartan allies had used the time that Nicias and his religious zeal had given them to close up the great harbor and force the Athenian fleet to hazard everything – their ships, their lives, the lives of all the soldiers who without those ships would never see Athens again – on a last attempt to fight their way out to the open sea. With more than a hundred ships, manned with archers and javelin throwers, the Athenians attacked the waiting fleet of Syracuse and its allies. With nearly two hundred ships crowded together in a harbor barely four miles wide there was no room for maneuver, no room for the skilled seamanship that had made Athens unbeatable at sea. The Athenians were fighting for survival; the Sicilians were fighting for both glory and revenge. This was not a day for mercy, this was war to the death; a war of sea-borne forces fought in front of tens of thousands of cheering, awe-struck spectators standing on shore. The harbor had become a great amphitheater in which a play, a tragedy, was performed in front of a crowd which, watching the battle, the action of the story, went wild with enthusiasm, or shed tears of lamentation, at what they saw.

I had made my way to the island of Ortygia, along the narrow street between the fortress and the water on which I had often walked as a girl, when the fortress was a castle and my father ruled alone. The water on the inland side that had made a gentle lapping sound I had so much loved and that had helped sooth or cushion the harsh, discordant words and acts of violence I had so often witnessed in Hiero's court, now churned with a violence of its own, banging broken boards and broken bodies hard against the rocks. The water, always so clear and sparkling, as green as the brightest emerald, had turned a turbid red, so thick with blood that it was a wonder any ship could sink. A severed arm, a severed head, floated by, and it was not long before dead bodies were commonplace, and instead of producing cries of shock and alarm went almost unnoticed. Too much depended on the outcome, too much hung in the balance, for the loss of life to seem important. The battle raged first one way then the other. Great cries of triumph and relief rang out from the low sloping hills on the other side where the Athenian army stood watching, when, for a moment, it seemed that the Syracusan line would not hold. But it did, and then, as the battle began to go against them, as it became obvious that the Athenian ships were being driven to shore, there was such a wail of terror, such heart-rending sadness, that alone among the spectators who filled the streets of Ortygia I began to cry. Athens, great Athens, had been defeated, and without a navy to protect it, Athens would be destroyed.

The army tried to get away. Forty thousand men tried to make their escape from Syracuse to the other side of Sicily. Only a few of them survived. Most of them were killed, slaughtered, as they passed down the narrow ravines or tried to cross the deep rivers that barred their retreat. The seven thousand who were left had no choice but to surrender. They were brought back to Syracuse and put into the stone quarries where they were made to wait while it was decided whether they should be allowed to live.

It is hard to describe the feelings I had, the conflict of emotions, at what I now observed. My life seemed to have moved in a great circle, or rather within a series of circles, each connected with the others; a spiral, if you will: an ascent from the immediacy of what I knew as a girl to what had become, if more complicated, easier to understand. This is not the paradox it seems. I had been taught by the greatest teachers of the age, and I had witnessed first hand most of the important events. Things made sense that, if you will forgive this way of putting it, did not make sense at all, the things that drive men, the things that draw them on, what I had learned about Eros and the different ways that desire, common to us all, finds expression. I could have written in advance the arguments I listened to as I returned again to the theater where I had once gone with my father to see a play written and produced by Aeschylus, the day I left for what I thought would be forever. They were there now, the citizens of Syracuse, not to take their lead from Hiero or any other tyrant, but to decide themselves what should be done with what was left of the Athenians who had come to conquer Sicily. I could have been back in Athens, listening to the debate about whether to kill everyone in Mytilene as a punishment for their revolt.

Someone called Nicolaus, who had lost two sons in the war, had the nobility of soul to insist that Syracuse should follow their better instincts and treat with humanity those who had fallen into their power. To my wonder and astonishment, he argued that they should "show mercy to men who offer their country as a school for the common use of mankind. For, what place is there to which foreigners may resort for a liberal education once the city of the Athenians has been destroyed. Brief is the hatred aroused by the wrong they have committed, but important and many are their accomplishments which claim goodwill."

This from a man who lost two sons in the war! There was greatness in a man who could say this, who could rise above his own anguish and suffering to see what was great and worth preserving even in those who had done him harm. He was specific in both his praise and blame. He pointed to Nicias who stood, bound and shackled, a prisoner like the others.

"It would be extraordinary if Nicias, the only man to oppose the expedition to Sicily, the man who looked after our interests as our representative at Athens, should be punished and Alcibiades, the man who brought on the war against the Syracusans, should escape his deserved punishment from both us and the Athenians."

If the vote had been taken then, at the moment Nicolaus had finished, the Athenians would have been released from custody and given safe passage home, but Glyippus, the Spartan, reminded them that the Athenians would never have shown them the same regard, that they had planned to sell the Syracusans into slavery, and that the Athenians had started the war in which so many Sicilians had died. He scorned what Nicolaus had suggested.

"Yet some have lost their reasoning power to such a degree as to assert that it is Alcibiades, over whom we have no power, who should be punished, but that we should release the prisoners, who are being led to their deserved punishment, and thus make it known to the world that the people of Syracuse have no righteous indignation against base men."

Like the assembly of Athens, the assembly of Syracuse was quick to change its mind; emotion, not reason, ruled the day. Nicias and the other generals were put to death and the thousands waiting in the quarries were left to die a slow death of starvation and disease. Athens, it was imagined, would be destroyed. There would be no place to which foreigners, or anyone at all, would be able to resort for a liberal education. I could not help but wonder whether for all his faults, for all his undoubted evil, Hiero, my father, the tyrant who ruled alone, would have been so willing to destroy the school that taught civilization to the Greeks, and that, among other things, had schooled the poet who had in words at least made him immortal.

I stayed in Syracuse; there was nowhere else I could go. I lived a private life, studying what I had learned, trying to learn more. Every day, in what became my morning ritual, I wrote out something of what I could remember of those timeless conversations in which Socrates and Alcibiades, Pericles and Aspasia, and countless others besides, had played their parts, learning a little more about their meaning each time I wrote down the words. I did not cut myself off entirely from the world. I heard the same rumors other people did: that Alcibiades had joined the Spartans, had in all his dress and habits adopted the style of their plain living, that he was now for all intents and purposes their leader, and that he had, in the king's absence, gotten the queen pregnant so that, as he was said to have put it, the Spartans would one day know what it was like to have a real king. I laughed when I heard this; it seemed so much exactly the kind of thing he would do.

I had the same thought when I heard later that he had left the Spartans and taken up residence with the Persian king whom he now persuaded to play one side off against the other and that way help weaken to his own advantage both the Spartans and the Athenians and become himself the strongest power. It was exactly what Alcibiades would do: orchestrate through a third party the outcome of the war until the Athenians would see that the only way to save their city was to call him back. Alcibiades was what Socrates had always known he was, and what I had always known he was as well. After everything I had seen, how easily our ambitions lead to war and murder, what other chance did Athens have than someone who had the intelligence to know what his own ambition lacked, who could feel at least a tinge of guilt that there was something better, something higher, even if Socrates was the only known example, than the popular applause he wanted and needed to have?

I live alone, but I am never lonely. I hear the voices I heard before; I read and write the words through which I sometimes have a glimpse of the things that never change, what things are in themselves. And each day, late in the afternoon, I go for long walks around the island where I lived when my face was as famous as my father's name. It is strange how often we can pass something and never notice it. Today, when I reached the far end of the island, the point where it reaches farthest out into the bay, I sat on the same bench I do every time I go for my walk. A young girl, about the same age I was when Herodotus helped me make my escape, and as pretty as any girl I have seen, was standing on the rocky beach just below, arguing with her younger sister. She looked up at me and asked if I could settle their dispute. When I walked down to where they were standing, she pointed to a tarnished bronze statue that had been placed there years before. It faced out to the sea.

"My sister keeps insisting that it is Helen of Troy, but it isn't, is it?" she asked.

Her large, laughing eyes made me smile. I turned and studied the inscription etched just beneath the sculpted face in weathered bronze.

"Helen, Hiero's daughter, gone to be Poseidon's bride."

I looked straight up into the cloudless, azure sky and threw out my arms as if to touch heaven and the gods, thankful for Herodotus and the path on which he had once started me.

"No, you're right," I told the girl. "It is not Helen of Troy; it is a different Helen. But she did not become Poseidon's bride; she did not marry anyone. She lived the only life worth living. She learned something of herself and something of the world. She might not even have been the daughter of Hiero after all," I said as I waved goodbye. "She may have been the only daughter of the sun. She had the gift of light."

The End